Praise for Meg Allison's *Dream Walk*

Rating: 5 Nymphs "...Dream Walk. It's the first in her new series, The Sentinels and if this intricately plotted and crafted book is any indication, the readers of this new contemporary paranormal romance series are in for an awesome ride."

~ *Mystical Nymph, Literary Nymphs Reviews*

Look for these titles by
Meg Allison

Now Available:

Secrets and Shadows

Alaina's Promise

Dream Walk

Meg Allison

A Samhain Publishing, Ltd. publication.

Samhain Publishing, Ltd.
577 Mulberry Street, Suite 1520
Macon, GA 31201
www.samhainpublishing.com

Dream Walk
Copyright © 2009 by Meg Allison
Print ISBN: 978-1-60504-317-3
Digital ISBN: 1-60504-191-2

Editing by Heidi Moore
Cover by Natalie Winters and Dawn Seewer

First Samhain Publishing, Ltd. electronic publication: December 2008
First Samhain Publishing, Ltd. print publication: July 2009

Dedication

For Marinda June, keeper of the muse, without whom this story would still be unfinished.

The Beginning

"And it came to pass, when men began to multiply on the face of the earth, and daughters were born unto them,

That the sons of God saw the daughters of men that they were fair; and they took them wives of all which they chose....

There were giants in the earth in those days; and also after that, when the sons of God came in unto the daughters of men, and they bear children to them, the same became mighty men which were of old, men of renown." (King James Version, Genesis 6: 1-2, 4)

These children of gods and mortals were born with special powers—*chosen* to fulfill a unique purpose on the earth with gifts given to help protect their human cousins from demons who prowled the land. Some were given unusual strength, others abilities beyond the mortal realm, a few were granted the promise of longevity and immortality.

The humans soon began to fear the Chosen, their protectors. Superstition and ignorance made these special beings targets of ridicule and scorn. Some of the weaker among them were hunted and killed. Others were made captive while their talents were exploited. Forbidden to kill their cousins, the atrocities continued as the older generations watched in desperate horror.

The persecution went unchecked until the strongest among the Chosen rose up to lead their brothers and sisters to a more secure land where they could live in peace. There they set up a secret society with a small but powerful army of warriors, the Sentinels, to help guard it. Their prosperity lasted a millennium, until pride stirred in the hearts of some of the Sentinels. Power like theirs could not be denied and they sought to regain their place on the earth by ridding it of the weak humans.

They required the power of their brothers to help them wipe out the human vermin—a need met by the most heinous of sins. Many stood against them and a great war raged in the shadows of the night, in the quiet valleys of the forgotten mountains, until those who rebelled were brought down for a time to be bound in chains forged from the mountains themselves. Knowing they would never be safe and loath to kill their powerful brothers, the remaining Sentinels scattered their people across the globe. Many of the Chosen rejoined human society, hiding their true natures to blend in with the others like chameleons.

The battle continues as their bonds are weakened and the ones who rebelled against their true mission are freed to walk the earth. They seek to conquer it and subjugate the lowly humans to their will. Many have joined with demons in an unholy alliance that grows stronger every day, fed by fear and nourished by blood. Only the faithful Sentinels stand in their way.

They are the stuff of legends and myth—the stuff of nightmares. They are mankind's only hope of survival.

Prologue

Tybee Island, Georgia
Ten years ago

He had failed. It stuck in his gut like a cold, sharp stone akin to the one that ended his mortality long ago and concluded his reign as a Sentinel. He did not savor the memory of the feelings it evoked.

Despite it all, he vowed not to fail again. This girl's power still called to him. He must possess her. His thoughts focused on none but her. His desire could not be redirected as her image seared itself into his brain.

Cursing the fates in his ancient tongue, he summoned the powers of wind and sea while he stood on the shores of Tybee Island, his boots sunk deep into the gritty sand. Energy gathered around him like a writhing, living thing. He raised his hands to the black sky and the wind wailed. Waves rose at his murmured command. It was not enough. He wanted more.

The momentum of his power pulled the water high on the beach. Cold and soaked from knee to ankle, he stopped to stare down at his hands covered in blood. The sight calmed his anger a bit. He took a deep, soothing breath. It would be folly to attempt his seduction again too soon. The encounter had left him weakened and they would guard her more diligently for a time.

What a cruel twist the fates conjured for him. The one human he needed above all others, guarded by a man whose life he had saved a century ago. The bastard would now rot in the cold, hard ground as he deserved.

Now he would bide his time until the girl's gift matured. Then her power would be his. Her essence would sustain him for many centuries. Once he had taken his fill of her flesh, the power in her soul would feed that eternal thirst he could not deny. They would be one. Then she would be no more.

The burning hatred of millennia swept away his self-control. He hissed in anger as the bloodlust set his body ablaze. She would suffer for her guardian's interference. He would find a way past her defenses if it took the rest of her life and he would make her pay dearly.

He had time. She was young.

Someday her gift would be his and his alone. The thought made his mouth water; his body grew hard and ready. He knew his eyes glowed with unearthly fire. The water reflected their hellish-red gleam. Once he would have feared such a thing, but now he reveled in its power. He basked in the horror it elicited from his weak and helpless prey.

He needed a plan...careful, measured and methodical. No one could stand in the way of his conquest a second time. Gods help the man who tried.

Chapter One

Savannah

Present day

Camille jerked awake, her breath coming in short, shallow gasps. Images from the nightmare hovered like nebulous ghosts in her mind. Long damp strands of hair stuck to her face, the thin cotton nightshirt clung to her skin. Kicking off the sheet, she swung her feet to the floor and took a deep breath.

Nightmare. More like night terror. She'd had them as a young girl—moments of absolute horror that had her seeing things crawling up the dark, empty walls. Camille remembered little except the transparent images superimposed on the real world, and her mother's soothing voice.

She clicked on the bedside lamp. Her shoulders drooped with defeat as she glanced at the clock. Five in the morning. She hadn't gone to bed until two. With a heavy sigh, she rose and crossed to the adjoining bathroom. She stripped off the sweat-soaked garment and climbed into the shower.

Over the past four months, she had relived the same terrifying visions with the same conclusion. Camille had all but lost her ability to sleep. Lack of sleep made it hard to think, let alone write. Work suffered, not to mention her sanity which hung by a thread.

"He's coming."

She jerked her head up from beneath the hot drizzle and glanced around at the swirling steam. With a sigh of relief, she shook her head.

"Don't scare me like that," she whispered.

"No worries, child."

She closed her eyes as a warm, peaceful wave filled her

from head to toe. Her guide, her spirit mentor, was the only man she trusted. The only *man* she'd let close since her nineteenth birthday over ten years ago.

As she allowed the blank screen in her mind to change, colors swirled like a kaleidoscope. An image formed of shoulder-length dark hair pulled back from a bronzed face. The features sharpened to reveal eyes as dark as pitch, a straight nose, heavy brow and full mouth. Camille's breath caught. He was beautiful and frightening all at once. This man would help her overcome evil? He looked like a warrior or a fallen angel, not a savior.

She shook her head and pushed the image away before turning off the shower. Beads of water dripped from her skin and hair. A whisper of cold air snaked through the white billows of steam to crawl over her bare flesh. She shuddered. The large beast who tried to devour her in sleep had to be a warning. Of what, she didn't know. But the dark stranger might keep the nightmare from playing out to its conclusion.

Camille balked at the idea. She held the reins where her life was concerned. For the past eleven years, she had refused help from anyone. She didn't need this man to intervene and protect her like a helpless child. But her guide insisted. The dream monster could not be faced alone and to do so would mean her destruction.

She whipped the shower curtain aside to grab a towel as impotent anger surged through her body. Her hands shook. She silently railed at the unfairness of it all. But the choice was clear—either trust the stranger or surrender to the monster of her nightmare.

Some time later, she paced the room in a soft crepe dress that spilled over her curves in loose folds to mid-calf. Its earthy color blended with her own. The murmur of traffic grew louder. Her sister, Ophelia, thumped along the hall, down the stairs to the kitchen below. Outside the sky began to lighten.

Camille desired little more than the freedom to write her books and live vicariously through the fantasies. If it lacked real happiness, it was a price worth paying. It gave her things she sorely lacked while growing up, mainly safety and peace of mind.

Fighting the urge to run and hide, she jumped as a tingle spread across her skin. The spirits of the house began to murmur in excitement when a black Jaguar pulled parallel to the curb.

Taking a deep breath, Camille silenced the voices of the dead with a simple command. "Be still."

A moment later, she watched the driver unfold himself from the sports car. He stood taller than she had realized, but the rest was the same as her vision. His long hair had been pulled back at the nape. Dark glasses hid the intensity of his gaze. She jerked back from the window when he tilted his head and looked up at her.

"Peace. No worries."

"Easy for you to say," she murmured. "You're dead. He can't hurt you."

Many of the spirits were enthralled with the idea of the Sentinels, an organized, albeit secretive society of men and women that protected the Chosen among them. Through the spirits, her guide in particular, she had learned much of their heroic acts and secret ways.

Sentinels were fearless, well-trained warriors like those of legends and myth. Although they were part human, they possessed special gifts or unique talents. Some were said to be immortal. She watched the man below, wondering if he might be an ancient one. The idea intrigued her.

Her dark knight shut the car door and the horn bleeped as he aimed a key chain at the hood. Long legs clad in black tailored slacks brought him up the walk faster than she could reach the hallway. The doorbell trilled.

"I'll get it!" Ophelia's voice carried up the stairs. Camille stopped short on the top step out of sight.

Part of her wanted to be the first to meet the Sentinel and take his measure. The other wanted to run and hide.

ſ

A young woman opened the door and stood there, speechless as she gaped up at him. Ian Spain almost sighed out loud at the look of bemused fear in her vivid blue eyes. This was not the woman he'd come to meet.

"I'm here to see Ms. Bryant."

Blood drained from her face. "I...uh, y-you mean Cami?"

15

the girl stuttered.

Ian quirked a brow. "Yes, Camille Bryant, the writer," he paused for a moment, irritation growing as the girl continued to stare. "She's expecting me."

That seemed to break the trance. "Oh! Really? Are you sure? I mean, she never said anything and Camille doesn't like... I mean she doesn't know too many, uh..."

"I'm sure," he said with a half-smile. From somewhere in the house, Ian could feel another watching expectantly...waiting. Maybe she thought he'd push past the younger woman and storm inside after her. The idea tempted him. It had been one hell of a drive and he didn't like being kept waiting.

"Um, okay," the girl murmured as she moved to one side. "Come in, I'll tell her you're here, Mister...?"

"She knows," he replied, ignoring her invitation to divulge his identity.

With a quick glance up the stairs, Ian entered the foyer and followed her inside. How long would his damsel hide in the shadows? The young woman led the way into a parlor, her long dark hair swinging loose about her waist. Her vivid blue eyes and tight, trim figure would have most men salivating. If the swing of her hips was any indication, she knew that fact all too well. But Ian didn't drool. Ever.

She turned, lowering herself onto the wide flowered sofa. Her gaze raked him from head to foot and he looked around the room to hide his disgust. Some lessons in seduction were needed. She licked her lips. *Subtlety would help, too.*

From Samantha's briefing late yesterday afternoon, he had learned a little about Ophelia Bryant. Although she was very much a woman at twenty-two, she still held on to childish ways, it seemed. She interested him in passing, but only because she had been raised by the woman he'd been assigned to protect. Knowing her better might give him insight into Camille's character, otherwise the younger woman meant nothing to him. However, he didn't want to have to worry about where Ophelia's hands might wander while he was trying to work.

The energy in the room shifted. He turned toward the hallway, the hair rising at his nape. An old reflex positioned one hand over the revolver holstered beneath his black jacket as a shadow drifted down the stairs. A figure swathed in floating folds of brown descended the narrow staircase. Ian pulled off his shades to get a better look.

His gaze flowed upward over a long skirt, full hips and bust all draped in enough fabric to disguise the exact form of the figure within. Before he realized it, she stood a foot away. He visually traced the curve of her cheek and soft pink lips, the tilt of her freckled nose, and dark purple crescents beneath wide-set eyes. She was a plain woman who wore little makeup and surrounded herself in dull color from the top of her shiny hair to the tips of her low-heeled shoes.

Then he looked into her eyes and his breath hitched in his throat. They were wide, pools of melted chocolate framed by spiky black lashes. The irises glittered with large flecks of deep green, holding him spellbound like the glimmers in a fortuneteller's crystal ball. Without thought, he stepped closer until he felt the warmth of her body and heard the soft rush of her breath. The peculiar shade of green reminded him of something, but before the memory formed, she blinked. Startled, he realized how close they were standing and took a hasty step back as he pushed the shades into his coat pocket.

"Ms. Bryant, I'm Ian Spain," he said, hesitating a moment before holding out a hand. He'd never felt anything quite so unsettling, despite witnessing some seriously weird stuff in the past seven years.

"It's a pleasure to make your acquaintance, Mr. Spain," she replied. Her smooth, warm voice poured over his soul like brandy on a cold northern night. It eased the tension coiled along his spine.

At the touch of her icy fingers to his, he frowned. She wasn't what he expected. This mousy, quiet woman wrote erotic fiction for a living? The contradiction intrigued him.

"The pleasure is mine." He stared for a moment, his usual easy manner short-circuited. The corners of her mouth lifted in a tentative smile and his heart skipped out of rhythm.

Had he thought her plain? She would stop traffic if she wore makeup and brighter colors. At the moment, her delicate features were almost lost in the sea of earth tones surrounding her.

Staring up at him, her eyes flickered with an assessing wariness he'd come to expect from timid women faced with his rather imposing appearance. Ian knew he looked like the big bad wolf or a biker in a suit. Her gaze drifted to his mouth and he had to fight the urge to lean forward to taste her full, pink lips.

She looked away, clearing her throat softly. "My agent told me she hired you. I'll be honest, Mr. Spain, I'm not happy with the arrangement. I don't need a bodyguard and I refuse to let anyone else direct my life, despite Samantha's concerns."

A slow smile lifted the corners of his mouth. The kitten was a tiger in disguise. *Nice camouflage.* It would be interesting to strip the fragile layers away and see just how sharp the tiger's claws were. In another time, another place, he might set out to do exactly that.

Ian shook the ill-timed thoughts away. *Business. Keep it professional.* He needed emotional complications now about as much a back-alley drunk needed another swig of cheap wine.

"Sam seems to think you have a problem, Ms. Bryant."

One delicate brow rose. "You know Samantha well?"

"We went to school together," he replied. The look in her eyes showed pure curiosity, but he refused to be baited. It was up to Sam how much Camille knew about her past. "I understand you've been receiving threatening emails and there was an attempted break-in several nights ago."

She shrugged. "Many people in the public eye get prank threats. I've heard of at least two other authors with similar problems. Our local police are still investigating the vandalism to the house. We don't know for certain that they were trying to break in, but even so, we have a few valuables...computers, televisions. I'm sure a couple of kids were out to make some easy money, nothing more sinister."

"Sam thinks otherwise."

"Yes, I'm aware of that. However, if you know her as well as you claim, then you understand she can be a little overprotective of her friends."

"Overprotective, yes, but she's also level-headed. Any idea why these coincidences worry her so much? She wouldn't call on me for help unless she thought it warranted my special attention."

When Camille folded her arms and looked away, he frowned. She was holding back. He'd asked Samantha Bays why the Council of Sentinels felt the romance writer needed protection, but she'd merely given him a basic rundown of the situation and Camille's talents. Samantha said he needed to ask Camille for more details. Did Sam have more faith in her friend than she should?

A disgusted grunt from the other side of the room reminded him they weren't alone. He glanced over his shoulder at Ophelia.

"Just tell him already," the younger woman demanded. "It's the dreams. Cami's been having horrible nightmares where she wakes up in the middle of the night, screaming her lungs out. Scared the shit out of me that first night."

"Lia."

"Well it did. They must be bad since you won't talk about them," Ophelia looked back at him. "For some reason Sam thinks they're prophetic or symbolic or something else to do with Cam's *gift*. That's why you're here."

"Please, Lia, that's enough," Camille implored.

He glanced between the two sisters, the tension between them thick enough to swim through. He sighed. If Camille didn't trust him enough to let him help her, what was the point? It would be an exercise in futility.

"It's not my fault you're a freak of nature," Ophelia complained. She sounded more like a whiny adolescent than a grown woman.

The whole situation begged for quick action. Like him jumping back into the Jag and heading for the nearest beach. Anything had to be better than babysitting a woman who didn't want him around while he dodged the younger sister's pathetic flirting.

Ian stuffed both hands deep into his jacket pockets. Change rattled and clinked against his keys in the silence as the women stared each other down. He had barely gotten a foot in the door and his temper was already on edge.

"Samantha is rather superstitious." Camille cast Ophelia one last quelling look as she spoke. "After the attempted break-in, I mentioned the emails and my sister inadvertently told her about my recent bout of insomnia and nightmares."

He frowned, now understanding the shadows he saw beneath her eyes and the reason he'd been chosen for this assignment. She downplayed the dreams, but they were a big clue to her problem. The dark circles spoke of sleepless hours tossing back and forth, of days on end with too much time staring at a computer screen. She might not realize how precariously she was balanced on the edge of sanity, but he could sense it. Hell, he'd been there often enough himself to recognize the symptoms.

While he could sympathize with her unhappiness over the situation, it had already spiraled out of her control. His presence here proved it. Samantha might be overprotective, but she would never send him to watch over Camille if her nightmares were simple dreams. Something outside of everyday fear must be causing them, something along the lines of demonic interference. Only a Sentinel with Ian's particular abilities could slay a dream demon. He knew one other who held such power but hadn't heard from the man in years.

"I don't want you taking over my life or my decisions," Camille insisted. "I can handle myself. I can protect myself."

"No. You can't. Not this time."

She stared at him, anger warring amid the weary confusion in her eyes. "I don't want help."

"But you need it, Camille. You can feel it. It's no use denying what your heart is telling you." He bent his head toward her, leveling all the intensity he could muster with one look. She had to listen to him. He would make her listen. "Sam has never asked me to help a personal friend before and she doesn't want to wait until the cops are drawing a chalk outline around your body. I wouldn't be here if you didn't need me. I can protect you, if you let me."

For a moment, he thought she would continue to argue. If so, he'd have no choice but to leave. He wouldn't force himself on her. Even if it meant her ultimate destruction, Ian could not make Camille take orders from him. His last job was a young man named Tom who possessed the extraordinary gift of languages. He spoke and understood more dialects than Ian had ever known existed. But the boy had refused to follow Ian's guidance—refused to believe a demon sought his abilities and his life. Tom died horribly as a result. The aftermath still haunted Ian. He held his breath, praying that it wouldn't be Camille's destiny.

The nod of her head was so slight he would have missed it had he blinked. He took a deep breath and smiled, tension easing from his shoulders.

"I won't take over," he assured her, at the same moment

wondering at the truth in those words. He wanted to lock her away in a room somewhere until they gave the all clear. Ian never backed down from a fight, but she ignited a primal, protective instinct that threatened to flare out of control. It set him even more on edge.

"You can go about your business as usual for the most part. Just think of me as your shadow or a new best friend."

She sighed. "For how long?"

"Until we're reasonably certain the danger is past," he hedged. "Then I'll move on and life can go back to normal."

"It doesn't seem that I have much to say about it," she said. "You may stay in the guest room at the top of the stairs. But I'm not changing my habits just because Samantha is paranoid."

"That'll work for a start," he agreed. "The fewer people there are that know why I'm really here, the better. So let's agree on a cover story. If anyone asks, I'm your boyfriend from Virginia. We had a fight before you moved back to Georgia a year ago. I finally admitted I couldn't live without you and followed."

She shifted on her feet, her eyes widening. Those arms tightened over her middle, better than any armored shield. "Can't you just be a cousin or brother or—or something?"

He smothered a grin, enjoying her discomfort and the faint blush in her cheeks. *This might be fun after all.* It had been a long time since he'd made a woman blush.

"I'm going to have to stay close when you're out, Camille. Very close. Too many people in the city know about your family. They'll know you don't have a cousin or brother, long-lost or otherwise. We all know how fast gossip spreads."

"He can be *my* boyfriend," Ophelia offered with sly smile. Camille frowned, her eyes flashing in annoyance.

"No, I can't," Ian replied. "Camille is the one I need to protect."

The younger woman narrowed her gaze as she lifted a stubborn chin. "And just what am I supposed to do while you two play house? Sit around this mausoleum and watch soaps?"

Ian stared at her for a moment, trying to look past the anger but her attitude made it difficult to stomach. Ophelia's eyes should be green instead of blue with all the jealousy that raged there.

"Lia, please," Camille said.

He turned back to her. Family dynamics were always a varied thing and apparently Ophelia's theatrics were embarrassing to her sister, but nothing new. As sisters went, they were as different as they could be.

Ophelia smoldered like a keg of fireworks—all flash and bluster, but no substance. Camille reminded him of a package wrapped in plain brown paper. He could imagine the lovely surprises hidden inside. It made her sexy...alluring. But those thoughts were inappropriate in the extreme. She was his damsel in distress, even a tarnished knight such as he adhered to the code of chivalry. She looked back at him, her mingled fear and irritation making him feel more like a demon instead of a rescuer.

"The last thing I want to do is cause more problems," he added, hoping to somehow reassure her. "I'm discreet in my work."

Her smoky gaze met his and she studied him for a moment, worrying her bottom lip with straight white teeth. For a moment, he couldn't seem to look away. Energy pulsed around him. It felt odd. Disturbing.

Vibrant, erotic images plowed through his brain. They featured Camille in his arms, in his bed. He could see the form of her body...feel the silk of her thigh at his fingertips, the touch of her breath on his bare skin. She had a small mole high on her inner thigh—he knew the taste of it, its texture on his tongue. Sensuous scenes with no right to be there played one after another like a lover's memories.

He shifted on his feet, trying not to let his discomfort show as he attempted to push the vivid fantasies aside. The collar of his shirt tightened. He reached up and thrust a finger beneath the starched material.

"Cami." Ophelia's voice was a harsh, urgent whisper.

Camille blinked and looked away, her face flushed crimson and her breathing somewhat erratic. Ian sucked in a rush of air, tension in his limbs flowing outward. He glanced around, feeling like an idiot. Where the hell had that come from? He wasn't a coward, but his intuition screamed at him to leave before he was pulled any deeper.

Walk away. Leaving was the only sensible course of action. He had his freedom, too. He could always say no to an assignment. Someone else would be sent in without a word of censure. He'd never asked for release before, but it wasn't out of the question, especially not after what happened to Tom. Ian pushed the memories aside and tried to focus on the present.

He gazed at Camille with her long sable brown hair cascading down her shoulders. The flush of pink in her cheeks emphasized the light reflected in her dark eyes. Her innocence seemed to mock him, but he knew she was no innocent. She couldn't be, yet he'd seen that look of fear move over her features. It made his gut knot.

She was a riddle he needed to solve. She had been placed in his care for safekeeping and he couldn't abandon her no matter what his instincts might urge. The biggest mystery of all—why did he find her so incredibly sexy? She had to be the furthest thing from his usual type of woman.

Distance. Damn but he needed some space right about now.

"I'll get my things and you can show me to my room," he said as he donned the shades and headed toward the door. Camille's stare bore into the middle of his back. The same vivid erotic images taunted him every step of the way through the courtyard, the iron gate and to the curb.

Aiming his key chain at the Jag's hood, he pressed the unlock button. The horn bleeped once and the headlights flashed. Another button popped the trunk. He retrieved his cell phone from the under the dash, a slim laptop and large duffel bag from the trunk before locking up again. The rumbling sound of hard plastic wheels on asphalt had him looking up in time to see five teenage boys riding skateboards down the sidewalk toward him. He nodded as the group slowed and checked him out, the oldest obviously impressed with Ian's wheels.

"Damn! That is one hot car," the kid said, flipping his board up with a toe and catching it mid-air. "Very nice...how fast can it go?"

Ian smiled. "Fast enough. I could outrun anything I needed to."

"Even the cops?"

"Now why would I want to do a thing like that?" Ian asked with a sly smile.

The kid grinned. "Hey, guys, check out the Jag."

The other boys ambled over to ogle the sleek vehicle. He

remembered what it was like to grow up on the wrong side of town, dreaming of fast cars while his father told him he'd never amount to anything. Ian proved him wrong in the beginning and took satisfaction knowing the old man hadn't been around during the bad years. Hopefully, these kids had someone to encourage them to follow their dreams in the right way.

"You guys live around here?" he asked. It might be a good chance to make a few connections to help him keep one eye open. Demons could enter their victim's lives through dreams, but they usually took human form in real life and used a host who looked like any other human being. Ian could sense demons...even smell them at times. But as they grew older, demons learned to mask their presence from those who hunted them.

"Yeah, we live in the neighborhood," the leader said, taking a slight step back, features shuttered. Ian cursed under his breath. It was good, really. Kids needed to be tougher these days, smarter and wary. But it ticked him off that he couldn't even smile at a child without him running to find mom or the cops.

Your choice, Spain. Big bad biker, remember?

He tugged off his sunglasses, snagged one stem inside the neck of his shirt and pasted on his most benign expression.

"I was wondering because—" he gestured toward Camille's house. "—you know the ladies that live here?"

The boy nodded, glancing at the house through squinted eyes. "Yeah, they haven't been here too long, but that one...man, she is hot."

"I hear that," another boy agreed while their friends chuckled in response.

Ian smiled, glancing around the circle of young faces still softened by baby fat but obviously eager to grow up. A little too eager.

"Yeah? Which one?"

"Black hair, kind of short? Damn, she's fine."

"Yeah, she's okay," he agreed. Of course they'd choose flash over substance. They were still kids despite the hormones kicking into overdrive. "But her sister is my lady and I'm worried about her. Someone tried to break into their house last week. You guys know anything about that?"

The boys shifted uneasily. Two of the younger ones glanced

down the street as if they wanted to bolt. Their leader stood his ground but couldn't hold Ian's gaze for long and looked down at his feet.

"I dunno. I heard some glass breaking in the middle of the night and saw the cops show up, but I don't know who did it. Hear lots of noises with the windows open." He looked up then, dark eyes blazing with anger. "It wasn't any of us. We just like to look at the ladies and ride our boards."

Ian held up both hands, palms out. "Hey, not accusing you of anything. I just thought since you know the neighborhood you might have heard about it. Maybe heard somebody bragging about scaring the women."

"Haven't heard anything like that."

Ian picked up his bag, hoisting the strap high on his shoulder as he tucked the laptop under the other arm. "Well, if you guys see anybody messing around, I'd appreciate it if you'd let me know. The name's Ian, Ian Spain."

"You staying here?" the boy asked, jerking his chin at the house.

"Yes, like I said, she's my lady. A guy protects what's his."

The kid tilted his head, eyes narrow in the sun's glare. "The one with brown hair, right?"

Ian nodded.

"She's nice. She's got class. Gave my mom copies of her books, autographed and everything, just 'cause I helped her carry boxes inside when they moved in last year. Mom likes those mushy things."

The boy stepped back a pace, shoulders squared as if he might have said too much. "Yeah, we'll keep our eyes open. Nobody messes with our ladies 'round here."

"Thanks...?"

"Jake." The kid dropped his board and led the others down the street.

He'd have to watch Jake carefully. He reminded Ian of himself at the same age. He knew there'd be some tough choices for the boy to make down the road. Maybe a voice of experience would help him make better decisions than Ian had made once upon a time. Of course, that might mean sticking around once Camille's demon had been laid to rest, and he had no intention of doing that.

Chapter Two

The man was a predator. Camille felt like the prey as she led him up the stairs, ever conscious of his gaze moving over her.

She took a breath, willing her pounding heart to slow. It didn't obey, couldn't obey with over six feet of hard, volatile male muscle practically breathing down her neck. Gorgeous and unyielding like the heroes in her books, Ian Spain set her on edge in a most primal way. He would be deadly to her peace of mind. Perhaps deadly, period.

She suppressed the urge to turn and face him. Camille lacked the courage to meet his disturbing gaze head-on for fear of what he might uncover. He might see the fear she tried to bury. He might realize she knew exactly what he was. She wasn't supposed to know anything about the Sentinels, but even they could not keep secrets from a woman with her gifts.

At the top of the narrow steps she moved aside, allowing him enough space in the hall so they didn't have to touch. But he moved closer. His body heat made her pulse spike.

"This will be your room," she said, avoiding eye contact as she gestured toward the closed door at their right.

She could smell the rich spicy aroma of his cologne mingled with the underlying clean of soap. His chest stretched broad and solid beneath the casual coat and white button-down shirt. She tried to look away, but her gaze flowed up his thick, bronzed neck. She could easily imagine nuzzling against the strong column, breathing in his scent and heat until it filled her with warmth. There didn't seem to be a safe place to let her eyes wander.

Coward.

She lifted her gaze and studied his features for the first time since he'd entered the house. He fit her earlier vision perfectly with his strong jaw, slightly shadowed even at this early hour, high cheekbones and sharp, straight nose. Crinkles about the eyes gave a clue to a more light-hearted side to this hard man.

"Are you afraid of me?" he whispered. His tone evoked reverence for the quiet rather than fear of being overheard.

"Should I be?" she challenged.

His gaze moved over her face before it settled on her lips. He leaned closer. "I'm not sure. Maybe we should both be. Do you feel it?"

If he meant the heat building like a blaze between them, taking with it every ounce of oxygen... Yes, Camille felt it. Suddenly the hall seemed even more dark and cramped like a tunnel. She swayed toward him while his gaze slowly penetrated her carefully chosen façade.

Dangerous described him as no other word could. Unlike her heroes, she couldn't control his actions, couldn't be sure what he would say from one moment to the next. She didn't know him at all and really couldn't trust him.

Camille blinked. "I-I don't know what you mean." She took a quick breath and stepped back. "There's an attached bath, it's small but comfortable. I'll bring you extra linens. If you need anything else, just let me know."

She turned toward her own room, reacting on instincts that screamed at her to run.

"Camille?"

She stopped short but kept her back to him.

"Ignoring it won't make it go away."

"I'm not ignoring anything, Mr. Spain. There's nothing to ignore."

She knew it to be a lie even as she dove into her room and shut the door. Now she had both the nightmares to conquer as well as her confusing attraction to the man sent to protect her. But she could do this. Letting him into her life wouldn't mean giving up control. Her heart, her decisions would still be her own. It would not be like before. No man would ever get too close after she'd been so thoroughly used and abandoned. Never again.

She straightened her shoulders, ignoring the quiet murmur humming between the walls of her rented home. Her bathroom was the only one with extra linens tucked into the tall built-in cabinet. Her bedroom acted as a refuge. She could spend days on end in her sanctuary without ever having to leave. Here were her dearest possessions and comforts including her computer, a small refrigerator, a television and microwave. This was home— or as close to it as she'd ever come.

Run. Hide. Fly, don't fight.

She sighed. It was no way to live. A small part of her demanded justice, cried for what she'd lost. But how could one really live while they jumped at shadows, spoke with the dead and feared a memory that didn't even exist? *Damn.* Maybe the dreams had already sent her over the edge.

Whatever the cost, she needed to avoid Ian Spain. Something about him frightened her. A powerful essence lurked within the aura of energy surrounding him from head to foot. It pulled at her, weakening her resolve to keep all men at arm's length. She made a fool of herself once, so long ago, and lived to regret every moment of it.

If I hadn't been such a trusting idiot... No sense going back there. The past couldn't be relived even if she wanted to do so. It seemed distant and foreign, consisting of little more than a few faded memories and one huge blank spot in her mind. Love had done that to her. It made her vulnerable, allowed her to be a victim.

Just like Mom. She cringed at the thought. She had loved her mother despite her faults and sordid past, but to know they were anything alike did not sit well.

With a sigh, she walked to the small bath and shut the door in order to access the cabinet. She hesitated a moment. The big man across the hall might not balk at rose pink towels, but he would look better in blue. A vivid image popped into mind of the Sentinel, wet and glistening, a short bath towel wrapped around his lean hips. She immediately shook away the impression. No, not a good idea to envision him in such a way. It would be all too easy to think of him as she did her heroes— all sex and testosterone, muscle and heated flesh. A shiver coursed down her spine.

Camille slammed the cupboard door, fighting for calm like a swimmer being pulled further and further out with the tide.

Struggle and drown. She clasped a stack of navy blue towels and crisp white sheets against her chest. Head bowed, she recited a quiet prayer for strength.

She knew with her abilities and her faith, her belief in one God had to be unique. But it had been faith alone that saved her after the betrayal. Faith combined with obligation kept her going as she fought for her sister's future and took them both away from the horror, memories and gossip.

She looked up to catch her own gaze in the mirror above the vanity. "You should have stayed away."

The longer she stared, the more her image became distorted like a fun-house mirror that somehow revealed inner ugliness to the world. Sins displayed for all to see. Horrors and shame clear to the naked eye.

"I will not live in fear," she recited the mantra taught her by her most supportive psychologist.

The doctor had helped her understand both her traumas and her gifts—had believed in her when few others had. A small number of people knew about her abilities, even less accepted them. Her mother had been the exception and the one woman who understood all too well. She'd once held a similar gift but lost it in the course of living and making one bad choice heaped upon another.

"I will not be afraid. I am in control." Camille stared at herself a moment longer. The chant did little to dispel her fear.

But what was she so afraid of this time? Being eaten alive by the monster of her dreams or losing some piece of herself to the dark knight come to rescue her from its jaws?

The bundle of towels held like a shield, she walked the long yards to her bodyguard's room. For a moment, she simply listened before tapping lightly on the door. Silence. She frowned. Perhaps he had gone back to his car for something?

She knocked louder. Nothing. With a shrug, she opened the door and stepped inside. It would be better to leave the linens on the bed and scoot out again. Without pinpointing the reason, she knew it wasn't wise to risk another confrontation so soon.

The room was small and sparse, furnished with only a dresser, a king-size bed and a nightstand. The muted eggshell walls and scuffed hardwood floors were less than luxurious, but Camille didn't care. A temporary address rented by the month from Samantha, it would never be more than shelter. She hadn't wanted to come back to Savannah even on a short-term basis, however much she loved the city. Too many ghosts drifted about, not so much the spirits that spoke to her, but the memories of a childhood gone very wrong.

She walked across the room and laid her bundle on top of the neatly made bed. Fatigue settled on her shoulders like a leaden weight. She stared at the king-size bed for a moment, longing to crawl beneath the quilt and hide from the world. Maybe the dragon wouldn't find her here. A door creaked open behind her. Camille froze like a burglar caught in the act. She felt heat rise in her face as she turned to face him.

Oh. My.

The Sentinel stood in the bathroom doorway, light from the window framing his body in a wash of pale yellow. His broad chest bare, long hair flowed loose about his shoulders like strands of black silk. Her mind flashed to an image of an ancient warrior—fierce and unsmiling as he painted his face in stripes of red and yellow. A rhythmic chant and the beat of a bass drum throbbed in her mind.

Ian continued to dry his hands on a small pink towel, an eyebrow quirked in silent question. She tried to make her mouth work, but couldn't quite manage it with him standing there half-naked, staring at her with a knowing look. A glimmer of some emotion darted across his features and a soft, low flame lit his dark eyes.

Staring into those eyes felt like looking into a deep well and glimpsing a bit of movement, a spark of light indicating the depths ended after all. Yet, it could never be reached without certain death to the seeker. Such were this man's secrets— dark, deep and guarded by both his warrior nature and distrust.

He swiveled at the waist and tossed the hand towel back into the bathroom. A white, slightly puckered circle drew her attention. It stood in stark contrast to his tan skin.

Shot, he'd been shot. Long ago...

The room seemed to fade, her peripheral vision going steadily gray as she stared at the old wound. There would be a similar scar beneath his shoulder blade. The bullet had gone through, barely missing his heart.

Blood...so much blood. Burning...agony.

She felt a muted version of his pain, his fear. The air

vibrated in rhythm to the frantic call of his heart. Then it slowed, measure by measure like a sonata played *adagio*...a lethargic, plodding funeral dirge.

A whiff of death, stale and sickly sweet. The pain lifted and in its place a peaceful nothingness. Empty, quiet, void of heat and sound. Cold, so very cold that it permeated through muscle and tissue, settling deep into bone. And then the darkness fell.

"Camille?" a voice called from somewhere outside the void. She couldn't answer, didn't have the energy or will. "Camille!"

Pressure built, consuming her. She was dying. No, it wasn't real. It was a memory. *His memory.* With the realization, Camille jerked her mind awake and fought up out of oblivion. This was not her reality, but a dream. *His nightmare,* she knew. One he had lived and now relived over and over.

Warmth surrounded her, supported her in the weightless vacuum. When she finally opened her heavy lids, she looked into dark, worried eyes. Camille frowned. Was this part of the vision or had she come back?

"Are you all right?" The dark man hovered above her, concern in each syllable.

It took a moment to realize she was in his lap, cradled to his chest like a child as he sat on the edge of the bed. Camille tried to push him away but the mental connection left her weak. She blinked in confusion, not quite understanding the experience. It was unlike anything she'd ever encountered.

"Don't struggle, I'm not going to hurt you," he assured. "You fainted." A small smile replaced his worried frown. "I know I'm kind of scary looking, but I've never had a lady faint on me before. Not in the bedroom, anyway."

She noticed the spark that flamed in his eyes, heard the soft, sensual edge to his words. She had no doubt he could make the most secure woman head for cover before she melted at his feet. Especially in the bedroom. Her cheeks warmed.

"I'm fine. Let me up."

A dark brow quirked. "Are you sure? You didn't seem fine two seconds ago."

"Well, I am," she insisted, moving one hand to his chest to push him away. Big mistake. She'd forgotten he was half-naked, had forgotten the smooth sleek look of his skin interrupted only by ripped muscle, a dusting of dark hair and... She sat up straight, heedless of his strong thighs beneath her bottom.

A scar.

Her hand drifted over his chest to his left side. She ignored his sharp hiss of breath as she searched for the blemish.

There...small, round and livid white against his tanned torso. A bullet wound.

"Who shot you?" she asked as she fingered the puckered flesh. His breathing quickened. He shifted his legs beneath her.

"Long story," he said and swallowed. "Another life."

She glanced up at his face and saw his eyes close, jaw clench. Before she could decipher the body language, he lifted her off his lap and set her on the mattress at his side.

"I'm sorry," she murmured, still somewhat dazed by the emotions of her vision. "It must have been a very frightening experience."

"No." He surged to his feet and strode across the room. Then he leaned both elbows on the dresser, his back to her as he breathed heavily. "Just another day in the life of a DEA agent. Hurt like hell, but I got through it."

Why is he lying? She'd experienced the moment, relived his pain and stark fear. Maybe he was a man who couldn't admit weakness. Or maybe he was telling her the truth. Could it have simply been nothing more than a painful experience that was all in a day's work? Somehow she doubted it.

"DEA...that's the Drug Enforcement Agency, right?"

"Yes. I retired years ago and went into business for myself."

Camille rose from the bed, her legs like rubber. She had never experienced such an overpowering vision. Her supernatural episodes involved speaking with the dead and her strange writing trances. Never this... Never a personal connection to someone's past. What was it about this man that turned her inside out with erotic visions one minute, painful memories the next?

"I'll leave you to settle in," she said as she made her way to the door. "I-I'm sorry about fainting like that. I haven't been sleeping well. I guess it's starting to catch up with me."

She reached the doorway and almost made it to the hall when he spoke. "What are your plans for the rest of the day?"

Camille turned to look at him, but he still had his back to the room. The ends of his hair brushed his shoulder blades.

She saw the exit wound—just where she had pictured it in her mind. The memory of his pain made her wince.

"I need to get some writing done," she said. "I'm on deadline. Lia wanted to go out this evening so I thought we'd have some dinner and hit a local club. The isolation has been hard on her."

He nodded. "Good. You shouldn't hide at home. It's best to draw him out in the open. Maybe we could shake some trees and see what falls out."

She raised a brow. "Interesting concept. Let's try for a relaxing evening, though. I'm really not energetic enough for tree swinging."

He turned and crossed his muscled arms over his chest. She fought the urge to squirm beneath his scrutiny.

"Do you have any idea who's after you, Camille?"

She licked her lips and shook her head. Truth...he wanted the truth and she had the feeling he wouldn't let her alone until she complied. The thought of Ian watching her, hounding her every moment with questions...it was almost more disconcerting than being swallowed whole by her dream monster.

"No, but I know he's getting closer." There. She finally admitted it. A small weight lifted off her shoulders. Maybe she wouldn't have to be alone in the nightmare any longer.

They stared across the room, a silent war being waged. She could sense his take-charge nature fighting with confusion and pride. He wanted to protect her and hide things from her at the same time. So much like a man of ancient times—a throwback to a bygone era. But part of her liked the idea. It had been so long since anyone had taken care of her. She grew weary of the battle.

"Who does Samantha think is after me?" she asked. "Did they tell you?"

He frowned, his arms dropping to his sides as he took a step closer. "What are you talking about—they? Samantha hired me to look out for you, no one else."

Disappointment made her shoulders droop. No, he wouldn't confide in her. It wasn't done. Ian might be a maverick of sorts, but he wouldn't break the strictest of rules. Only a select few knew of the Sentinels and their existence. Usually the list included those who were one of them and those they killed. Rarely did a Chosen One ever receive any kind of confirmation until their life was in danger, although rumors often abounded. Apparently, he meant to keep her in the dark unless he had no other choice. Maybe that meant her life wasn't in danger after all? She grasped at that straw and held on tight.

"Of course, Samantha," she murmured. "Does she know what's going on?"

He searched her face without answering. Just when she thought he would ignore her question, he took three long steps and stood looking down at her. His chest only inches from her face, she had to tilt her head to see his eyes. Shimmers of awareness played along her spine.

"She knows you're special and that you're in trouble, Camille. But the only way for this to work is for you to tell me everything you know."

"But I—"

He placed a finger across her lips. "Everything. No lies."

She fought the urge to taste his skin. She longed to lean into his broad body, to let him support her tired limbs. It would be easy to let this man hold her...love her. The thought almost made her laugh out loud. What would a stern loner like this know about love? She wrote about the emotion day in and day out and still didn't have a clue. It was all make-believe, a fantasy. Perhaps that was all it ever would be.

His intense expression deepened the frown line between his full brows. From the moment he had entered the parlor, he'd taken her breath away. He filled the house with his tall, intense presence like a flooding river fills the countryside. Ian's eyes were so dark she could barely make out the pupils. She couldn't look away. He wanted something from her. A fire burned deep in those eyes, a lingering desire she sensed had never been fulfilled. She could see it all so clearly reflected in the black depths. The notion terrified her more than the bad dreams.

"We have time," he murmured. "You *will* talk to me, Camille. Together we'll figure out what's going on. Until then, go about your business as usual. Think of me as your shadow."

§

But shadows didn't change the feel of a house. They

invaded dreams or sent imaginations flying. Sometimes they offered a place to hide. With the presence of Ian Spain, the entire aura of the building changed.

She would have felt his proximity even if she couldn't hear the heavy tread of his footsteps and the deep rolling timbre of his voice as he spoke on the phone. A subtle tingling filled the air like the moments before a thunderstorm. Never before had she been so completely aware of another human being. She didn't know if she liked the sensation.

Camille tried to work but the blank white screen mocked her futile efforts at finding that place where the words poured into her mind and out again. The zone, she called it. It hovered just beyond her grasp while her thoughts raged with visions of the Sentinel.

She periodically paced the floor of her small bedroom, rubbing the gooseflesh on her arms. Should she give up and go downstairs, despite the risk of having to spend more time in the man's presence?

No, let him hang out around the house, trying to detect the presence of whatever kept creeping into her dreams. She didn't need to get close to him, didn't want to be anywhere near him. This whole mess was likely fueled by her hyperactive imagination coupled with Samantha's overprotective nature.

Camille sighed. Somehow, she knew that wasn't the case. Evil lurked in the shadows behind the memories she'd hidden for over ten years. She couldn't shake the feeling her misguided college romance was somehow connected to her current distress. But maybe the feelings were the remnants of emotions surrounding her mother's brutal death. Everything had to surface at some time. The fear lingered for months after Camille left Georgia with Ophelia in tow. Maybe it had simply returned.

The second hand ticked slowly by as time dragged on. It seemed to stand still as she watched the hands move around the face of the small brass clock on her dresser. No matter how hard she tried to ignore it, the soft tick drew her attention again and again as the sun moved over the sky toward the west.

A well-stocked mini-fridge meant she didn't have to venture out of her bedroom office. She had music to inspire her, peace and solitude to create the right mood, but still the words wouldn't come. Ideas in short supply, she soon surfed the web and found other ways to procrastinate.

Computer mahjong lost its appeal after eight straight loses. None of her cyber friends or critique partners were online and her website guestbook was as silent as a tomb. She laughed at the thought. Since when did she ever equate death with silence? Graves were quiet because the spirits mingled among the living. The dead didn't hang out in cold, musty cemeteries. But ghosts were far from silent. They loved to talk, and talk...to anyone and everyone, even those who couldn't hear them.

She clicked off her website, making a mental note to update the contest page, when a thought struck. Anything and everything from candy bars to bored teens had websites. Why not the Sentinels? Curious, she typed the word into a search engine and waited.

Over 600,000 references?

She sighed. Even if the one she wanted was part of that enormous number, it would take days to narrow the field. She doubted they would be careless enough to let their secret organization be so vulnerable, anyway. Too many lives would be at risk—those like her, whose gifts set them apart; men and women like Ian, whose abilities made them formidable allies and deadlier foes.

An image flashed across her mind. The Sentinel dressed in a white poet's shirt and tight black trousers, a cape swinging from his broad shoulders as he smiled to reveal straight, white fangs. She shivered. He'd make a perfect vampire, like the one she'd been thinking of these past two months. This one was much more intense and focused than the hero of *Healing Touch*. Ian had the same essence about him, like a solid brick exterior surrounding a lonely, forgotten heart. A heart he'd long ago given up on healing.

Why did the bodyguard have an air of loneliness about him? He couldn't be lonely. He was the epitome of a virile man. Men like Ian made women stop and stare as they walked down the street. His kind made them sigh and dream. Women threw themselves at men like him in crowded bars. He was a man's man and a woman's dream.

No, he can't be lonely. He wouldn't know the meaning of the word.

§

By six o'clock that evening, she was beginning to feel like a caged beast. It was too early to sleep, but she couldn't concentrate enough to work and she had promised Ophelia a night on the town. But Camille couldn't shake the feeling of something approaching. Something for which she couldn't possibly prepare. In the past ten years she had fought every moment to keep her life ordered and under control. So far, so good, until now.

A light tapping on the door had her spinning around. She stared at it for a moment without moving, her breathing shallow and erratic. Could it be him?

Camille swallowed. "Yes?"

"Come on, Cami, I'm starved and you said we'd go out tonight," Ophelia complained. "Are you lying down again?"

"No, of course not." She slid off the lock and opened the door, plastering on her best smile in order to keep her sister pacified a bit longer. Ophelia had to keep believing everything was under control and that moving back to Savannah had been worth everything she'd given up in Virginia. Camille only wished she could truly have faith in the decision herself.

"What did you have in mind?" she asked. "Nothing too rich or I'll never sleep."

Ophelia grimaced and waved a hand in dismissal. "Nonsense, we're young and healthy. I don't think a little barbecue is going to keep you up all night. Well, not that you sleep half the time anyway. Come on, let's go."

Camille hesitated, her gaze skipping across the dim hall to Ian's door. "I'm not sure this is such a good idea with everything that's been going on. Why don't we just order some take-out and rent a movie? Mr. Spain must be very tired."

She felt a hand on her arm and before she realized what was happening, Ophelia dragged her out of the bedroom toward the stairs.

"Oh, give me a break. We haven't been home in over five years and I am not going to waste my time hiding away in this oppressive old house. Now, let's go check out the action and see if the bodyguard can keep up."

"I'll give it my best shot."

They both jumped, turning to see Ian leaning against the doorjamb. A lazy, sardonic smile curved the corners of his mouth. Dressed in black slacks and a dark red pullover, he looked good enough to grace any men's magazine cover. He looked good enough to eat.

Ophelia laughed. "Busted."

"I understand you ladies are going out this evening. I've been waiting to hear the details."

Camille glanced at her sister and tried to tamp down the erotic images skimming through her mind. Why did she feel so unsettled with him? "We haven't been home in a while."

"And," Ophelia added. "I haven't had hardly any fun since we moved back."

Camille gritted her teeth as guilt and anger mingled. Her sister could still be incredibly selfish at age twenty-two. But whose fault was that? She'd been the role model for the last ten years, no one else.

"Lia, you've been out almost every night of the week just in the past month." Camille sighed at her sister's petulant expression. "All right, we'll go because I promised, but I need to get some work done tomorrow. How about if we agree to be back by midnight?"

"Midnight? Are you nuts? That's when everything starts hopping. Make it two."

Camille shook her head. She wasn't getting any sleep anyway and the writing had suffered. But when Ophelia got in one of her moods there was little she could do beyond locking her indoors. There was no way she could let her sister go out alone. Too many things could go wrong even if the bodyguard shadowed Ophelia like a bird of prey. Camille knew he'd insist on staying with her, anyhow. She just couldn't take a chance of letting her sister go out alone.

"Let's compromise and say one o'clock," Camille offered.

Ophelia's blue eyes narrowed, her mouth twisting in disgust. "Oh, fine. Take what's left of the fun out of my life."

Camille smiled at the familiar line. "That's my job. Fun killer."

She turned to glance at Ian who stood a few steps behind. Something in the way he looked at her made her stomach flutter. "Are you sure this is okay? You must be tired after your long drive."

"Let's go," he insisted. "I'm in the mood for some good food and music. Just stay close, ladies. Remember, I'm your shadow."

Chapter Three

Something in the crowded nightclub shifted. Its essence changed, transformed with warm, kinetic energy that vibrated along with the rhythmic southern rock and conversation. Camille knew somehow that Ian watched her from the bar. She felt it to the marrow—his gaze like the caress of a warm hand on chilled skin.

The Blue Moon Tavern resonated with the laughter of friends out for a good time. But she sat alone at a small table, cradling a glass of red wine between her hands. Her heart thundered as she glanced around the jammed room in an effort to avoid the Sentinel's gaze.

At one end of the bar, she spotted her sister flirting with a flock of admirers. She watched Ophelia laugh for a moment, somewhat envious of the ease with which she made friends. The hair on her arms lifted as the crowd parted to her left and Ian's dark, brooding gaze clashed with hers. She looked away, feeling suddenly breathless. Heat rose in her face.

She wondered if he also felt the strange, almost unnatural pull between them. It was like fighting against a primitive force of deadly proportions. They were so different, like positive and negative charges bouncing through the same space, unable to resist the compelling energy drawing them together.

But fight it she must. There was too much to lose—too many secrets that a man like Ian could uncover. He possessed a curious nature and a calling to seek the truth, of that she was certain. Besides, she could never let a man close to her again. Her judgment proved faulty when it came to the opposite sex.

The muted, neon glow surrounding them enhanced his dark looks. It wasn't fair, her heart mourned. He so precisely fit that two-dimensional vision of the perfect man, the perfect hero who could sweep any woman off her feet and toward a passion unlike any other. But real men were not perfect.

She feigned interest in the blood-red depths of her glass before lifting her gaze again. Ian had looked away. Lost interest, no doubt, as a young waitress in tight jeans and red cropped T-shirt stopped at his side to flirt. Jealousy stabbed through her when he smiled back at the twenty-something girl. She was everything Camille was not—vibrant, ultra-young, reed-thin and confident. The girl obviously knew her way around men and was the type to go after what she wanted. The thought made her slightly sick inside.

But what did it matter? She wasn't interested in the Sentinel even though she could easily imagine him whispering sweet seductive words in the dark. Even if she couldn't help but imagine his hands caressing her...moving over her with deft, erotic strokes. A hazard of her profession, it meant nothing on a personal level. Nothing.

She chose not to pursue the tall, dark knight. Ian was a stranger. Men were treacherous. She'd yet to meet even one she could trust.

Her attention back to the wine, she noted the waiter who served her. He walked by, one brow raised as she poured another glass from the bottle. No doubt he wondered if they'd have to pour her into a cab later. He must already think her a bit of an oddity since she insisted he bring a full, unopened bottle to her table.

Little could he know that she would finish less than half the burgundy, leaving the remains for him to drink or discard. Ever since that night ten years ago when she'd been drugged into oblivion from a spiked can of cola, Camille insisted that any drink she ingested be opened by her own hand. She wouldn't let herself become vulnerable ever again. The obsession was easier to hide when Ophelia shared the wine, but tonight her sister had opted for stronger stuff and more masculine company.

Raising the glass to her lips, Camille took a long sip. She jerked when a searing pain blazed across her shoulder blades. Scorching anger slammed into her. The air wrenched from her lungs and strength bled from her limbs. Someone else watched from the crowd. Someone she hadn't sensed until it was too late. Her gift had failed her.

Reciting a silent prayer for protection, she inched her chair backward. She could feel the malevolence digging into the center of her spine. Her stomach rolled in protest as she brought the glass to her lips and emptied it in one gulp. Her heart leapt to a frenetic pace. Feigning casualness she didn't feel, she turned.

It took a moment to sweep her gaze over the dozen or so faces at the opposite side of the club. Her breath caught, heart seizing in mid-beat as a face from her past came into view.

It must be an illusion, a trick of the light or memory. A doppelganger come to haunt her at a stressful hour. Camille blinked, but the man remained. Their gazes held and she knew with a certainty that it was him. The man she had once trusted. The one who had tricked and deceived her. The one who had taken that trust and twisted it, abused it beyond redemption.

Time seemed to stand still around them. Voices and music drifted down the dark tunnel into which she had fallen. Like a prisoner awaiting execution, she stared at the man in mute horror. Then his thin lips turned up into a smile and he raised his beer in mock salute. The spell shattered, Camille turned away.

She couldn't breathe. Her throat tightened as panic twisted through the fringes of her mind, freezing her body to the spot. Glancing at the bar, she saw Ophelia in deep conversation with a blond man, their heads bent close together. Her gaze flew to Ian, still laughing with the flirty waitress.

Camille's stomach tightened until it became a throbbing ache. She was alone. Always alone to face...

"Welcome home, sugar."

The past.

She didn't look up, didn't dare.

"What? No hello kiss for your old beau?"

Her cold fingers squeezed the stem of the empty wineglass.

"Leave me alone, Drew." She cringed at the note of panic in her voice.

He chuckled—a deep, chilling sound devoid of humor or warmth. How many nights had the memory of that laughter haunted her dreams?

"Now, now, sweet sugar," he said, leaning near her ear. His

heated breath washed over her neck with the smell of stale beer. "What kind of greeting is that? Seems you've lost that southern charm since we last met. You remember don't you? Was a night to remember, but if you don't, I'd be happy to repeat the experience."

He reached out, trailing his fingers down her bare arm. She jerked out of his reach; the glass stem snapped in two. The remnants fell to the table and shattered on the tabletop. He wasn't deterred. He twisted a chair around and sat so close that his knee brushed hers.

For a moment, Camille stared at him. Goosebumps rose over the flesh of her arms. She had once thought him the most handsome man she had ever seen. Now she searched his cold blue eyes for some sign of the person she had thought him to be. Nothing but arrogant humor looked back at her. She didn't have to open her senses to know he was toying with her as he used thinly disguised charm to set her on edge.

Power and intimidation turned him on. She would have realized that from the beginning if she had been stronger. But things had changed.

"If you come near me again—"

"You'll do what? Call the police?" The corners of his mouth turned up in a mocking grin. "I don't think so, sweet cakes. Not then and not now. Or would you like the world to see just how passionate you can be? I'm sure the ladies who buy those little books you write would just love to know all about your colorful past, don't you? They do love a good sexy story."

Her stomach tightened as bile edged up her throat. *Oh, God.* He wasn't bluffing. *If anyone ever knew...ever saw...* They would never understand, never give her a chance to explain what had really happened ten years ago.

"You have more to lose this time 'round, sweet sugar."

He was right. She couldn't stomach another scandal in her life or one more round of roasting on the front page of every newspaper and tabloid in the state of Georgia. This time her name just might make the national news as well.

Why had Drew come after her now? At nineteen she had merely been a pawn to him—an easy mark and an even easier lay. He must have found a better target for his degenerate needs by now. Camille fought back the panic and straightened her shoulders.

"I'm willing to risk it," she lied. "Stay away from my sister and me. I'm not a scared nineteen-year-old anymore."

"No, you sure aren't." His gaze slipped down her body, hot and intense in its scrutiny. Revulsion slammed her in the stomach like a fist, threatening to bring up the wine. "And you have aged mighty well, sugar. You're just at your peak, aren't you now? Godamighty...I bet you're even better in the sack. I read your little books. You damn well know your way around a man, you sure ain't no shy little virgin anymore. What lucky buck taught you all them tricks, huh? Or did your mama give you some pointers before your old man sliced her up?"

She flinched at the memory. Her stomach churned with hate and grief as her fingernails bit into her palms. "What do you want?"

His gaze returned to hers, the anger she'd sensed earlier burned like fire beneath the blue ice. "Cooperation, sugar. Give me what I want or I'll make your life a living hell. I kept the pictures for sentimental reasons, but I'm willing to sell them to the highest bidder. Then again, I might just post them free on the Net...depends on my mood."

Her blood ran cold. "Why are you doing this?"

"Because I can, and because your daddy owed me big." The flare of hatred in his eyes made her shrink back. "I'll just take my payment out of your sweet hide. I've been waiting on this day for over ten years."

She surged to her feet as his last words demolished the last shreds of her self-control. Her chair clattered to the floor. From the corner of her eye, she saw a tall, dark figure pushing through the crowd toward them.

Coming to the rescue or to join the hunt?

Panic gripped her by the throat as Ian's intimidating presence rushed closer. She felt trapped between the man she hated and the one she didn't trust. She turned and ran toward the door like a fox chased by a pack of hounds. A taunting chuckle underscored the noise around her; the sound of her name followed her out into the night.

"Go back!"

She shook her head, ignoring the small inner voice that most often gave her the best advice. She couldn't go back and face Drew alone, and she didn't trust the Sentinel. She didn't know Ian, but she had experienced Drew's cruelty up close and personal. She'd be damned if she'd ever let the man touch her again.

Camille knew Drew wouldn't hurt Ophelia—his obsession lay firmly at her feet. A tremor washed over her and she sprinted down the street in the general direction of the house. She glanced back every few steps to see if anyone followed. She had to get away from that bastard and the gauzy memories that dogged her every waking moment. If Ian were any kind of bodyguard, he'd never have let the other man get so close. It always came back to relying on her own strength. No one else ever gave a damn long enough to help.

Soon the darkness seemed to swallow all sense of direction. She found herself at an unfamiliar intersection. Where had she made a wrong turn? Camille stopped, glancing left and right as she wrapped her arms about her middle. It would be stupid to lead Drew home even if she could figure out how to get there.

Footsteps in the distance made her panic further and she turned right toward the riverfront. A streetlight at the end of the block seemed to beckon. She slowed as she neared it, approaching warily. Her gaze darted around for some point of reference. Somehow this place seemed familiar. She closed her eyes and listened. The spirits were quiet, except the one that led her. He beckoned her onward, toward the alley.

Strange how the only man she trusted was a dead one she'd never met. *The dead wouldn't hurt you,* she reasoned. *Most of them have better things to do.*

Camille swallowed, wishing she could go back, but unable to ignore the guidance this time—so strong was the compulsion. Her low heels clicked on the pavement as she neared the corner and turned into the deserted back alley. Stepping gingerly over a broken piece of cement that jutted up at one end, she continued. A cold chill prickled down her spine.

The short alley smelled of rotting garbage and river water. It ended with the back wall of a tall, brick building. There were only three doors off the alley and all of them were boarded up. She almost turned around until a soft glow of light from one dirty window caught her attention.

The sign over the door read *Second Sight.* A black silhouette of a cat lounged beneath the words. The animal looked as if it would jump down and run at any moment. She almost swore she could see the feline move, ears flicking in annoyance.

Camille heard footsteps coming from the main street. She glanced around, taking less than a second to make a decision, before she pushed open the door and stepped inside.

The first floor looked like an empty storage room. The pungent smell of mold and river water filled her nostrils. She wrinkled her nose as she shut the door and looked around. A single bulb hung from the center of the room, casting its yellowish light over the bare cement floor and brick walls. She could just make out a watermark high on the faded brick, indicating the building had flooded at least once.

"Hello?" she called, almost afraid of being answered. Her voice echoed around her.

Then she heard the faint sound of music coming from above. Curiosity and the calm she sensed around her gave her a boost of courage. Camille moved forward as she searched the empty room for stairs. She found them at last, crawling up the back wall like an ancient twisted centipede slinking toward the second floor. After a moment's hesitation, she began to climb the wooden treads, holding fast to the shaky handrail as she went.

At the top landing, a red-painted door barred her way. A small sign reiterated the shop's name. Camille hesitated, but thinking of the climb back down the splintered steps, decided it would be better to brave whatever lay ahead. There had to be another way out, one that would take her more directly to the main street.

She turned the knob and entered a long narrow room amid the sound of bright, tinkling bells and the distant strains of stringed instruments. As she stepped inside the threshold, the music stopped. The sweet scent of jasmine mingled with the musky blend of mildew.

Shelves lined the walls of the shop. They spilled over with books, glass bottles and cardboard boxes. At first glance, nothing in the shop seemed very expensive or unique. It was more like the jumble left over after a yard sale.

A long glass display case edged one side of the narrow aisle. The other was lined with more bookshelves. The case held a haphazard display of chunky jewelry, silken scarves and various items labeled as charms. The shelves were filled with small ornate bottles of numerous shapes, sizes and colors. Each container seemed to reflect the muted light and magnify it somehow as the colors swirled and danced around them.

Overall, there was a gentle hum about the room—a peaceful energy that reached inside Camille's defenses to calm the shaking inside. She found herself drifting down the aisle as she examined the small treasures tucked behind the glass partitions.

"May I help you?"

Camille spun around, heart hammering. "Oh, I'm so sorry. I-I didn't think anyone else was here. Are you still open? I mean, the door was unlocked, but..."

"Yes, of course, child." A small woman, not much taller than a young child, gazed up at her. "I'm always open to those in need. You come on in now and make yourself at home."

The edge of panic continued to blur as she looked at the woman. Her dark blue eyes twinkled up at Camille from a round face. Hair as white as new snow framed the woman's golden brown features. It had been pulled up into a small bun at the crown while soft, wispy tendrils curled about her high forehead and plump cheeks. The small figure was swathed in a voluminous caftan in jewel shades of purple and blue. The garment shimmered and glowed with reflected light.

"What are you doing out here all by your lonesome on such a pretty evening?" she asked, her lilting accent making the words sound like music. "There be a lover's moon out tonight. A sweet thing like you should have a beau."

Camille shook her head, fighting to order the thoughts that floated there like disembodied spirits. "I was with my sister but we were separated."

A wrinkled hand reached out from beneath the folds of shimmering material. The woman patted her arm. "Well, you're safe now, child. Why don't you come on in the parlor and have a seat? I was just about to pour myself a cup of chamomile tea."

"Oh, but I couldn't."

"Of course you could." The woman smiled. "I'm closed now and you can use my phone to call your sister if you think she's worried."

"But, I thought you said you were open?" Camille turned toward the red door she had come through. It wasn't there. She frowned, glancing about in confusion. She must have gotten turned around somehow.

At her left she noticed a small flight of stairs with another door at the bottom. This one had a large glass window over which a shade had been pulled down along with a closed sign.

"How...?" she began, but the woman was gone. She disappeared somewhere among the hodgepodge of trinkets and books. A tingle spread over the back of Camille's neck. It didn't feel evil but left her uneasy all the same. She glanced around the chaotic shelves and counters, half-expecting to see someone lurking in the shadows. She was alone.

"Hello?"

"Back here, child, behind the curtain," the woman called. Camille hesitated a moment before following the sound. Her sense of direction must be completely fouled up.

Too much wine, after all.

She skirted around the counter and pushed a deep purple velvet curtain aside. It hid a small back parlor from the rest of the crowded shop. She was sure the curtain hadn't been there before, but that was absurd.

The old woman sat on a high-backed chair at a small round table near the center of the room. She glanced up from pouring tea into two mismatched cups.

Camille's gaze roamed around the room. Bookshelves lined a wall to her right. The others were covered with knick-knack shelves that glittered with bits of ceramic, crystal and glass figurines. A small air conditioner whirred in the lone window, the only view above it was that of the dark night sky. The smell of jasmine, musk oil and mint permeated the room, carrying with them a sense of peace that drew her inward even before the woman spoke.

"Come, come," she admonished as she flicked a delicate hand toward the loveseat nearby. "Do have a seat and join me. It isn't often I get to entertain anymore."

Her grandmotherly smile drew Camille forward another step, banishing the last niggling doubt. She sank down onto the loveseat and smiled. "Thank you."

The fragrant aroma of chamomile filled the steam that wafted up from the thin porcelain cups. Camille shook her head when the woman silently offered her cream or lemon. She picked up her cup, careful not to grip the slim, tapered handle too firmly as she blew across the golden surface. There was a small chip in the rim, a vein-like crack marring its white surface. Another breath drew the aroma of the soothing herb deep into her lungs but she couldn't bring herself to drink.

"My mother used to make us chamomile tea," she murmured.

"Yes, and double-fudge brownies. Then she'd read to you from the *Tales of Beatrix Potter*."

Camille's eyes flew open wide, tea sloshed over the rim of the cup and burned her fingers. She hastily set it down and grabbed a cloth napkin to dry her skin.

"How did you know that?"

Her hostess smiled and chuckled softly. "There's nothing to be afraid of, child. I knew your mother."

"But—"

"You don't look much like her, except the way you carry yourself." The woman sat back for a moment. Her deep blue eyes studied Camille's features with shrewd intelligence. "Yes, you're Marguerite's daughter. She often visited and brought your pictures along. She was very proud of you and your sister, though the little one gave her a tough row to hoe."

"I...I don't even know your name."

"Virginia, *Madame* Virginia to those who seek guidance. You are Camille. I know of your return after so many years. The papers are full of stories of your success. The spirits are tense with excitement." She waved a hand in the air. Her eyes sparkled like sapphires in the moonlight.

"But they be anxious for you. Something's coming. Something we can't change for it was set in motion long ago."

Camille blinked and the hair at her nape lifted. She accepted her gift—understood it to some extent—but this was too much, even for her. It felt as if the woman's gaze tunneled right through her, seeing much more than she could allow.

"I think I better leave." She began to rise.

"No," Virginia commanded gently. "You've come seeking guidance and that's what you'll have. I won't hurt you, child. I know I seem a mite odd, but if you reach deep inside, you'll see the truth."

The small woman's eyes seemed to hold the wisdom of the universe. Camille couldn't drag her gaze away. The secrets there pulled at her senses, begging her to stay and discover them for herself.

"You will never know peace of mind until you trust what is

in here." Virginia pressed a finger to her chest. "And until you find faith in yourself and the Creator. You can never find peace until you trust."

"You believe in God?'

"Of course, child." Virginia laughed. "Where do you think my gift came from? And yours?"

"But...I just assumed..."

"That I wouldn't be God-fearing 'cause I believe in magic?" She glanced around the parlor as if trying to confirm or deny Camille's suspicions. Finally, the woman shrugged. "I haven't always relied on Him. But my power is stronger now that I do. We all have to follow our own ways."

A dark feeling settled over Camille. She'd never possess enough faith in anything to make it through this ordeal if the darkest moments of her life were displayed like an open book. Drew had come back, slinking out from beneath his rock to demand payment for sins committed by another. How could she ever face those kinds of ghosts? What would become of her now? Somehow, she knew this was only the beginning.

"Give me your hand," Virginia commanded.

She held it out, unthinking. The woman turned it over in hers, smoothing a finger across her palm. "You are strong...a long life is ahead of you. You have a good heart."

Virginia closed her eyes, her face going still as she laid her other hand over Camille's palm. The light touch sent a jolt of heat, a spark of power tingling across her skin. She stared at the old woman's delicate fingers, the deep copper hue such a contrast to her own pale skin.

"You are very lonely...except in your work. You see the possibilities through him, your guide. The spirits of the past...souls of the lost and forgotten. Those that hide in the shadows and are misunderstood, feared. They need you to tell their stories, to bring their sorrows to life. They need to know love waits...they need hope. They need *you* so they can find peace."

Virginia opened her eyes and smiled broadly. "You write stories of love."

Camille nodded, her voice caught behind the lump that had formed in her throat. How could this woman know these things? No one knew about her guide or the way she wrote. Not Ophelia, not even her agent, Sam. But despite her inspiration, the stories were still fiction. Weren't they? This woman almost made them sound like prophecies.

The all-seeing eyes closed once more. Silence filled the room, interrupted only by Virginia's steady breathing, until she spoke again.

"You are a chameleon. Your colorless image hides your true soul from the world. You are...frightened...wary. You fear rejection. You fear love and letting yourself care. You fear losing control by giving power over your life and heart to another. You fear...men."

The eyes flew open, spearing her with a look that simmered with anger. "The man should have been punished for hurting you so! He uses others in a way that is evil to the core."

"No. It was my fault." She tried to look away but the small woman held her gaze captive. "I made mistakes. I was young and stupid."

The woman shook her head and closed her eyes again.

"You are afraid of this man who's come back. He wants something...but what?" Her delicate brow wrinkled. "I cannot tell. He is shrouded from me." Virginia shuddered.

"You are afraid to tell anyone of your past...afraid of what the evil man will say and what they will believe. But there is another who will believe you. He is dark, tormented. So alone.

"He frightens you and yet you long to trust him. He intrigues you, this man of your visions, this protector of the Chosen. He is a chameleon, like you. You can help each other if you trust yourself. You can save him from his own darkness as he walks your dreams."

The old woman dropped Camille's hand and jumped to her feet, her eyes alight with excitement. "I know what to do. I know how to help, but you must trust me, yes?"

Camille felt the fear drift away like a trail of smoke. "Yes, all right."

Was that her voice? Why was she agreeing to anything this strange little woman had to say? What was she getting herself into?

It didn't seem to matter. Camille knew deep inside that she didn't have much of a choice. The aching burden of her past lay heavy on her shoulders. A foreboding chill seeped into her body, penetrating her very bones. She didn't have a clue how to stop the evil that hovered on the horizon.

Virginia shuffled out of the parlor, the curtain whipping about as she pushed through it. A few moments later, she returned. Her hands clutched a small velvet bag and her eyes sparkled like those of a child on Christmas morning.

"This is for you," she murmured, opening the bag and extracting its contents with great reverence. "It has been waiting for you, I think. Here..." She pressed something cold and hard into Camille's palm. "Take it, child."

Camille looked down at her hand. A round pendant shone gold in the muted light of the sitting room. Two lizard-like creatures formed the two-inch circumference, each holding the tip of the other's tail in its mouth. A dark red stone glistened in the center, its many facets catching and reflecting the light.

"It is the Chameleon Talisman," the woman said. "It's very, very old. I've had it for many years but never had a reason to use it myself. I think it's been waiting for you, child."

Camille frowned. "But, what is it for?"

She shrugged slightly. "It draws power from whoever wears it. The result is different for each person. Legend says it was blessed with extraordinary power by the one who crafted the amulet. He made it to protect the woman he loved."

Camille stared at the old woman. Her senses tingled as the pendant lay heavy in her palm, the long gold chain pouring out to snake around her arm. But she couldn't shake the doubts that assailed her despite the power shimmering within the blood-red stone.

"I don't believe in magic talismans, Madame."

The woman chuckled and shook her head. "Neither did I, until I had need of one long ago. Take it, child. Wear it. But beware how you use it. Don't let the power take over. Be true to yourself when you feel ready. Just don't wait too long 'cause you might lose your way back."

"But, how can it help me? *How* do I use it?"

Virginia smiled. "Sometimes we need to hide for a spell. We need time to face who and what we are so we can fight another day. You'll understand when the time comes. The magic will be there when you need it most." She folded Camille's fingers over the chameleons and patted her hand. "Go. If you need me, you know where to find me. But now it's late and someone is looking for you."

She drew Camille to her feet, turning her toward the

curtain. A moment later, Camille found herself ushered back out into the street through the front door. She blinked, disoriented and somewhat dizzy. The lone streetlight near the alley entrance cast a dim, gray glow on the pavement at her feet.

A tinkle of the silver bell, and the shop door closed tight behind her. Camille turned to say good-bye, but the shop was dark and deserted. She frowned. The sign above the door was almost identical to the one in the alley. But this placard hung limply by one corner, swaying slightly as if a breeze blew against it. The cat silhouette had vanished, like the strange impish woman, leaving only a vague feline outline in its place.

Camille's thoughts churned with the knowledge that her sanity hung by a thread. She had come in another way...through an alley, but now she stood on a main street. The entrance was the same, but different. Had it all been a dream? A hallucination? Had she finally snapped?

Something hard and cold pressed into her palm. She glanced down, opening her clenched fingers. In the dim light, the talisman seemed to glow with some inner warmth. She walked toward the street lamp, her gaze riveted to the golden chameleons—the blood-red stone between them winked at her.

A black cat leapt hissing from the shadows when she narrowly missed stepping on its tail. Camille watched in stunned amazement at it galloped off down the alley. Her toe snared on something hard and she cried out as the world tilted, the sidewalk rushing up to meet her.

She caught herself with her empty hand, twisting the wrist at an odd angle. The cement scraped away a layer of skin. She rolled over on her side and tried to catch her breath. Tears stung her eyes.

"Camille!"

She jerked up to see a dark figure rushing toward her. *Ian.* He stooped down beside her and gently lifted her injured hand in his. She gasped at the feel of his warm, rough skin enveloping her cold fingers. The scent of his cologne filled her nostrils while he leaned close. A tremor coursed through her body.

He glanced up to meet her gaze. "Are you all right?"

"I tripped." She looked behind her, noting the broken cement. "I wasn't looking and..." She stared at him, a tendril of fear snaking around her. "How...how did you find me?"

Chapter Four

"I saw you fall." He fought to keep his anger in check. The stubborn, difficult woman was going to get herself killed.

Damn it all, not on his watch! *Not this time.*

He rose slightly, the pavement hard against his knees as he pulled a bandanna from the back pocket of his jeans. Careful not to touch the torn flesh, he wrapped it around her bleeding wrist. Ian had to clench his jaw shut to keep from cursing.

"What happened at the bar?" he asked finally. "Why did you run off without me? I had one hell of a time picking up your trail."

She looked away. "I had enough and decided to go home. You were both enjoying yourselves. I didn't want to ruin your fun."

Ian gazed at her in disbelief. Did he hear a bit of jealousy in her tone? Hurt? He pushed the thought aside and focused on what was important. She didn't trust him and acted carelessly.

"Who was the man?"

Her body went rigid beside him. "No one important, just some guy. I told him I wasn't interested."

Liar.

"Why did you run from me?"

She looked down. "I wasn't running from you."

"I know a hunted look when I see one, honey. Something scared the hell out of you and I'd hate to think I almost ripped a man's face off for no good reason."

Her head jerked up, eyes wide. "Did you get into a fight with him? Oh, God, tell me you didn't!"

He searched her face for a hint to the thoughts flitting

behind her dark eyes. "No, I didn't get in a fight. I asked him why you left."

The memory made him clench his jaw. Nothing would satisfy him more than laying the bastard out flat after what he'd implied. If he ever saw the son of a bitch again, he might follow through on the impulse.

"He made a crude comment, then I came after you. I've been searching the streets for the last half-hour, Camille. I had Lia call the police. Where have you been hiding?"

She stared at his hands holding hers. He followed her gaze and noticed the way her ivory complexion almost glowed against his darker skin. It could have been a photographic study in black and white—the rough hands of a warrior holding the smooth fingers of a porcelain doll. The shadows made the image all the more surreal.

Ian had a hard time keeping control. The urge to shake her until her teeth rattled almost overtook reason. As did the other urge...the one that demanded he gather her close and press her body to his. His protective instincts were always on high alert, but coupled with these strange surging desires they were making his head spin.

"Where's Lia?" she asked.

"She's safe with a friend of mine," he said as he pulled off his jacket and wrapped it around her trembling shoulders. She glanced up into his eyes, the streetlight revealing her swirling emotions.

"But...how?"

"He was the tall blond-haired man at the bar, Brent Adair. I called him earlier and asked him to keep an eye on her for me. Didn't you see them together?"

Camille frowned. "Yes, but I just assumed she made a new friend."

"Or conquest?"

She nodded. Ian tried to ignore the way his pulse raced at her nearness. He slid his hand beneath her elbow, the other arm across her back as he helped her stand. He thought again how Ophelia and Camille were as different as night and day. It still amazed him that they could be related.

"Is your sister in the habit of picking up strange men?"

"No!" she exclaimed, jerking around to look at him over her shoulder. "Of course not. It's just that..." She sighed. "She hasn't been out in a while and she likes men and flirting. She's always been popular with men but my sister is *not* a tramp."

"Calm down, I didn't say that." He felt her shiver before her body relaxed a little against his. The warm, soft weight of her pressed into his rigid muscles sent waves of pure desire through his body. Maybe not pure...there was very little purity in the thoughts this woman evoked.

"You shouldn't be out here, wandering around dark alleys on your own," he murmured. Her scent filled his nostrils with vanilla and spice. Warm, sultry like a summer breeze washing over the shore. Ian swallowed back the longing to bury his face in the cool silk of her hair.

"It's dangerous," he muttered thickly. "Anything could happen."

"I'm fine." Her eyes darkened and for a moment they gazed at each other, the quiet interrupted only by the thundering pulse of his heart.

"Why did you leave without me?" he asked again.

"I can take care of myself, Mr. Spain." Somehow she sounded a little less sure of herself. "This is my hometown after all and—"

"Ian."

She blinked. "Excuse me?"

"The people I put in jail call me Mr. Spain. The paperboy calls me Mr. Spain. My name is Ian. We're going to be spending a lot of time together, Camille. Formalities will get irritating."

It shouldn't be so important, this urge to hear his name on her soft pink lips. But it felt vital. As did the quickening in his blood, the rush of heat to his extremities as he stood there in the lamplight, holding her. She peered up at him through dark, fathomless eyes while she leaned against his chest. Her round bottom hovered just inches from his groin, sending waves of heat spiraling to his cock. God, how he wanted to pull her against him...to feel the weight and warmth of her pressed to the building ache.

"All right, Ian, if you insist. But I do think you're overreacting. I wasn't in any danger."

"Then why did you run?" he asked. She was lying. She'd been scared to death when she ran from the club as if she'd seen a ghost or the devil himself. "Who is he?"

He felt her move away as she shook her head. She

hesitated. Was she trying to decide how much to tell him?

"Just someone I knew a long time ago."

A jealous ache gripped his gut. The realization hit him like a bucket of cold water. Ian slid his hands from her and stepped back. He must be losing his mind. His reaction to her mimicked a teenager with his first major case of lust. She was a client— one who was hiding something. One with gifts he couldn't quite comprehend and who had attracted some sort of evil like a homing beacon from hell. He couldn't let her charms reduce his good judgment to mush.

"Old boyfriend?" he asked, trying to convince himself that he didn't care. He only needed to know in order to protect her. Somehow Ian couldn't persuade his chaotic emotions to that effect.

"He thought so." She increased the distance between them and folded her arms across her belly. "I'm tired. I'd like to go home now."

If he'd been a man who cared about such things, he would have felt dismissed. As it was, her abrupt change in demeanor intrigued him, which was more than a little annoying. He did not want to be intrigued by anyone, let alone an uptight romance writer. Already his unprofessional feelings toward her were getting in the way. How long before his judgment clouded completely?

"Fine. Let's go."

He thought he saw a glimmer of hurt in her eyes before he turned away. But he forced his feet to keep moving down the sidewalk in the direction of her house. He didn't turn to see if she followed. The soft click of her heels sounded behind him as they neared the busy main drag. An occasional glance in a passing shop window showed him she was close enough to be reached if anything happened. Laughter and the occasional burst of music serenaded them along the way.

She still feared him and watched him carefully with large, wary eyes. Not a problem. As long as she showed a healthy amount of fear over something there was hope for her. It's when the fear vanished that things happened...bad things. Things that took life careening out of control.

Getting her to trust him with both her life and her secrets would be her salvation. He somehow knew this woman draped in drab brown material did not easily give trust. If she feared him, at least then she might listen to his orders, if only because she couldn't predict what he'd do when she disobeyed. Looking scary had advantages.

He pulled his cell phone from his jacket and dialed. "It's me. Found her. Yes, she's fine. I'm taking her home. No, stay for a while. We're good. We'll talk tomorrow. Call off the locals for me. Thanks, good night."

He turned off the phone and slid it back into his pocket, intensely aware of Camille's scrutiny. But he refused to look at her. He needed time to think and couldn't seem to do so with her gaze challenging his.

Traffic zipped by as they turned another corner, the late hour doing little to put the buzzing city to sleep on a Friday night. How he loved Savannah, even after spending months and years away fighting for his ideals in some of the best and worse cities across the country. Ideals faded. Reality set in.

Time and experience, the sense of his own superiority, had dulled his senses until nothing made a difference anymore. The bad guys became just as appealing as the good, or maybe the other way around.

He had lost perspective long before the shooting slammed him into years of constant pain. Long before the prescribed drugs became his haven. Then the world had gone insane from within the misty, dream-like view that clouded his thoughts.

He hadn't cared until a rookie on his operation took a bullet. A bullet meant for him. And then he'd learned life wasn't as simple as it seemed. Monsters lurked in the dark and he had nearly become one of them.

"Slow down!"

His pulse jumped and he stopped short. He'd forgotten her for a moment. Some bodyguard he turned out to be. Camille jogged up to him, her chest rising and falling with each breath.

"I can't keep up," she panted.

"I thought you didn't need my help," he said, knowing the dig was childish at best.

She crossed her arms over her stomach and glanced at the traffic. "I don't..." She stopped and sighed, her gaze finally meeting his. "I'm sorry about the way I've been acting. It's just...I'm used to dealing with things on my own. I guess I don't like someone else taking over."

He nodded and took a deep breath. "I know the feeling all

too well." He held out a hand. "Apology accepted."

She laid her small, cold hand in his. Their bodies communicated on some primitive level. He could hear the hitch in her breathing. They stood there staring into each other's eyes as the world streamed by.

"Truce?" he asked.

Camille smiled. "Yes, for a while anyway."

"Until we find out who's stalking you."

"There's no one—"

He quirked a brow and her mouth snapped shut. "Just because you want to be in control, doesn't mean you are. It's not a weakness to admit you need help, Camille. The weakness is refusing to ask."

She tilted her head. "The voice of experience?"

He studied her for a moment. "Yes. Now, as you said, it's getting late. Let's go home."

They reached the old Victorian with Camille leading the way inside. His gaze traveled down the length of her long unbound hair, past her waist to the curve of her round hips. The brown material floated around her like an ethereal shroud of protective armor. The subtle message broadcast too loud in the intimate silence.

Hands off. Don't look. Never touch.

How did such a rigid woman write about love and passion? He began to wonder about her work. He'd never read any of her books, not even the one that had rocketed her to a sort of local cult status as well as putting her name on several best sellers' lists. What had he been missing? Maybe he'd pull the copy out of his bag tonight and see what other secrets this quiet woman hid beneath her fragile shielding.

He paused as she pulled a key from a pocket hidden in the folds of her dress. The lantern hanging from the ceiling of the old porch cast harsh shadows around them. He couldn't keep from staring at her profile as she fumbled to fit the key in the lock. Her skin would be cold and smooth like a gemstone. He longed to reach out a hand to see if his instincts were right.

He felt drawn to her like an addict staring at the ultimate drug, the most exquisite high. But Camille was the farthest thing from his type. She was innocent. Secretive. A woman in distress who was either too stubborn or too dumb to see the danger.

He shook his head, his gaze catching hers when she turned her head. *No. Not dumb.* Intelligence glittered within those dark eyes. She was assessing him at the same moment. Camille might be reckless or she had her own agenda in not admitting the danger around her. But she was nobody's fool.

She turned abruptly, twisted the knob and pushed the door open as if the hounds of hell nipped at her heels.

"Thank you," she said once they stepped into the narrow entry and he closed the door. Her hand fluttered at her side while her gaze skittered about the small space.

"For what?" he murmured. Unable to resist the impulse, he stepped closer, crowding her against the hall closet. She was so tempting with her sweet bakery scent and wide doe eyes. He heard her small gasp of surprise as he laid a hand on her shoulder. The strength he felt beneath the thin material seemed inconsistent.

On the surface she projected such a timid, fragile image. But there was steel beneath the softness. A will of iron gleamed from the depths of her dark eyes. She blinked up at him and Ian forgot for a moment what he had intended to say. The realization hit him deep in the gut and he jerked his hand away.

"For-for coming after me," she stuttered. "Even after everything I said about not needing help."

He swallowed. "I'd say you have been very welcoming, all in all. These situations are never easy, Camille. Everyone reacts differently."

She twisted her hands together—chances were she didn't realize the inner turmoil she displayed to him, a stranger. She still didn't trust him despite her agent's confidence in his abilities and the erotic energy that swamped them every time they came close. Heaven knew what it would be like if they really touched. Skin to skin...limb to limb...her hips nestled in his lap.

Ian turned and locked the door with a shaking hand.

"Good night," she murmured. A moment later the sound of her soft steps disappeared up the stairs. Ian leaned his head against the solid door, his pulse hammering in his ears. He took a deep breath and let it out in a frustrated rush.

What the hell was wrong with him? He hadn't lusted after a woman since he was seventeen years old and never for one that embodied everything opposite his normal one-night type.

Focus. He had a job to do. Someone or something was coming after Camille. It was up to him to solve the mystery and keep her from becoming a victim. She had some powerful abilities and valuable secrets. Too many people had expressed concern about her welfare for him to take her protests seriously.

If anyone hurts her... He pushed the thought away. It wasn't going to happen. He would protect her with his own life. After all, that was his job.

Ian thought of the man he'd seen talking with her at the club. He was trouble, that much had been obvious from the few sentences he had uttered and the cold, malicious glint in his eyes. Camille dismissed the individual as unimportant. Ian knew better. He hadn't survived this long without good instincts. Tonight they were telling him the man was dangerous.

The fear in her eyes hadn't been an illusion, but neither had the impression she was hiding something. He'd find out who was threatening her and why. With or without her help.

§

Lying across the borrowed bed, Ian stared at a crack in the white plaster ceiling, his cell phone clenched in one hand. He had calls to make, some digging to do. But all he could think of was the way he'd panicked when Camille ran out of the bar.

He could still feel the unnerving wave of fear that had set in after he ran into the street and found her gone. Disappeared like an image from a dream.

The last time he'd felt so vulnerable, a stupid mistake blew his cover at the crack house he'd infiltrated. Then his life flashed by in a pathetic parade of mocking images. Tonight, he'd pictured large smoky green eyes, open and lifeless. All because he'd insisted on creating a little distance between himself and a woman whose scent had haunted him from the moment her hand touched his.

She made him hunger, made him want things he should never imagine. Because of that, he'd been careless.

The phone rang and he jerked violently. Cursing himself, Ian answered with a less-than-civil tone.

"Yes?"

"Well, hello to you, too," a familiar voice said, a soft chuckle easing the tension in his shoulders.

"Sam, I was just about to call you."

She laughed again. "I hope so, Ian. I was beginning to think you'd left the country to avoid me."

"Now why would I do a thing like that?" he asked with a smile.

He enjoyed sparring with Samantha Bays. They'd known each other since high school and he had once thought himself in love with the spirited redhead. But they had both known it would never work between them and had remained friends. Only back then, he hadn't known about the Sentinels or her family's long tradition of being councilors to them.

"Where are you?" she asked.

"I'm at Camille's." He wondered if his casual tone sounded as strained as it felt. "In the guest room, to be more precise."

The long silence that followed had him sitting up. He waited even as he wished he could see the expression on her face.

"Wow, she actually agreed to this?"

"Isn't it what you wanted? What the council wanted?"

"Well, yes. I mean, of course it is. But, knowing Camille I thought we'd have a fight on our hands. She's one of the most independent people I've ever met."

Ian laughed out loud. "Tell me something I don't know."

"I guess the Spain charm isn't a legend, huh?"

"I wouldn't say that."

As close as they were, he could never tell Sam about the attraction that sizzled and swelled between him and Camille. It simmered like magma just below the earth's crust, searching for a fault that could send it rocketing sky-high. One weak moment would mow down every ounce of his common sense.

"Ian?"

"Hmm? Sorry, what were you saying?"

"I asked how you pulled it off? How did you get her to agree to let you stay?"

"I'm not sure, actually. I think she's more concerned about the situation than she'd like to admit."

"I hope so, this whole thing has had me worried sick. The

nightmares are getting worse and I'm sure it's only a matter of time before something happens. There's something there. We're not sure what, but something is causing this."

"How long have you known Camille?"

"We met about eight years ago when she first submitted a manuscript. I couldn't put it down—read all four hundred plus pages in one night. I knew she'd make it big someday, so I signed her on. We've been friends ever since, but..."

Ian frowned at her sudden reticence. "But what?"

"She's very nice, don't get me wrong, but she isn't the easiest person to get close to. I think that's why I'm really surprised she let you stay. That's more of an accomplishment than you realize, Ian. She's very shy and holds her privacy dear."

He thought of the man at the club and wondered just how well Camille knew him. "Has she ever discussed her past with you?"

"Well, not anymore than necessary for her author bio. Everything else we know is just public knowledge. Why?"

Ian rubbed his forehead with one hand. "I'm not sure. I just have this gut feeling there's something else going on here. Samantha, what exactly are her gifts besides talking to the dead? I've been experiencing some strange things around her."

She was quiet for a minute. "What kind of *things*?"

The erotic vision of her naked and in his arms passed through his mind. Ian swallowed hard. "It's hard to explain," he hedged. "She had a vision while we were together earlier of something from my past. She seemed to know all about the last bullet I took in the line of duty. I tried to play down the incident but she wasn't buying it."

"Huh, that is strange. As far as I know her gifts don't normally involve any connection with the living. Her gift is quite strong but not unique in and of itself, except I suspect she uses it to gain information on others of the Chosen. Ian, have you read the book I gave you?"

"No, not yet. After tonight I might have to." He thought of the man at the club and his own strong physical reaction to Camille's presence. Would there be hints in her writing as to how her mind or powers worked?

"You were supposed to read it!" Sam admonished. "That would have given you a lot of clues. It's about a friend of yours."

He frowned. "Friend?"

"Yes, take a look at it, you'll understand. Even the cover is quite an amazing likeness."

"Hang on..." Ian laid the phone on the bed and retrieved his duffel from the small closet. The thick paperback was right where he'd left it. He pulled it out, collapsing back on the mattress as he sought the phone with his other hand. The image on the dark blue cover made his breath catch.

"My God. It's Gabriel."

Samantha laughed. "Yes. I had Camille change his last name. Until this past winter, the story itself was still fiction. But it is him, right down to some of his more peculiar habits."

Ian couldn't suppress the nostalgic smile that tugged at the corners of his mouth. "I'll be damned. Gabriel's a romance cover model."

They both chuckled—it felt good. It had been too damn long since he last had a good laugh.

"It's not him, exactly, but I did manage to find a model that looks enough like Gabriel to be his twin."

"Shit, Sam! How can you let her write about him? Isn't that dangerous?"

"It can be," she agreed. "Fortunately very few people believe beings like Gabriel really exist. They belong to that mythical world of fantasy and folklore, too far beyond the grasp of human understanding.

"But I had the same initial reaction when I read her first book—that and being blown away by the writing itself. I knew the man she wrote about by reputation only. When I checked it with the other council members they were rather astonished at the amount of accurate detail in her story."

Now some things were starting to make sense. "And that's why you signed her on? To figure out where she got her information and bury it somehow?"

"It crossed my mind," she admitted. "Although, I was very happy when the individuals involved gave me permission to let the story be. Of course, I had her change some key, identifying details in all three of her books. She's a talented writer, with or without her gift. I knew the story was golden."

"Hey, hold on," he interrupted. "You said Gabriel's story *was* fiction until last winter. What does that mean?"

"Gabriel wasn't involved with a woman at the time Camille wrote the story. Then about six months after it was published, he actually *met* the heroine. She had the same name, same physical description—everything right down to a small scar and her personal history. It was unbelievably eerie, to say the least. Similar situations arose from her first two novels as well."

"She wrote about the future? Then she has the gift of prophecy."

"No, I don't honestly think she does. I'm quite sure her gifts are speaking with the dead and writing fantastic stories. We've spent too much time together for me not to get a sense of something else going on in her life. I don't understand how it happens or where her inspiration comes from, but it's definitely unique."

"Wonderful," he muttered. "Have you ever thought the briefings could be a little more detailed? Were you planning on telling me this, eventually?"

"Ian, you were given the basic facts and clues you needed, as always," she lectured. "You're usually the first to figure it all out. I'm surprised you didn't do your detective work before you left Pennsylvania."

"I've been a little preoccupied," he admitted quietly, knowing his long-time friend would keep his weakness secret. He had been through his own personal hell and back after losing his last assignment to a horrific death. While Ian had been unable to stop the carnage, he still felt keenly responsible for the young man.

"It wasn't your fault," Samantha said softly. "Tom knew the risks involved when he refused to cooperate. It happens to every Sentinel at one time or another."

"That doesn't matter. I was supposed to protect him and I failed. He was just a kid...a baby."

"He was twenty-five, hardly a baby by any stretch."

Ian sighed. "I can't lose another one, Sam. I *won't* lose another one. Not without one hell of a fight."

"Listen, maybe it was too soon to send you out again. Maybe—"

"No. You need a dream-walker and I'm all you've got right now. You sure as hell can't send Gabriel in with all she knows about him—not until we understand what we're dealing with on all fronts. Just make sure someone is close enough to watch my back if I call for help."

"Now you've got me worried," she said. The light teasing tone barely hid true concern. "I don't think I've ever heard you admit to needing back-up."

"And you never will again. But right now I already feel like I'm in too deep. Something isn't right here." He stared at the paperback and smiled. "So, this is Gabe's story."

"That's it, with a little poetic license naturally. Read it and I promise I won't ever tell him you called him *Gabe*." Sam laughed. "This novel is even better than her first two. It's one of the most powerful stories I've read in years. She did a masterful job telling it."

Ian frowned, still unable to take his eyes off the air-brushed image of the Sentinel who had saved his life seven years ago. "I don't get it, though. How the hell does she know? Where does she get her information?"

"I wish I knew. Camille isn't the easiest person to get close to. She's got this thing about her privacy, which I can understand, given her talents and her past. But she won't open up to me and from what I can tell I'm one of her closest friends aside from Ophelia."

Ophelia a friend? He doubted it. The sisters shared little that he could see except a last name and address. Something inside him twisted at the thought of Camille being so very alone in the world. They did have a lot in common.

"Is that something the councilors want me to investigate while I'm here?" he asked. "Do you want to know exactly how she gets her information?"

"If you can find out, yes. We're a little concerned others might be able to tap into the same source. But that's not your mission, Ian. We need you to flush out whoever...*whatever* is after her. Many more sleepless nights could result in horrible consequences. I'm worried she can't handle it."

"I'll do what I can. I just wish she'd open up to me. It would make this whole thing a hell of a lot easier."

"I know."

"There's something that bugs me, though. Why would Gabriel or any of the other Sentinels allow you to publish a book about them? I'm not sure I'd like my every move in the bedroom splashed on paper for anyone to read."

"You should ask Gabriel sometime," Samantha insisted. "In

the meantime, read the book and I think you'll understand why he gave the okay. Besides, I'm not sure they believed these were their stories until after the fact. Like I said, the books are more prophecy than anything. I do want information on Camille's writing, but promise you'll watch your back, Ian. Keeping you both safe is the number-one priority. I couldn't bear to see anything happen to either of you."

"Do you trust me?"

"With my life, you know that."

"Good. Then consider the job done. Nothing will happen to the lady while I'm here. I guarantee it."

"All right then, we want you to use your talent as soon as possible. Say tonight? You need to get into her dreams and figure out what's going on, what we're fighting here."

Nervous energy filled the room. He had discovered his dream-walking abilities long before Gabriel saved his life—long before he realized he wasn't the only oddity in the world. But it still bothered him to use the "talent", as Sam called it. To him it had always been an irritation. For years he had been unable to control whose nighttime fantasies he entered. He'd never been able to deal with his own dream demons.

But he knew that was why they'd called on him, even so soon after he lost a protected one. Some of the councilors might not trust him at this point, but he was the only one they had who could enter Camille's dream. Walkers were not in abundance for it was a rare gift. He alone could help her overcome the demon that threatened her life and sanity. But the idea of failing again scared the hell out of him.

"It's too soon, Sam." He scrubbed a hand over his jaw. "I need a little time to get a feel for the situation."

"There might not be much time left. She's operating on two or three hours of sleep a night—has been for at least four months as far as I can figure. It started long before I realized anything was wrong. You know what that can do to a person."

Delusions, paranoia, violence, insanity... Yes, he knew all the possibilities. He'd been there himself and if it hadn't been for a dream-walking ancient by the name of Gabriel Bonnett, he might have wound up dead or mentally crippled.

"All right," he relented. "I'll try a small reconnaissance tonight."

"Thanks, I feel a lot better knowing you're on the job."

Ian grunted. "Don't go singing my praises yet. If I can't earn her trust I could lose her."

"I know the Spain charm. I've seen it in action. If you've gotten this close so fast, I'm betting she'll be following your instructions without a second thought. If anyone can help her, it's you."

"I'll do my best. I'd better go and prepare. If you think of any other details you failed to mention, please give me a call."

"Will do, and Ian?" She hesitated. "Be careful. Don't get *too* close."

He laughed. "Invading someone's dreams is about as close as you can get, Sam."

"You know what I mean. Don't do anything that'll get you personally attached."

"Why do you think I would do that? It goes against everything you taught me."

"I think it's possible because you're human and she's an attractive woman. And..." she sighed. "And I get the impression there's more going on than you're telling me. I have the impression your emotions are already entangled."

"Ah, yes. I tend to forget you have your own talents, don't I?"

"I just don't want to see you hurt again."

"Thanks for the concern, but I'll be fine. This is a job, nothing more."

"Good, let's keep it that way. I want Camille whole and alive, but I need you the same way."

"Stop worrying. I'll be in and out, slay the demon and we can all go about our lives. Now, it's late. If I'm going to make the first show, I need to get off here."

"Okay, good luck."

"Good night."

As he turned off his cell phone, Ian couldn't help but think of the worry in Sam's voice contrasted with the stark fear in Camille's beautiful eyes. He went to the door, opened it and listened to the sounds of the old house. Traffic noises rumbled softly beneath the clicking sound from across the hall. She must be working after all, writing another of her sensuous stories. Possibly another true story, according to his friend.

He wondered how any of the Chosen could let their

intimacies be exploited? Why would they allow such private emotions put on display? Their futures paraded for all to see? Sam had told him to ask Gabriel. Maybe he would do just that one of these days. Until then, she had also insisted he needed to read the book to understand his charge.

With a sigh, he decided to make himself comfortable on the large bed after leaving the door ajar. Reading always helped him relax, and soon he would need to sleep, before he could enter her dream.

Piling both pillows against the headboard, Ian stripped down to his boxers and climbed into bed, the copy of *Healing Touch* in hand. He was hooked from the first line. The imagery was so intense, so focused that he had the feeling of being swept away through time and into the private thoughts of a man and woman falling in love. When he finally turned the last page, it was almost five in the morning.

His eyes burned with fatigue even as his mind whirled with the images Camille's words painted. Yes, he would have to talk with Gabriel. To thank him again for all he had done...and to meet the amazing woman who had turned his friend's life upside down. If this story was indeed true, she had not only given him love, but a reason for continuing his immortal existence.

Ian became aware of the thick silence that had fallen over the house. Rising from his bed, he looked out into the hall. No sounds from Camille's room; no light peeked from beneath the doorframe. He closed his own door and went back to bed after switching off the lamp. Hopefully, he could make his way inside her dream without setting off any of her intuitive alarms. This first time he would simply observe and get the lay of the land, so to speak. His next venture could be more intrusive once he knew what to expect and how she might react to his presence.

Lying back on the pillows, he allowed his mind to drift, reaching for that meditative state that freed his spirit. Ian let his body relax as he silently counted backward from one hundred. His essence floated upward, tugging at the bonds that held body and soul together. Then his spirit lifted free and he felt the rhythm of the house, the ebb and flow of emotions embedded in the walls and floorboards. He looked down at the body he vacated and watched the steady rise and fall of his chest. This experience, this separation, still had the power to make him reel in wonder.

One glance around the room ensured there was no danger. He could leave his body behind for a while. Then he went in search of Camille, hoping her defenses would let him inside.

Chapter Five

Heart pounding a *staccato* beat, Camille rushed down the dark alley. If she could just find the little shop again, she would be safe. Madame Virginia would give her shelter—she would know what to do.

A sound grabbed her attention and she almost stumbled as she glanced behind. Shadows moved, slithering over the sidewalk toward her. They extinguished the glow of the street lamps one by one as they drew closer. Like a massive storm, the darkness would soon blot out all light. She would be stranded. Alone.

This time the dream brought her to a different place, but the demon followed, his form concealed in the heavy shroud of black fog. Something hissed. A misty shape reached out of the shadows to touch her skin. A cold, sharp object pricked her arm and she bit back a scream, her feet moving faster. Could she outrun a nightmare?

"Camille."

She jerked to a stop, scanning the alley before her. She was alone. Something fluttered by her ear and she screamed. Instincts took over as she ran into the alley. The blank brick wall rose up before her, barring the way to any kind of safety.

Oh God, he had her cornered. She had always escaped before, had always been able to hide long enough to pull herself from the dream. Heart pounding frantically, she braced her back against the wall and faced her dragon.

Instead of the dark, mythical beast, Ian stood before her. Tall and unyielding, feet planted shoulder width apart, he gazed at her with such intensity she couldn't draw air into her lungs. He wore a black leather jacket that hung open to reveal his bare chest, and skin-tight pants of the same material. A gleaming saber clutched in one hand, his mane of dark hair blew about granite features. His gaze held hers for a moment before he looked down at the clothing. With a twist of the wrist, he lifted the weapon and turned it so the faint light glittered off the blade. He frowned.

"Is it a knight you've conjured, Camille, or a vampire slayer?" He looked at her. "I'm not quite sure I fit the part either way."

She shook her head. "I didn't summon you. I've never been able to summon help before."

One corner of his full mouth quirked into a half-smile. A dangerous smile.

"It seems I'm here now, whatever the reason." He bowed slightly at the waist. "Where is your demon, my lady?"

A hiss filled the air and orange flame shot between them. The rotten-egg smell filled the alleyway. Camille choked on the rancid fumes.

"Please, Ian..." A sob ripped through her. She swallowed and blinked back tears. "I can't do this again. Make it leave. Just make it go."

He gazed at her silently and she wondered at the wariness in his expression. "I thought you didn't need me."

"Please..." His features softened at her desperate plea. Then he nodded, stepped toward her and turned.

"Stay behind me, Camille. Whatever you do, don't run. Demons thrive on fear and you cannot outrun a nightmare."

All Camille could think of was hiding behind his broad back as darkness descended around them. The flutter of wings and a snarling growl echoed off the tall brick walls. Her body shook. Blood pounded in her ears. She could smell the brimstone mingling with sweat and the musty mildew of the alleyway.

Ian stood at the ready, sword clasped in both hands, blade pointed straight up. "Who is it, Camille? Who is your demon?"

"I don't know," she whispered, clutching at the leather coat. "It can't be real. It must be symbolic—"

"Camille..."

She jumped at the sound of her name whispered from the shadows. Ian went rigid, but she couldn't see his face.

"Camille, come to me."

She shook her head even as her feet seemed to follow a will of their own and stepped around her protector.

"Get back," Ian commanded, his gaze never wavering from the writhing shadows before him.

"I...I can't."

Another step and he turned, his weapon clattering to the cement below as he grabbed her arms with both hands and pushed her back against the wall. Rough brick pressed into her spine, Ian's chest against her breasts. She looked up into his eyes, feeling only the rise and fall of their lungs in unison as they stood crushed together.

"I'm sorry," she murmured. His eyes darkened to pitch and his gaze slipped to her lips. He swallowed hard.

"Don't let it control you. Think, honey...who is it? Who is trying to drive you insane? Is it someone from your past? An old boyfriend or lover?"

"I don't have anyone like that."

They stood in the churning darkness, hearts pounding as one. Ian held her pinned to the wall, his body hard and shaking. She wondered at the panic she saw flare within the dark depths of his gaze.

"I'm not prepared. Camille, I'm not ready for this. You weren't supposed to see me this first time."

"What are—?"

A roar shook the building at her back. He spun around, keeping his body between her and the shadows. She could see devilish-red eyes gleaming from darkness now thick as tar. Sulfur made the air hard to breathe and the heat pushed down upon them, coming closer with each rumbling breath the great beast took.

"I'm not ready," Ian murmured as if talking to himself. "This was *not* a good idea."

He grasped her by the arm, all the while his attention centered on the dragon. The beast seemed to grow, his silhouette undulating higher and broader with each snarling exhalation. Ian's grip tightened until she winced in pain.

"Take us out of this, Camille, I can't focus. End the dream."

"I can't!" Panic gripped her by the throat.

"You can, and you must," he insisted. "Think...where are

you? Feel the sheets...feel the mattress beneath you...hear the sounds of the house, the traffic outside. This is not your reality, Camille. Send the beast away."

She shook her head frantically. The fear held her in place. It couldn't be just a dream. Bile filled her throat; her body shook in seizure-like tremors. It was vivid and horrifyingly real.

"Try," he entreated more gently. "I can't protect us both."

She didn't think she could die in her own dream, but could the Sentinel?

"Leave! I-I'll be okay," she insisted. "I'm always okay. I don't want it to hurt you."

"No. Leaving you alone is not an option."

The dragon roared, the sound making her ears ring.

"Remember Camille...remember..."

She shook from head to toe but fought to subdue the fear. It filled her so fully she knew this had to be the end. A clawed foot reached from the darkness, cutting Ian from collarbone to navel. He dropped to his knees, a groan of pain the only sound he made.

"Ian!"

He looked up, teeth clenched, his color fading quickly as blood trickled from the gaping wound.

"Take us...out!" His head drooped forward and Camille closed her eyes. Tears coursed down her cold cheeks.

She could feel the hot rancid breath of the beast fanning her hair. But she reached past that, past the malevolent image to the reality that would provide refuge. And then she began to remember...a vague sensation of her body pressing into a firm mattress, the cool linens caressing her heated skin. A familiar hum rumbled beneath the noise of the growling demon. The sharp retort of a car horn sounded.

"Awake!" Ian's strangled command sent a jolt through her and in the next moment, Camille sat straight up in bed, blinking at the soft gray light that filled her room.

She looked down at her sweat-soaked nightgown, the gauzy material transparent where it clung to bare skin. Breathing as if she'd run a marathon, she sat there and shivered as wave after wave of unspent fear coursed through her.

She was whole. She was awake. The dragon had gone.

A glance around the room confirmed the Sentinel had left

as well. Had he ever truly been there? She half-expected to see her dark knight standing in the corner, watching. Disappointment made her shoulders sag. Of course he wasn't there. It had been a dream, her nightmare. Yet, this time she had not been alone. In her night terror she had a champion—a biker masquerading as a knight of the realm. It was strange, this end of her isolated dreams. Strange and somewhat comforting. Would it last?

Rising from bed, she stripped naked and walked to her bathroom, then went through the same routine as the morning before. Icy water fell from the shower nozzle in a dull, limp patter. She gasped as its temperature sent a shock wave through her system. The drops warmed and quickened when the ancient pipes pulsed to life. She felt her aching shoulders relax, unwinding inch by inch under the rhythmic beat of the hot water on her skin. After several minutes, a thick white fog obscured the white tile walls, commode and sink.

The laundry hamper in her bathroom almost overflowed even though there were still three days until the normal washday. Maybe she should just sleep in the nude and save herself work later on. The thought of Ian across the hall made her quickly dismiss the idea.

After the shower, Camille chose a pair of faded blue jeans and a favorite T-shirt with a cranky looking alligator emblazoned across the front. The simple message of *Back Off!* should give fair warning regarding her mood. It seemed each night got shorter, each day longer. She was at a brittle point. Pity whoever dared push her over it.

Memories of the night before rushed in one after the other, though the dreams were beginning to merge with reality. She looked at her nightstand drawer, hesitating a moment before sliding it open to retrieve the golden talisman hidden behind a box of tissues and several unread books. Slipping the chain over her head, she tucked the pendant inside her shirt. The sturdy chain felt heavy around her neck, the medallion cold and foreign against her skin. Yet, it provided some measure of comfort, although she didn't know why.

She finished her grooming in short order, doing little more than pull her long hair into a braid and slather on some moisturizer that promised to erase signs of aging. After four months of nightmares and insomnia, she needed all the help she could get. At least the cream added a bit of a glow to her sallow complexion. A nice day out in the sun and fresh air would be better, but she was so far behind in her work it didn't seem prudent to take even a couple of hours off.

A knock on her door made her jump out of her skin and set her heart loping. When she opened the door Ian gazed down at her as if he waited for something. His complexion seemed a little pale. Tired lines edged the corners of his mouth and eyes. She couldn't keep from glancing at his chest, half-expecting to see the red, angry mark of the dragon marring his bronzed flesh. But he wore a black T-shirt that covered him completely and would hide any mark the beast may have left behind. Realizing the foolishness of her thoughts, Camille felt her cheeks flame.

"You're up early," he observed. "Another nightmare?"

She glanced away, the memory of his presence in her dream caused strange little tremors to course through her body. Of all the people she knew, she'd never pulled anyone's image into her terror. Never had she begged anyone to save her from the demon bent on possessing her. Why now? Why him?

It could only be because of her initial thoughts of him being a dark knight sent to the rescue. It was only a dream, but the passion that had flared between them in that fantasy made her shy in his presence.

"Camille?" He stepped forward and she jumped back in reflex. Ian froze. "Are you all right?"

"Yes," she said, adding a nod more to ease her own mind than his. "I'm just tired."

His gaze searched her features, looking for clues, no doubt. He thought she knew more about the danger around her than she let on. How to convince him she knew even less than he did?

"What are your plans?"

"Work."

He tilted his head, one corner of his mobile, sensuous mouth curving upward. "All work and no play. How about we take the day off?"

"But, I have a deadline. Sam—"

"Will understand."

She shook her head. "No, my publisher is expecting another best seller. I can't let them down and I'm so far behind as it is."

"I have a feeling you won't be getting anything done today with those bloodshot eyes and dark circles. Take a day off, Camille. You need fresh air, exercise, a little fun."

His observations stung no matter how accurate they might be.

"Thanks," she mumbled. "If I look that bad I'd better stay home. Wouldn't want to frighten any little children."

His laughter rippled through the air like a warm burst of August wind. She couldn't resist the gleam in those dark eyes or the way he held out his hand.

"Come on," he coaxed. "I'll bet you never played hooky even once in your life. Give it a try."

Camille hesitated before she gave in and placed her cold fingers in his. The contrast between dark and light, cold and warm, intrigued her so thoroughly she simply stared at their joined hands for a moment.

"Ready?"

She looked up and caught his gaze. It seemed to hold a promise and a warning. Was she ready to let herself get closer to this man? She'd almost rather brave the dragon in that darkened alley. Almost.

"No," she admitted. "But let's go."

Halfway down the hall, she remembered the outfit she'd chosen and pulled to a stop with a grimace. "Wait...I need to change."

He turned, her hand still held firmly in his. A devilish smile curved his mouth as he glanced at her shirt. "You look great. It's good to know you have a sense of humor. Come on, the day is wasting. Let's get some sun before the tourists soak it all up."

§

Ophelia opened her eyes and groaned as the sunlight burned her retinas. Another night out drinking herself into oblivion meant another day with one hell of a hangover and a whole lot of dark spaces in her memory. When would she ever learn?

"Never," she whispered as she pulled her legs from the clutches of the twisted sheet and sat up. The room spun dizzily for a moment.

Squinting at the digital clock on her beside table, she wondered what had woken her up so early. But the inclination to lie back down dissolved as she remembered at least some of the events of the night before—in particular, a drop-dead-gorgeous bodyguard who had freaked out her straight-laced sister. The thought brought a smile to her lips. If anyone needed freaking out, it was Camille. She sure as hell needed something in her life besides make-believe heroes and writing perfect sex.

Not that Ophelia had anything against sex, but "perfect" anything was non-existent. She'd much rather have the real, sometimes bumbling, often messy, deal, than none at all.

Speaking of sex...

She sat still for a moment and tried to remember what had transpired between herself and the tall, blond hunk she'd made friends with at the Blue Moon. Um, yeah, picked up would probably be a more accurate term, but he did confess to being a former colleague of Spain's. An old friend from college, she'd discovered. How much more harmless could the guy have been?

Still, Ophelia couldn't remember too much after her sister had run out of the bar like a bat out of hell. What had happened next? A few more drinks, a call to the police when neither Camille nor Spain came back, then the bodyguard calling Brent to let them know he'd found her sister.

Why the hell hadn't they come back for her? Then again, Ophelia hadn't minded all that much when Brent looked at her with that sexy lopsided grin and winked. Her body tingled at the memory. But after that, the rest of the night seemed very hazy. What had they done? She concentrated on her anatomy, pushing the headache aside in order to decipher any other aches and twinges she might be feeling. Especially any twinges that might have something to do with getting up close and personal with Mr. Nordic hot-bod.

None. She frowned.

That must mean he brought her home and left, because as long as it had been, she knew she'd be able to tell. Had they even kissed? No way to know, but Ophelia hoped she had enjoyed herself and hadn't acted like a total slut. Brent had been nice—a little too nice, maybe.

A shower, clean clothes and four aspirin helped her regain

enough equilibrium to venture downstairs. As she passed her sister's suite, she stopped to knock but realized the door stood slightly ajar, the room empty. Ophelia stared into the bedroom, her gaze roving over the familiar furnishings, organized shelves and cluttered desk. Her sister had gone out without telling her. Camille never went anywhere. Never.

Without thought to her pounding head, Ophelia took to the stairs, bounding down the first five before the jackhammer on steroids shot off another round against her skull. She jerked to a halt and sank down on the carpeted treads, her head held tight in both hands, eyes closed.

After a minute or two, she managed to get to her feet and carefully walked down the remaining steps with less bouncing this time around. The silence suffocated her. Where had her sister gone? Ophelia walked through the downstairs hall, glanced in the parlor and the adjoining den, then stopped outside the kitchen door. Her hand hesitated over the push plate and she swallowed back the bile that edged up her throat as memories bombarded her. Horrible, gruesome memories of blood and carnage spread across her mother's immaculate kitchen floor.

Another kitchen, a different house in another time.

At twelve, Ophelia had been the one to find their mother crumpled in a heap of mangled flesh and blood-stained clothes on the pristine white tiles. Ophelia was supposed to have come home early the night before, having been grounded for one reason or another, something to do with school. But she had come home late the next morning from her friend Jessie's house. Home too late to do her mother any good.

She'd walked into the kitchen of their silent home, ready to face the lecture on responsibility, etc., etc. She hadn't expected to meet with a corpse bathed in blood and lifeless blue eyes staring at the ceiling. She hadn't expected the white-on-white kitchen to glow pink in the morning sunlight peeking through the window.

Ophelia shook her head as she forced the images back into that dark place where they hid. Then she pushed open the door with such force that it slapped against the wall on the other side. The empty kitchen mocked her racing heart. She took a breath, stepped in the doorway and glanced around for some signs of life or a note of explanation. Nothing. No dirty dishes in the sink or newly washed ones in the drainer. Not even a fork or dishtowel out of place.

She walked carefully across the kitchen floor to the coffee pot. The timer had gone off as usual at seven, and the pot seemed untouched. She flipped off the switch and filled a large mug with the dark brew. The first sip burned her tongue and the bitterness almost made her spit it back out. But she drank it down, hoping the caffeine would kick in to clear her fuzzy thoughts.

"Camille, where the hell are you?" Her voice sounded hollow in the empty room, the slight echo making her feel even more ill at ease. Ophelia filled her cup to the rim once more before she turned and hurried back out into the hall, pursued by ghostly whispers of the past.

Further inspection of the house showed the bodyguard had left as well. She wasn't sure if that was good or bad. She had seen the way Spain looked at her sister and heard them talking quietly in his room after he arrived. Only an idiot would have been immune to the sizzle in the air when the two of them stood toe-to-toe in the parlor. Yeah, there was a man who just might get hands-off Cami in the sack. But what would happen if he did and then left?

Meltdown, that's what. Her sister's sanity hung by a thread as it was, one push and she just might crash and burn for good.

Ophelia paced across the small parlor floor, her bare feet slapping against the smooth wood. Every turn she stopped to peer out the front bay window, hoping to catch a glimpse of her sister strolling down the walk or through the garden gate. The phone rang and she jumped, staring at it for a moment before rushing over to the end table to answer.

"Hello?"

"Hey, Lia, darlin', how are you?"

She didn't recognize the number on the caller ID, but the voice sounded very familiar. "I'm fine, Brent."

"You sure? I was worried about your head this morning. You must have finished half a bottle of scotch all by yourself."

Ophelia cringed. Yep, maybe it was time to cut back on the booze before her liver gave notice. "I've got a hangover, but nothing serious. How are you?"

"Just fine," he replied. Damn, but the man had a voice just

made for phone sex or long, steamy nights writhing between the sheets. "Is your sister all right? I know you were pretty worried about her."

"Uh, I'm not sure actually. She wasn't home when I got up.'

"Oh?"

"The bodyguard is gone, too. Do you have any idea where they might have gone?"

"No, I don't. Spain and I haven't talked much in recent years. He just gives me a call when he comes to town. This is the first time since he's retired that he ever asked for my help."

"He did what?" she interjected. "You never mentioned he asked for your help."

Silence.

"Damn," he muttered. "I wasn't supposed to say anything, but he called yesterday and wanted to know if I had an evening or two free. He doesn't want to leave you at loose ends while he keeps an eye on your sister."

Ophelia didn't know whether to laugh or cry. Damn but life loved to kick her in the teeth. "I don't need a babysitter, so you can just go screw with somebody else's head for a while."

"Hey, come on, Lia. I was there to watch over you, but that didn't include staying out all night dancing and talking. I really enjoyed your company and I'd like to see you again."

Something in his tone grabbed at her heart, but she refused to believe his crap. Men were nothing if they weren't dishonest.

"I don't think I should believe you, Brent. Is that even your real name?"

He chuckled, the low seductive sound sending tingles down her spine. "Yes, it's mine, unfortunately. My mama had a thing for soaps when she was a teenager."

Ophelia couldn't hold back a smile.

"Please, Lia, I want to see you again. Don't make me suffer because of my lousy taste in friends. After all, if I hadn't said yes, we would never have met. I think maybe I owe Ian a big thanks."

Now how could a girl resist something like that?

"So? Will you meet me? Do I need to beg?"

She laughed out loud as she twisted the phone cord around her fingers. "No, you don't have to beg...not now, anyway.

Maybe later."

"Promise?" The innuendo his voice made her hot. The man's charm should be illegal.

"That depends."

"On what?"

"Now it wouldn't be much fun if I gave you all the answers, would it?"

His responding chuckle reminded her of hot fudge—warm, sinfully decadent. Yes, Brent Adair had definite possibilities. Ones she would pursue as soon as possible.

"When I hear from Camille, I'll call you back," Ophelia said. "We can make plans then."

"Sounds good. Don't keep me waiting too long. I'm sure Spain has her well in hand."

Why didn't that comfort her?

"It'll be worth the wait, Brent."

When she hung up the receiver, her hand shook. Was it the hangover, her overdose on caffeine or Brent's deep, sexy voice?

Definitely the voice.

Her stomach growled and she thought about grabbing a snack, but she just couldn't quite make herself go inside that kitchen again. It was a completely different house, but similar enough to spark the horrific memories. Memories that belonged locked tightly away in their hiding place.

Either the booze or general lack of sleep allowed them to surge from that dark little corner. Maybe it was just the whole nightmare scenario kicking her imagination into overtime. If it was the liquor, then all the more reason for her to dry out.

Chapter Six

It had to be the hottest day so far this summer, but she didn't care. For a woman who lived her life feeling like a walking popsicle, heat had become a treasured commodity—even in excess. Camille closed her eyes and let the hot summer sun pour over her face. She took a deep breath of air that smelled of river water, gasoline fumes and the faint tinge of flowers.

"Don't you ever get tired?" Ian stopped beside her on the sidewalk.

She turned away from the river to look at him and smiled. Every ripple, every hard curve of his masculine torso was neatly outlined by the T-shirt he wore. She knew he was smooth and sculpted like a statue of old. She could almost feel the firm, sleek texture of those muscles beneath her fingertips. Imagination was a wonderful thing.

"No, never," she managed despite the fine, distracting picture he made. "I love to walk. It helps me think."

"Well, I need to sit down before I fall down. It's hotter than hell and we've been out here for over three hours."

She tried not to let her disappointment show. "Yes, you're right of course." She glanced at her watch and started to walk back to where they'd left his car. "It's late and I've got a lot—"

Ian grabbed her hand when she passed, bringing her to a halt "I didn't say I was ready to go back. Let's get some lunch first. I'm hungry and I doubt you eat much more than rabbit food up there in your little hideaway."

"Okay, but somewhere casual."

"Naturally. I don't do formal." He winked and her pulse quickened. She told herself it didn't matter how gorgeous he was, Ian wouldn't be around for long. Once he left, her life could go back to normal. Letting anyone close wasn't a good idea—especially not a man who wouldn't even remember her name a year later.

He drove them to Liberty Street and parked. Then she found herself ushered through a door and into a small restaurant that looked like a greasy spoon. Not a place she'd expect him to notice, let alone eat. The moment they entered, the enticing aroma of grilled meat and fries sent almost erotic signals to her brain. It had been a long time since she'd indulged in a really good, greasy burger.

"Well, bless my soul if it ain't Ian Spain," a short, motherly woman greeted him with a hug and laughter. Camille stood a step back while the scene played out before her. She noticed Ian's answering smile and faint blush that stained his high cheekbones.

"It's good to see you, Mama C." He hugged the woman back, lifting her off her feet in the process. She squealed with delight when he set her down again.

"Now, now...where has my best boy been all these months?" She reached up and playfully patted his face.

"Business. Keeps me hopping."

"Not another woman?"

He grinned. "Impossible! No one can hold a candle to you."

The woman's throaty laughter resonated off the diner's creamy white walls. Camille noticed several of the other customers were watching the byplay with bright smiles and avid interest. A younger woman near the back wall seemed to be taking Camille's measure. The sensation of being scrutinized from head to toe made her feel like hiding behind Ian's bulk.

"Ah..." The older woman's bright eyes moved beyond Ian and pinned Camille to the floor. "So, no other women, eh? Then who's this lovely stranger?"

Ian turned sideways and pulled Camille forward. "This is a client of mine, Mama. Camille, this is Celeste Carter. Celeste, meet Camille Bryant."

The older woman stuck out a hand, her smile friendly. But Camille couldn't help but notice a curious, speculative look in her sea green eyes.

"I'm sorry, dear. Have we met before? You seem familiar."

"No, I don't believe so. We just moved here last winter. I haven't been around town much."

Mama C shook her head, blond curls bouncing. "But I'm sure..."

Ian leaned down close to her ear and whispered something that made the older woman's cheeks glow pink.

"Ah, mercy sakes." She turned a brilliant smile in Camille's direction. "Why didn't you say so, child? I'm a big fan. This is so exciting. A real live celebrity in my restaurant."

"Well, how about serving a real celebrity one of your famous cheddar bacon burgers?"

"Yes, of course. Now you two just sit yourselves down wherever you've mind to. I'll be right back."

With a large hand on the small of her back, Ian led her down the narrow aisle to a booth at the back of the diner. The red vinyl seats crunched and squeaked in protest when she and Ian slid down the narrow table until they sat facing each other dead center.

"What did you tell her?" Camille asked across the shiny black surface.

Ian shrugged. "Just who you are. I had a feeling she might be a fan."

"She seems very nice. Have you known her long?"

The younger blond, who had been watching, walked to their table. Her gaze sought Ian's to no avail. She thumped two large glasses of ice water on the tabletop. He didn't look up, but murmured his thanks and took a swig from the glass. The girl's face darkened before she spun around, storming back to the kitchen with her long mane of hair flying out behind her.

"For a few years," he said, seemingly oblivious to the woman's anger. "I used to live in the neighborhood. Mama C gave me my first real job."

Camille wondered how he could be so insensitive to the waitress. She obviously knew him, but he acted as if they were a total strangers. Yes, Camille had a feeling she'd been right not to let herself too close to the man.

"She seems very fond of you," she observed. "You must have been a good worker."

"Not sure about that. But she was always very kind to my mother and me."

"What about your father?"

"Camille, I didn't bring you here to talk about my past."

She wanted an answer, but his less than subtle evasion was a clear signal to let it alone.

"Then why did you bring me here?" she asked.

He tapped his fingers on the table, his dark gaze skittering about the room until it rested once more on her face. "I brought you here because I think you need some time out and away from work. It might be part of what's causing your nightmares. If you don't start getting more sleep there could be serious consequences."

She waved a hand in the air, reaching for nonchalance that she didn't possess anymore. She was so used to taking care of herself, to keeping order and maintaining the image of a relatively normal, healthy woman, that it was intimidating to admit that she had stopped feeling in control many months ago.

"My health is fine, I'm just tired. Why do you care so much? You're a bodyguard, not my doctor. If the insomnia lasts much longer I'll get some sleeping pills or something."

"It won't work."

She raised a brow. "How do you know? Maybe the problem is all in my head."

"I'm not a doctor, but I'm pretty sure you aren't mentally deranged. My job is to make sure you're safe and to find out who's been threatening you and who or what is causing the nightmares. It's all tied together."

"What do you do, exactly?" She held her breath, waiting, hoping he'd confide in her about the Sentinels. If he would only show her that small amount of trust, then perhaps she could loosen her own rigid control and confide in him as well. Twisted logic, but the instinct of self-preservation had become deeply ingrained in her mind. Nothing less than his own confession could break down her defenses, even if she so desired.

"I try to keep innocent people from suffering," he said. "I try to make sure they don't get hurt. Sometimes the police really can't step in until it's too late." He shrugged. "Blame the laws or politicians, but it happens. I do what I can to make sure at least some victims have a fighting chance."

She nodded and looked down at the gleaming black Formica. She should tell him everything. Drew was trouble, dangerous. But what would this man think of her if he knew? Somehow, she couldn't quite bear the look of pity and disgust she might see in his dark eyes.

"Camille?" His hand covered hers and warm fingers gently squeezed her cold ones. "Let me in. Tell me what's going on."

She shook her head. "I can't. I don't know."

He searched her eyes for a long moment, his thumb stroking the knuckles on the back of her hand. She felt guilt well up between the delicious tingles that spread throughout her body at his touch. Suddenly she wanted to talk to him, needed to tell him her secrets no matter how hard it might be.

"The guy at the Blue Moon last night—his name is Drew Lee," she confessed. "We dated for a while during college."

Ian gazed at her with keen interest. Was this what he wanted all along? Was curiosity or duty the only reason for this invitation? She took a deep breath and continued, conscious of every word she chose, careful not to reveal too much.

"He treated me well at first, but then he started acting erratic. He wanted to have sex and when I refused he seemed fine with that but..." She licked her lips. His hold tightened over her hand.

"Did he hurt you?"

Camille couldn't look him in the eye as she told another half-truth. "No, not really. I eventually gave in like many girls do and he got tired of me. About a week later my mother died. As soon as the police were satisfied we had nothing to do with her death, I packed up my sister, our clothes and relocated to Virginia. I had to get us away from the memories, the gossip."

She glanced up to catch him frowning at her. She thought a bit of disappointment flickered in the depths of his gaze. Was he sorry there weren't more sordid details?

"Why Virginia?"

"That's as far as Mom's life insurance money would take us and I always loved the mountains. They're peaceful, safe."

He squeezed her hand once more and pulled away. "I won't hurt you. You can tell me anything. I hope you'll realize that sooner rather than later. You have to trust me."

"I want to."

"But?"

"I'm not sure I know how. I haven't confided in anyone in a very long time."

"Okay, I promise not to push so hard. But I have been wondering about something else."

She raised a brow. "Go ahead, ask away. I don't promise I'll answer, but you can try."

His mouth turned up into a heart-melting smile. "Honest and straight-forward, I like that. Okay, then tell me why you don't use a pen name."

"Ah, you've been briefed on my sordid background, haven't you? Sam told you the story of Dad murdering our mom and his drug-dealing?"

"Something like that. If nothing else, using a pen-name might allow you more privacy."

She took a deep breath and gazed over his shoulder. She could see the afternoon traffic whiz by, people walking to various destinations—all unaware of others around them. As always, the scene made her feel like an outsider.

"I thought about it at first. Actually, I almost changed our names when we moved to Virginia. I was so afraid the whole mess here would follow us forever like a plague."

The memories were so fresh, so clear. The pain still hadn't faded. Having her mother murdered had been horrible enough, but then having her entire life scrutinized, sensationalized by every television station and newspaper in the city? It had made life unbearable.

"But Lia wouldn't do it and then when Samantha took me on, she said it wouldn't do any good in the long run. She insisted that somehow, someday people would find out my secret. She told me owning up to my past is just better for business. After all, I hadn't done anything myself, so there was nothing to be ashamed of. It was merely a tragedy beyond my control."

A small smile curved her lips as she remembered the day she and her new agent had discussed the idea of pseudonyms.

"If they don't like it," Sam had said. *"Then they can just kiss my ass and lose their jobs when the next editor makes a mint off your books."*

She nudged the memories aside and looked back at Ian. "I have a rather pleasant name. It's easy to pronounce and remember. Sam convinced me the disreputable past would help sell books."

Ian chuckled and took another drink of water. "Did it?"

"I'm not sure it helped, exactly. I guess it might have. I was still in Virginia working on the sequel the publisher requested so I didn't spend much time worrying about anything else except maybe the reviews. But the Savannah papers did mention the scandal. How could they not? It's part of my story, after all."

"Write what you want about me, just spell my name correctly?"

Camille grinned and leaned back in her seat. "Something like that." Diner sounds hummed around them. Dishes clinked together, voices lifted in friendly conversation, the sound of the front door bells jingled as more of the lunch crowd entered.

"I don't suppose you've ever read a romance novel?"

"Yes, I have," he said with a bit of pride. "I actually read one of yours."

She raised her brow. "Seriously?"

"Yep, seriously." He chuckled. "Okay, I read it because Sam made me."

It was her turn to laugh. "She did, huh? I always knew she used some strong-arm tactics, but I didn't know it spread to expanding my fan base."

Ian's smile lit his dark eyes and took her breath away.

"Yeah, well she thought I might get to know you and the situation better if I read the book. I've learned it's best to listen and obey. Samantha isn't called 'she-devil' for nothing."

Camille laughed. "Oh, I haven't heard that one. Who has the guts to call her that?"

The smile faded a bit and he looked at his glass as he absently wiped a bead of water from the side.

"A few business associates of mine. Don't get me wrong, we love her like a sister, but she has a tough side you don't want to cross."

"That I can believe."

Were these business associates other Sentinels? Camille couldn't help but speculate just how deep her friend might be involved with the secret society.

"So, what did you think?" she asked, her stomach tightening a bit at the thought that he might have hated her book. Though she logically knew the difference between personal and professional criticism, any bad review of her novels still hurt. It was a bit like standing naked on a street corner and asking onlookers whether or not you were beautiful.

He sat for a moment, not looking at her as he twirled the water glass in one hand. The ice cubes clinked together in an almost musical rhythm.

"It was good," he finally answered. Camille's ego thoroughly deflated.

"Oh."

His gaze met hers across the table. "*Really* good, I couldn't put it down."

"That's nice to know." She took a quick sip from her own glass and found herself trying to decipher every word and nuance of his tone.

"I read it last night," he admitted.

"All of it?"

"Yes, I told you I couldn't put it down."

They stared at each other for the longest time. Camille's thoughts tumbled as she focused on what he was telling her between the lines. He liked her story a great deal if he read it all in one sitting. A small bit of warmth burgeoned in her belly as the world revolved around them. Why it meant so much that Ian liked her writing, she wasn't sure. But it gave a much-needed boost to her sagging ego.

Mama C bustled up to the table, two large plates in hand. Each held a mountain of thick cut fries with an enormous burger nestled in the center. Camille breathed in the heady aroma of freshly grilled meat and tangy cheese.

"It smells delicious."

Mama C smiled and set the plates on the table. "The best cheddar-bacon burgers in town. Now you two eat up and let me know if you need anything else." She hesitated. "Ms. Bryant, I know it might be an imposition, but I was wondering..."

"Yes?"

The lady glanced at Ian, a blush staining her round cheeks. "I have one of your books in the office. I've been reading it again 'cause you ain't got nothing new out yet. But, would you mind autographing it for me?"

A mixture of pride and embarrassment churned inside her at the request. She still had a hard time understanding anyone wanting her autograph. It had become a somewhat common request after her novel's leap onto several bestsellers' lists, but it still left her feeling like an imposter.

"Of course, I'd be more than happy to sign it."

The woman clapped her hands together and grinned. "I'll be right back. Thank you so much."

Camille turned to her lunch and eyed the huge burger with some misgiving. "I hope she's not offended if I can't eat all of this." When she looked up, she found Ian staring at her with a speculative look.

"What?" she asked, somewhat unnerved by the scrutiny.

He shook his head. "No, nothing, just...thanks for being nice to her. It means a lot to me."

Without another word, he picked up his burger and started eating as if food were the only thing on his mind. Maybe it was. She'd always heard men could compartmentalize aspects of their life, keeping business, physical needs and love separate so one rarely interfered with another. As she watched him eat, she wondered just how far down love was on his particular list of priorities. Not that it mattered to her except in a professional sense. She was forever watching people, cataloging various quirks, mannerisms and personality types.

A crash sounded from behind the kitchen doors. Everyone in the restaurant stopped and turned toward the sound. Voices were raised from behind the stainless steel doors, the words unrecognizable. A moment later, Mama C swished out of the kitchen, a book held tightly to her breast.

"Sorry about the noise, folks, just some old dishes, no need to worry," she called with a smile. Camille noticed the expression didn't quite meet her eyes.

"Here you are, Ms. Bryant...I really appreciate this," she repeated as she laid a well-read copy of *Healing Touch* on the table beside her plate.

"I'm sorry, Mama—" Ian began softly but she cut him off.

"Don't you worry, boy. We all gotta move on now, don't we?" She handed Camille a pen.

"No hard feelings?" he asked with a lopsided smile.

"With you? Never." She patted his shoulder affectionately. "You ended it and moved on, now she needs to do the same. You two just weren't good for each other, Ian. That child has a lot of growing up to do and it's 'bout time she start."

Chapter Seven

"Well, well...finally back are we?" Ophelia's snide tone spun Camille backward, right into Ian's solid chest.

"We've only been gone a few hours for lunch."

"I was up at ten and it's now..." Ophelia glanced at her watch, "...four o'clock. Lunch, huh? Is that what you call a nooner these days?"

Camille's eyes went wide. "Lia, what's gotten into you?"

"I've been stuck in this godforsaken dump all morning, alone. After you made your grand exit last night, I'd think you'd have more sense than to roam the street with a total stranger. Don't you have a deadline to meet?"

"Just what is your problem, Ophelia Lynn?"

"Oh, stuff the mothering attitude, Camille. I haven't needed a mother in over ten years."

"What are you so angry about?"

"You! And him!" Ophelia jabbed a long red fingernail in Ian's direction, hatred burning in her eyes. "Traipsing off together and leaving me high and dry without a phone call or even a note. Without telling me where the hell you've gone. If I pulled a stunt like this you'd have a cow. So what's the deal, sister? Are you researching your next novel? Maybe a takeoff on *Beauty and the Beast*? Only the beast is an aging stud muffin and beauty is a shriveled up old virgin?"

"That's enough!" Shame blazed in Camille's cheeks, made her stomach churn. "Just keep your filthy mouth shut. Whatever I do and who I am with is none of your damn business. Now, if you don't mind, I have work to do as you so eloquently pointed out. One of us has to pay the bills."

She turned to Ian, unable to hold his gaze. "Thank you for

a lovely morning and for lunch. I'll be upstairs the rest of the evening."

Holding her head high, Camille walked up the steps and into her room. As the door closed quietly behind her, she collapsed against it. Her knees gave way and she slid down its surface until her bottom hit the floor. Tears rolled down her cheeks, hot and fast like rain on a southern July evening.

§

Anger made his blood simmer as he listened to the silence from Camille's room. He'd stood there, helpless, as she ran up the stairs, unsure for the moment if he should go after her or give her time alone after the nasty scene her sister caused. Hands clenched, jaw set, he kept his back to Ophelia until he thought he might be able to look at her without giving in to the murderous rage her words had ignited.

Ten... Twenty... He counted silently, temple ticking in time to the clenching and unclenching of his jaw. Finally, when he felt he had some control, he turned. The girl flinched and a wave of satisfaction washed over him. It did nothing to dispel the anger, however. Ophelia took a step back, crossed her arms and waited.

"What the hell is your problem?"

Ophelia raised her chin and glared at him. "I don't have a problem, Mr. Spain. My sister does. Why don't you just mind your own damn business?"

He raised a brow. "You insulted us both. That makes it my business."

"We don't need you here. Everything was just fine until you showed up and now she's running out of bars in the middle of the night and taking days off to go do who the hell knows—"

"What's got you so upset?" he interrupted. "The fact that your sister has a life or that maybe, just maybe you don't have to be a part of it? What would happen if your meal ticket decided to kick you out on your ass?"

Ophelia's eyes narrowed. "Don't lecture me! You don't have a clue about our relationship. And just for the record, my sister *has* no life. If it weren't for me, she'd be totally alone in this world, sitting in her room day after day writing her damn fantasies in spiral notebooks and shoving them under the bed. She wouldn't be published if it hadn't been for me pushing her to send her stories out.

"What kind of life is that? It's nothing. It's *pathetic*. She's one of the oldest living virgins in America and she sits there all day and night writing about sex and love."

"I don't believe what you say about Camille. But, even if it is true, it sure as hell isn't anyone else's business. What gives you the right to stand there and judge her, to judge *us* about whatever might have happened?"

"Life has given me that right," Ophelia answered. "Watching her suffer and wallow in loneliness for ten years gives me that right! You're here for what, one day? And you think you have it all figured out, don't you? Well let me tell you a thing or two, Mr. Bodyguard, Camille has spent her life trying so hard not to be like our mother that she's become a female eunuch. And it's not the lack of sex that's pathetic. She doesn't have any real friends and she's afraid of men, for God's sake!"

"Your mother?"

Her pretty, flawless features twisted with bitterness. "Yes, dear sweet Mum—a fifty-dollar whore in her younger days. Oh, and that was how she met our dad. Did him a favor for a hit of some fine coke, as the story goes. Not much of a romantic fairy tale, but then, that's the one thing my sister and I do have in common. Neither of us believes in fairy tales."

"You had a rough life, Ophelia," he conceded. "But you've got to let go of that bitterness before it eats you alive."

Her red-painted mouth curled in a sarcastic smile. "Bitter? Oh, no, not me. I'm practical. Camille is the bitter one. No one else sees it, but I know that bitterness is there. I felt it whenever she looked at me after...after the great tragedy."

Did he imagine the slight catch in her voice? The glimmer of tears in her eyes? Ophelia turned and strode toward the front door, snatching a purse off the armchair on her way and slinging the strap over her shoulder. When she turned back to him her features were smooth like granite, her jaw set in anger.

"When you're a whore's daughter there are only three ways to go, Mr. Spain. Walk the streets, give it away when you want to, or be like Camille and hide from life, all the time praying no one will figure out who you really are behind the mask."

"Which did you choose, Ophelia?"

"I enjoy life and I damn well make sure I don't give too much of myself away. Cami lives a lie. No, strike that, like I said before, she doesn't really live at all. Hell, her best friend's a dead guy."

If Ian thought she was done as she opened the door and took a step out, he was wrong. She stopped, hesitating a moment before she turned sideways to look at him.

"By the way, Brent's great. I like him, but I don't need a babysitter so unless he's really interested, call off the guard dog. And if you hurt Camille you'll be the one needing protection, because I will kill you myself. Nobody messes with my sister and walks away. Nobody."

Long after the shotgun echo of the slammed door faded, Ian could feel Ophelia's anger. It filled the room, bouncing off the walls like a bullet in a steel chamber. He shook his head and thrust both hands into his jeans' pockets as he began to pace.

Could Camille be as filled with venom as her sister? Or had she been the one to overcome the horrifying images of their past?

Nightmares were usually the manifestation of fears and hopes, nothing more. But that was for normal people. Camille was not normal. She was a chosen vessel—the direct descendant of those ancient ones who first walked the earth and planted their seed in the daughters of men. She was a powerful woman. Her gift could serve a great purpose.

Her dreams might be remnants of anger and fear brought on by the move back to her hometown, but he doubted it. The dream demon he encountered had been extremely powerful. Someone sought her gift the only way it could be harnessed—by making her a slave and siphoning off her power one drop of blood at a time. Or maybe the demon meant to take it all at once after he finished playing this frightening mind-game. It could be the only way to destroy her great resistance was to destroy her sanity first.

That dream had been very real. The dragon was very much alive, although Ian had not yet deciphered its true form. Identifying the demon would be the first step to solving the puzzle and keeping her safe. He touched his chest over the beast's mark. Even with the material in-between, the slight pressure stung and he winced. Yes, the demon was real and he would bear the scar to prove it.

After debating what to say, he headed up the stairs and stood in the dark hall for a moment, staring at her closed door. Ophelia's comments struck Camille where it counted. Her sister had known the words that would hurt the most. The thought made him curse the other girl anew. It figured something like this would happen when he was beginning to make progress. She'd opened up to him today and now he feared the door would be firmly bolted shut again.

"Camille?"

No answer. He frowned at the closed door, fighting back the urge to pummel the hard wood with his shoulder until it crashed down around him or his collarbone shattered, whichever came first.

"Please, let me in," he murmured, his forehead pressed to the smooth paneled surface.

He knew she would hear him, knew she waited on the other side, fighting the demon on her own even while awake. Ian clenched his fists, frustration mounting. He had to protect Camille no matter what. But how the hell could he if she kept throwing up walls between them?

$$\S$$

Hunger gripped his gut like a fist. The girl had escaped him far too long.

Time to feed.

Luckily, the streets were filled with others who could satisfy his thirst. They wouldn't have the strength she possessed but they also wouldn't have a Sentinel shadowing their every step.

He picked a street with plenty to offer. Dozens of men and women hurried along the thoroughfare, some on their way home after a long day, others just beginning their labors, still more out to enjoy the entertainment offered in the local clubs and bars. Like most large cities, Savannah never slept completely. He fancied it his own private buffet.

He hugged the edges of the crowd, more comfortable with an easy escape than the confinement of the throng. The press of warm bodies inflamed his appetite but managed to scrape at his nerves, as well. He could never stand being toe-to-toe with humans for long. Perhaps that part of him had made his transition from protector to predator that much easier.

In the beginning, the kill had made him retch until his stomach heaved on empty air. But he had grown immune to such frailties. He had no choice when death was the only alternative. The scent of blood became more pleasant over time, until it no longer made him ill.

Now the odor stirred his senses and made his mouth water. Now he craved the chase, dreamed of the kill. He could feel his prey's fear as he stalked them through the shadows. He savored the adrenaline of each victim as it spun through the air like small bolts of electricity. He could feel it zing through his own body as they fought for one last second of life and the warm, coppery liquid poured over his tongue and down his throat.

His mouth ached for that feeling again. *Tonight.* He had to feed tonight.

A scent rose above the others as he scanned the crowd. Someone with a small gift roamed near. It was hard to tell these days when the bloodlines of the Chosen had been diluted until few with true gifts remained. The decimation of his race stirred his anger. The Sentinels had allowed the mingling of their blessed children with the dregs of human society. Now there were precious few who understood their powers, even less who could actually use them in any way.

But on the street before him there sparked a flare of that long-ago divinity. He drew the air deep into his lungs, all senses on full alert as he isolated the myriad of odors one by one. Magnolias bloomed with the hyacinth and orchids in a nearby square, fumes from automobiles and city buses polluted the sweet scent, fish fried in a nearby restaurant, wine, whiskey and beer poured freely everywhere. Around it all hung the stench of human sweat and pheromones.

A couple walking arm in arm had just had sex. He could smell the sickly sweet stench on them both. His mouth twisted in disgust and he glared at the tramp as they walked by. Her fear jumped out at him. She whispered to her lover and they hurried on, the man glancing behind them as they went.

It didn't matter. They might notice him, might fear him, but they could do nothing to stop the inevitable. One day they would pay for their insolence. One day they would all understand how truly worthless their feeble lives had become. If he allowed them to live that long.

The Chosen One drew closer, her scent stronger on the night air. He lifted his head, eyes wide and alert.

There! At the corner.

He pushed through the crowd, slowing his steps as he reached the woman dressed in a nurse's white uniform. She smelled of disinfectant, blood and fatigue. She wouldn't fight him—not for long—and she would taste sweet, oh so sweet.

He followed close behind as she moved through the crowded street then turned the corner and left the others behind. The road stood almost deserted as traffic in all forms took another route toward the bustling nightlife. The woman's soft-soled shoes padded on the pavement as a fine mist filled the air around her. She hesitated at the mouth of a dimly lit alley, one hand clutching the strap of her shoulder bag as if it were a lifeline. The other hand held a can of pepper spray.

"Help."

She jerked to a stop and squinted down the alley. After a moment, she shrugged when a voice soft and weak whispered on the breeze.

"Who's there?" she called. "Do you need the police?"

Silence.

She took a small step onto the gravel and waited as she glanced up and down the vacant street. Her hesitation sent adrenaline coursing through his body.

Another moan, softer, fainter than the last. She reached into her bag as she moved forward and pulled out a cell phone. The blue light glowed dimly against her pale skin.

She dialed as she moved forward, her eyes scanning the shadows ahead. A pebble skipped across the concrete and clanked against a garbage can. The woman stopped in her tracks.

"Hello?" She glanced down at her phone and cursed. "Damn battery."

He smiled. Cell phones were so unreliable.

She turned around and slammed into his chest. Her face went white as she looked up into his eyes. He grinned wide enough to show his fangs, reveling in the way her heart sped at a frantic rhythm.

"Boo!"

She gasped and he laughed aloud at the terror in her eyes.

Then, with preternatural speed, he ripped the scream right out of her throat along with her jugular vein. It was time for the feast.

§

Ophelia pushed open the door and dove into the crowd already forming at the Blue Moon. Canned music swirled around her. The familiar odor of cigarette smoke and sweat filled her nostrils.

Several people gave her startled looks and backed away as if her mood were directed at them. The anger that coursed through her must clearly show. *Good.* She wouldn't have to fend off any unwelcome advances tonight. It had taken her three hours of shopping and walking the city streets to let go of some of the rage and fear. But she'd be damned if she let all of it free. Anger alone had helped her survive this long.

Hell, anyone would be lucky to get within ten feet of her.

The sight of Brent Adair sitting at one end of the long bar brought her up short. She hadn't really expected to run into him since she hadn't returned his call once Camille came home. He looked up while she was trying to decide what to do. His wide, sexy grin calmed the tumultuous churning in her gut and she found herself zigzagging through the throng to reach him.

"Hey, gorgeous," he greeted, then pulled her close and pressed his lips to her cheek. She could smell the whiskey on his breath. "You didn't call back but I was hoping you'd show up after all."

A small shiver moved down her spine at his touch. *Damn, the man is good.*

His gaze narrowed. "You did find your sister, didn't you?"

Ophelia took a deep breath before answering. "Yes," she said and slid onto the stool next to his. "She and the bodyguard finally came back a while ago."

He raised a brow. "Why are you upset? Did something happen?"

"No," she squirmed on the stool for a moment, feeling like an idiot. She tried to find the words to express how she had been feeling all afternoon. How could she tell this man—a complete stranger—what it had been like to lose her mother? To be the subject of gossip and pointed whispers? How could she explain the unreasonable fear that somehow, someday, she would lose the only family she had left in the same brutal manner?

An image of her mother's kitchen flashed through her mind and Ophelia shoved it away as she flagged down the bartender. "Rum and coke, please—make it a double."

"Coming up."

She felt Brent's stare and swiveled to face him. "She and Ian went out for the afternoon and didn't tell me. I'm just a little ticked they couldn't bother to phone or anything."

"Ah," he said with a grin. "You sound like an overprotective mom."

"It's not that," she brazened, unwilling to give him any points for seeing through her act. "It's because I've spent the last ten years doing everything she said. I gave up my social life to follow her stupid rules. Now she's not even bothering to follow them herself. I hate double standards from anyone."

Brent nodded and took a long drink from his glass. "I can understand, Lia, but Ian's a good guy. If anyone can protect Camille, it's him."

"Yeah, well who's going to protect her *from* him?"

He eyed her sharply. "Has he made advances?"

"Oh, I don't know," she admitted with a shrug. "I don't think so. But even if he doesn't...well, there's like this chemical thing going on when they're together. I don't want to see her get hurt."

"Physical involvement isn't allowed."

Ophelia frowned. "For who?"

"That's one of Ian's first rules of business—no physical involvement. I'm sure he wouldn't break his own orders. You can't keep control if you say one thing and do another."

"Is that right?"

He nodded and took another drink. "First rule of running any kind of business—any successful one, that is."

"Guess it depends on the business," she muttered and took a sip from the tumbler held tight between her hands.

"And what does that cryptic comment mean?"

Ophelia shook her head and took a long gulp. The rum slid down her throat while the bubbles tickled her nose. "Long boring old story."

The memories earlier had been too vivid, too real to simply lock away. They haunted her in formless, invisible shadows whenever she let her mind wander for even a moment. She finished the drink in record time. Immediately feeling the effects of the rum, a light buzzing feeling hummed through her mind. It might help drown the memories if it didn't kill her liver first.

She lifted her hand to order another, but Brent's strong fingers closed around her wrist. "Don't you think you should slow down a little?"

She scowled at him. "Why? I'm here to have a good time and relax."

"You're going to drink yourself into a coma if you don't take it easy."

Ophelia stared at him. Why did he care? No one else ever had.

"Do people in comas dream?"

His brow creased. "I'm not sure. Why?"

"I don't dream when I drink."

"Is that what this is about? Avoiding dreams?"

"No, of course not," she lied. "But you're right, I should slow down. I need the lady's room, excuse me."

She weaved her way to the restroom, the flashing lights and throbbing music making her head spin even faster. Once inside, Ophelia found it a bit easier to think, but the headache creeping up the back of her neck wouldn't be stopped. At some point she would have to give in to the pain and ride it out. But not yet. If she had her way, she was going to enjoy this night despite her sister and the tall dark beast guarding her like a dog with a bone.

A few minutes later, she was feeling a bit more refreshed and ready to face the night and the gorgeous man waiting for her at the bar. She started across the room, but a man rammed her from the side and she almost ended up on her butt. He grabbed her by the shoulders.

"Geez," he slurred, weaving and obviously already deep in some bottle. "I'm sorry, sugar. You okay?"

Ophelia pulled away and rubbed her arm. "No problem, I'm fine."

He stumbled off toward the men's room. Ophelia frowned.

He seemed familiar somehow. *Probably another regular.* With a shrug she turned back to see Brent bending over to pick up a napkin that had fallen to the floor. The man had fine, tight glutes. She grinned and snuck up behind him.

"Do you want to dance?"

He straightened up in surprise and laughed. "Sure thing, babe. Here, I ordered you another. No more doubles, though."

She grinned as she grabbed the glass from his hand and took a long swig. Brent was a man who seemed to go with the flow and take life in stride. Just her kind of guy. She led him through the throng of people to the small, empty dance floor near the stage and walked into his arms.

Everyone might watch, but Ophelia didn't give a damn anymore. Let them look. Let them see that Marguerite's daughter had survived. Let them spread their gossip about her supposed sins. She had survived hell on earth and no one would take that victory away from her now.

A slow, smooth song played on the jukebox. Ophelia sank against Brent's tall, lean form. She liked how he tucked her head beneath his chin when he held her close. He was warm, sweet and smelled like fresh spring mornings.

"What do you dream about, Lia?"

She sighed and pressed her cheek into his chest. The tempo of his heart rose. A smile tugged at her mouth.

"I don't dream," Ophelia said. "That's Cam's problem."

They swayed together in a slow, endless circle. "Problem?"

"Nightmares...she has horrible nightmares."

"Has she seen a doctor about it?"

Ophelia closed her eyes, content to be rocked in Brent's arms even as part of her wished he'd stop talking about her sister. *Why the hell does everyone want to talk about Camille?*

"No, no doctors for the wonder girl," she said the words without thought, without conscience. "She doesn't trust them or drugs. Me, I don't dream. I just remember."

"Remember what?"

"Mom...and the kitchen...all the blood."

The music seemed to go on forever. Ophelia fought to open her eyes. Her limbs grew heavier and heavier. She shouldn't have finished that second rum and coke. She should have slowed down.

Shit!

She was turning out just like the old lady after all.

"Lia?"

Brent's voice sounded hollow and far away. She tried to answer but could only manage a slight shake of her head before everything went black.

§

"You okay?"

Camille spun around at the sound of the deep, familiar voice. Ian stood in the doorway to his room, arms crossed over his chest as he stared at her with those dark eyes. They seemed to swirl and dance with small sparks of light that had to be an illusion.

He could look right through a person and know everything about them, she thought.

He could know just how he made her feel. How he made her want.

"I'm fine," she lied before her thoughts could turn down that sensuous path. But he continued to stare, unmoving. "I apologize for what Lia said earlier. She can be a little—"

"Overprotective?"

She glanced up at him in surprise. How had he figured it out so quickly? What were the Sentinel's gifts?

"I take it you had a different word in mind?"

Camille chuckled despite herself. "I was thinking *bitchy*, but you're right. She is protective of me. Has been ever since..." she swallowed and looked away, "...ever since our mother died."

"No one has the right to talk to you like that," he insisted. The tone of his voice sent butterflies swirling over her skin. She felt the tremor in her hands and the warmth in her cheeks.

She could get used to being looked after...cared for. Camille shook the thought away as she pulled her gaze from his. It would be stupid to let herself believe she meant anything to this man. To him, she was an assignment, a job.

"It's not that easy," she murmured, groping for words she knew would sound lame.

Ophelia's attitude and behavior had gone drastically down

hill in the last two years. It was one of the reasons Camille had agreed to move back to Savannah. She hoped if they faced their past together, they might be able to finally banish the ghost.

"Why isn't it that easy? It should be. She's your sister, for God's sake. You earn the money she's living on, make it possible for her to play the party girl. A little common respect shouldn't be too much to ask."

She studied his strong features—the brow drawn down into a tight frown. Anger glimmered in his eyes while his arms were locked tightly about his torso.

"How much do you really know?"

"About?"

"Our past...our mother?"

He looked away for a moment and then shrugged. "I know she was murdered and the police blamed your father."

The word "father" sounded so false, so wrong when even remotely connected with the man.

"Maybe we need to sit down and have a little chat," she said. "You've been dragged into this mess, like it or not. You may as well know everything you're dealing with."

He nodded. "I'd appreciate that."

"Okay," she said and sighed. "I was just going to make myself some tea. Would you care to join me?"

Again the silence wrapped around them as his gaze held hers. "Sure...let me grab some shoes."

He reappeared a second later wearing a pair of black sneakers. "After you."

Minutes later, they sat together over cups of steaming chamomile tea. He watched her expectantly, as if he'd been waiting for this conversation. Camille fought back a sudden, strong urge to plop herself into his lap and bury her head against his broad chest. She sighed. Such weakness would never do. Instead, she took a sip of tea and let the soothing herbs fill her senses.

"Lia was in junior high when I started college," she began, staring at the table. She hated telling only part of the truth, but how could she do otherwise when she didn't even remember it herself? "I lived on campus and came home most weekends...except, I didn't make it that time. Mom and I... Well, I didn't make waves and we got along okay, but we weren't what you'd call close. Lia...Lia was a different matter altogether. She'd been fighting Mom's rules since the day she turned eleven and insisted on wearing makeup. Their relationship went downhill from there."

"And your father?"

She flinched a little. "He rarely entered the picture after Lia was born, thankfully. He was a very unpleasant, loud man, with a lot of scary friends."

Ian lifted the mug and took a drink. "The police believed he killed your mother."

"Yes, because he had a reputation for being abusive," she admitted. "The neighbors called the cops on him more than once, though I don't think he ever spent one night in jail for hitting her. But the cops couldn't prove he killed her—there wasn't any evidence to go on—and he was never seen again. Rumors later surfaced that he skipped the country with a bunch of drugs. Later, I heard the story changed to where his drug cronies got tired of him and dumped his body in the ocean. No one knows the truth."

"Camille, I understand you both went through hell, but how—"

She held up a hand. "Let me finish." She cleared her throat. "Lia was supposed to be home the weekend Mom died. Mom grounded her for some reason or other, but she snuck out and spent the night with a friend." The pain of the past ached in her gut—dull and endless, like a wound that could never heal.

"Lia came home and found Mom in the kitchen." She swallowed down the tears that suddenly sprang up. "There was so much blood...I heard they had to tear everything out and redo it. The cabinets...the tiles. It soaked right through."

He grimaced. "I'm sorry."

She smiled softly, but couldn't hold his gaze. It would be too easy to break down if she allowed herself to dwell in the sympathy there. God, she seemed to be getting weaker by the moment.

"So, you see," she continued. "Lia carries guilt with her constantly and she won't let it go. I'm not sure she knows how to. She hates therapy. When I finally forced her to go, she wouldn't say a thing to the doctor. Now...now it's like she's still this little girl, thinking Mom died because she disobeyed her. I really think she believes Mom would be alive now if it weren't for her. From what I can tell—from things she's let slip—she thinks she has to watch over me, *be* there for me or I might wind up dead, too."

He leaned back in the chair. "Guilt can make a person do some stupid things, I'll grant you that. She is trying to protect you, Camille, but I'm not the enemy. We both know that."

"Do we?" She looked away and set her gaze at the depths of the golden liquid in her cup. "Lia senses that I'm very attracted to you. She worries about me getting hurt. Yes, she was nasty about it, but that's the way she is. When she feels cornered or frustrated, she lashes out and it's rarely pretty."

The silence between them stretched taut and thin as the clock on the wall ticked like a metronome. Camille braced herself, hoping she at least wouldn't see pity or disgust in those dark chocolate eyes. She needed him to understand before he condemned her sister and her physical reaction to him had to be obvious anyway. Lia was all the family she had. But she hated to contemplate why it was so very important for Ian to get a clear picture of the situation.

"She is right to worry about us."

Camille's gaze flew to his. "Why?"

"Because..." He stared into her eyes, the emotions there saying more than words. They both excited and scared the hell out of her. "We both feel it, Cami. It shouldn't be happening between us, but—"

She stood and rushed to the sink with her cup, the delicate porcelain clattered on the polished metal with a threatening clang. The voices in her head exploded into a cacophony of noise until his warm hands grasped her shoulders.

"Don't be afraid," he murmured near her ear as the scent of him and his warmth surrounded her. "I'm not going to attack."

"I know," she whispered.

"I won't hurt you," he continued. "I won't do a thing you don't want me to do. But you need to know...you *have* to know what you do to me. How much I want to touch you."

"Don't," she begged, her voice lacking any true conviction.

Strong hands slid down her arms and he leaned closer until she could feel his warmth at her back. He pressed against her—rigid steel to soft curves, flame to ice.

"I've never wanted a woman the way I want you." He breathed deeply and sighed. "Never."

She could feel the hesitation, the regret with which he uttered those words. Was it because he couldn't have her or because he knew their relationship must soon end?

"I...we can't." His lips brushed the curve of her neck and she shivered.

"No, we can't. We shouldn't."

His fingers entwined with hers. She leaned back into his tall, solid body.

"Ian—" She murmured as he nuzzled her neck. Camille felt the heat rise in her belly. Her limbs grew heavy and weak. She was losing control from just his kiss, his touch. His hands moved around her waist, his breathing labored as his chest rose and fell against her back.

"You smell good," he murmured, his warm, strong hands slid slowly, ever so slowly to her aching breasts. "Good enough to eat."

Touch me, her mind begged. But she couldn't seem to form any coherent words. Her mind languished in a sensual fog, her body heavy and aching. It was as if his mere touch drugged her beyond reason.

The thought made Camille catch her breath. She blinked her eyes, the window above the sink coming into slow focus as she realized where she was...what she was doing. What she was letting Ian do. He was a stranger...a man.

No man can be trusted.

She jerked away from his embrace and scurried to the other side of the room, arms crossed over her middle. Ian stared at her—his eyes dark with passion.

"I'm sorry, honey," he reached out a hand and she jumped back. He frowned. "I'm not going to hurt you, Camille."

Her cheeks burned with embarrassment even as her body ached with the need for his touch. She shivered.

"I know. I'm sorry. It's not you. I...I just can't."

"No, you're right." He rubbed the back of his neck with one hand, his mouth twisted in self-disgust. "This shouldn't happen. I promise to keep my hands to myself."

She nodded sharply. "Okay, good, and I'll try not to provoke you again."

He looked back at her then, his grim expression melting into a heart-stopping grin as he chuckled. "Honey, I'm not sure you can avoid that. I seem to have developed a deep-seated yen for a petite brunette with big hazel eyes."

His gaze moved over her body from head to foot and back. Fire glittered in his eyes and made her stomach leap. Maybe she was wrong? Maybe this wasn't such a bad idea? Panic flooded her at the thought of taking things further.

"I couldn't possibly be your type," she blurted without thinking.

"And why not?"

"I'm...well, I'm overweight and—and plain." There, she finally stated the obvious. Now any strange illusions he had conjured would be vanquished. But the most miraculous thing happened. Instead of turning away, Ian smiled.

"Oh, honey, you must be using a fun-house mirror if that's what you see." He moved to stand before her, one rough palm cupping her cheek as he held her gaze. "You are a beautiful woman," he murmured, silencing her protest with the caress of his thumb across her bottom lip. "You are captivating, intelligent and creative. I can't stop thinking about you. No, this shouldn't happen. It's against every rule I've ever made for myself. But it will. We both know it will."

She blinked up at him, fighting the urges that bombarded her at the sound of his words, the feel of his skin on hers. Everything in her wanted to melt into his touch, to simply become a part of him. His warmth. His strength.

"You have to trust me, honey," he coaxed. "You have to open up and let me into your world. I won't touch you until we're both good and ready, but I'm still going to protect you—if you let me."

"I *let* you stay."

"I need more."

He gazed at her until she could almost feel his thoughts. She didn't want to admit there might be something more to her nightmares than unresolved fears, but they were getting to her. They felt real and were making it impossible to sleep, to think, to function. Maybe if she trusted him this much...maybe he'd be able to stop the nightmares.

"Where do you want me to start?" she asked.

He smiled softly. "Tell me how your gift works."

She stared at him in confusion. "Didn't Sam tell you? Don't they tell you who you're babysitting?"

"I want to hear it from you."

"I talk to dead people. Some would say I'm a medium—a gateway between our two worlds."

Ian looked up at the ceiling for a moment as if he were listening for something. When he glanced back at her, the passion had faded. "How do you speak to them?"

"I hear their voices in my head. I talk to them—sometimes verbally, often in my thoughts, and they respond. Why are you asking me this? Why didn't they tell you?"

"They?"

She made an impatient gesture. "The Sentinels, I know about them—well, I know a little. My guide told me. He wanted me to trust you and he told me about what you do, although I'm sure he left out some details. He can be very stubborn."

"Your guide? Is he your mentor?"

Her face flushed anew and she moved away from him. "He's a spirit. Someone who lived long ago, I think. He protects me from the voices. He showed me how to channel their energy and how to use my gift."

When he looked confused, she continued on a sigh. "Sometimes the dead are quiet, and other times, they're very lonely, needy. Before he came to me I had a hard time listening. I couldn't filter out the bad ones or keep them from bombarding me. I had a lot of headaches and blackouts that got worse as I got older. I had no idea how to control it all.

"Then Josiah spoke to me one day. He promised to help me if I would listen to him and obey no matter what."

"And you agreed—just like that?"

"It was either agree or wind up in a nut house. My mother had just been murdered, I—" She looked away and hugged herself. "I didn't feel like I had any choice, really. He's kept me safe, kept me sane, ever since."

"Josiah..." Ian frowned and moved a step away.

"Yes, that's his name. Why?"

A distant look on his face, he rubbed at the stubble on his square jaw. "The name sounds familiar."

Silence filled the room as she stared at him. If only she could read his thoughts as easily as she heard the voices of the dead. But the living had always been a mystery to her.

"Did you know someone by that name?"

"No." He moved back to the table where he gulped down the last of his tea. His gaze wandered around the room as if something distracted him. "It wasn't this house—where your mother died?"

Camille blinked, thoughts upended by the sudden shift in topic. "No, of course not. I could never bring myself to go back there. Lia finds it too similar, though. I think that's partly why she wants to go out so often."

"Had you ever been here before?"

She frowned. "Not that I can recall. The house has been in Sam's family for years." But he should know that, shouldn't he?

"I was just thinking that this—" he waved a hand at the walls, "—this might be where the nightmares are coming from. Houses tend to hold on to the past."

He turned back to her suddenly, his features dark and brooding. "You have to be careful, Cami. Even in your dreams. A woman with your talents can be very tempting."

"Tempting? To who?"

He took a deep, slow breath and sighed, his brow relaxing so quickly that the change in him gave her pause.

"To wolves like me." His small smile took some of the edge off his words, but she couldn't help the little tingle of awareness that slipped down her spine.

"Wolves are the least of my worries at the moment," she said as she turned to leave. "Dragons are much more frightening."

The door swung shut behind her. The thin barrier gave her peace of mind and a small reprieve from the mercurial man on the other side. Swallowing back the fear that edged up her throat, Camille walked to the dark stairway and slowly climbed. The carpeted treads muffled the sound of her steps as a dark fog seemed to envelop her. A murmur, soft, low but insistent, penetrated her crumbling barriers. She paused, took a deep breath and closed her eyes.

"Be still," she demanded, her tone as a mother reprimanding a wayward child. The murmurs ceased and she continued up the stairs. If only she could silence the nightmares as easily.

Chapter Eight

Soft morning light filtered around the yellow curtains draped over the lone window in her room. Traffic hummed in the distance, the subtle tremor of tires on asphalt reverberating through the walls. A voice sung softly...its ethereal tone at the very edge of normal human hearing. A child laughed, sweet, innocent clear notes carrying above the darker noises that rumbled around her.

Camille took a deep breath, closed her eyes and released the air in a slow, steady stream. The voices grew louder, more insistent.

"Enough!"

Silence. She stared at the wall, wishing there were some kind of magic that could get her through this. Why couldn't she make her problems vanish as easily as she sometimes banished the voices of the dead? But she knew deep in her heart that magic didn't exist, it was all an illusion.

What was Drew's game? Her father had been a low man on the drug-dealing ladder. So many rumors had spread about his fate, but no one confirmed anything. At least, not that she knew of. Yes, she'd heard that some cocaine disappeared at the same time. But as far as she knew, her father never met her one-time boyfriend. She had rarely had contact with her father herself, except for rare visits when he needed a place to crash and someone to knock around.

Roland Dupree took the one chance she and Ophelia might have had for a normal life that warm September night. When he killed Marguerite Bryant, he'd also killed any respectable existence they might have had in Savannah. The scandal of her mother's brutal death and her father's crimes and flight from

Georgia had destroyed any chance of normality.

The drug pusher's whore and his bastard children made a delightfully gruesome and tragic tale for a city that embraced its eccentricities. Camille and Ophelia had been embraced and thrust directly into a sordid free-for-all. For a brief time their house had even been a stop on the Most Scandalous Homes of Savannah tour, directly following a former bordello. Camille didn't know when the furor died down since she'd taken every last dime of her mother's insurance settlement and fled to Virginia with Ophelia in tow.

This whole thing was her fault. She should have turned down Samantha's insistence that she move back to Georgia. Tears burned her eyes and she swallowed back the sob that edged up her throat. Why had she taken such a chance?

Damn!

A trickle of ice slithered down her spine, flowing outward to encompass her limbs to the tips of each finger and toe. She'd made the decision because *he* had told her to. He had encouraged her, assuring there were *"no worries"*.

"No worries my ass!"

He had appeared somehow when she needed him most—shortly after her betrayal and mother's murder. Innocence used by one she trusted and her mother brutally killed, Camille had accepted the spirit's guidance because she had been afraid of trusting her own judgment. It had seemed almost natural, inevitable. Speaking with the dead had been a part of her life since she was old enough to hold conversation. Her friends were mostly of the spirit world until she realized not everyone spoke with ghosts.

Her guide or muse, as she often referred to him now, kept her from leaping into that dark place that beckoned in times of desperation. He was the spirit who whispered hope and inspiration in her thoughts. He warned her of danger and trials to come and guided her path in so many ways. She relied on his judgment. Like a fool, she had given over her life to another. Even dead men could not be trusted.

He hadn't warned her about Drew at the bar. Her senses themselves had failed her, too. A man who embodied pure evil slithered out of the shadows and almost to her door without the smallest warning. She hadn't even been aware he was back in Savannah after all these years. The last news she'd heard of

Drew Lee, he'd been convicted of armed robbery and assault with a deadly weapon. She thought he was still serving a long sentence at the state pen.

A knock made her jump. She stared at the closed bedroom door, heart pounding as she wondered who else could possibly be up this early? The sun had barely risen.

"Camille?"

She let out a deep breath as Ian's voice reached through the barrier.

"I need to speak with you."

She bit her lip. Maybe she could pretend...

"I know you're there," he said as if he could read her mind. "Open up."

She slid off the lock and opened the door. His presence filled her room even as he stood in the hallway, gazing down at her with those midnight-black eyes. A woman could sink into those eyes and gladly drift away toward the promises lingering in the shadows. But she had always been afraid of the dark.

He searched her face like a seer divining tea leaves. From the way his jaw clenched, he didn't like the revelations. He stared at her a moment and it seemed as if she could feel his mind reaching into hers—seeking the truth. She blinked in surprise. Did he have a psychic gift as well? He gave her a half-smile that didn't quite reach his eyes.

"I need access to your website. I want to see if my tech boys can trace any of the threatening messages."

"You can use the computer in the study downstairs, but I deleted them all a long time ago."

"I imagine they'll hit a brick wall, but it's worth a try. I need something to occupy my time while you're writing."

"All right, I'll be here if you need anything else."

"What's your password? They'll need it to access the site as the administrator."

She hesitated for a moment—not because she was giving him admittance to another portion of her life, but because she was afraid. Would he laugh? Judge?

"Beatrix Potter."

He frowned. "Excuse me?"

"The password is Beatrix Potter." She sighed when he continued to stare. "She wrote children's stories about animals.

Peter Rabbit?"

He held up a hand. "Yes, I know who she is. I was once a child myself, believe it or not." This time the smile lifted the corners of his dark eyes where it glittered like stars in the deep-night sky. "You continue to amaze me. You aren't anything like what I expected."

"Oh, and what did you expect?"

His smile broadened to a full-fledged grin. Her heart skipped a beat and then raced like a jackrabbit fleeing a wolf. *God. He's beautiful.*

"Well, honestly, I expected someone more like Ophelia." He winked and turned away.

She watched him saunter down the hall and back downstairs. Then she felt her own mouth curl into an irrepressible smile. For some reason she couldn't quite fathom, Camille found herself chuckling. She closed the bedroom door, her thoughts filled with Ian. He not only changed the essence of her home, but he was beginning to change her, as well. She felt lighter, somehow. Less stressed and unsure. Less afraid.

She sat back down in front of the computer screen. The white page and black cursor mocked her. *No talent...worthless...how could she ever write again?*

Camille shook her head in disgust. This was getting old.

"Knock it off!" she demanded aloud.

It had taken over a year before she realized the demon voice of self-doubt was exactly that—a demon who preyed on creative energy and self-esteem. One who gloried in the depression and hopelessness of mankind. Since that revelation, she'd become adept at turning it away, though it still snuck under her defenses now and then. The sneaky creature didn't like being recognized or told what to do.

Camille took a deep breath and stretched her arms toward the ceiling. She reached upward until the bones between her stiff shoulders popped softly back into place, new blood hummed through her muscles. Fingers poised over the keys, she closed her eyes.

"Guide me," she whispered. On cue, the images sprang to life in a slow-motion montage played out on the movie screen within her mind.

Words flowed like ink spilled over clean white paper. The click of the keys ebbed and surged. The images translated in crisp detail as she described the emotions and actions taking place. For a moment she couldn't make out the faces of the lives she watched, then she gasped as her new hero came into sharp focus. He had the eyes of an angel, his hair as black as a raven's wing. He looked so much like Ian that she blinked and brought herself out of the trance-like state.

Camille glanced around the room, but she remained alone. With a sigh that touched on regret, she closed her eyes and conjured up the image once more. Then opening her eyes again, she gazed at the computer screen. Her mind and hands worked in sync as the words brought the visions to life.

This new hero was very strong, ancient, a loner. He made her previous heroes seem almost sissy by comparison. He would be impossible to reach. Camille frowned as his thoughts and emotions filled her. He was a shape-shifter, a man who lived a violent life and who seemed to follow destruction as if he'd been born to it.

He was angry and alone. His past held horrific images that made her cringe. *So much blood and death.* How could this man be saved? How could she invent a heroine strong enough to brave the darkness that surrounded him? Why would any woman want to try?

She stopped typing, her fingers arched above the keys as she waged a silent battle in her mind. This man could not be a hero. He was unworthy of the title with the amount of blood he had spilled. He could not have a happy ending and that was the only kind of story she would write.

"No worries," her guide whispered. *"All is well. Trust me."*

Camille ground her teeth at the smug, masculine voice and pushed her chair back from the desk. *"I'm not listening to you. Not now...not today. Maybe never again."*

The voices stilled for a moment and then a cacophony of sound began to swell. She was losing control. After her mother's death and her own bitter betrayal, Camille had been unable to stop the tidal wave of voices that barraged her from the other sphere. But she had learned to stifle it with years of practice and the teachings of her guide. Now it felt as if the barrier she'd erected crumbled at her feet.

She had insulted Josiah and he was showing her what it would be like without his guidance, without his force standing between her and the others who longed for attention. He acted as a sort of filter, a sieve that separated the wheat from the chaff. Now he left her alone to prove a point and as a reprimand for her pathetically adolescent behavior.

Camille bore the noise, anger making her more stubborn than usual. She covered her ears with her hands when the pain intensified. Sound and emotional energy bombarded her. Tears welled in her eyes before she admitted defeat.

"I'm sorry," she whispered.

The sounds stopped. Again she heard the soft whir of the air conditioning, the growl of traffic outside. The child laughed, the woman sighed. She was alone...or as alone as someone with her gifts could ever be.

"There is reason in all things," she echoed as the familiar refrain whispered in her thoughts.

She stretched again and took several deep breaths before immersing herself into the world that grew in her thoughts. The words poured from her fingertips, cushioned by the faint whisper of Madame Virginia's voice, *"They need you to tell their stories, to bring their sorrows to life. They need to know love waits...they need hope."*

The words continued to flow even as one part of Camille's mind pondered the meaning of the old woman's strange turn of phrase. Her stories were fiction, pure and simple. Images created by some part of her brain or conjured by the ancient spirit that helped her stay in control. The woman must have gotten her own images confused.

Vampire-like creatures weren't real...nor were shape-shifters, witches or fallen angels who gave up heaven for love. It was fantasy that helped Camille keep the delicate balance between life and complete insanity. None of it was real. It couldn't be.

Her fingers stumbled and she shook her head to clear the confusion. With another breath, she continued, the words seeming to write themselves as the sad drama played out in her mind. It did bother her that her new hero looked so much like Ian. But that had to be because his image remained indelibly etched in her brain. Such a man would give any woman hours of heated fantasies. His was a face and form impossible to forget. His voice was a siren call to all lonely hearts.

He probably had a girlfriend, several of them, in fact. A twinge of jealousy twisted in her stomach. Camille could safely say a man like Ian would have a different woman in every city—a different partner for every night of the week.

He would be an extraordinary lover. Giving. Sensuous. A man that knew his way around a woman's body and took pride in bringing his partner pleasure. That was one thing her heroes did have in common—they all prided themselves on helping their lovers achieve an almost spiritual climax. Not that Camille knew about such things. Not firsthand, anyway. But some part of her knew it as fact—either the natural intuition of a woman or her own, more distinct gifts. Beneath Ian's large, rough hands, a woman could find paradise.

She cursed herself and pushed the keyboard away. No sense in continuing when she was so preoccupied. She checked her page count and grimaced. Ten pages in about an hour—not terrible, but not her best. She could usually churn out twenty or more when the words flew like they had at first. But she was way behind schedule thanks to all the distractions.

Ian Spain was one monster of a distraction.

With a sigh, she rose from her desk and flicked the television on before grabbing a diet cola from the mini-fridge that acted as a nightstand. The early morning newscast was just beginning and she grimaced at the lurid headline accompanied by a blank silhouette.

"The body of Millicent Graham was found early this morning in an alley near River Street. A registered nurse at Savannah University Hospital, Ms. Graham was last seen yesterday evening when she left work after completing her usual shift. The police refuse to release any specifics about the death except to say foul play is likely. The forty-two-year-old was the mother of three and a lifelong resident of Savannah. No other details are available at this time.

"In other news..."

Camille changed the channel quickly. The short speech reverberated through her mind. A woman's life summed up in less than two minutes. It seemed wrong and incredibly sad. The world was such a dangerous place. She supposed it had always been that way, but for some reason the senseless violence seemed to stand out in her mind lately. It had to be the nightmares and the creepy emails. She tried to tell everyone it didn't matter, that it meant nothing, but she didn't quite believe it anymore. A person could only stick their head in the sand so long without having to come up for air.

With a sigh, Camille readied for the day ahead, all the while trying not to think of the monster that haunted her dreams or the ones lurking outside in the real world. Life had turned into a scary proposition no matter which way she turned. It seemed she was running out of places to hide.

§

The world drifted in and out of focus for a long time before Ophelia finally realized she rode in a car. She opened her eyes, the effort almost exhausting, and looked around. The lighted dash blurred and shimmered, shadows and colored lights whizzed by the closed windows. Cold air blew across her skin, sending goosebumps crawling up her arms. She could hear a soft male voice humming next to her in the dimly lit vehicle. The tone was happy and cheerful, as if the man didn't have a care in the world. She couldn't quite make out his face.

"Where am I?"

"Oh, good, you're awake," Brent said as he reached a hand out to her and brushed her forehead.

She jerked away and quickly regretted it as a thousand hammers started beating inside her skull. "Where are you taking me?"

"Nowhere in particular. I was driving around until I could figure out what to do with you." The corners of his mouth turned up slightly, but the smile didn't reach his eyes. A dark look passed over his gaze, sending a chill down her spine. Before she could decipher the emotion there he turned away.

"I wanted to get you to the hospital but you kept insisting you didn't need a doctor. I thought if you fell asleep long enough I wouldn't have to give you a choice." He stopped at a red light and took that moment to examine her face. The soft pink rays of the sunrise made everything glow in surreal monotone. "Are you okay now? I've never seen anyone go down as fast as you did."

"Go down? Did I faint or something?" She sat up straighter, her head pounding and stomach whirling as if she'd just been through a hurricane at sea. "Oh, I don't feel so good."

"Shit, I knew it! We're going to the emergency room."

"No," she said, somewhat panicked. That was the last thing she needed. Camille would lock her in her room until she turned forty if she ever found out. "I didn't eat today and all the booze on an empty stomach just did me in. I'll be fine after I eat a little."

He frowned at her, jerking in response as the car behind them honked. The light had turned green. Brent stepped on the gas, zooming through the intersection as his jaw clenched and hands tightened on the wheel.

"You scared the crap out of me, Lia. You were so white I didn't know what the hell to do, but you kept saying, 'No, no doctors.' Damn, I was never any good at dealing with illness."

She smiled and laid a hand on his arm. It was kind of nice having a guy worried about her. The novelty of it could grow on her.

"Just feed me and take me home, Brent," she said. "I'll be one hundred percent by the afternoon, I promise."

He sighed. "Fine, I guess I should get one last meal, too. Ian is going to skin me alive when he finds out what happened."

"Who says he has to know?"

He glanced at her sideways as he drove. "I'm not going to lie to the man."

"I didn't suggest you lie, just omit a few facts. You don't even have to talk to him—just drop me off and leave. There's no harm done and no reason for anyone else to find out."

"I don't know—"

"Please?" she interjected. "Neither one of us needs that kind of headache right now. I swear I'll be more careful from now on and we'll just pretend this never happened, okay?"

His silence made her uncomfortable. Then he sighed and she felt a weight lift from her shoulders.

"Okay, we'll do it your way this time. But if this ever happens again, you're on your own."

"Fair enough. Now how about a burger? I'm starved."

"There's bound to be someplace that'll serve you a hamburger at six a.m.," he said. "But then I'm taking you straight home. I suggest you spend the day resting, Lia. You're going to wind up in an early grave if you don't take better care of yourself."

She leaned over and kissed him on the cheek. "Thank you."

Brent grinned back at her. "About time somebody appreciated me."

An hour later he left her at the curb in front of the old house she'd come to think of as an antebellum fortress. Ophelia insisted he let her face the music alone, but promised she'd call later in the evening once she'd gotten some sleep. She stared at the wrought iron fence hung thick with ivy and grimaced. They only needed a good thunderstorm and a dog howling in the background to complete the impression of an old gothic novel. She hated this place, hated Savannah if the truth be told. Not because it was a bad city...there were just too many memories. Camille thought coming home would help somehow, but it had the opposite effect. If only her sister would listen to her now and then.

Sneaking inside proved easy since she had remembered her key. As she stood in the entryway, Ophelia could hear the faint sounds of tapping from upstairs. Camille was writing again. Good thing, too, she needed to get that next book done. She had talent and wrote one hell of a love story. Ophelia didn't want anyone to forget that fact ever. Sure, they needed the money and the fame was kind of cool, but Camille needed her outlet most of all. Sometimes Ophelia was positive the writing was all that kept her sister from jumping off the edge.

She noted the sound of another keyboard from the den off the parlor. The bodyguard must be occupied, too. She could easily slip upstairs and into bed without having to face either of them. *No lies, no harm, no foul.* Yes, she might be a chicken, but she also had a strong sense of self-preservation. Cami could be a truly formidable witch when provoked.

Lia slipped off her shoes, leaning on the banister to keep from falling on her butt, and smiled. Maybe she had overreacted. Brent was fantastic—sexy, fun and considerate to a fault. The bodyguard must have something in common with him if they had once been friends. Maybe it wouldn't be so bad if big sister got herself a man after all these years. Hell, it might even take the edge off her uptight, pain-in-the-ass tendencies.

Great sex...that could be just what Camille needs.

Ophelia snuck up the staircase, avoiding the spots she knew would squeak and attract attention. In another minute, she was in her room, the curtains drawn tight against the morning sun as she slipped out of her rumpled clothes and climbed into bed with a sigh. Her last thoughts were of Brent and the way he had kissed her goodbye. There had been a bit of heat in his gaze and more than a hint of promise in his kiss.

Imagine that, she thought drowsily. *The Bryant sisters going out with decent, respectable men for a change. What would Mom think?*

Chapter Nine

The phone rang, piercing the still night with its cry. Camille sat up straighter, the muscles along her spine bunching in protest to both the late hour and sudden movement. She stared at the white receiver. Her heart hammered as she reached out to answer. No good news ever came after midnight.

"Hello?" she said, her voice barely above a whisper.

"Hey there, sugar," The deep familiar voice rumbled over the line. Her stomach clenched and unclenched.

"What do you want?" she demanded.

"Ah, now, not a very warm hello. Did I interrupt something? Maybe a little late-night research?"

Camille's flesh tingled as goosebumps broke out over her skin. Drew had an aura about him that reeked of evil. A power fueled by darkness lurked behind those carefully chosen, suggestive words. She hadn't seen that blackness in him when she was nineteen and desperate for love. God, what a blind fool she'd been.

"How did you get my number, Drew?"

"I have friends all over Savannah, despite the little trick you and your daddy played."

She shivered as his hatred slipped beneath the controlled façade.

"What are you talking about? I never played any tricks on you. You were the one who drugged me."

He laughed, the sound bringing to mind the dark place she'd seen in his eyes two nights earlier—the twisted anger and lust that lurked behind the blue ice.

"Don't play dumb, sweet sugar. We all know what your

daddy left behind. I was supposed to get my fair share, but the bastard left me twisting in the wind. Now I'm here, you're here, and I want what's mine."

She shook her head, frowning as she tried to make sense of his proclamation. "You didn't even know my father, what are you—"

"Don't play dumb, bitch!" Fear slithered through her veins at the blatant hatred in his voice. The charming Andrew Lee had his limits. "I want the merchandise, baby, and you're gonna help me get it."

"I don't know what you're talking about."

"Right," he drawled, all southern charm once more. "Such a shame really. I suppose I'll just have to get my money some other way. I wonder...just how much do you think I could get for the pictures I took? I'm guessing, now that you're famous and all, why I could pretty damn near name my price in the right market."

She swallowed down the bile, wishing this were just a dream, wishing she knew what to do. Call his bluff? Could she risk that? What if that filth made its way to the public? The humiliation was too much to contemplate.

"You don't have to do that, Drew," she said, grateful that she could manage to keep the panic from her voice. "Besides, there's not much market for ten-year-old amateur porn. I'm not exactly famous."

"Ah, come on, baby. Just how dumb do you think old Drew is? I've made a nice sum of money off skin flicks and photos. Hell, you'd be surprised how big the market is, especially on the Net."

She bit back a curse as tension crept up her neck and along the back of her skull. "I was drugged out of my mind. That doesn't exactly make for exciting entertainment."

"Don't be so sure," he said with a low chuckle. "Takes all kinds to make the world a cesspool. I think your little spread will give a lot of men a good jolt. Hell, baby, maybe your daddy will even get to see his girl in action."

"You slimy bastard—"

"Now, now watch your language. I'm surprised at you. Whatever would your sweet mama say?"

"Leave her out of this," she ground out through clenched teeth. "Tell me what you want. How much to buy the photos?"

"More than you got now, baby. But from what I heard, there's a bright future ahead. I think we could strike up a nice long-term partnership. I'd even be happy to help you research those sex scenes. I got the best porn collection in all of Georgia."

"Shut up! I won't listen to this and I will not do business with you for the next ten minutes, let alone years."

"Don't mess with me, Camille. I'm not bluffing. The whole world will see you screwed."

"I'll give you five thousand in cash."

He laughed. "I don't think so. Make it twenty and your daddy's stash."

"I told you before, there is no stash."

"Then where the hell did a kilo of pristine coke disappear to?"

"How do I know? Maybe he took it with him or-or dumped it in the Gulf."

"I'm not buying, baby. He left it somewhere in Savannah. Either you help me find it or you will be making your centerfold debut on a global scale."

"Go to hell."

"Yes, ma'am. I most likely will. But I'm gonna enjoy every moment 'til I get dragged under, and you'll be crawling down there beside me if I got anything to say about it."

She slammed the receiver down, the base crunched beneath the force. Camille stared at the wall. Her chest tightened until her breath came in short, hollow gasps. She closed her eyes and fought against the panic. With the voices ringing in her mind, she managed to slow her breathing down bit by bit. She pulled the air more deeply into her lungs, blowing it out again in a slow stream as she released some of the tension. Her heart began to thud more easily, her pulse no longer hammered in her ears.

Camille beat the panic attack, but she couldn't stay in her room and sit there as if nothing had happened. Sleep wouldn't come—it hadn't for days now, except for an hour here and there. She needed time to think. Time alone. But how could she ever be alone with the voices of the dead whispering in her thoughts?

With jerky movements, she pulled off her nightshirt and fumbled with the jeans she'd worn earlier. She left her bra in the dresser and slid on an extra-large shirt that fell loose around her bottom. The comforting weight of the pendant nestled between her breasts. Sneakers, socks and a ponytail later, she made her escape down the front stairs, out onto the stoop and across the garden path.

The cool breeze lilted through the crowded streets from the waterfront. The air smelled of exhaust and the heavy, sweet odor of summertime. Above the noise of traffic, she heard the sound of music and voices. Dead or living, she couldn't be sure and refused to listen closer to find out.

Alone. She wanted to be alone. But it seemed even her thoughts were always crowded with the minds of others. Privacy was non-existent in her world. Yet, somehow, loneliness permeated every cell of her being.

It had always been a companion in her friendless childhood. It had been hard to make friends as the daughter of a self-proclaimed psychic who once sold her body to pay the bills. Self-disgust welled in that dark place, that small portion which harbored even the faintest memories of her mother and her childhood. The rest had been banished or suppressed long ago according to one therapist she'd seen.

If you can't deal with it, forget it. Worked for her. Sometimes.

She hugged herself as another cold chill buffeted her bare arms. There was so much emotion in this city—remnants of fear, hate, love and loss, but little happiness seemed to linger. The more negative emotions, except for love, were stronger somehow. Intense passion, boiling anger, livid hate...they all lingered like the mists that lay heavy over the streets after a steamy rain. Joy, sweet and simple, could not fight the more passionate emotions. It dissipated like a puff of smoke.

Camille walked through the streets of the historic district beneath the towering maples, her mind whirling with the sounds and muted colors of the night. For a time, the voices ravaged her brain, but finally they seemed to show mercy and grew still. Silent. The shadows around her darkened even in the array of incandescent and neon lights she passed.

"Go home, little one."

She shook her head, refusing to answer her guide even in her mind. She'd had enough of taking orders, following advice, being the one to take care and watch her step in life. Where had it gotten her?

Alone. Unable to sleep. Terrorized by horrific nightmares. No friends to speak of except the disembodied voice that flitted in and out of her head at whim. The only family she had left was her younger, prettier sister who, for some reason, resented the hell out of her.

Camille blinked at the tears burning her eyelids. *Damn.* Wasn't she a pathetic sight, wallowing in self-pity? She stopped at the next corner as a couple holding hands pushed past, the woman giggling as the man drew her close to his side. Camille had a sudden impulse to tell them to go to hell.

Nice...real nice person you've become.

With a deep sigh, she glanced around and made note of where she'd wound up. Far from home, that was sure, but she knew Chippewa Square would be close. She could sit beneath the trees for a time and think. After she crossed the street, she felt a stronger sense of peace wash over her. He was trying to speak...trying to guide her, though she stubbornly refused to let him in. But she knew without Josiah in her corner, life would be an even bigger hell on earth.

A sultry summer breeze swept across the grass, serving as a balm to her anger. Camille sank down onto a hard bench and stared at the statue of General Oglethorpe, the bronze metal dull and lifeless in the intermittent lamplight of the park. The man had been revered by many and a standard subject of study in Georgia schools. Camille could remember little about him.

She thought of her childhood and the few happy times she could recall—times spent without the specter of Roland Dupree hovering in the background. He had been frightening, and yet she'd always hoped with the simple faith of a child that he would someday love her. Her mother had told her it would be okay. But it never had.

"Your daddy loves you, baby girl...don't you worry, we'll be a good family someday."

At six, she had believed her mother implicitly...had counted on her and knew someday, somehow, her father would come home again. Someday she'd figure out how to make him smile. But that day never came. Roland Dupree was a player in every sense of the word—he could never be a father.

"He didn't deserve you...or your mother."

"Stay out of my thoughts!" she snapped aloud, just as an older couple strolled by. They jumped a little and walked quickly away after looking at her with a mixture of sympathy and fear. "Great, the whole world is going to think I'm insane before this is over."

"You are not insane, little one. No worries."

She snorted. Although she usually believed and relied on his soothing words, Camille knew without a doubt there were many things to worry about. For one, how to get the photos from Drew without exposing herself to the world. Literally.

"Tell Ian."

"No!" she shouted, then glanced around to make sure they were alone. "He's the last person I want to know about those...things. About what happened."

"He won't blame you. He'll understand."

He might, but it wasn't a risk she'd be willing to take. Somehow the thought of being humiliated in front of the Sentinel made her want to curl up and die. Camille hadn't felt this weak and needy in a lot of years. She'd be damned if she'd give in to those feelings at this point in the game.

There was a chill in the air that hadn't been there before. Camille sighed. They were waiting...wanting to speak to her, longing for a listening ear. But she just couldn't deal with it tonight of all nights. She didn't have the patience to listen to their stories and was sure she lacked any semblance of wisdom for those needing advice on getting through to those they'd left behind.

"Josiah, you talk to them," she whispered. "Send them to someone else...there has to be someone else who can hear them. I can't do this now. I'm sorry."

Disappointment and anger filled the void around her and she sighed again. She hated letting anyone down, knowing all too well how much it hurt a human soul, but it couldn't be helped.

"Not tonight."

"Cut the melodrama, little one," Josiah admonished. *"This, too, shall pass."*

"I'm supposed to find comfort in that?" she retorted. "You sound like a damn fortune cookie."

She thought he chuckled but couldn't be sure. A man walked by at that moment and cast her a rather startled look before hurrying down the path back to the street. Camille sighed as she sank back against the hard bench, the slats biting into her back. She wiggled around, searching for a more comfortable position but found it impossible. The bench was meant to look good—not made for comfort.

§

He woke in sweat-soaked sheets with his heart pounding in his ears. Ian sat up, wiped damp hair back off his face and sighed. Even his own dreams were in turmoil but he knew why. His demon sprung from the shadows of his past—mistakes made and paid for years earlier. Mistakes he still couldn't quite forget, no matter how his body had healed and how much time passed.

He remembered the fiery sting of the bullet piercing his side, heard the clatter of his own weapon as it fell to the ground, useless. Worst of all, he heard the moans of his one-time partner...and the silence that followed. That had been the loudest sound of all.

Knowing Camille had somehow witnessed his shame dredged it all up again. He sat up, throwing off the sheet and blanket despite the chill in the air. *Why did she keep the house so damn cold?* When he stepped on the cool floor, his side began to ache anew. The doctors told him it should have subsided long ago, that there wasn't any physical cause for the pain. He knew better. The bullet may have missed anything vital, but it took a piece of him that would never fully heal.

Ignoring the goosebumps that pebbled his naked skin, he went into the bathroom and snapped on the light above the white pedestal sink. The face staring back at him from the vanity made him blink. God, when had he gotten so old? It seemed just yesterday he was a cocky, know-it-all rookie with visions of the F.B.I. etched in his mind. He had goals, ideals. Now all he had to show for his life were some scars, a boatload of guilt and nightmares that wouldn't leave him alone.

He opened the cabinet door and faced yet another demon. A simple bottle of aspirin sat on the middle shelf above his razor and shaving cream. It seemed to mock him and he felt the old familiar twinge of shame. He'd beaten his addiction to painkillers, but ever since that humbling experience, the idea of getting hooked again—on anything—scared the shit out of him.

He'd spent many days and nights riding out the pain of even the worst headaches because he couldn't take a chance. Ian would never allow himself to be controlled by anyone or anything as long as he lived.

Fear dogged him every step of the way. Fear that he possessed his father's abusive temper or that he'd never be able to control the addictive disposition he had inherited from his mother. The only good that had come from Ian's own addiction had been the discovery he wasn't a freak, after all. After hitting rock-bottom, he'd discovered his ability to walk through the dreams of others was a gift—and one he could use to help others.

Gabriel Bonnett entered Ian's dream after he'd been shot. The Sentinel not only healed Ian's battered body, but taught him the secrets of the Chosen. He taught Ian to use his abilities instead of hiding inside a bottle. The man saved him from a life of torment and isolation, and for that he would be forever grateful.

Since becoming a Sentinel himself, Ian had found a reason to live instead of merely surviving. He'd found a purpose—to protect those who couldn't help themselves. He wasn't the useless human being his father had accused him of being. He mattered.

Ian chose to forgo a shave. Instead, he splashed icy water on his face and the back of his neck. A shower would feel good, he decided. Since it was early, he might as well get the necessities taken care of before facing Camille.

Her beautiful face flashed in his mind, setting off more turmoil for his guilty conscience. He'd crossed the line with her in more ways than one. God help him, but he knew he'd do it again. No matter what his head told him, the rest of him knew better. Those erotic images of them in bed together making love were prophetic. They were inevitable. He honestly had no desire to stop them from coming true. On the contrary—he wanted those images to become real. He wanted the woman more than he'd wanted anything in his entire life, including the booze and drugs which once held him prisoner.

His body hardened at the memory of the erotic images of their naked skin pressed together, the feel of her mouth as she moved down his body, kissing and tasting every part of him. He stared into the reflection of his own eyes. Should he fight it?

Was this passion between them something the demon wanted? Was he playing right into his hands?

He turned from the mirror and started the shower. Hot water soon filled the small room with heavy steam. He stepped in to stand beneath the dull patter of water, hands braced on the wall beneath the shower spray, head bowed. He stayed there a long time, until the water began to run cool, his hair dripped and his skin had taken on a slight pink tinge from the heat.

Tension ebbed and he turned off the water. It was then that the feeling hit him. He was alone. No, not completely...there was a presence here like he was being watched. But something—someone was missing. He wiped the water from his face and stood, naked and wet, listening intently for a sign or signal to let him know what he was feeling. The silence weighed heavy in the quiet of early morning. Then he knew, without a doubt, what it was.

Camille's gone.

Panic and anger followed in close succession as he stumbled out of the tub and hastily dried his body with a towel. Five minutes later he was dressed, hair still wet and plastered to his skull. He loped down the stairs and outside. Only when he reached the Jag did he realize he had no idea where to start.

He slammed the hood with his fist. "Goddamnit!" he snarled, angry at himself and her.

"You looking for your lady?"

Ian spun around, hand reaching halfway to the gun in his boot before he realized who had spoken. "Jake, you scared the hell out of me." He didn't bother to ask the kid what he was doing outside at one in the morning. "Did you see her leave?"

Jake nodded. "Yeah, about half an hour ago. She looked kind of, you know, spooked. I wasn't sure what to do... You asked me to keep my eyes open and I thought—"

"Thanks, man," Ian clapped him on the shoulder. "Did you see which way she went?"

He wasn't sure, but he thought the boy blushed. "Uh, I sorta followed her. She wound up at Chippewa Square near old Oglethorpe's statue. She was sitting on a bench when I left."

The way the boy hesitated made his gut tighten. "And?"

Jake shrugged. "She was talking to herself. I think she was crying."

That stopped him cold. "Are you sure she was alone?"

"Yeah, it kind of freaked me out. I didn't know what to do so I decided to come back and find you." He looked at him again, his eyes wide and round. "Is she gonna be okay? I really like her."

Ian smiled. "Yes, she'll be fine. Thanks to you. Go on home, Jake. I'll bring her back."

"No, I'll take you there—I know this town inside and out. It'll take you longer in the car and it looks like it's gonna rain soon."

"Won't your mom worry?"

The boy looked away. "Mom has a friend over. I don't wanna be there right now."

Ian could hear the pain in the boy's voice but didn't comment. "Okay, then lead the way."

Fifteen minutes later, they approached the dark, shadowed park. Jake led him to the statue where a few benches sat in a wide circle, surrounded by trees. *Great place to get ambushed.*

The boy stopped and pointed to one of the benches set back in the shadow of a large willow. "There."

Ian saw her then. Wound up in a tight little ball, her feet were on the bench, arms encircling her legs as her forehead rested on her knees. From her pose, she looked as if she could be asleep or deep in prayer. His gut tightened. She looked so damn helpless and alone right now.

"Thanks, man," Ian murmured as the tension slowly uncoiled within.

Jake didn't say a word. He silently stood on the fringes as Ian made his way to Camille's still form.

"How did you find me?"

He started a bit. She'd been so quiet he thought her oblivious to everything. Good thing she wasn't. Anything could happen to her out here alone in the middle of the night. Anger veered its ugly head and overcame any relief he'd been feeling at finding her alive and well.

"Do you have a death wish?" he demanded, taking no satisfaction when her shoulders jerked in response. Then she looked up at him and he could see the tears glittering in her eyes.

"I had to get out. It felt like I was suffocating—I could

hardly breathe."

He waited. That was it? No explanation? Remorse? An apology for scaring the shit out of him? He clenched his jaw and drew in a long, deep breath as he fought to dissolve the fury heating his veins. But it didn't help.

"Next time open the freaking window!" He felt a hand on his arm and jerked around.

Jake glared up at him. "Chill, man. Can't you see something is bothering her? I didn't bring you here to yell at her—you're supposed to help."

Beneath the anger, Ian heard the other emotions...the betrayal, the slight edge of fear.

Damnit to hell. Acting just like the old man. Ian took a deep breath and closed his eyes.

"I'm sorry, kid. I was just—"

"Scared?"

"Yeah, scared."

Jake nodded and they both looked back at Camille. She hadn't said a word as he bawled her out.

Ian cleared his throat. "Are you okay?"

Camille shook her head and tears slipped down her cheeks. *Damn.*

He took a tentative step toward her, his logical mind telling him to haul her pretty ass out of there before something happened. The other part—the soft, protective, foreign side only she seemed to call—urged him to be careful. This woman was quickly approaching her breaking point and he wasn't sure anyone could put her back together again when the pieces shattered. He'd sure as hell try.

"Did you have another nightmare?"

She shook her head and dropped her chin to her knees. Ian frowned as he reached her side. The bench looked damn hard—she couldn't possibly be comfortable sitting in that position. A sudden gust of wind brought with it the smell of rain. A crack of thunder sounded in the distance.

"Honey, let me take you home," he spoke softly like he might to a frightened child. The way his mama spoke to him after one of his dad's rampages. "It's going to rain soon. You could wind up sick."

"They stopped," she said, her brow wrinkled as if she were

trying to solve a puzzle.

Ian hoped to hell she hadn't already snapped.

"Who stopped?"

"The voices..." She looked up at him and he sunk down on one knee to look into her eyes. "Whenever you come close they stop talking to me. They leave me alone."

He blinked. "Is that good or bad?"

She tilted her head to one side as if considering his question. "Good, I think. It's the only time I have real peace. Even Josiah can't do that very often."

She lifted a hand and reached out to touch his cheek. Her fingers were soft and cold on his skin. He closed his eyes as a shudder coursed through him. Soft, light raindrops began to drop on their heads.

"You're cold," he murmured, eyes closed, heart pounding faster. Ian swallowed. "Honey, let me take you home. You need to be safe."

"I am," she said. "You're here."

They stared at each other until Jake stirred as the rain grew heavier. "Hey, uh, you two ready to go back? I'm getting wet."

Ian pulled his gaze from Camille's and turned his head. "Sure thing, kid. Let's go home."

Ian stood and put his arm around Camille, gently urging her to her feet as the warm summer rain soaked their clothes. She seemed almost incoherent—as if her mind were a thousand miles away. The easy manner in which she gave in to him made him worry. She had none of her usual fight in her. Anything could have happened while he was at the house fantasizing about getting her naked.

He tucked her securely against his side, one arm around her shoulders as they headed back the way they'd come. The rain played hide and seek through the thick growth of trees overhead, but they still managed to be dripping wet by the time they neared the house. He glanced down and immediately noticed her tight nipples pushing at the transparent material of her soaked shirt. He wrenched his gaze away and set a faster pace.

Don't let your mind go there, Spain. Not now.

Jake trailed somewhat behind like a quiet shadow. When

they reached the iron gate of her courtyard, she stopped and looked at it as if facing an unknown obstacle.

"Where are we?" she asked, blinking as the rain dripped down her lashes.

"We're home."

Camille frowned and tilted her head to look into Ian's eyes. "No...this isn't my house."

"Honey...you're renting this from Samantha, remember? You've lived here for almost a year now."

Camille stared and Ian knew a moment of pure fear. Had he been too late? Had she reached the point of no return while he slept?

"Oh, of course, I'm sorry." She turned to the boy and smiled apologetically. "Thank you, Jake. I'm sorry if I frightened you. I've been having a bad time lately. Things are kind of screwed up."

The kid shrugged. "Yeah, I understand. I'm just glad you're okay."

"Are you going home now?"

"Nah," he looked at his shoes. "I can't. I'll find a place to crash."

"You can sleep on our sofa," Camille offered and he looked a little eager but quickly dismissed the idea.

"I'm okay, really. A buddy of mine lets me stay at his place sometimes. Y'all don't need me hanging around."

"Sure we do," Ian added as lightning flashed across the sky. "You shouldn't be on the streets this time of night in this storm. It's not safe for anyone."

"But I—"

"No, we insist," Camille interjected. "Come inside, help yourself to anything in the kitchen and sack out on the sofa. I'm sure Ian can find something dry for you to wear while we wash and dry your clothes. You're more than welcome."

Jake shrugged. "Sure...okay. I guess it wouldn't hurt. Bubba's old man might have a cow if I wake him up this late." He nodded. "Thanks, I am tired and I could help you look after things."

Ian smiled. Seemed he was going to get his chance to look after the boy despite his earlier reluctance. He owed Jake a lot. If the kid hadn't been awake and watching over the neighborhood, he might never have found Camille before dawn.

Or before something happened to her. The thought made his gut knot.

After getting the teen settled in the living room with dry sweats and a blanket, Ian made his way upstairs. He'd sent Camille up twenty minutes earlier alone. He needed time to think away from her and the temptation she presented with her figure outlined in crisp detail. He had a lot of soul-searching to do. Unfortunately, he quickly ran out of excuses to remain downstairs and was forced to leave a sleepy Jake on his own.

Chapter Ten

"You need to get out of those wet clothes," Ian said. It took all the will-power he possessed not to drag her into his arms and taste what the wet t-shirt so aptly displayed. "I appreciate the view...but you need to rest."

She looked up at him, eyes wide with fear so stark that it made his gut twist. He'd give anything not to see that look in her eyes again.

"Honey, I'm not going to hurt you," he whispered as he sank to his knees by the bed. He took her hands in his and smiled. "You need to change before you get chilled. I'm a lousy nurse, believe me, the last thing you want is for me to have to take care of you."

She blinked and smiled softly. Relief flooded him.

"I bet I'd make a worse patient," she said.

He stood and pulled her to her feet. She swayed a little and he held her firmly by the shoulders.

"You aren't going to pass out on me, are you?"

"No, I'm okay. Really." She smiled up at him and he felt something deep in his chest crack. *God.* He'd never wanted to feel this way for anyone—especially not her.

"I'll change," she said and turned from him to make her way to the bathroom.

He watched as the door shut softly between them, then sighed and toed off his damp boots. She'd gone out alone again despite the danger she was in, despite the severity of his warnings regarding what could happen to her. He should be mad as hell. He should be bellowing like a bull, not wanting to hold her close and whisper words of comfort. How the hell had he fallen this deep when he'd never taken even a small tumble before?

He felt like he was losing his freaking mind. The bathroom door opened and she came out swathed in the deep blue folds of the softest looking bathrobe he'd ever seen. She stopped just outside the doorway, her cheeks flushed as her gaze skittered away from his blatant perusal.

"You don't have to stay," she said. "I'll be fine now."

Yes, she probably would be, but there wasn't a force on earth or in hell that would take her out of his sight for the next few hours...maybe days.

"No, I'm not taking any chances," he insisted. "Now climb under the covers where it's warm."

She obeyed almost automatically, hurriedly slipping off the robe before she lay back against the pillows. The brief image of her in a short nightgown was almost his undoing. Now he had the sight of her long, bare legs to add to the image of taut nipples and rain-drenched skin. Ian tried not to let his lust get away from him and instead focused on how vulnerable she looked with the shadows beneath her eyes and her damp hair splayed across the white pillow.

"Where do you go?" she asked.

"What do you mean?"

"When you dream? Do you even have dreams? Nightmares?"

"Yes, both sometimes. But not like yours. Mine are usually the past coming back to bite me in the ass."

She chuckled softly, her eyelids drooping closed. "Such language," she murmured.

"Sorry."

"Didn't your mama teach you not to curse like that in front of a lady?"

"She taught me every word I know."

"Huh, why do I find that hard to believe?" Camille yawned and rolled over on her side facing him.

"I don't know, ma'am. Now why don't you stop interrogating me and go to sleep?"

He started to move away and she grabbed his arm. "I know I keep telling you I don't need you around..." She sighed. "It's a lie. Please stay."

He cocked his head to one side and studied her face. "I'm

not going anywhere, honey. You're stuck with me 'til I say so."

"No..." She looked down at her hand resting on his arm and bit her lip. "I'd like you to stay *with* me tonight. I don't want to be alone."

His mouth went dry and he realized all she was saying and not saying. Staying with her was what he wanted, but he suddenly wasn't sure he could trust himself so close to her all night long.

"Honey," he licked his lips, "I'm not sure that's such a good idea after—"

"Please?" she begged in a small, throaty whisper. The sexy tone sent blood racing through his veins and straight to his cock.

"Are you sure?"

Camille nodded.

"Okay, I suppose I can do that," he said aloud, more to reassure himself than her. "I'll take the chair."

"Don't be silly, the bed is a queen size, there's plenty of room."

He chuckled nervously. "Samantha likes big beds, doesn't she?"

"I think she comes from a family of giants."

"Yeah," he replied, thinking of his old friend and her six-foot-plus brothers and father. "You wouldn't know it by looking at her, all of five six and—"

"Ian?"

He shut his mouth and stared as he noticed the hunger in her eyes. *Damn.* How the hell had he gotten himself into this mess?

"Come to bed."

Amazing how three little words could give him such a fast hard-on.

"Cami—"

"I won't attack, Ian. We'll just sleep."

He swallowed. "Do you think we can? I sure as hell don't."

She smiled then—the smile of a woman very pleased with herself. "I'm willing to give it a try."

He stood and pulled the wet T-shirt off over his head and let it drop to the floor. Her gaze lingered the entire time. It felt a bit like performing at Chippendale's. He'd done that once during his first year at the police academy. A buddy bet him he didn't have the balls to take it off on stage in front of a bunch of horny housewives. He not only went through with it, but he went home with four phone numbers, one very interesting proposition and enough cash to live on for a month.

But this was far more enticing with those big hazel eyes staring at him. She didn't say a word as he opened the snap and zipper of his jeans then slid them down. He'd almost gone commando when he realized she had left the house earlier. Now he was immensely relieved that he'd had enough foresight to pull on a pair of black boxer briefs.

"You're staring," he pointed out.

"You're beautiful."

"Men aren't beautiful. Now move over, honey."

She scooted to the far side of the bed and he thought he saw a faint blush color her cheeks.

"Change your mind?" he asked as he slid under the blankets beside her.

"No, of course not." But she was retreating again—pulling away from him both physically and emotionally.

"Camille, I'm tired, you're tired." He slid down onto the pillow but kept a small space between them. "Sleep...I don't expect anything else, honey."

She reached for him then, a determined look lighting her dark eyes. "But I don't want sleep. I want you."

She pulled him to her. The shock of her cool skin against his heated torso set the beast within free. Camille tasted of sweet tea and woman, a tempting combination that fueled his hunger. Her arms wrapped around his neck and she moaned softly beneath him. After what seemed an eternity, he managed to raise his head and look down into her eyes. He swallowed.

He was hard and aching for her. It would be the best sex he'd ever had... Somehow he knew that from one kiss. But he also knew once he had her, he'd never be able to walk away. Ian had to walk away. Anything else wasn't in the cards.

"Sleep..." He rolled off of her and lay at her side. "I'll stay with you until morning."

He pulled her body close to his, her back to his front as he spooned himself around her soft curves. She felt good pressed to the heat in his chest and the throbbing need in his groin. Ian clenched his teeth to keep from groaning aloud. He closed his eyes and waited for her reaction.

With a soft, wistful sigh, she nestled deeper into his embrace. Soon he felt her body relax until her slow, careful breathing told him she'd fallen asleep. When he was satisfied the nightmare hadn't returned, he allowed his own muscles and limbs to uncoil one by one. Soon his mind drifted and floated in that gray region between life and dreams. At one point he thought he could hear voices—soft, distant, but somehow close at hand.

"Thank you," a deep male timbre rose slightly above the others.

Ian tensed, his arms automatically tightening about Camille as his eyelids fluttered open and closed.

"Take care of her."

The words followed him into oblivion as he wondered what the speaker expected of him.

ξ

At the edge of conscious thought, her body felt warm and heavy even as her mind seemed to float. Soft voices flitted in and out of hearing—the words garbled. They clearly didn't speak to her and that was all that mattered. She relaxed a little more as she let her mind drift unhindered, unafraid. None of the usual darkness colored her dreams like an old movie. This one might be calm. Peaceful.

She felt her feet alight on a soft warm surface that seemed to suck her down. Camille opened her eyes and looked around. The beach on which she stood seemed to stretch for miles beneath the cold silver glow of the full moon. White sand warmed the soles of her feet and pushed between her toes. Waves rolled over the shoreline nearby, their rush and pull like a lullaby to her tightly coiled spirit.

Come and play. Come and play, the water seemed to call as the white-capped peaks rolled, faded and lapped over the sand then retreated.

She stared at the scene, breathing the salty air that smelled of seaweed and sand. A smile pulled at her lips and she shivered as a soft breeze blew off the ocean to caress her bare arms and legs.

Paradise at night, she mused. *This is what it would be like.*

The moonlight caressed the waves, sparkling like fireflies dancing on the water. Her gaze traveled down the rolling expanse of sand and water until she spied a dark form huddled at the edge of the shore. It should have scared her, but it didn't. Somehow she knew this wasn't one of her nightmares.

Camille walked slowly toward the figure, her toes pushing deeply into the warm, wet sand as a breeze lifted her hair from her shoulders. The rush of the waves filled her ears along with the pulse of her heart. Finally, she stood but few feet away and could see the man more clearly in the soft moonlight.

He sat with his head on bent knees, immobile but for the wind that ruffled his dark hair about his shoulders. Tanned forearms clasped around his legs bore witness to his underlying strength—even in repose, the outline of tendon and muscle was clearly visible. She recognized him. He lifted his head to look at her as if he had sensed her scrutiny.

Ian. His eyes were as dark as the sky. Then his lopsided smile slid into place and she felt a spark zing in her belly like a light electrical shock.

"Are you in my dreams, now?" he asked, his voice husky and smooth above the sound of the pulsing waves.

"I think you're in mine."

His grin broadened and he shrugged his shoulders before he moved to lean back on those powerful forearms.

"I don't think so, honey." His gaze slipped over her from head to foot and back again. "I'd know if I was dream-walking, and I'm not." He tilted his head to one side. "This is my private place. I come here to be alone."

She glanced around them at the utopian scene. "Is this real? I mean, does it exist somewhere or only in your dreams?"

Ian shook his head, a frown sliding into place. "I'm not sure. Either way, you're the first to visit it with me."

She wrapped her arms about her middle to quiet the uncomfortable swirling in her belly. The wind picked up off the ocean and swept through her thin dress.

"Are you cold?"

"A little."

"Sit beside me," he offered. "We can keep each other warm."

She bit her lip, unnerved by the chaos erupting in her gut.

Sitting beside him could well be the most dangerous thing she'd ever done. *But it's just a dream,* she chided herself. *What happens in dreamland, stays in dreamland.*

Camille dropped down beside him on the soft, warm sand before she could have second thoughts, but kept a reasonable distance between them. He chuckled softly.

"What's so funny?"

"You. Even in dreams you're the most uptight woman I've ever met."

"That's not true," she snapped. "Just because I don't fall over myself to get into your bed doesn't make me uptight."

He quirked a brow. "Now who said anything about you getting into bed with me?"

She felt her cheeks warm and turned to gaze out at the water. "That is what you were implying. Besides, I know your type."

"Oh, I have a type? And just what is that, may I ask?"

"The wham-bam type. You find a woman you want, get what you want however you can and then it's on to the next one."

"Seems you have a rather low opinion of me, Ms. Bryant."

She shrugged. "Not a low opinion, just a realistic one."

He seemed to consider her words as he stared out at the darkening waters. "I'll admit I used to be free and easy when it came to relationships and sex. But people change. At least, I hope I can change someday. No, I'm not in a position to settle down with one woman today...but someday I might change my mind. I think I'd like to give it a try, actually."

"Not likely," she said. "In my experience people don't change in the ways that really matter."

"So, you think I'm *incapable* of making a commitment, right?"

"Yes."

"And you are such an expert because...?"

"I've observed and written about your kind for the past ten years," she said. "I've seen the broken hearts men like you leave behind—the unwanted children, the haunted, betrayed women who thought they would be the one to change the bad boy into a one-woman man."

"If such a man is unredeemable then why do you put them

in the starring roles in every one of your novels?"

She sighed. It crossed her mind many times over the years. Why did she glamorize the type of man she secretly detested? Why couldn't she seem to write about the good guys? The betas out there who knew how to treat women with kindness and fidelity?

"I write fiction, Ian, and in fiction no one is unredeemable." She shrugged. "I wish I could write about a different type of man but for some reason this is what comes to me. These stories are what my muse gives me and I really can't change the basic facts."

He studied her face intently. "You make it sound like you're taking dictation instead of making up stories."

The idea rattled her a bit. Camille pushed to her feet and walked away until the cold water lapped over her toes. Would she be able to write without Josiah? Was he truly the one with the gift others praised her for? The thought pricked at her conscience.

"Sometimes," she admitted softly. "Sometimes it feels that way."

She faced him after blinking away the tears that had formed. "Are your dreams always so serious?" she asked, hoping to deflect his attention from such a difficult subject. "No wonder you seem so intense. I thought I was the one who had a hard time letting go. At least I used to be able to play in my dreams."

His dark eyes narrowed beneath his furrowed brow. Camille balked at the glimmer she saw there—the predatory glow.

"Actually, I'm not much of a talker in dreams," he said. "You seem to have that effect on me."

He stood slowly. His body seemed to tense like a big cat ready to pounce. The glitter in his eyes made her take a step back until the hem of her dress floated in the water.

"Do you want to see how I normally act in my dreams, Camille?" he asked, his voice low and seductive. Dangerous.

"Show me."

Her breath quickened, fueled by the look of hunger in his eyes as well as her own boldness. But it was only a dream. Whatever happened here couldn't matter. He stepped toward her and she jumped, eyes widening.

He'd never know what happened here. No one would. If it were her secret alone, her private little fantasy, then who could possibly judge her? For years she had stayed hidden from the stigma of her parentage, she had tried to pretend that it didn't matter and the gossip didn't hurt, didn't wound. But it was a lie. So she had acted like the sweet, shy and virginal big sister—the responsible one. The one who always did the right thing no matter how difficult or lonely it might be. The one who thought everything, every problem and emotion to death.

She moved forward and reached for Ian with both hands. The look in his eyes went from predatory to surprised and then satisfied as she dragged him into her arms.

"You were saying?" His large, warm hands moved down her back.

Camille closed her eyes and stood on tiptoe, stretching to brush his mouth with hers. He groaned. The deep feral sound vibrated against her chest and lips. His reaction sent a jolt of need low in her belly.

"Now this," he whispered against her cheek. "This is more like it."

"Shut up and kiss me."

Ian chuckled softly and did as she demanded. Any illusion that she had been kissed before soon vanished when his lips took full possession of hers. His mouth moved over hers with small, soft strokes at first, each coaxing a response from her that she couldn't deny. A gentle sweep of his tongue and her lips parted, eager and willing to allow his invasion. The heat grew, the fire roared to such intensity it burned through every defense. Their tongues dueled in hot, chaotic strokes. Her hands grasped at his shoulders, his demanded surrender as he cupped her bottom and pulled her tightly against his swollen cock. She could feel him through their clothing—hard and ready. Ready for her.

Camille shifted a bit in his arms and gasped as her sensitive nub came in contact with the hard, rigid part of him. She moved her hips in slow, sensuous strokes forward and back. Each motion made her tingle, shocking her body with small, electric charges. Ian groaned again and pulled back from the kiss.

"Honey...I'll self-destruct if you keep that up."

She gazed into his eyes. "Promise?"

He groaned and kissed her deeply, his tongue seeking hers with a tempo that grew stronger and faster until she had to pull away to catch her breath.

"Do you always have sex on a first date?" she panted.

Ian stared her for a long moment. Then he smoothed a strand of hair off her cheek.

"No, and I won't start with you."

Disappointment made her stomach drop and she tried to pull away. His arms tightened around her waist.

"You and I would make love, not have sex."

She blinked, still trying to catch her breath. "There's a difference?"

A slow, sensual smile curved his mouth. "Of course," he said, then leaned forward and suckled the sensitive skin on the slope of her neck. Camille's head fell back as she moaned.

"I'm surprised a romance writer doesn't know that. Here...let me show you."

The next moment she lay on her back in the sand, the warmth of Ian's body covering hers. He felt heavy but she liked the sensation. He slid over her, teasing and caressing until she thought she'd spontaneously combust. She ripped at his shirt, needing to feel his flesh against her own, needing to touch him and taste him. He unbuttoned her dress, peeling it down off her shoulders as he pushed the fabric away.

The waves sounded in time with the beat of his heart against her chest, the flick of his tongue at her breasts, her stomach, and lower. Camille gasped with disbelief at the hunger he ignited as he lifted her hips and pulled the dress off before tossing it aside. His hands drifted slow and sure up her legs, heedless of her muttered cries. His fingertips played at the backs of her knees and inner thighs. The air seemed heavy and warm—so much so that she couldn't draw in enough to satisfy her starved lungs.

Then he touched her where she ached and the stars above seemed to swell before they fractured into a million tiny shards. He moved again, climbing higher until his hard, muscled chest pressed into her tingling, swollen breasts. He gazed down into her eyes, his hidden by the darkness of shadows.

"Are you okay?" he whispered. She smiled at the words and the unsteady cadence of his heart thudding so near her own.

Camille brushed a lock of hair back from his eyes. "Yes,"

she whispered. "Very okay."

His full mouth curved and she noticed a dimple there. She lifted her head and placed a soft kiss on the spot.

"I've never met anyone like you." Ian's frown conveyed he didn't like the idea. Her insides seemed to tumble down.

"You mean uptight?"

He shook his head. "No, addictive." He twirled a lock of her hair around his finger and brought it to his lips. She watched as he breathed in the scent with eyes closed. "I could get very used to having you in my dreams."

"I like it here," she admitted. "I feel safe with you. I don't want to leave."

He studied her face before lowering his mouth to hers. She felt his tongue trace a sensuous pattern over her lips. It was a long time before he lifted his head, breathless.

"But you can't stay here," he said. "And the more I dream of you, the more danger there is."

Camille frowned. "Why? You'd never hurt me."

"Not here...here we're on equal ground. But if I think of this too often, if I think of you like this—" He sighed and rolled off of her to lie on the sand. "Damn. This is going to get one of us killed."

"Having sex in a dream will get us killed?" she asked incredulously.

Ian chuckled. "No, me thinking about making love to you might. I won't be able to look at you without getting a hard-on. It's not easy to concentrate on other things when I can barely walk."

She felt the fire in her face and looked away.

"And would it be so bad to want me?" she whispered, hardly aware that she'd spoken the thought aloud. Her cheeks burned hotter when he chuckled.

"Oh, honey, it would be fantastic." He sighed again. "But I need to keep my mind on business. I need to keep my mind on protecting you, not laying you."

"They're only nightmares."

He turned his head to look at her, the moon and stars reflected in his dark, fathomless gaze.

"And this is only a dream. But it sure as hell feels real, doesn't it? There's a lot more to the world than you seem willing to believe. It's time to admit there are boogey men in the shadows."

"I don't want the dragon to be real."

"If wishes were horses—"

"Then beggars would ride," she finished. They stared at each other for the longest time until Camille swore they breathed at the same intervals. It was as if they were becoming two halves of a whole. She liked the sensation.

"Come, it's time to go."

"I don't want to leave," she whispered as unbidden tears filled her eyes. She felt safe here in this dream with Ian at her side. She felt at peace and at one with another human being for the first time in her life. Even if it were a fantasy, she didn't want to let it go. Not yet.

"I know, honey," he murmured, his gaze moving to her lips. "Neither do I, but we don't always get what we want. Not even in dreams."

She wanted to change his mind, wanted to show him how it could be between them, uncaring about the reality or the dream. But she never got that chance. The gentle throb of the surf grew louder and louder until it became a roar of sound. She sat up and watched as the dark sea before them began to churn and dissolve into a fractured mist of color and light.

"Ian?"

She turned her head but he was gone, vanished into a glittering void that swirled like stardust around her. Floating along in the emptiness, her heart leapt in fear. Then the heaviness crept back over her, dragging her under and deeper into the dark. Further and further until she no longer felt the peace and serenity of the dream.

Camille sat up, eyes wide as she panted desperately for air. The early morning light crept beneath the curtain at her window, bathing the room with a pink glow. She managed to slow her breathing before she got out of bed. The floor seemed to roll beneath her feet for a moment and she dropped back onto the mattress.

She had known all along. It had been merely a dream. A lovely, warm and sultry dream. But it had seemed real. Even more real than the nightmares that plagued her nights for the last four months. Rolling around in the sand with her bodyguard held much more appeal than hiding from a bloodthirsty dragon. The ringing phone jerked her attention away from the sweet memories and she picked up the receiver.

"Hello?"

"He'll never stay."

Camille frowned. "Excuse me?"

"He'll never stay with you. You aren't even his type for a one night stand."

"I'm sorry but I think you have the wrong—"

"You think just because you're a famous writer that Ian will stick around, fall in love and carry you off into the sunset? I saw how you looked at him at the diner. But he doesn't feel the same."

Camille recoiled at the venom underlying the unfamiliar female voice.

"He'll be gone before you know it. Before the sheets cool he'll be out the door and on to his next lay."

She couldn't seem to think, couldn't react as the hateful words filled her ear.

"I'm just warning you, Ms. Bryant, as one woman to another. Believe me, you don't want to wind up as one of Ian's used-up whores."

"I don't know why you're calling me, but there's some mistake," she replied levelly.

"The only mistake is that a man like Ian never gets what he really deserves."

A click and the line went dead. Camille stared at the wall, her mind reeling. It had obviously been someone who knew them, someone who had seen them together. The waitress at Mama C's? It made sense. Camille hung up and took a deep breath as she fought to dispel the images the woman's cruel words had dredged up.

Ian had an enemy. One who held a lot of bitterness toward him. But who could really blame her? A man like him would get deep into a woman's blood—especially once she let him inside her body.

She shook the thoughts away and went straight for the bathroom. As the hot spray pelted her skin, she closed her eyes but couldn't block out the echo of the woman's voice on the phone. Camille wondered if she should tell Ian about the call. The caller had sounded bitter, but she didn't actually threaten either of them. Telling him about the call might do little more than embarrass them both.

She rinsed the shampoo from her hair and turned off the water before wrapping herself in a towel and climbing out. Her thoughts whirled with questions she was afraid to ask. When she opened the bathroom door, she heard a small grunt of surprise. Ian stood near the head of her bed, staring at her as if she had sprouted two heads. His hair was still damp from an early shower. He wore black slacks that hugged all the right places and a white polo shirt that stretched across his solid chest and abs.

"I left my watch." He held up the object that glittered a dull gold in the dim bedroom light. He looked down at it as he fumbled with the clasp. "Sorry."

"That's fine," she lied. For some reason, something wasn't fine but she didn't know why. God, the man drove her to the brink of what sanity she had left. How could she possibly trust him when his moods changed so quickly that she wound up with whiplash?

"Did you sleep okay?"

She shrugged. "No nightmares this time."

He nodded and finished fastening the band around his left wrist. "Your sister's home."

She nodded back and cringed at the picture they made. *Two bobble-heads in the back window of a Buick.* Where the hell had their easy camaraderie gone? Had everything about last night been a dream?

"Is she still in bitch mode?"

His gaze jerked back to hers then and one corner of his mouth curled up into a reluctant smile. "Not sure. I haven't actually spoken to her."

Camille sighed. "Well, I guess I can't hide forever. I'll have a talk with her."

He cleared his throat as his gaze slid over her in slow perusal. "Maybe you should get dressed first. Brush your hair so you don't look like you've just been ravished. We wouldn't want a repeat performance of her tirade."

She felt the heat flame in her cheeks and looked away. They'd come very close to making love last night before he'd pulled away. He must know she wouldn't have stopped him, *couldn't* have stopped him with the way his touch burned through her defenses. Being so vulnerable didn't sit well.

"Last night—"

"Let's say we forget all about it, okay?" he interrupted.

She stared at him for a long moment but couldn't read the clues in his eyes. He had a shield up again—his "no trespassing" signal that stopped her cold every time. Camille wished she had enough courage to kick the damn thing down and demand some truth for a change. But she didn't. Not now. There was no way in hell she'd approach him about her dream after this.

"Fine with me," she lied and turned away to head back into the safety of the bathroom. "Now if you don't mind, I'll get dressed. I have a lot of work I need to get done."

She closed the door behind her and leaned back against it as she held her breath, listening. Silence. Just when she thought she'd have to face him again wearing the towel, booted footsteps sounded to the door and out into the hall. The bedroom door shut softly behind him.

Camille sighed. If it was arm's length that he wanted, then that's what he'd get. Maybe her mysterious caller had done her a big favor with that reminder. Players never changed, they only played harder. Those left in their wake were the ones to wind up suffering the most.

§

Camille was filling the kettle at the sink when Ophelia slammed the kitchen door against the wall. Camille jumped at the sound, then gritted her teeth and took a deep breath. God, she was so not in the mood for one of her sister's tantrums today. Not after that dream and the phone call—especially not after that horrible story they kept rehashing on the news. She couldn't turn on the television or radio without hearing about the poor woman left dead, almost bloodless in that alley. A woman who had hopes and dreams—a family who needed her. There was just too much death and violence in the world, and all Ophelia seemed to care about was herself.

"Is there anything to eat around here?" Ophelia flung open the refrigerator door and scowled at the contents.

"There's eggs, sausage and fruit," Camille replied calmly.

"I'm sure you can find something to eat from all that. But if you'll make out a shopping list I'd be happy to—"

"Forget it!" Ophelia slammed the door shut. She began opening and closing cupboard doors, the sound growing louder and louder with each one. The last door slapped shut with such force that Camille thought the wood might splinter.

She took a deep breath and searched for something to say that wouldn't start another argument. Verbal sparring sat low on her list of things to do. The safest choice seemed to be silence, so she continued with her morning ritual and pulled out a canister of tea bags, then placed one in her large mug as the pot started to simmer.

She could feel Ophelia staring at her back, could almost hear the questions rattling through her mind. Tension billowed around them like a thick veil of smoke. It wasn't all that different from most mornings, really. Anger always seemed to take the place of other feelings in her sister's life. Anger seemed to be the only emotion Ophelia expressed anymore.

"So," Ophelia broke the silence. "What do you and the *bodyguard* have planned for today?"

Camille clenched her jaw at the nasty little jab apparent in her sister's tone. Ophelia didn't like Ian—or maybe she just didn't like having to share Camille with another person. Either way it didn't sit well today. It was about time the spoiled little girl grew up.

"I plan to write for a few hours and then I have a book signing at Tamara's shop later," she said, fighting to keep the anger from her voice. "I have no idea what Ian plans to do other than follow me around."

"Seems like a pretty decent gig, considering the fringe benefits."

A shrill whistle began to build from the kettle as Camille held her breath and counted slowly. She had almost reached twenty when her sister opened her mouth again.

"Not that I blame you," Ophelia continued with saccharine sweetness. "I mean he's not bad for an old man. He's got a great ass."

Camille spun around, oblivious to the pot shrieking behind her.

"What the hell is wrong with you?" she demanded.

Ophelia glared back at her through hate-filled eyes. They

were the same color as their mother's, right down to the long black lashes. Camille wondered if Ophelia realized just how much she looked like Mom.

"My problem is that you're setting yourself up for a big fall, sister dear. That man isn't going to stick around no matter what incentives you offer."

Her hand flew out and caught Ophelia across the cheek. They both stood like stone statues as the sound of the slap reverberated in the air. Ophelia's cheek turned red, her eyes narrowed with anger.

"Don't you ever talk to me like that again," Camille said. "I haven't done a damn thing to earn this malice from you and I refuse to take it anymore. If you're bored, get off your ass and get a job somewhere. If you need a man, I'm sure you won't have any trouble finding one to accommodate you. In the meantime, if you have a legitimate complaint, I'd be happy to hear it. But now, if you'll excuse me, I have things to do."

She carefully turned off the fire beneath the kettle and waited as Ophelia walked to the kitchen door. Just when it seemed she'd had the last word, Ophelia hesitated.

"He'll leave," she said softly. "They always leave. But just know I'll be here to pick up the pieces."

"You've never had to before," Camille reminded her. "I've always taken care of myself."

"You wouldn't let me help," she answered, her voice suddenly young and forlorn. "But I listened to you cry."

The door creaked shut behind her, leaving Camille alone. She stared out the kitchen window as her vision blurred with tears. The sky outside grew heavy with thick, gray clouds that blotted out the sun.

Had she really pushed her sister away like that? Her mind felt so clouded, her memories covered with shadows. She couldn't be sure, but it was possible. Ophelia had known about her tears. There had been so many of them, but she thought she had hidden them from her little sister. She had tried to protect her from the pain.

§

Half an hour later, Camille had dried her tears and tidied

up the kitchen before heading back out into the parlor. Ian sat on the dainty flowered sofa reading the morning paper, looking perfectly at home despite his size. The sound of her footsteps drew his attention and he looked up. He folded the newspaper and laid it on the table before rising to his feet.

He said nothing, only watched her expression as he walked across the room, almost floating as if his feet never touched the floor. *Do real men move like that?* She'd never thought it possible. Smooth, powerful, so at ease in his own skin, he seemed to mock mere humans and their unflattering gaits. He would make a great hero for one of her books. An otherworldly air hung about him like an aura.

Camille rubbed her fingers together wishing she had a keyboard or a pen and notepad. His gaze slid over her from head to foot. She felt a wave of heat buffet her cold flesh. How could this man alone make her so warm? Make her ache with one glance? She forced a smile onto her face and glanced over his shoulder at the empty parlor.

"She went upstairs," he announced.

But she didn't want to talk about Ophelia. She didn't want to talk about anything with this man that made her body tremble with need. It frightened her. The melting heat that bubbled around them had her feeling jumpy and unsure of herself. It seemed to mock her self-control.

"Camille, have you eaten yet?" His deep voice broke into her reverie.

She stared at him. Had there been a note of uncertainty in his voice? Mr. Smooth, a man of the world? No. She had to be imagining things again.

"No, I haven't." She waited for a response, afraid to infer more meaning into his words.

Always leave them a way out, so no one gets hurt.

The fewer chances taken, the better. She couldn't afford risks—not in real life. Those were left for her characters to deal with. Through them, she could take a risk, laugh at fate and put herself on the line. In real life, the potential pain would be unbearable. But in her stories, the heroine could be put through hell while always knowing that a happy ending lurked a few pages away.

He glanced at his wristwatch. "It's almost ten. You have a book signing at three, right?"

"Yes, three to six at my friend Tammy's shop. I'm sorry to put you through it, but you can blame it on Sam."

He chuckled softly. "I wouldn't miss it. I don't think I've ever attended one before." He looked away and cleared his throat softly. "Would you have lunch with me?"

The question took her by surprise. He sounded...uneasy, almost as if he were afraid she'd refuse his offer. Could the sexy bodyguard possibly worry about rejection? She doubted it. No woman with a breath of life left in her could refuse him a thing. The knowledge that she would gladly have given him anything last night made her want to curl up and disappear.

"Don't worry about me," she insisted. "I'll just make myself a sandwich before we have to leave for the signing."

He stared at her a moment, the groove between his thick dark brows deepening. "It's my job to worry."

She glanced down at the loose red T-shirt and faded jeans she'd put on after her shower. "I'm not really dressed for anything but fast food."

"You look fine," he assured her as he looked her over from head to foot. She thought his gaze lingered a moment on her hips, her chest. An answering rush of heat filled her cheeks.

Camille couldn't think of a plausible excuse to stay home. Not when he looked at her with those dark eyes sparkling with a secret, knowing smile. She didn't want an excuse, she realized. She wanted to be with him.

"Okay, but I really need to change and freshen up first—maybe answer some emails, too. Then we can just drive over to Tammy's for the signing after lunch and not worry about coming back here." She turned and bolted up the stairs before one of them could change their minds.

Anticipation hummed along her nerve endings as she changed her clothes and freshened her makeup. As she unbound the tight coil of her braid, the long waves of hair fell over her shoulders and flared a bit as static and her excitement seemed to buoy every cell in her body. Camille stared for a moment at the results of her primping. She sighed. Her plain features and dull brown hair would never catch his eye. Ian was more than likely used to vibrant, self-assured women with trim bodies and classic beauty.

Not that she cared. No. It didn't matter in the least. She had no desire to enter a romantic relationship with the man.

Meg Allison

Liar.

Chapter Eleven

"I hate these promotional events," she murmured as the city streets and stately old houses sped by her window.

"Why?"

Camille twisted her hands together in her lap and sighed. "I'm not good with strangers, and they act like I'm something special. They treat me like a celebrity or a freak in the sideshow."

Ian chuckled. "I really doubt any of them see you as a freak, but a celebrity, yes. You do something very few people can."

"A lot of people can write."

"True, but few of them get published."

"Yeah, well that was the hard part, believe me. I have a stack of rejection letters about an inch thick." She shrugged and wrapped her arms around her middle to ward off the chill of the air conditioner. "I'm not really that special. I just refused to give up on myself. Besides, without Sam in my corner, I doubt I would have gotten this far."

He glanced at her with that sexy half-smile of his. It sent a tingle over her skin. "That alone makes you unique. Very few people are able to hold on to their dreams when things get tough, no matter who's helping."

She tilted her head to one side, ignoring the compliment and concentrating on the words instead. The meaning beneath them.

"The voice of experience once again, I presume?"

He grinned wide and slid his Ray-Bans on with one hand, eyes now trained on the surrounding traffic. "If you say so."

And that, she knew, would be the end of that...at least until she had him alone later. If he thought she was giving up, he was sadly mistaken. For reasons she couldn't quite fathom, Camille had developed an acute interest in the Sentinel—who he was, how he became the man he was. That interest grew measure by measure each day, until it all but consumed her. She had to know what made Ian Spain tick, no matter what the consequences.

The small bookstore teemed with people, the crowd so thick that no one could move more than a foot in any direction without stepping on someone's toes. The butterflies in Camille's stomach put on cleats and stomped around her innards in a rather bad *Lord of the Dance* imitation.

She fought back the urge to run as she entered the store in front of Ian. He immediately placed a hand on her lower back and she knew, despite the dark glasses, that he was dissecting the scene for possible risk. Somehow, the idea both soothed and annoyed her. The only risks she needed protection from involved the dragon in her nightmares and the erotic images Ian evoked.

"I don't think this is a good idea," she murmured.

"Like it or not, we're here," he replied. "Don't worry, I'm not letting you out of my sight."

He didn't quite understand. It wasn't really the living that she feared, or the crush of bodies that surrounded them. It was the voices. The dead lingered around those they had left behind—some needing closure, some unable to give up love, others unwilling to forsake their hatred. If these people knew what or who hovered around them, getting her autograph would be the least of their worries.

"The voices..." She rubbed her temple, squinting in an effort to block out the migraine that hovered at the fringes of her brain. She could almost feel the blood vessels constricting; the pain behind her eyes began to build as the bolder of her fans moved forward.

"Ms. Bryant?" a young woman asked hesitantly. "I just love your novels. I've read all of them at least three times. Could you please sign my copy of *Healing Touch?*"

Camille forced a smile. "Of course, just let me grab a pen."

"Ladies, excuse me, please...let Ms. Bryant catch her breath." Tamara King parted the crowd with an ease that would have inspired Moses. She'd been running King's Book Nook for the last ten years and was savvy enough to keep the small establishment in the black despite competition from the big-name chains in the area.

Tamara stood in front of her and took Camille's hand with the smile of an old friend. "Sorry, girl, but apparently my PR manager really did his job this time. Can you handle it?"

"Of course, Tam, anything for you." Camille knew she wouldn't be here today without her old high school friend—the one who had stood beside her and hadn't judged her because of her parentage. Tamara was one of the few she counted on as a true friend.

She noticed Tamara's interest in her companion.

"This is Ian Spain," she said, turning slightly to glance up at the man who hadn't taken his hand from her since they entered the crowded room. "Ian, this is Tamara King, owner and manager of King's Book Nook."

"And an old friend," Tamara added as she extended her hand. "Pleased to meet you, Mr. Spain."

"Ian," he interjected. "And it's good to meet a friend of Cami's."

Tamara's pencil-thin brows shot to her hairline. Only very close friends used that nickname and Camille was sure she could see the wheels turning in Tamara's eyes.

"Yes, well...let me get the two of you to the table we've set up and I'll find another chair."

"That's not necessary. I prefer to stand."

Camille looked up at him with a frown. "I'm supposed to be here for three hours, at least. You can't just stand there the whole time."

"Sure I can."

They followed Tamara to the back of the store where a place had been cleared between the aisles and a table set up with copies of her books. Camille took her seat on the folding chair and nervously rearranged the pens and bookmarks lined up in neat little rows.

"You'll be fine—much better than our first time," Tamara said near her ear, then gave Ian a sassy smile. "Especially with your gorgeous friend hanging around." She laughed and moved around the table, instructing the gathered onlookers to form a line and that they should bring their books to the front register once the author had signed them.

"If you two need anything, just holler."

The first reader approached with a shy smile and grabbed a copy off the top of a stack. "Could you sign it for Mandy?"

"Sure," Camille said with an automatic smile.

She knew by the end of the afternoon her face would ache, her smile feeling more like a plastic grimace than any kind of true greeting. How she hated being in the spotlight—on display like a performing bear at the circus.

Seventeen autographs later, Camille had to put down her pen and try to uncrimp her fingers as she took a swig from a bottle of water.

"What did Tamara mean about the first time?" Ian asked, somewhat startling her. She'd been so engrossed in the proceedings and questions asked her that she had almost forgotten him standing there at her side like a Roman general.

"Oh, when my first novel came out, Tam wanted to support me, of course," she said. "So she talked me into coming back to Savannah for a weekend book signing. It wasn't very successful."

"Not much of a crowd?"

She laughed at the memory. "Um, no...I sold five books in three hours, and one of those was to Tam's sister-in-law who absolutely hates romance. I doubt she's read the book to this day. Anyway, it was a dismal failure and I swore I'd never do it again."

"Something must have changed your mind." A small smile tugged at the corner of his mouth. It fascinated her...he fascinated her. She glanced away and picked up the pen, swearing silently as she realized her hands were shaking. How did the man tie her into so many knots?

"Yes, Sam insisted they were necessary." She shrugged. "They have gotten better," she admitted as another line began to lengthen in front of her table. "This has to be the best turnout ever. I never expected this many people."

She signed a few more books, answered very familiar questions the best way she could, before she dared another glance at Ian. Didn't the man ever get tired of standing in one place? For someone who moved with the grace of a panther, she thought he would be stalking the store by now, instead of lounging against the wall behind her as if he had nothing else in the world to do.

"Are you sure you don't want a chair or some water?" she asked.

"I'm fine," he assured.

The afternoon dragged on...the line filling, dwindling and filling again, until Camille wished she could just sneak out the back door. It wasn't that she didn't appreciate it all, but she didn't think she'd signed her name so many times in her entire life. Her head pounded, her fingers ached, her butt felt numb pressed against the hard metal chair. Just when she was about to get up and excuse herself for a run to the ladies' room, Tamara sauntered up to the table.

"Well, I think we've tortured you long enough," she said with a wide smile. "Take a break, we'll have you read an excerpt and then call it day. How about it?'

Camille felt the butterflies rev up for a cha-cha. "A reading? Oh, come on, Tam, I don't think—"

"They'll love it. I've already picked out an excerpt, all you have to do is lend the voice."

"That's what I'm afraid of. What part did you choose?"

Tamara's grin made her want to groan. "Not the really juicy stuff, you know I like the buildup better than the climax."

"Tammy, you're outrageous." Camille could feel her cheeks flaming as Ian's gaze raked her body from over the top of his dark lenses.

"Come on, it'll be fun," Tammy insisted.

"For who?"

"I'd enjoy it," Ian said.

Something in his voice made her pulse race. Yes, he would just love to have her in that position—reading some sexy snippet out loud while a room full of women sighed and dreamed. All the while Camille knew she'd picture Ian as her hero, imagine his hands on her body, his lips... She cleared her throat and looked away.

"I just don't like the idea of reading in front of so many people without any notice."

Tamara touched her arm and smiled softly. "I understand, believe me. But you need something extra right now. It's been a long time between books and, well, the words just wouldn't sound right coming from anyone else."

Still, Camille hesitated.

"Please?" her old friend begged in earnest. "For old times?"

Camille sighed and let her head fall back to stretch out the kinks. "Okay, if you put it that way, how can I refuse?"

Twenty minutes later, Camille sat on a high stool at the edge of the crowd. While the numbers had substantially dwindled since they first arrived, it was easy to see that the popularity of *Healing Touch* had not ebbed. Eager, expectant faces from almost every walk of life stared up at her...waiting. They looked both curious and excited—except for the man in black who held her own attention. Her body and senses seemed cued to every move he made as he slowly circled the crowd, hands clasped behind his back in a casual manner she wished she could adopt.

Camille felt as if she were going to faint. Stage fright could be a bitch.

"I want to thank you all for coming by today," she began, cringing inwardly at the slight tremor in her voice. She cleared her throat. "I hadn't planned on doing a reading but Ms. King was very persuasive."

"She means pushy," Tamara called from the sidelines. Laughter filtered through the crowd and Camille found herself relaxing a bit. She had always envied Tamara's easygoing manner.

"So, my pushy friend..." Camille continued, cuing her own round of giggles from her fans, "...has chosen a very nice section for me to share with you today—lucky for me, it's not one of the love scenes."

Several mock-groans of disappointment filled the air. Camille smiled, picked up the book and opened it to the place her friend had marked. It just happened to be one of her own favorite parts—one written with the ease of pouring water into a glass. The words had come directly from her writing zone.

She lay before him helpless and in such pain her body shook in small tremors. By all the gods, how could he continue to let her suffer? Beth had come to him on her own, seeking help as she stumbled through his doorway and into his arms.

She was so light...so weak and helpless. The plea for mercy had been there in her tear-filled eyes. He'd known this kind of pain before, over a thousand years ago. No one had offered him mercy then until his savior had shown up and offered him life instead of certain death. He'd chosen life and he had not regretted it.

Or so he told himself over and over. In truth, he often wondered if it had been for the best. Had death been so frightening compared to an eternity of solitude?

Gabriel pushed the memories aside and concentrated on the twisted features of the woman on his bed. She made a small, keening sound like the wind through the thick forest on All Hallow's Eve.

"No worries, child, I will take care of you."

"Please…" she whispered. "The pain…"

He felt it radiate from her like steam from a kettle ready to blow. He had to release some of the pressure before he lost her. For some reason he didn't wish to examine too closely, he couldn't bear the thought of losing this woman he hardly knew. Since they had first met, she'd become vitally important to him.

Gabriel laid his right hand on her forehead—the fire from her fever scorched his skin. The other he placed between her breasts where her heart lay. It pounded beneath his palm in a strong, almost frantic beat that spoke of the ordeal her body must be going through.

Then he closed his eyes and began to pray in gentle words that whispered through the night. The words were forgotten long ago, remembered by but a few. A few like him who could heal with a touch.

He continued on, heedless of the fiery tendrils that fed through his palm, up his arm and then dissipated throughout his body like an electrical current. He could feel a dark presence hovering nearby. It wasn't unusual, but he and Beth were protected by the blessings he'd placed on his home after it was built.

The tenor of her breathing began to change as her heartbeat slowed from its frantic pace. Her fever broke and sweat beaded on her high brow. Sweat coated her skin and plastered her thin shirt against her breasts. After another moment, he ended the prayer with an expression of thanks and opened his eyes to find her staring up at him.

"Thank you," she murmured. "I think you just saved my life."

The emotions in her eyes made Gabriel uneasy. He shrugged and moved away. "I only did what was necessary."

She grasped his hand in hers and brought it to her lips. Her *skin was so soft, so sweet against his that for a moment he held his breath as her kiss lingered.*

"Thank you," she said. "I'm in your debt, Gabriel. Forever."

The chapter ended and Camille lifted her gaze to the listening crowd. Some had tears in their eyes, others wore wistful, dreamy expressions. All at once, they erupted into applause, several standing on their feet and the others following suit. Camille couldn't help smiling—and blushing—as she rose to her feet and nodded to the cheering audience.

"Thank you," she said, but was sure no one could hear above the tumult.

She scanned the faces, marveling at their depth of appreciation and looking for Ian. In her heart, she hoped he had also felt something from her words. She hoped, like Gabriel, there might be a way to reach such a reclusive hero in the real world. Her thoughts careened to a sudden halt when another face peered back at her from the throng. Goosebumps pebbled across her arms and her pulse quickened. Tall, blond and as big as life, Drew Lee simply smiled back at her, blew a kiss and vanished into the crowd as quickly as he'd appeared. She felt the blood drain from her face while the bookstore seemed to waver around her.

"Are you okay, Cami?" Tamara asked, pulling her out of the moment. She glanced at her friend's concerned frown and nodded.

"Yes, I think I'm just a little tired. Do you know where—?"

"I'm here, honey." She felt his warm hand at her back and leaned into him thankfully.

"Can we go?"

"Of course."

Camille turned to her friend. "Thank you, Tammy, but we need to leave."

"Oh, are you serious?" Tamara stepped closer, her usual ease overshadowing the faint concern that lingered in her expression. "I should be thanking you. You've always been a good friend to me, Cami. Take care of yourself, okay?"

"Of course, and as soon as the next one comes out, we'll do this again," Camille promised.

Tamara gave her a big, sisterly hug. "You can count on it. Then we'll have a night on the town after, okay? Just us girls."

Ian led her through the store and outside. As soon as they hit the pavement, his arm slipped around her waist, gathering her close to his side. The contact sent her cluttered thoughts in a whole different spin.

"What are—?"

"I'm your boyfriend, remember? Good a time as any to act the part."

"Oh," she said as she tried to keep in step with his pavement-eating stride.

"What happened back there?" He asked as he unlocked the car door, his gaze moving back and forth from her to the traffic and the sidewalk. Camille prayed for a steady voice. She didn't want to mention Drew being there, especially when the image had been so quick, so fleeting that she wasn't sure now if it had been real.

"Nothing happened, I'm just drained. It's been a long day."

"I saw your expression, Cami. Something scared the hell out of you."

"No, you're wrong. I just need something to eat and a nice long nap."

"Didn't you sleep well?"

Great, he'd jumped from one topic she wanted to avoid right into the fire.

"Yes, I did," she hedged, memories of the dream making her face warm.

"Obviously not." The sarcasm was subtle but it cut all the same. Did she really look as wrung out as she felt? It was a wonder no one had measured her for a casket, yet.

"Hey, come on," he added. "I know a great place for barbecue—how about we stop and have an early dinner?"

"I'm still pretty full from lunch." Her stomach growled and she pressed a hand to her middle. Ian chuckled.

"Your stomach doesn't seem to agree," he said with a smile. "That salad you insisted on couldn't have been too filling. Come on, let's go grab something hot and spicy."

Heavens, she hoped he couldn't tell what sorts of thoughts those words evoked. If the man got her any hotter, she would go up in flames at any moment.

"You're right," she admitted. "And if there's one thing I can't resist, it's great barbecue."

"Glad to hear it, now climb in, Ms. Bryant. I think it's about time you got a little pampering."

Silence hung between them on the rest of the drive, filled only with the sound of soft jazz from the car speakers. The bluesy notes of the alto sax struck a chord within. Its smooth melody soothed Camille on such a deep level that she felt her body grow heavy, her thoughts calm. The scenery passed by in a soft blur of muted colors and motion. Her eyelids drifted closed and she gave in to the undeniable urge to slip from conscious thought to oblivion. This time her moment of panic at entering the realm of dreams passed quickly when Ian's warm, gentle voice offered her comfort.

"Rest, I'll watch over you."

Her head jerked, eyes opened then shut again. The lure proved too strong to resist. She could sleep—just for a while. No demon would dare seek her out in the presence of the formidable Sentinel. With a final sigh of peace and resignation, Camille fell into a deep sleep. The next thing she knew, Ian gently shook her awake.

"We're here," he said. She blinked up at him. "You still with me?"

Camille yawned and stretched as well as she could in the cramped car. "Sorry about that. I couldn't stay awake."

"No problem..." He seemed poised to say something more, but merely gave her one of those heart-melting, sexy half-smiles before he climbed out of the car and walked around to open her door. "The service is great and the food will bring you back for more."

"It will, huh?" She couldn't resist a smile. He seemed so lighthearted and carefree that being near him lifted her spirits.

"I guarantee it," he insisted. "Be warned, you'll crave it in the middle of the night and that craving won't let up until you drive over for a bite."

"Sounds like an addiction."

His smile slipped a little. "It may be."

They were seated quickly at a small oak table that rocked a little until Ian stuck a matchbook under one of the legs. By the time their waiter arrived for their order, at least four people had stopped to say hello to the Sentinel. Most of them were women, much to Camille's dismay.

The meal passed with easy, if intermittent conversation. It

didn't have that uncomfortable feel to it, however. It was as if they'd done this a hundred times before and simply didn't have to talk. The decadent, fat-laden barbecue pork tasted like heaven on a bun. Camille wolfed down half of the huge sandwich before she slowed down.

"Dessert?" the efficient waiter asked as he scooped up their plates and silverware. "We have the best pecan pie in the state."

"Oh," Camille moaned, a hand on her stuffed belly. "That sounds so good. I haven't had pecan pie in years. But I just don't have any room."

"How about some ice cream?" Ian asked with a child-like grin.

"Nope, no room for ice cream."

He gaped, eyes wide in mock horror. "There's always room for ice cream. It melts around everything else."

Camille laughed. "Really, I'm stuffed. But you go ahead, Ian. I don't mind."

He raised a brow in disbelief, but soon relented. "I'll have a scoop of chocolate ice cream with hot fudge."

"Yes, sir, coming up."

The sudden silence between them made her shift uneasily in her seat. Ian sat watching her as if he were waiting for something.

"Now will you tell me what spooked you earlier?" he finally asked.

"I saw someone in the back of the room," she admitted.

Ian stared, his entire body suddenly tense and alert. "Who?"

"The man from the Blue Moon the other night—my old boyfriend, Drew."

"I didn't see him. I was the only man there today, and believe me, I was watching closely."

She felt the panic twist in her belly. Could it finally be happening? Was she losing her mind?

"I thought..." She shook her head and swallowed back the tears that clogged her throat. "I'm sorry. I really thought he was there. I feel so odd, so edgy lately. It's like someone's right behind me and then I turn to look and they're gone." She hugged herself and blinked to clear her vision. "I'm finally going over the edge."

"No," Ian said. "You may be feeling a lot of things, but you're not going crazy. This thing is pushing you in that direction. I'm telling you you're still sane. You do need rest and you need to let someone else worry about things for a while."

She couldn't hold back the smile that tugged at her lips. "You, for example?"

"Yes, me." He stared at her for a long moment, the depth of his gaze drawing her deeper, calming her even as it stirred her senses. "I won't let anything happen to you," he promised. "But you have to trust me. You have to do whatever I say."

He clasped her hand across the table, his expression filled with determination and something else. Something she longed to cling to. Camille closed her eyes and sighed. She was in so damn deep now, she wasn't sure she'd ever be able to claw her way out.

Chapter Twelve

Her eyes filled with tears as she stared at him. The scene hadn't changed since the first dream walk. They stood in the shadows, the lamplight dimly illuminating the street. Old brick buildings towered above them like stone giants. The city stood still, silent but for the beat of his heart and the air rushing in and out of his lungs.

She had been so frightened, so vulnerable all evening. He had longed to pull her into his lap right there in the restaurant, in front of the customers, waiter and everyone. The urge to protect, to comfort had never been so strong. It had never been a part of his nature—at least, not since the day his mother had given up on life and died.

But Camille needed him and for some reason he wasn't prepared to identify, he needed her.

"Why are you here?"

"It's my job, Camille."

She shook her head, tears glittering in her eyes. "No Sentinel can save me from a nightmare. Not even you."

"Maybe I'm the one that can. One of the few."

She moved closer, the usual caution gone from her beautiful hazel eyes. She wasn't afraid of him in her dreams because she still didn't understand. The knowledge that he would have to tell her the truth made his gut knot. But he didn't have to tell her now.

"You don't belong here," she insisted. "This is my battle, my demon. Leave, please. I-I couldn't stand to watch you die."

"I told you last time, leaving you alone is not an option."

She tilted her head and smiled, spurring his heart to a gallop. "Such a gallant knight, Ian Spain. You were born centuries too late. But this is a dream...only a dream, and you are an illusion."

She moved as if to walk away. He reached for her and gathered her into his arms, their bodies flush from chest to hip. Camille's eyes went wide, her gasp echoed off the rough brick walls. Then he felt her press against him as she slowly relaxed into his embrace.

"Does this feel like an illusion?" he demanded. "It may be a dream, but I am very, very real. So are you."

Here in his arms he held a body made for love, designed for him. Lips that begged to be kissed, eyes that promised something that both beckoned and frightened him at once. He hadn't seen it coming, hadn't looked for these feelings—if anything, he'd avoided them like the plague. But they wouldn't be denied anymore.

Camille. His woman. He'd never have believed it just days ago, but his words to Jake and his skateboard buddies had been right. She was his woman in every sense of the claim. Passion darkened her eyes and he felt a surge of pleasure as her arms twined about his waist. Vaguely aware of the malevolent beast drawing closer, Ian lowered his head inch by inch until, at long last, their lips met.

A touch, a mere caress and the beast within his own body roared to life. Primitive, powerful emotions swamped his self-control. The beast in him demanded all from the soft, beautiful woman in his embrace. He groaned, a sound to express his desire and his despair. But there was no turning back. He might try to deny the attraction while awake, but here in her dream, there would be no lies. Ian wanted her, needed her like earth needs water, like a vampire needs blood and the darkness of the night. Somehow, Camille had become essential to the very beat of his heart.

Even in her dream she tasted sweet and warm. The feel of her hands on his back, moving in slow, hesitant caresses had him drawing her closer. Her whimper made him pause, but when he tried to pull away, Camille made another sound, one of protest, and dug her fingers into the muscles of his back as she pressed tighter against him.

His body grew hard, throbbing where her pelvis molded to his. Grasping her bottom in both hands, he lifted her off her feet then thrust up to meet her perfect heat. Grinding in slow circles, he held her so close it was a wonder either of them could breathe. She moaned and her tongue met him stroke for stroke, deeper, almost frantic in the need to get closer until he had to break contact to breathe.

"Camille," he murmured, one cheek pressed to the top of her head. Her soft hair tickled his nose. His body burned for her. This should never have happened, not even in a dream.

"I'm sorry," he added. But it wasn't quite true. He'd wanted that kiss since she first walked down the stairs in that brown sack of a dress.

"Don't be," she whispered, tilting her chin to peer up at him. The emotions shimmering in those amazing eyes all but brought him to his knees. "I just wish..."

Ian frowned at her hesitation. "What, honey?" He smoothed a strand of hair back from her face, uncaring how his hand shook. "Tell me what you wish."

Her sad smile made him ache deep inside. "I wish this wasn't a dream."

A crack of thunder made her jump, but he held her tight to his chest, not allowing her to move away. Ian looked up into the churning mass of blackness that had surrounded them, jaw set as he reigned in his passions.

He must vanquish the demon, but could only do so if he remained in control. While he longed to strike out and kill the beast, he knew they must identify him first. It was no ordinary dream demon—he had the feel of someone with great power. Such power could be deadly, if not for Camille, then for someone else with psychic gifts. Ian could not lose to another monster. He would not be responsible for the death of another Chosen One.

"Reveal yourself, demon," he commanded. A sound between a laugh and a hiss vibrated off the alley walls.

"Go to hell, Sentinel," a raspy voice replied.

He felt Camille's arms tighten around him.

"Give me the woman. She is mine."

"Never."

"Oh, I think you will. Once you learn the truth. She does not deserve such a warrior as you. She is defiled. She is marked. You will let the woman go or suffer for her sins."

Ian shook his head. "She is under my protection. You will

not have her."

A rush of wind whistled down the alleyway, blowing her hair around his face. Ian carefully untwined her arms from about his middle and turned to face the dragon, tucking her securely behind him.

"Then we fight, demon. I will not give my woman to you. You will die."

That laugh again. It pricked at his nerves, set the hair on his arms at attention.

"You cannot kill me, Sentinel," the demon growled. "Neither could her last protector and he paid the ultimate price. Is that to be your fate as well?"

Her last? He pushed away the questions that sprang up. "I will not let you have her."

"Then so be it, mortal. She will watch you die...and then she shall be mine."

Ian raised his hand and from the mist, conjured a sword much like the one Camille had unwittingly fashioned for him during that first dream walk. But this one felt more familiar in his grip. Its heft and weight like an extension of his own hand.

The black mist billowed and curled, a thin tendril reaching out from the massive cloud as Ian stood at the ready. The narrow wisp moved toward them, pulling more with it as it thickened and spread. A beast began to form in the inky vapor. His edges sharpened to scale and talon, legs and neck. A long, massive tail and glowing red eyes took final form. The beast's jaws opened to reveal long dagger-like teeth. Camille gasped and her fingers clawed the leather at Ian's waist.

"You do not frighten me, demon. Show your true form...or are you such a coward that you must use this childish disguise?"

"I am no coward," the dream demon said with a growl. His jaws jerked like those of a marionette. "This is what I am, Sentinel. You should be afraid. Only a fool would be otherwise."

"Do exactly as I say, Camille. Do you understand?"

"Yes," she whispered. He only hoped she understood the urgency in his command, though he kept his tone steady. A wrong move now could mean his death and hers as well. Neither of them would awaken ever again.

Without warning the beast lunged. The thrust of his giant head slammed into Ian's shoulder. He flew up into the air and careened into the brick wall. Camille's scream pierced the resonate thud of his pulse, the vibrating roar of the dragon. As his body slid down the rough brick, Ian fought for breath.

"Be still," he whispered. Camille stood like a statue, a fist pressed to her mouth as tears welled in her dark eyes.

Ian winked at her, satisfied when her eyes widened. "You've got to do better than that, demon."

He pushed to his knees then rose. The sword lifted off the ground where it had fallen and rushed through the air to be caught in his grasp. He felt Camille's gaze upon him but kept his on the adversary.

"Now you've pissed me off. Royally. Not a good move."

He raised the weapon and with an ancient war cry his Celtic ancestors would applaud, Ian moved forward. The blade whistled through the damp air, sending ribbons of vapor twisting in the night. A surge of adrenaline and pure rage filled his veins.

He saw the dragon move, felt the slice of his claws but not the pain. Leather ripped as scale tore it in two, but they fought on. Forward, thrust, feint to the left and slice. A ribbon of blood burst across the beast from neck to groin, marking the path of Ian's sword. The demon's howl of pain pierced Ian's eardrums, but he continued his assault.

He raised the blade and brought it down to the left and across again. Another stroke swept to the right and up. Not every lash connected, but those that did met with scale much softer than he thought possible.

Blood spurted, bathing the alley with a dark crimson stream that hissed and bubbled against the brick and stone. The monster shrieked. Each blow made him stumble backward as he reeled in pain.

"I banish you, demon!" Ian roared, the sword aloft. His muscles clenched, quivering beneath the weight of the tempered blade that now dripped with blood. He brought the sword down in an arc, a cry of triumph wrenched from his gut. Steel hit pavement—the impact ricocheted up his arms.

Ian stumbled and fell to his knees on the uneven cement. He blinked at the empty space where the dragon should be.

"What the hell...?"

"Ian!"

A soft touch on his shoulder made him flinch.

"You've been wounded." The sting of sweat dripping into a large cut accompanied the observation. Until that moment, he hadn't felt the pain. The burning sensation that spread through his system made him wish he couldn't feel it now.

"I'm fine," he lied. When he tried to stand, pain ripped through his side and he fell back to his knees with a grunt.

"Fine, huh? Sure you are." Her hands sought hold on his upper arms where the leather sleeves hung in gaping shreds. Those hands were so small, so cold against his skin. How could this fragile thing help him to his feet?

But then he stood erect, her shoulder beneath his. He looked down at her with wonder while he panted for breath and fought to still his racing heart.

"You could have been killed," she murmured. Tears glimmered in her eyes, her voice wavered like a sail on the breeze.

"No, he can't kill me, Camille. I won't die that easily."

She turned her head and looked at the place where the dragon had collapsed. Only the dark red stain of his foul blood remained.

"Is he dead?"

Ian shook his head. "I'm not sure, but I don't think so. It was too easy somehow. I think he'll return."

"Are you so sure the demon is male?"

The question took him by surprise. He hadn't realized it until now...but he knew in his heart the demon obsessed with Camille held a man's soul. Or what had once been a man and now was little more than a force of pure evil.

"I can tell by the voice, by its presence. Do you disagree?"

"No...I've always thought of it as male. I just wondered. You seem so sure, so at ease battling a dragon. I just wondered if you had done this before."

He stared at her, unsure how to reply. She knew of the Sentinels, that much had been made clear, but he was forbidden to tell too much. It could prove deadly to them both. The spirits of the dead spoke to Camille. How many others might they tell the secrets of the Sentinels?

"We need to get you bandaged up," she said, letting him off the hook for the moment. "But...I'm not sure how. Should we go somewhere special?"

She glanced around the dim alley and he had to smile. Faced with unspeakable terror, unrivaled evil and she still let her mothering instinct shine through.

Selfless, nurturing...he'd never met anyone quite like her.

"I'll be fine, Camille. Maybe it's time to end the dream."

She shook her head. "Will he come back?"

"Yes."

The sadness in her eyes made his chest tighten. "Will he come back tonight?"

He took a deep breath and let his senses flow outward along the sleepy streets of her dream Savannah.

"No, I don't think so. He'll need to rest. That battle must have taken a lot of his energy."

She nodded then and smiled. "Then I just might get a decent night's sleep out of this. I'm staying, Ian. But you can leave whenever you wish. I release you."

He took a step closer and gazed down her. "You haven't been listening, honey. Leaving is not an option. Quit trying to get rid of me."

"All right, Mr. Spain. But it's my turn now. You need to be bandaged and this is my dream. We're going to have it taken care of now."

She grasped his hand in hers and closed her eyes, head tilted back a fraction. The scene around him went out of focus; he swayed at the sensation of movement. Then he shook his head and looked around to find them in Camille's house...in her bedroom.

She opened her eyes and smiled. "Sit down."

"Camille, this isn't necessary." But she had walked into the bathroom and opened the cabinet. He watched her rummage through the contents.

"Like I said," she began as she gathered first aid supplies in her arms and came back through the bathroom door. "This is my dream, and I want to take care of my knight. Now sit."

Fighting back a grin, he obeyed, and then steeled himself for her touch. Camille dropped the bandages and ointment on the bed beside him before returning to the bathroom for a small plastic tub of water and a washcloth.

"This is going to hurt," she warned him a minute later. She bit her lip as she took a gentle swipe at a deep laceration across his left biceps. When he flinched, she pulled back, a look of worry and sorrow in her dark eyes.

"I'm sorry," she murmured.

Ian shook his head. "It's okay, honey. I'm a big boy. I can take a little pain."

The ministrations continued, her gentle, hesitant touch soothing something deep inside him. Ian closed his eyes as the tension within began to uncoil stroke by stroke.

The scent of vanilla and some spice filled his nostrils with each breath he took. Her warmth reached out to him, stirring the hunger deep within. The erotic montage that had invaded his mind the first time they met replayed through his thoughts.

His breath quickened at the vision of her smooth, ivory skin. He could feel the silk of her skin...the soft coolness of her long hair caressing his bare chest. But it wasn't real. It was only an illusion. One he longed to make a reality.

"You know what I am," he said. It seemed the time had come for some information exchange between them. Anything to keep his thoughts from straying to the images of their naked bodies entwined. "You know a lot about the Sentinels."

"Yes," she allowed. "The spirits speak to me about many things. I think they like the way I listen."

"How do you mean?"

She shrugged. "Without judging them. Most of them were good people, but not all. Many were quite wicked from time to time. Of course, the truly evil ones aren't allowed to reach me."

He smiled at her gentle expression. "And you, Camille...were you ever wicked?"

She glanced up at him, her eyes haunted. "Not willingly, no. I'm not perfect, but I've always tried to be kind. It doesn't always help, though, when all is said and done. Bad things still happen to people even if they try to do the right thing."

He wondered at the pain lurking in her eyes, longed to soothe away the worry and nightmares that dogged her every step. Without thinking, Ian cupped her cheek with his hand.

"Who hurt you, honey? What bastard put that shadow in your beautiful eyes?"

She smiled softly. "You are such a unique man, Ian Spain. So unlike what I expected of an ancient warrior."

"Do I really look that old?"

"No, you look about thirty-five. But, you are a Sentinel?"

"Yes, though not one of the ancients. I grew up right here in Savannah. I never knew about my ancestry until one night when another Sentinel saved my life."

"The night you were shot?"

"Yes." She knelt on the floor at his feet, her body positioned between his thighs. So close...so many erotic positions he could picture in his mind. Ian cleared his throat. "I was undercover, working to bring down one of the many crack houses in that particular neighborhood. My cover got blown and the next thing I knew, I had a hole in my side the size of a small canyon. A Sentinel came to me. He told me of my heritage, my powers, told me I was meant for better things than a nightly bottle of scotch and living with criminals for weeks on end.

"He explained my true purpose, my worth in the grand scheme of things. And then he set about to heal my battered body. The soul healing took a bit longer."

She looked away from him and continued to clean the wound. Something cool poured over his biceps. He hissed in pain when it settled in the cut, fizzing and burning the torn flesh.

"What the hell is that?"

Camille laughed. "Peroxide, we can't have you getting an infection, even in my dream."

She dried the surrounding skin and applied several butterfly bandages over the cut. He watched her hands during the process. They were a study in graceful, fluid motion. He grimaced when she carefully pulled together the torn edges the dragon's claw had ripped.

"There," Camille announced. "That's the worst of it I think. Let's get this vest off so I can see what else the dragon did."

"I'm sure he looks worse."

She smiled. "I hope so."

Several minutes passed in silence except for the ticking of the bedside clock and the whoosh of cool air through the vent in the floor. Her touch became firmer, bolder with the cleansing of each nick and gouge. He watched as the water in the tub turned dark with his blood.

"You know what my problem is?" Camille sat back on her heels and packed away her first-aid supplies.

He raised a brow. "I didn't think you'd admit to having one."

"My problem is that I've always played it safe. The one time I ventured into the unknown, I was badly used, so I let that convince me life's dangers are best left for other people to live. Now here I am...embroiled in a dream with the sexiest man I've ever met, and I still do absolutely nothing about it. I still play it safe even when there are absolutely no consequences to fear."

She looked up at him then, her dark eyes shining with possibilities. His conscience demanded he tell her the truth, tell her of his gift and the fact that this encounter was more real than she thought. But curiosity overrode all moral objections. He longed to see her just once with her guard down.

She moved toward him, rising on her knees between his legs. Her hands teased his thighs with soft, hesitant caresses. Her touch sent blood rushing right to his groin.

"I want to do something about it, Ian."

Tell her.

"Camille, I told you about the Sentinel..." She leaned forward and pressed her lips to his chest, a scant inch from the healing wound of his first encounter with her demon.

"Camille..."

She trailed kisses up his throat and Ian clenched his hands at his sides to keep from grabbing her and ripping her clothes off.

"Please...honey, you've got to listen."

She shook her head, hair whispered across his jaw as she nuzzled the sensitive skin beneath his chin.

"I don't want to talk," she murmured. Her warm breath on his neck sent an electric jolt down his spine. His body shuddered in response.

"He was a dream-walker, Camille. Do you..." Another kiss, a flick of her tongue and he almost groaned out loud. "Do you understand? Honey...please listen to me, I'm a man, not stone..." Though he was getting harder by the second.

Then to his relief, she stopped. Her body held so still for a moment that he thought she'd stopped breathing. Then Camille pulled away, her large dark eyes filled with confusion and wariness.

Damn. He was afraid of that.

"You're...you're a dream-walker, too. Aren't you?"

Ian nodded.

"That's why you're here...to vanquish my dream demon, not to protect me."

"I'm here to do both. But the demon is my main purpose."

Her gaze wandered about the room. "This isn't just a dream? It's all real, somehow?"

"Yes, in a way."

A soft exclamation of panic escaped her. She scrambled to her feet and backed as far away as the perimeter of the room allowed.

"I just made a total ass of myself?" She stared at him in horror, arms tight about her middle. "In my own dream?"

"No, honey, it's not like that." He started to rise, to explain. "But I couldn't let—"

The room wavered like a mirage beneath the desert sun. Ian fell back against the mattress. The dream image went from soft waver to full Tilt-A-Whirl. Then with a violent jerk, he felt his essence fly through time and space. His soul met body with jolting speed and the bed bounced, its frame shrieking in protest.

He gasped in alarm, heart thudding wildly at the ride just taken. But he didn't have time to recover before the bedroom door flew open and slammed into the adjoining wall.

That'll leave a mark.

Camille stared at him, chest heaving, eyes flashing fire. She just might leave a mark of her own if that seriously pissed look was any clue to her temper.

"Camille..."

She strode to the bed, leapt upon it and straddled him, cold hands pulling at his shirt. But before he could make sense of her actions, he felt the fabric rip apart. Camille stared down at him. Emotions washed over her pretty face. He held his breath and waited. In any other circumstance, with any other woman, this position would lead somewhere very satisfying. But not with her. Camille was special. Different. And madder than hell.

"The beast marked you. It was all real. Why didn't you tell me?"

Her hands clenched on his belly and he knew she was fighting the urge to hit him. The look of hurt in those dark eyes almost made him beg her for one good punch—just one to absolve him of some of the crushing guilt. Instead, she jumped off him and ran back out of the room, her short nightshirt swishing about every round curve in the most provocative way. The slam of a door down the hall shook the house like an earthquake.

"Good job, asshole," he muttered out loud, one arm over his forehead. Pain began to throb behind his eyes. At least the post-dream headache might override the now uncomfortable ache in his crotch.

Then again, maybe not.

Chapter Thirteen

He stumbled along the shadows of the town square, his side aching. The Sentinel had been faster than he realized...stronger. Compared to him, Ian Spain was still little more than a child playing with his powers, yet the bastard had managed to wound him. The loss of blood made him weak with pain and hunger. Although he had fed only days ago, he would have to feed again. It was the only way he would heal properly.

"This death be on your head, Sentinel," he muttered as he slunk across grass, the smells of the city strong in his nostrils.

It was easy to find victims but harder to get one alone. In his current condition, he couldn't handle more than one human at a time. He needed to find an isolated spot—one that would yield a decent meal while allowing him some solitude. He sank down on a bench and closed his eyes. First, he had to rest.

It's that stupid girl's fault! he thought as he clenched his fists and hissed anew at the pain knifing through his chest. He'd make the Sentinel suffer for his insolence. If he had his way, the girl would watch him die in slow, agonizing detail. That would be sweet revenge indeed.

"Are you all right, Mister?"

He drew in a ragged breath at the smooth feminine voice to his left. A smile curled his lips but he kept his head lowered.

"I'm hurt," he murmured, letting some of the agony leak into his tone. "Can you help me?"

Silence. Then he heard the girl shift from one foot to another. He cursed to himself. This one was skittish, wary. He'd have to play it carefully.

"Never mind," he amended and let a cough roll from deep within his chest. "I just need to rest."

He tried to rise and yelled out in surprise as the pain bent him in two. Arms wrapped around his middle, he fell back onto the cold bench. He needed this girl—needed her blood, but he would never be able to chase her down if she chose to flee. He had to draw on her sympathy. If she thought him helpless....

"What happened to you?" She took a cautious step closer and his pulse quickened.

He shook his head. "Somebody...didn't like the way I looked. Story of my life."

"Maybe I should call the cops." She didn't sound as if the idea appealed much.

"No, they'll just hassle me," he said. "All I need is some whiskey and a good night's sleep."

A soft sigh and the girl moved to him, reaching out with compassion that overrode reason. "How about I get you to the street and into a cab? Do you have somewhere to go?"

He nodded, groaning aloud as he let her drag him to his feet. She was small, young. She couldn't be more than eighteen. The knowledge made his heart pump faster.

So careful, but not careful enough.

"Thank you," he muttered, his mouth watering at the scent of her skin.

"No prob—" Then she looked up into his eyes and froze, mouth gaping.

"Yes, it is...for you."

§

"I don't want a bodyguard, Sam." Camille paced across the plush gunmetal blue carpet.

"I told you before, no bodyguard, no contract."

She spun around to face the red-haired woman sitting quietly at the massive oak desk. It was the only piece of furniture that didn't seem to fit in with the modern office or the woman who occupied it.

"That's blackmail," Camille snapped, unable to hold back her temper. "I can't live like this with him..." she waved a hand in the air, frantically searching for the right words, "...hovering in the shadows and breathing down my neck. He's not necessary. The only thing that could possibly help me is a good dream dictionary or a fifth of scotch at bedtime."

Samantha's green eyes narrowed. "Are you drinking heavily?"

"No," Camille assured, then let herself fall into the overstuffed chair her agent had offered when she first stormed into the office. "I'm not drinking anything but a glass of wine once in a while. I'm not using. I'm not sleeping. About the only thing I *am* doing is eating and writing—that is until Mr. Tall Dark and Brooding entered the picture." She studiously ignored her friend's slow grin.

"He hovers day and night. The whole essence of the house has shifted. Even the spirits are quiet. It's as if he scares the hell out of them, too."

"Ian scares you?" Sam leaned forward a bit, a frown creasing her smooth brow. "I'll admit he can be intimidating, but—"

"No, not me," Camille interjected. "But I think he scares Ophelia. Oh, she tried her usual come-and-get-me-big-boy crap, but he didn't even bat an eye. She seems to disgust him more than anything." She didn't admit it out loud, but for that alone she felt more than a small amount of gratitude and grudging respect. "Lia doesn't trust him. She's been on pins and needles since he showed up, acting like a real bitch. But what really worries me is that he scares the dead. The *dead*."

She waited for her meaning to sink in, but Samantha seemed particularly dense on the subject. "The voices are silent when he's around," Camille continued. "My guide is silent when Ian's near. It's as if he doesn't want to tread on the big bad bodyguard's toes."

"You need Ian, that's the bottom line," Samantha interrupted. "And if he scares the hell out of a few spirits, then he just might send this demon back to where he was spawned."

Having her tormentor named in such a blatant, matter-of-fact way made her heart race. Panic sent her directly into self-defense mode. She sat up straight and slid to the edge of the chair.

"I want the man gone and I want him to leave now. I can't live like this indefinitely."

"No," Samantha rose, hands planted firmly on either side of the ornate desk. "He stays and you let him help you or I swear I'll cancel your contract in a heartbeat."

Camille's throat tightened as her body shook with a sickening combination of fear and anger. "I thought we were friends."

"We are, but friends don't watch each other put themselves in danger without stepping in. Believe me, Cami, if there were another way—"

Camille was through listening. She turned and she headed for the door. Hand on the brass knob, she hesitated and looked back over her shoulder.

"I know what he is," she said quietly. "I don't know how you know a Sentinel, Samantha, but I'm having simple nightmares. I don't need a bodyguard with special abilities. I can handle this myself."

"Cami, I can't tell you everything but I will tell you his help is vital."

Camille's mouth twisted into a grim smile. "The dead have no secrets from me, unlike my friends. They hear and see a lot more than anyone realizes."

Sam studied her face for a moment. "Give him a chance. I'd trust him with my own life."

"It doesn't seem as if I have much of a choice now, does it?" She watched her friend's expression as she considered calling her bluff. "I could take you to court if you try and cancel our contract."

"Yes, and you have that right, but I'm not going to sit here and mind my own business until you wind up dead."

A chill passed over Camille's skin. Samantha believed everything Ian had tried to tell her. Camille couldn't refuse to face the facts any longer—her worst fears were being realized. If she didn't cooperate, Samantha would cut ties with her, and after last night, she had to admit the thing haunting her dreams held more substance than she'd like to think. But could it really be a demon? Did such things exist? Sure, she believed in the self-doubt demon, so it only stood to reason there were other monsters prowling the earth. Her stomach knotted at the thought.

The nightmare had been incredibly real, terrifying and sensual. But it had been so vivid it felt like a memory instead of a vague collection of disjointed images as most dreams were. The touch of Ian's hand...the heat of his lips pressed to her skin...she could still feel it. As crazy as the whole idea seemed, it was no less bizarre than her ability to talk with the spirits of the dead.

"Fine, have it your way," she conceded at last. "He stays. But this isn't over—not by a long shot."

"That's precisely what worries me the most."

Camille slammed the door behind her, but the acoustically designed hallway muffled what otherwise might have been a satisfying crash. *Failure, again... Damnit to hell!* She was so sick of screwing up, of losing the fight.

She trudged to the elevator and stabbed the down button. If Ian were bent on making her life difficult and humiliating her, then maybe she could give it back to him in spades. While the very idea of disobeying the man made her uneasy, it was all she could come up with at the moment. Camille had never been much of a rebel. Her teenage years were spent trying to be invisible, trying to pretend her parents weren't the reprobates others whispered about. She fought to shake their stigma by blending into the woodwork. It hadn't been a very successful plan, even then.

But Ian...he was more than she could handle. His presence sent her libido into hyper-drive while the moments of compassion and vulnerability he tried to hide tugged at something deeper and more dangerous in the long run. She found the man spoke to her own heart. As if on cue, the elevator opened and he stepped out. It was a wonder his towering frame fit into the small rectangular chamber.

"What are you doing?" he demanded, his face dark as a thundercloud as he took a step to tower over her. Camille was not in the mood for intimidation.

"I came to get Sam to call off my guard dog," she snapped. "Why the hell are you following me?'"

"After everything's that happened, I think that should be obvious."

She moved to walk past him but his hand shot out, grasping her by the arm in a vise-like grip. "Get your hand off me," she growled.

"From now on, baby, you don't go anywhere or do anything without my say so, understand?"

Her brows shot to her hairline. "Baby? Where the hell do you get off calling me that? I am nobody's baby."

"Then quit acting like a child, Camille. You're too much of a woman for the role to suit you anyhow. Leave the pouting to Ophelia—she's had more practice."

The comment almost made her want to smile...and that ticked her off even more.

"Let's get one thing straight, *Mr. Sentinel*, I am fully aware of what you are, but you are not needed. What I need is peace, quiet and a nice long nap, not some freak of nature trespassing in my nightmares."

His eyes narrowed. "I've been hired to keep you safe and that's a job I take very seriously. So get used to it, honey. I'm your shadow, remember?"

How could she ever forget? God, he made her angry. He'd stolen into her dreams, snuck past her unconscious defenses and let her make a royal fool of herself. Her cheeks burned with the memory and she looked away, trying to free her arm as she stepped toward the waiting elevator.

"I don't need your kind of help."

He loosened his grip but didn't release his hold. She led him inside. "I'm exactly what you need, like it or not."

"You lied to me." She punched the button and the doors slid shut, the car suspended for a breath while she stared at their distorted images in the polished steel doors.

"I never lied," he murmured, his voice suddenly quiet and gentle. The contrast made her train of thought slip a little.

"Let's call it a sin of omission, then." She spun around, arching a brow at him and silently daring him to talk his way out of it.

Ian frowned. "All right, let's say I did omit a few things. They weren't things you needed to know at first."

"Excuse me?" Her voice cracked. "I didn't *need* to know that you could enter my dreams? Manipulate them and me? I didn't *need* to know that this...this monster could be real? That what I do in these dreams is real? Like hell."

"Calm down."

"How am I supposed to do that?" Tears threatened just below the surface. But she refused to let them fall. *Hold on to the anger...don't cry.*

"Everything was fine until I came back here. I need to leave. I need to get out of Savannah and forget all about this dragon."

He stepped closer until she found herself pressed between

him and the elevator wall. "It won't leave you alone, Camille. Not until it gets what it wants. It found you here, but it can and will follow you. You can't hide from the devil. I've been trying to tell you that from the beginning."

The soft, rumbling timbre of his voice sent a shiver down her spine. She closed her eyes and took a deep breath. The scent of his skin invaded her senses with the aroma of leather and spice and just a touch of soap. Heat radiated from him and she felt her body sway. She looked at him just as he pressed the stop button on the gleaming metal panel. His gaze captured hers and suddenly she was drowning in the dark night sky.

"You need more in your life than imaginary lovers and adoring fan mail."

"How do you know what I need?"

"I've been in your dreams." He cupped her cheek, his palm warm and rough against her skin. "I think you've somehow been in mine. I've felt the passion you hide and run from. You need someone to watch over you. You need someone to take care of you."

She swallowed. "I don't want anyone in my life."

"Are you sure about that?" He gently traced her lips with the pad of his thumb. "I almost made love to you the other night. I've never crossed that line with a charge but you...you make me want to forget the rules. You make me *want*."

"Don't..." she pleaded even though she melted into his touch. Her body ached for his. Some primal part of her—some uninhibited part wanted him to take her now, in the elevator where anyone could discover them. She didn't care. All she could think of was the feel of his hands on her skin...the taste of his kiss.

As if he read her thoughts, he leaned down and pressed his lips to her forehead. Her eyes closed. Every nerve in her body jumped in response to his caress. The space around them shrunk to unbearable proportions. Her breathing increased measure by measure until she was sure she'd be gasping for air if he didn't move.

Ian drew back and peered down at her. "I would rather die than hurt you...you know that don't you?"

"Yes." His gaze held her spellbound. Nothing could break her free. "I know."

He slowly bent toward her, allowing her time to back away,

giving her one last chance to avoid the unavoidable. The kiss. The one they had both contemplated from the moment they met; the one without restraint that must inevitably lead to those erotic images thrust upon her at their first meeting.

His lips brushed hers with such gentleness that it took her by surprise. It was a simple touch, the endearing sweetness wrapped around it reached deep into her heart. Camille fisted his cotton shirt and drew him closer. Hunger clawed at her belly, sending waves of heat lower and lower until she ached for him with feral, urgent need.

He braced both hands against the elevator wall on each side of her head. His heat reached out to envelop her. It radiated around her, pulling her closer, drawing her to him. Here was warmth...sensation. The closeness of another human being—of this man who attracted her on so many levels. She'd lied before. He did scare her. The way he made her feel frightened her even more than the demon who haunted her dreams.

Ian groaned deep in his throat. The sound vibrated in her mouth as his tongue dueled with hers. His arms wrapped around her and he lifted her off the floor. His lips moved from hers, teasing the skin at her throat...nipping at the curve of her neck, the upper swell of her breasts exposed by her plain cotton shirt. She let her head fall backwards, encouraging his sensuous exploration. Her heart thundered in her chest. Wave after wave of sensation built to an ever-heightening crescendo. His hand moved beneath the hem of her skirt, seeking her flesh beneath the fabric.

She caught sight of their entwined image—distorted and misshapen on the reflective metal surface above. It was like being doused with ice water. Passion morphed to panic and Camille let go of Ian's shirt, twisting away from his touch while an embarrassed heat replaced the lovely feral warmth.

"Stop...Ian. Stop."

He lifted his head, eyes clouded, lips still parted as they had been against her skin. Camille looked away and swallowed. He let her body slowly slide down his until her feet were back on the floor. But she held on since her knees had the consistency of warm jelly.

"We can't...we can't do this."

"Why not?"

When she didn't reply right away, he lifted her chin. But she kept her gaze pinned to his chest. If she looked into those eyes again she wouldn't have enough strength to stop this craziness.

"We barely know each other." It sounded lame even in her own ears. "And you said yourself that you can't...that you aren't supposed to—"

He placed a silencing finger to her lips.

"You're right." Ian drew in a deep breath and let it out in a rush. "I'm sorry."

"I... It's not your fault."

"Maybe, maybe not. Either way I know better. I can't seem to help myself when I'm with you."

Camille couldn't hold back a smile. "I'm flattered."

"Don't be." He took a step back and hit the ground floor button on the elevator panel. The car jerked and shimmied before it renewed its downward trek. "My lack of self-control could get us both killed."

He frowned at the doors with such ferocity she briefly wondered if they'd melt. Sure, she'd been mad at him before, but the attraction that blazed between them wasn't a one-sided deal. Her stomach twisted with guilt. He shouldn't blame himself for the small indiscretion. It didn't seem fair. The car came to a bouncing stop and the doors swished open.

"Ian—"

"Save it." He stepped out in front of her, scouring the area with another hostile glare before allowing her to step into the hall. Anything dangerous likely curled up and died on the spot thanks to the look on his handsome face. The man was way past intimidating—he had crossed over to lethal.

"Clear, come on. I'll drive you home."

"Would you wait a minute?"

He grabbed her arm and hustled her down the hall, out the door and into the busy pedestrian traffic. The vibrant July sun seared her eyes as the heat hit her full in the face like a sledgehammer. She stumbled a bit, squinting against the glare. Ian led her to his Jag parked on the street a few spaces from the front door.

Camille took a moment to study his sharp profile while he unlocked the passenger door. He clenched his jaw with such force that she winced thinking of the headache he'd likely have in the morning. She placed her free hand on his arm and he turned. A glimpse of self-loathing he quickly hid behind his shades made her ache inside.

"We both wanted that kiss," she said. "I don't think you should take all the blame here—there's something going on...something I can't really explain. But it's...it's been there from the beginning." She swallowed. "It's been there since the first day you walked in my door."

He gazed down at her and Camille felt a sudden rush of relief, knowing she finally admitted her feelings out loud.

"Did you—" He stuttered to a halt, then sighed. "Did you somehow put those images in my mind?"

She frowned at him. "What images?" Something in his look registered. "Do you mean...?" Camille glanced at his hand on her wrist, her cheeks warming. "Did you have the same vision? Us...together like...like..."

"Lovers."

She looked up to find him watching her over the top of his sunglasses. The glimmer in his eyes sent another wave of fire up her neck until her face glowed hot like a Roman candle.

"No, I didn't. I don't know how."

"But you had them, too?"

"Yes, at least I think they were the same." She closed her eyes for a second and sighed. "We were in bed together...but I didn't see much, um, detail."

"I did. You have a small pink mole on your inner thigh, left leg."

"You have a tattoo on your right hip—a Celtic cross."

They stood there, staring into one another's eyes as traffic rolled by. Camille couldn't make herself look away. Where had the visions come from? Were they as real as they had felt?

"You kissed me there," he added softly, heightening the blush in her cheeks.

"I don't understand." She swallowed and licked her dry lips. "If neither of us can project images or see the future, where did they come from? Could someone be manipulating us?"

Ian shrugged. "Another mystery to solve. But first we find your demon before he finds you."

"I have a feeling he already has. I didn't have these

nightmares until I came back." She glanced around them at the busy street and the people leading their normal, if somewhat mundane lives. What she wouldn't give for one ordinary, dull day. "He found me—but I don't know what he wants other than to drive me slowly insane."

He took her gently by the shoulders and pulled her into his arms. Camille stiffened for a moment before allowing herself to accept his comfort.

"I'm here to keep him from hurting you," he said. "But you have to trust me."

She tilted her head back to look at him. "I have trust issues."

That brought a small smile to his lips...such warm, sexy lips. Camille shook the thought away.

"I noticed," he replied, then pressed a kiss to her forehead. "Seems we both have issues. We'll work on it together."

She breathed deeply, savoring the scent and warmth of him. "Okay, I'll try harder."

He raised a brow and waited.

"Promise," she vowed with a smile. After a moment, he seemed to accept her word and stepped back to let her slide into the Jag.

§

"She had a Sentinel before." Ian waited for Sam's reply, knowing Camille was just two doors away and might overhear the phone call. It couldn't be helped. He needed answers and he needed them now.

Samantha's silence spoke volumes.

"Yes," she finally affirmed. "Did she remember him?"

"No, but the demon did."

"We were afraid of that," she murmured.

"Of what?"

Sam sighed. "Josiah Kane was one of the ancients, a councilor."

"He was sent here to protect her?"

It was unusual for the ancients of their race to take any real part in the protection of fledglings. Because of their status and vulnerability, they normally stayed out of harm's way and spent their time guiding and training others to do the dirty work. If this man had taken an active role in Camille's safety, it could only mean she was an extremely powerful woman *or* a direct descendant of the ancient Sentinel's clan.

"Is she his great-great-granddaughter or something?"

"I don't know," she admitted. "This was a little before my time on the council. My father might know more. All I remember is the disturbance when Josiah disappeared. They never knew what happened. He insisted on being sent to a young fledgling and vanished soon after. He sensed she was in danger."

"Sam, damnit!"

"I couldn't tell you, Ian, you know that. Believe me, I fought against the rules this time, but it's a strict code. The past is the past—don't let it affect the present."

"And maybe I could have *learned* something from the past. Maybe I wouldn't be stumbling around in the dark rehashing what you already know."

"We don't know what actually happened to Josiah. We don't know what went wrong or how the demon defeated him. Even our own forensics people couldn't piece the clues together. All they could ever be sure of was that he died in the line of duty."

"Well, I don't know how he died, but I do know this demon killed him. He's after Camille again, and he's not going to give up this time."

"How do you know for sure?" Samantha asked.

"He told me."

"Josiah?"

"No..." Ian corrected. "The demon told me about the first Sentinel. But Josiah is here...somewhere. I can feel him."

"Wait...you just said—"

"Yes, Josiah is dead, but he never left Camille. I think he's moved on to a new position as her spirit guardian. He's the one that helps her write her stories."

Sam gasped. "That isn't possible."

"Are you so sure about that?" he asked, unable to contain his temper a moment longer. "Maybe you aren't being told everything, either.'

"This is insane," she insisted. "My father would have told me."

"Would he?" Silence met his query. "This secretive *'past is past'* shit isn't working, Sam. I think you and the other councilors might want to reconsider it before someone else winds up dead."

She sighed heavily. "Someone already has, Ian. There have been two murders in Savannah in the past week."

"That's not so unusual in a city this size."

"True, except that the two women were found with their throats torn open and their bodies almost completely drained of blood. The cops are baffled."

He went still. The enormity of Sam's disclosure sent an icy chill over his skin.

"Let me guess, there was little or no blood at either crime scene."

"Exactly."

"A demon."

"I'm afraid so. He's feeding and being very careless about it. The council is concerned."

"About the innocents killed or the risk this monster is taking at being discovered?" He let the bitterness out, knowing full well he shouldn't vent his frustration on the messenger. Samantha may be a councilor, but she was the youngest and that put her very low on the totem pole.

"Both, honestly," she admitted. "None of us want more innocents to die but we don't need the police asking too many awkward questions or looking for things we don't want them to find."

"Does it matter? How could they connect the Sentinels with two random murders?"

"They probably couldn't unless the demon wants them to connect us. We're worried about his motives. You don't understand what his kind are like, Ian. You've been lucky to never come across one. They feel they should dominate the earth—they believe they are the rightful rulers and heirs. Secrecy was never part of the game plan with the renegades. The true protectors decided to mix and mingle since it seemed the easiest way to live in peace with the humans."

"Don't ask, don't tell."

"Yes, exactly. It worked for long time, but now..."

He shook his head. "Shit, Sam. If the cops somehow catch

this demon there'll be a whole other can of worms opened up. He'll either slaughter them like sheep or tell the world about us. How am I supposed to watch over Camille and keep the bastard from killing again?"

"We're sending in reinforcements."

"Now wait just a damn—"

"Not for Camille. She's still your priority, Ian. We need others in there to watch the streets and search the city block by block if necessary. If we have patrols out there's a chance they'll spot the demon before he can get close to Camille or anyone else. He'll either lay low or go after her sooner. Either way we can win this thing."

"This isn't a game, it's war."

"Tell me something I don't know," she snapped. When she spoke again, she sounded calmer. "With each victim he grows stronger. We can't let that happen. He'll be nearly invincible and I'm not sure any one of us is strong enough to fight that kind of power."

"Fine, let's say we go with this. You do realize if he lies low we have little chance at catching him, right?"

"He won't stay off the radar forever. He's fixated on Camille. I don't think he'll rest until he's had her."

"She's the main course, then." God, how he hated this. No matter which way he turned, the only option for destroying the demon involved using Camille as bait. "From what I can tell this bastard is the same one that tried to kill her ten years ago—he admitted as much in her last dream."

"You have to talk to her, Ian. It's time to explain things. She has to understand everything."

"I've explained some of it, but she's going to think I'm a raving lunatic after this."

"Not necessarily. I think she trusts you more than she has anyone in a very long time. She'll believe it coming from you."

"That's the point, Sam. How well do you think this story is going to go over when she's finally accepted me? Especially after discovering my talents. She's still wary."

"I think you underestimate the attraction," she said. "I sensed it when she stormed into my office trying to get you fired. Part of her wanted you out on your ass but the other...the other wanted you naked and chained to her bed."

Ian chuckled at the visual. Camille taking off without a word had made him madder than hell, but when he'd seen her in that elevator—eyes blazing, temper seething, he had known then and there he was in big trouble. He'd fallen in hip-deep without waders.

Hook, line and sinker.

"Ian?"

Sam's voice drew him back to the present. "I'll talk to her in the morning."

Her silence held a world of meaning.

"I know..." he said on a sigh. "I've screwed up."

"No, I wasn't thinking that. Not in the least." She hesitated. "But are you sure you know what you're getting into?"

"It's a little too late to shut that particular door," he admitted. "I couldn't leave her now if my life depended on it."

"Does it?"

This time he didn't know what to add.

"Ian, she's a great lady but..." She sighed.

"But?"

"You've been through a lot in the past six months. Maybe what you're feeling—"

"Is exactly what I don't need right now." He smiled to himself. *Shit.* He seemed to jump from one fire into another.

"I was afraid of that when you first called me," she admitted. "That's why I tried to warn you."

"Yeah, with all the subtlety of a sledge hammer," he remembered. "Don't feel bad, Sam. I think it was already too late."

"Love at first sight?" she scoffed. "I never pegged you for a romantic."

"I'm not...at least, I never thought so."

The more he thought about it, the more he wondered how much those initial visions had played a part in what he felt for Camille. A niggling thought began to burrow deep into his brain. Was it all a matter of suggestion? Did this attraction have any real substance behind it?

"What was Josiah's gift?"

"What? Oh...uh—" she stuttered, seemingly thrown off by his change in topic. "He was a seer—a prophet. His gift was strong but he was known for keeping things close to the vest."

"Why do that? Why not share his knowledge?"

"The more people know about their future, the better chance they have at screwing it up. At least that's what my father always said. Josiah was very well-respected, even revered among the Sentinels. We lost a great warrior when he died."

"He's not lost, Sam," Ian murmured. "He's only moved on." A door slammed somewhere downstairs. "I have to go. Let me know when reinforcements set out. We have plenty of room if they need a place to sleep."

Ian hung up without letting her question him further. Yes, he was sure now. Josiah still watched over Camille and his powers were intact. That in itself was comforting. Except it also meant he now knew where the erotic visions had come from. Camille's guardian had somehow projected the images into their minds, probably the same way he provided the inspiration for her novels.

But, why? Why would he interfere in such a way in death when he never would have done so in life? Why had he given them both this enticing view of what they could be to one another?

Ian clenched his jaw, the muscle ticking painfully at the pressure. He never had liked being manipulated, for whatever the reason. He wasn't about to fall in line with Josiah's scheme, even if the outcome seemed highly desirable. There had to be a better reason for him to take Camille to his bed. He would never hurt her just to scratch an itch created by an X-rated vision. She was worth so much more than that.

Chapter Fourteen

"Why was she here?"

The old woman stared at him with those dark blue eyes that once haunted his dreams. The ancient one held unimaginable power in her frail body. She'd once been considered a witch, and in another time, another place, a voodoo priestess. Some even thought her the bride of Satan himself. But he knew better. This one would never side with evil.

Once feared by many, admired by all, she had finally grown old and weak. Now was the time to take what he needed. She would be unable to defend herself, despite her power. He was finally stronger.

"What did you tell the gifted one?" he demanded.

The woman stared. "There are many gifted souls in the world, demon."

Anger pricked at his self-control, but he took a deep breath and held his temper firmly in check. He didn't have time for this.

"Don't play stupid. Don't you know who I am?" He leaned closer, drawing within an inch of her dark, round face as he let every ounce of hatred radiate from his being. "Do you not know what I can do?"

Silence met his query instead of the fear he expected. Her expression remained as placid as ever...as if she were examining a merely curious insect.

"I recognized your stench the moment you entered our city," she replied at last. "You've changed your hosts many times, but I remember your evil essence. It has not altered."

He ground his teeth together and pulled his body up to his

full height. She was so small...so insignificant in comparison. How could she act so calm? It infuriated him further.

"Am I to believe you do not fear me?"

She shrugged her thin shoulders. "I do not fear anything. It be hard to fear when a body's seen so much evil in a lifetime."

Again, he grew impatient with her manner. He would have the girl and anyone who stood in his way would be destroyed for their trouble.

"Tell me where she is or your life is over."

"So be it," she murmured. "But mark my words, demon, you will not survive the dream-walker."

He laughed, the sound echoing off the walls of her shop, shaking the glass bottles and chimes like a small earthquake. He took a calming breath and narrowed his gaze as he recalled the bit of power he had inadvertently freed with his anger.

"I've killed dozens of his kind over the centuries—many much older and more powerful than he. What makes you think this fledgling Sentinel can take me down, old woman?"

She smiled then—a slow grin that lifted her round cheeks and sparkled like shards of glass in her blue eyes. Those fathomless eyes had seen the world from near the dawn of time. It seemed almost a shame she would see no more.

"I *think* nothing. I *know* it to be." She leaned closer, her expression triumphant, defiant, even while facing her death. "I have gifts of my own, demon. I have seen you die."

$$\varsigma$$

Another peaceful dream passed without the presence of the dragon. Camille still found herself wide awake after only three hours of sleep. She stared at the shadowed ceiling, dawn hours away. Thoughts swirled through her head one after another, overlapping and merging until the chaos began to fray on her nerves.

God, I'm going insane.

The blankets weighed down her limbs. Her nightshirt rubbed the wrong way. No matter which way she turned, she couldn't find a comfortable position. A scream split the night, jolting her up out of bed and onto her feet. Her body shook, her heart raced as she listened and waited for another to follow.

Silence.

Camille swallowed and inched her way to the bedroom door. She opened it, gritting her teeth together as its squeak echoed down the narrow hall. The house remained still and for a moment she wondered if she had imagined the scream. Could it have simply been a product of her overactive imagination?

"Josiah?" she whispered then listened for her guide. Nothing. There was something wrong.

The stairs looked darker than usual, but she crept down them at any rate, certain the scream had come from below and not the same floor. The worn carpet felt rough on her bare feet, the banister cool and smooth. At the bottom, she stood in a pool of silver moonlight beckoning from the large window above the doorway.

"Is anyone here?" A chill washed over her skin through the thin nightshirt. "I won't hurt you." Camille knew the intruder had to be a spirit. She'd had similar experiences many times. "Please, tell me what you want."

The clock ticked above the mantel, a car drove by, the sound of the engine fading as it rolled down the street and beyond. She held her breath, listening, waiting for a reply. A few minutes later, her patience wore thin and she sighed. *It must have been a dream after all.*

"Great, now I'm imagining ghosts when there are none. How crazy is that?"

She turned to go back to her room and walked right through a woman on the bottom step. A scream caught in Camille's throat as she jumped back, hand to her neck, and stared at the apparition. The young woman stared back.

"Who...who are you?" she asked once she had caught her breath.

The girl blinked as if she didn't understand. Camille could see there were tears in her translucent eyes.

Odd. She never realized a spirit could cry real tears.

"Tabitha." The soft, reedy voice surprised her a bit. It held a faint accent—one she couldn't place without hearing more.

"Hello, Tabitha. I'm Camille."

The ghost nodded. "Yes, I know. They sent me here to find you."

Her stomach knotted. "Who sent you?"

The girl stared, sorrow etched in every shimmering line of her features. *British,* Camille thought. The girl must have been a beauty in life, though a servant if her clothes were any indication. Her hair pulled up beneath a plain white cap, she wore a stained apron over a dark calico dress. As she stood there in her ghostly form, the poor girl lifted her hands in a gesture of defeat.

"She's dead."

Camille stepped closer. "Who's dead?"

The girl continued to stare as if she hadn't heard the question. Camille felt her control stretch thin like elastic being pulled at both ends.

"Tabitha!"

The spirit blinked again and seemed to focus back on Camille's presence.

"Who died? Please, tell me."

"The ancient one," the ghost replied, her voice cracking. "He killed her. He cut her throat from ear to ear and I couldn't do a thing."

"Tabitha, I don't know anyone called the ancient one. Why are you telling me this?" Suddenly she had another thought. "Is she the one who screamed? Is she close?"

"Nay, 'twas I who screamed when he murdered her. We're alone. Where will we go? Who shall talk to us now? I don't want to be alone." The girl sobbed and wiped at her tears with an edge of her sheer apron.

"Tabitha, you have to tell me the ancient one's name."

The girl sniffed, then her attention seemed to drift again. Camille's patience snapped. She grabbed at the specter, her hand passing straight through. It had to be the most frustrating encounter of her life.

"Virginia," the ghost said.

Camille wavered on her feet as her vision grew dim.

"Virginia? *Madame* Virginia? Is she the ancient one?"

Tabitha nodded, her face still twisted with unearthly grief and pain.

"And now we're alone...all alone. You must stop him. She said only you can stop him from killing them all."

The spirit vanished.

§

A persistent pounding roused Ian from a deep sleep. He blinked at the faint light from a nearby street lamp. It beamed through the small windows and cast silver shadows across the room, leaving most of the perimeter in darkness.

In a moment, he shoved up to his feet and staggered to the door. When he opened it, the sight of Camille in a nightshirt that reached mid-thigh, hair tousled and sexy from sleep made his pulse race. But the deep frown on her pretty face brought him to full alert.

"What's wrong?"

"I'm not sure, but I think someone died tonight."

His gaze flowed down over her full curves and he forced his mind and eyes to focus on her face. Her brow dipped sharply into a deeper frown and she clasped her hands together as if to keep from coming unraveled.

"I think you need to sit down and start from the beginning." She nodded and followed his lead as he sat at the edge of the king-size mattress.

"I woke up and couldn't get back to sleep. While I was lying there a woman screamed."

"I didn't hear it. Are you sure you didn't just dream it?"

"Yes, I'm sure. I came downstairs to investigate and walked right through a ghost. She told me the ancient one is dead. He killed her."

"Who's dead?"

"I didn't know who she was talking about but—" her eyes welled with tears and she turned her head. "—she said the woman's name was Virginia. That they sent her to tell me he had killed her. She said others are going to die if I don't stop him."

She looked back at him. "When I left the Blue Moon the other night I wound up at an occult shop on River Street. The woman there was named Madame Virginia. I think she's the one the spirit spoke of, Ian. I think someone killed her."

He closed his eyes, breathing in and out slowly to focus his thoughts. "I've heard of a Madame Virginia, she was an older sentinel. I never met her, though. Are you sure this wasn't all part of a dream?"

"Yes, I wish it were, but I'm sure. Tabitha was petrified and grieving. She knew the woman somehow."

"Tabitha is the ghost?"

"Yes."

He didn't know what to believe. Over the last seven years he had learned there were many strange and wonderful things in the world beyond his comprehension, but he had never seen or spoken to a ghost. Demons, yes. Shape-shifters, healers and other dream-walkers, of course. But never spirits such as Camille described. It seemed they both had their own thresholds of disbelief and they were being stretched the distance.

"You never mentioned seeing ghosts before."

"That's because I never have until tonight," she replied. "I speak to them, but seeing one is a whole different experience." Her hand on his wrist felt cool and firm. "Please, we have to find out. Can we go there? Now?"

"We should call someone...the police, Samantha—"

"No! We have to leave. I have to see for myself if this is true." She hesitated, her confusion and fear clearly displayed on her lovely face. "I feel like I'm losing it, Ian. I have to know if I'm going crazy or if what I saw and heard was real."

"Okay, honey, we'll go." He stood and drew her to her feet. "We'll drive over and find the shop."

Her soft smile melted a little corner of his heart.

"Thank you."

"Let me throw some clothes on first." He glanced down at her, amazed that even in such a situation he could still feel a surge of lust for her. As if she sensed the direction of his thoughts, she moved back and crossed her arms, her cheeks flushed.

"I'll meet you downstairs." She turned and all but ran out the door.

§

They first drove to the tavern and Camille attempted to guide him. Trouble was, she had been panicked that night and not watching every turn she'd made. Luckily, Ian's skills as a tracker came in handy. He retraced her movements as he had that night with precision.

When he spotted the lamppost he'd found her sitting under, he pulled the Jaguar parallel to the brick building and cut the engine. It didn't look like much from the outside—the sign dangled askew and needed some cosmetic repair. The space next to it stood empty, the windows boarded up to prevent vandals from breaking them. Someone had spray painted insulting epitaphs across the crudely hung plywood.

Ian grimaced. "This is the place, but it looks deserted."

"It did that night, too." Camille shook her head. "Virginia's here. I can feel it."

Ian frowned. "I thought you could only speak to the dead."

Camille took a deep, shuddering breath and let it out. "I can talk to them *and* sense their presence. She's among them now."

He could hear the pain in her voice and feel the sorrow rolling off her. It took every ounce of strength he possessed to keep from pulling her into his arms. Ian turned and scanned the empty street, reaching out with his own senses to get a feel for things.

Death. He had sensed it many times, even long before his indoctrination into the Sentinels. It had a distinct energy—an unmistakable odor about it that made even the strongest man weak in the knees. Along with death, he felt the presence of Camille's dragon. The demon had been here in some form or other. Ian suspected he had somehow taken out one the oldest living Sentinels of record. He had never met the woman personally, but he knew her by reputation. This demon must be one powerful bastard to have been able to kill her.

"You feel it too, don't you?" she asked quietly.

He looked at Camille to find her staring, her brow creased with a worried frown.

"I feel something," he hedged. "Let's go, but stay behind me."

He didn't want her alone on the deserted street, though he sure didn't feel good about leading her into what may well be a trap. Ian reasoned that if the demon had wanted Camille dead, he could have done the job easily months ago. He wanted something from her—something he could only obtain after stripping away her sanity. Ian guessed the beast craved Camille's power.

They climbed out of the Jag, both shutting the doors quietly as if they were afraid of disturbing the neighbors. Ian grimaced. The only neighbors they might wake up were some rather large rats he noticed scurrying toward the alley.

"I don't like this," Camille whispered. "Maybe you were right the first time. Maybe we should go back home and call the police."

"No," he said as he checked his gun and flipped off the safety. "They aren't equipped to handle demons even if they believed us to begin with. I don't want to give him a chance at changing hosts before we discover his current form. When they switch it's harder to track them—they can hide for a time."

"What good will a gun be?"

"Silver bullets," he replied with a wink.

He moved toward the front door of the shop. Later, when they were alone and safely behind blessed doors, he would answer the questions swirling through that pretty head. But now, there wasn't time for better explanations. Now they needed to find the demon or the remnants of his trail. Sometimes he could catch their scent and other times they left an electrical energy trail behind. So far he hadn't detected either near the little shop.

Keeping his gun hand low, Ian approached the glass door. The shade covered the window and displayed a closed sign. He stood to one side of the opening with Camille tucked behind him, and pushed on the handle. When it moved easily inward, Ian glanced at Camille and nodded.

In the utter stillness surrounding them, he could hear little but the beat of his own pulse and the soft rush of Camille's breath at his back. Ian closed his eyes briefly to help focus his senses, then pushed the door open a scant inch. Air heavy with jasmine and sandalwood filled his nostrils. He opened the door further and stepped inside, but an underlying scent set him back on his heels. *Blood.* It was strong...a recent kill. He could also feel an undercurrent of rage bouncing around the small room.

Steeling his nerves for the onslaught to come, Ian slipped silently up the short flight of stairs and through the front of the shop, careful not to touch any of the shelves or items lining the narrow aisle that led to the counter. Deep gray shadows were illuminated by faint light coming through the grimy front windows. He clenched his jaw and stopped for a moment, allowing his eyes to adjust as he listened intently. Gabriel, his mentor and savior, had taught him how to use all of his senses—including those most humans had long ago forgotten they possessed. But there was nothing in the little shop to sense.

Nothing living.

Something touched his shoulder and he spun around, pistol aimed straight at Camille's heart. Her eyes went wide.

"What the hell are you doing?" he snapped as he lowered the weapon. "Damnit, Camille! I could have killed you!"

"Tabitha told me there's nothing here—the killer left," she told him calmly. "She said we need to look in the back room."

He frowned at her for a minute and nodded. "Don't ever do that again, do you understand?"

"Yes."

He turned back toward the counter and made his way through the maze of displays. The shop was deserted and quiet except for the light chime of bells emanating from behind a dark purple curtain at the back of the counter. Ian followed the sound, his gut tightening with every step. He knew whatever lurked behind that rich fabric would not be pleasant, but he had no choice. He couldn't afford to miss any valuable leads because of a little squeamishness.

The heavy curtain felt slick and cold to the touch and when he lifted it aside, a cloying scent of jasmine and some other flower choked the air from his lungs. Ian pushed through the barrier and slid into a crouch, his gun arm braced. For a moment, he stopped and stared at the room, mind reeling. It was surreal and grotesque.

Bright white walls were spotted with dark crimson, some of it already a rusty brown where it had begun to dry. The stuffed chairs and love seat had been shredded and the stuffing strewn about the tiny sitting room. Tables and shelves were overturned, objects lay crumpled, shattered and broken in heaps of shimmering glass and ceramic. Ian rose to his full height and lowered his weapon as his gaze swept the room. He heard a gasp behind him and turned to find Camille had followed.

She stared at the destruction, her chest heaving as she fought to breathe in the heavily scented air. When she placed a hand over her mouth, Ian followed the line of her vision. A gnarled, dark hand protruded from behind the upended loveseat, fingers curled like talons.

He shoved his gun into his waistband and picked his way through the debris, careful not to disturb anything or tread in the pools of blood on the carpet. When he could see around the loveseat, he didn't need to search for a pulse. The woman had to be dead. Her dark blue eyes stared in glassy unconcern at the ceiling that held spatters of blood. Her body had been twisted and bent—her head tilted at a very unnatural angle. If he were to guess, Ian would say the demon had broken the old woman's neck after slitting her throat. The blood had been deliberately splattered from wall to wall after. But why? Why didn't he take her power? The powers of the Chosen were said to be transferred by blood—and judging by the amount of gore present, this demon could not have taken enough of Virginia's blood to do him any good. Had she put up a fight? Or had he simply lost control?

"Oh, God in Heaven," Camille murmured on a sob. "Why did he do this? What did she do to deserve this?"

"I don't know."

She stared at him. "That isn't good enough, Ian. Did he come after her because of me? Is this my fault?"

He wrestled with his conscience. How much did he dare tell her? Would it do more harm than good? But the look in her eyes—the stark fear and confusion, helped him make the decision he'd been leaning toward. She needed to know the truth. If she knew, she'd be in a better position to fight for her own life.

Ian glanced down at the lifeless corpse and sighed. It was time to call in some help and to train his damsel as a warrior. But first they needed to get the hell out of Dodge.

§

They waited three blocks up from the crime scene as police cruisers and an ambulance swarmed River Street and converged outside the brick building. An anonymous tip brought the cops, paramedics who wouldn't be needed, and a coroner who would. Ian watched the commotion from his rearview mirror while Camille sat silent, hands folded, in the seat next to him. She had agreed the police wouldn't believe her story and might hold them as suspects, but he could tell that leaving the old woman behind had been difficult.

"Are you okay?"

She lifted her shoulders slightly. "I guess. I was just thinking about my mother. The whole thing is just too similar."

He hadn't thought of that, but now some pieces were beginning to make sense. Camille had been stalked before. It was the same being after the same thing. Could her mother have merely gotten in the way? What of Josiah? What part had he played in that long-ago confrontation?

"How did your mother die?"

She looked at him and swallowed. "He beat the hell out of her and then slit her throat. Her blood coated the walls and the floor—everything in the kitchen."

He hated to press the point since he had already figured it out, so he let it drop.

"I'm sorry you had to see that." He said softly.

"Was it my fault?" she asked again, her eyes wide and pleading in the light of the dash.

For a moment, he wasn't sure which murder she meant, but he shook his head. It didn't matter. The demon might have Camille blame herself, but he would never allow it.

"No, and never think that. You can't stop anyone from making their own choice whether it be a demon or a man. Sometimes the good guys win, sometimes they lose."

"Virginia didn't speak to me," she told him. "I thought she might be lingering behind to tell me who did this, but she didn't say a word. I felt her presence, and then the feeling just vanished. I don't get it. When I *can* help they don't turn to me. It seems the only time the dead do speak is when I can't do a damn thing about their problems."

"I don't get it either, honey. Virginia was a strong woman. I would have bet on her winning against anything thrown at her any day."

Red and blue lights strobed off the buildings around them and a few curious citizens began to mill about the corner. The crowd seemed to grow by the second and was getting dangerously close to their position.

"We'd better get out of here before someone notices us," Ian said.

"If they haven't already," she added. "This car isn't exactly low profile."

"True." He turned the key and the engine roared to life.

Chapter Fifteen

They returned home near dawn, only to find Samantha sitting in the kitchen. Across the table from her sat an enormous man with skin the color of mocha latte, his black hair shaved close. He gazed at them through eyes so dark that they seemed to have no pupils. When they entered the room he stood, his solid frame towering above them all. He looked like a giant warrior from an old fairytale.

Ian's jaw clenched, his fingers flexing at his sides. The two men stared at each other, neither speaking. Samantha finally rose from her chair.

"Camille, this is Davu Johnson," she said. "Davu, Camille Bryant."

"Yes," the newcomer's voice was deep and lilting with a trace of accent she couldn't identify. He took a step toward her and held out an enormous hand. "I've heard much of you, Camille. I'm glad we have finally met."

She nodded slightly and shook his hand, unsure of what to say. His presence had a way of making her feel at ease and wary all at once.

"Davu is such a poetic name. I'm not sure I've ever heard it before."

"Not likely," Ian spoke up, his eyes narrow. "Mr. Johnson is one of a kind."

She wondered at his churlish attitude. The two men continued to stare each other down.

"You heard about Virginia already?" Ian asked Samantha.

"Yes, we were on our way here when I got the call. The Sentinels have a few friends at the police department." Sam's gaze faltered. "She was a good woman. We don't mean to barge in, Ian, but the council feels the situation is out of control. This creature must be stopped before more good people are killed."

"Do you know who he is?" Camille asked.

"Not yet," Davu replied. "But we know who he was."

"Amazing," Ian murmured. "I always thought you were perfect."

Sam sighed and moved around the table. "Don't start this now, gentlemen. We have enough trouble brewing without you two staging a pissing contest."

Davu flinched at the comment while Ian lowered his head to hide a grin. Camille wondered at the tension between them. It wasn't hatred, exactly, but she could tell they had some sort of history. She'd have to question Samantha about it later.

"You're right, Sam." Ian held out a hand to the dark man. "Truce?"

Davu narrowed his gaze and Camille held her breath as she waited for his response. He stood at least four inches taller than Ian and looked much stronger. How would a physical confrontation between the two end? Her stomach clenched at the thought of her hero being beaten to a pulp or worse. Then they were shaking hands, as both eyed each other with a small amount of distrust.

"What's the plan?" Ian asked.

"We need to lure him out of hiding and trap him before he switches hosts."

"Wait," Camille interjected. "Ian mentioned that before. What does it mean?"

"A demon is either created as such from the beginning or becomes so," Samantha told her. "Humans without our unique ancestry are preyed upon and killed by demons—in the old days, some of the rebels among the Chosen joined the hunt.

"However, when a Chosen One or a Sentinel is injured and dying, a demon-born will sometimes offer them eternal life for their continued servitude. Some find it irresistible and they become a new-found demon. There are two catches, if you will. First, if the new-foundling's body is beyond repair, they must find and possess a host. Most often it is someone highly suggestible and mentally weak."

Camille frowned. "Do you mean mentally impaired?"

"No, more along the lines of someone who has severe,

uncontrolled mental illness or someone high on alcohol or narcotics," Samantha explained. "Habitual users are more prone to prolonged hostile possessions in which their own spirit dies. At the point of intoxication, for example, their minds and souls are vulnerable to attack."

"If the new-found demon doesn't find a host?"

"Their spirit moves on to the next life as it was meant to do."

"Okay, but if you kill the host, does that kill the demon?"

"Normally, unless it's able to find a new host before the demon's essence weakens and dies."

"How do you keep that from happening?"

"We have to keep the demon as isolated as possible while we attack, then salt and burn the physical remains immediately after the death of the host body...unless, of course, the demon's spirit can be killed in the dream realm."

Camille cringed. "Sounds nasty."

"It is," Sam agreed. "But it's necessary."

"So you can't just rush in and shoot the host because the demon could escape."

"Exactly, and then you have to uncover his or her new identity which often takes time, especially after an initial transfer."

"Why?"

Ian cleared his throat. "The demon is weak at that point and it's almost impossible to detect his unique scent or energy."

She gazed at him, knowing without a doubt that at some point in his career Ian had lost a demon's trail. Then she looked back at Samantha.

"You said there were two rules," Camille asked her. "What's the other?"

"To continue the life cycle, they have to periodically change hosts—some think because the human body wears out easily, others think it's to hide their identity from Sentinels." Samantha glanced in Ian's direction. "To continue the cycle and add new strength to their powers, they have to have blood to survive and allow their powers to flourish. They don't have to feed very often, but some of them seem to enjoy the process a great deal."

"We will kill him before it comes to that," Ian spoke up, his glare daring the others to refute him. "We won't let this bastard hurt you or anyone else, I promise."

She fought the urge to run into his arms and walked to the sink instead, where she filled a glass with cold water. Her hand shook as she gulped it down. Then she turned to the others, shoulders squared. It was time she stopped running from who she was. It was time she learned the truth.

"This is my heritage." She faced Davu, somehow knowing he could answer her questions the best. "I need to know more. I want to know everything you can tell me about the Chosen, the Sentinels and demons. Everything. I need to be familiar with all aspects of what's going on here."

Davu looked at her for a moment, or rather through her as he seemed to be focused on some far-reaching vision. Everyone watched the man, waiting. Camille's body filled with restless tension and she had to make herself take slow breaths as the anticipation rose.

"Very well..." he motioned to a chair. "...sit and we will talk."

"Everything...from the beginning," she repeated.

He closed his eyes for a moment and sighed. When he opened them she could have sworn there was a depth there that she hadn't seen before—colors and lights that seemed to swirl in his black irises. It was as if the ends of eternity were suddenly laid open and bare for her to view. Camille shivered as he took her hands in his. Then he began his story of the sons of God and daughters of men...their love...their children and the unique gifts with which they were born.

"When the Chosen separated themselves from humans, they formed their own society high in the mountains of Asia. There they found peace for a time."

"How long did it last?"

He shrugged impatiently. "I'm not sure the exact length of time. Others can fill in the small details."

"Fair enough."

"A part of them—those with great strength, size and cunning, for example—were selected as warriors. They were set apart to protect both humans and the Chosen from the demons."

"These warriors are the Sentinels?"

"Yes. Only there were a few among them who felt they

shouldn't have to hide or serve humans. They felt it was their birthright to rule the earth because they were gifted, they were stronger. That's when a civil war began among the Chosen.

"It may have ended quickly, but for one of the rebels, a very old Sentinel. Legend says a demon visited him in his sleep and whispered the great evil into his mind. He learned how one may drain the power of another and take it as their own by drinking the blood of the gifted one."

She fisted her hands and fought back a wave of nausea. "Go on."

"They must first weaken the subject," Davu continued. "They kill them quickly, usually by slitting the throat. Afterward they drain as much blood as they can stomach."

She swallowed back the bile that rose up her esophagus. "Then they..."

"They drink."

Strong warm hands on her shoulders sent the panic away. She stood and turned into Ian's arms as she let him embrace her. It didn't matter what Davu or Samantha thought, right now she needed this. She needed this man's comfort to keep her from throwing up on the kitchen floor.

"The power is in the blood," Davu added. "It is the life force. In it are contained most of the genetic coding for a Chosen beings' powers and skills. It is likely where the *vampyr* legends originated. Some even say Vlad the Impaler himself was a Chosen One turned demon. I personally think the man was merely an insane degenerate."

"Is that why this demon wants me?" she interrupted. "For my power? My blood?"

"Yes, you're a very talented medium, Camille. This isn't the first time this demon has stalked you and it may not be the last. I will admit this one seems to have a certain affinity for you—for whatever reason."

"He killed her mother, didn't he?" Ian asked as he held her tight to his chest.

"Yes, I'm sure of it," Davu affirmed. "He sensed the power within the house but did not know which woman held the most strength. Then he battled Josiah and won, but he must have been wounded somehow. It was enough to send him back into hiding—perhaps to await another victim or a better time to return. Camille's gift is much stronger now than it was ten years ago. The power around her is quite intoxicating. I do not think she even realizes the extent of her abilities."

Camille turned her head to look at him. "Was it my fault? My mother's death? Virginia's?"

Davu shook his head. "No. The demon chose another because he had been thwarted. Your mother knew what he was. She distracted him and it made him angry."

"I don't understand."

"She fooled him into thinking it was her power. She did it to protect you and your sister, Camille. Marguerite was a good woman who made some bad choices."

"But she redeemed herself in the end."

Davu shrugged. "Yes, I think so, but few regard my opinion very highly."

Ian snorted softly and she looked up into his face, but he was staring at the dark man sitting at the table. "Don't let him fool you, honey. His opinion is held in high esteem by many."

Davu ignored the comment. "Are you willing to put an end to this?"

"How?" she asked with a frown. "He's so powerful. We don't even know who he is or how to find him."

"I believe I will know him," Davu said. "From all he's accomplished, he must be an ancient one, but I must be older. If I'm close enough, I will sense his presence. He is going to make a move soon, and when he does, I will be there. We won't have to find him because he will find us...he will find you."

"But what if he knows you're there? Won't he stay away?"

The man chuckled. "I am stronger than that, child. I can mask my presence from almost everyone."

"All right, what do I do?"

"Wait," Ian interjected. "Maybe there's another way. This just feels like an accident waiting to happen—it's too dangerous. The demon must know we're on to him by now if he's killed Virginia."

"I have to do this, Ian—for my family, myself. I can't let this thing kill others if I can stop him."

He turned a frustrated stare on Davu. "Is there any other way?"

"If he learns of my visit, he may change hosts and be lost to us for many more years," Davu said. "How many more should die by his hand? How will we know Camille will ever be safe? He's fixated on her and won't give up now when he's come so far."

Ian's jaw worked as he ran both hands through his hair and sighed. "Okay, but I'm staying close."

"Good," Davu replied. "It is just as I would have it."

"But what I don't understand is why he comes to my dreams? Why hasn't he just attacked me outright?"

"He wants to weaken you both mentally and physically," the ancient Sentinel replied. "He must be afraid of failing again."

"Ian was wounded in my dream. Does that mean I could die there? Could Ian?"

"It's possible, yes. The dream realm is unusual in the minds of the Chosen. Instead of simply being another state of consciousness, a part of our spirits, if you will, visits another plane of existence. Some say we can live out fantasies there, learn new skills, even die. Many believe if a person dies in the dream realm, their physical bodies die as well."

"But the demon can die there, too?" She looked at Ian for confirmation. "Is that why you enter my dreams and fight it? Can you kill it?"

"I should be able to," he hedged. "If nothing else, I can force him out of your dreams and keep him from driving you insane."

"But, you've killed demons before?"

"Yes."

"In dreams?"

He looked to Davu as if seeking guidance. "Yes, in dreams and otherwise."

"Couldn't we just let you kill him there? I could go to sleep and—"

"No!" Davu said. "At this stage, fighting in the dream realm is too risky for both of you, Camille. He's already weakened you beyond a safe level. It is better to draw the demon out where we can control the environment."

"You don't think I can control my dreams?"

"Few of us can," Ian interjected. "It takes years of practice. This bastard knows what frightens you. He knows how to push your panic button. Davu's right—it would be safer to fight him in reality."

"All right, I'll trust you know what you're doing." She turned to Davu then. "Before this goes on, I want to know one more thing. Who is Josiah?"

He stared at her, his black eyes unfathomable, his expression suddenly shuttered. "It is not necessary."

"Yes!" Camille interjected as she moved away from Ian and faced the ancient one. "It *is* necessary. More than that, it's vital. You know the truth and I want it. Now."

He sighed, his shoulders drooped a bit. "Josiah was an ancient Sentinel—a seer of great power..." he hesitated, "...he was also your true father."

Breath caught in her throat and for a moment, Camille felt the pain all over again. The shame of her mother's past, the gossip, whispers and laughter. The man she had thought of as her father—his violence and cruelty. *It had all been a lie?*

"The same Josiah? My spirit guide? He's my father?"

"Yes, although he hid his new position in your life, even from me."

"Why was I never told?" she asked. "Why did they let me believe that bastard Roland Dupree was my father? Or wasn't I good enough to be the daughter of a Sentinel?"

"I do not know the reasoning behind his and your mother's decision, but I do know Josiah was a good man. He held power in his hands to surpass all others. He was kind and patient, a true warrior."

"And yet he died."

"I believe he gave his life willingly so you and your sister might have a reprieve from this demon. The demon defeated your father not because he was stronger, but because they were too evenly matched. Your father chose to give up and let the evil one take his life to spare you both yours. And perhaps so he could guide you more effectively in the use and control of your gift."

"It doesn't make sense. The demon is still here. He came back to finish the job he started. What good did Josiah's sacrifice really do?"

Davu gazed at her for a moment, his head tilted to one side. "How do you know this is the same monster?"

Camille blinked. How did she know? It felt like the truth. Somehow she knew this demon tried to kill her ten years ago. This demon...

"It took Josiah and my mother," she murmured. "I...I saw it, didn't I? That's what I don't remember about that night. I was at home."

She slumped down onto the kitchen chair, her mind reeling, body numb and disconnected as little flashes of memory leeched through that dark barrier that had shielded her all these years. She saw bits and pieces like a surreal kaleidoscope. *Her mother's face... Someone screaming...the bellowing of a great beast... Running...running...she had to get away.*

"Oh, God. I remember. I wasn't with Drew." The realization hit so hard that she felt a piece of her inner core snap beneath the weight. She giggled—the sound more hysterical than humorous. "All these years I believed..."

Ian knelt down at her feet and took her hands in his, stroking her wrists with his thumbs. "Cami, are you okay?"

She looked into his eyes and felt a bit of the panic ebb. "I've never been able to remember exactly where I was the night my mother died." She closed her eyes and swallowed as a sick feeling twisted in her gut. "I woke up alone in a hotel room. I was so confused...then I went home and Lia was there with the police—lights flashing, yellow tape everywhere... For some reason I always thought Drew must have done something to me...I thought that was why I couldn't remember. He'd drugged me before and I only recalled bits and pieces of that night, too."

"It doesn't matter now, Camille," Ian interjected. "I won't let the bastard near you again, do you understand? No one is going to hurt you ever again."

"Yes, I understand." She smiled softly. "I'm all right, really. Maybe this was too much too fast but I'll be okay." She looked up at Davu. "Was Josiah Lia's father, too?"

His gaze flickered from hers and he paced to the other side of the kitchen, his back stiff. When he reached the sink, he paused and stared out the small window for a few seconds. His shoulders rose and fell as he took a deep breath, and then he shook his head.

"I'm not sure," he finally replied. "That image isn't clear."

"Speaking of Lia," Samantha interjected. "Where is she? I'm not sure how much we can tell her, but I think we need to get her somewhere safe until this is over."

Camille and Ian jerked around to face her.

"Isn't she upstairs?" Ian asked.

Samantha glanced at Davu who shook his head. Camille felt a chill slither down her spine.

"Oh, God," she whispered. "Where's my sister?"

§

Ophelia flinched away from his touch, unsure what the feelings meant, but certain it had something to do with him. All she knew was that she had to get away from this place, away from him.

"What's the matter, babe?"

She blinked against the light. Her head felt like it was stuffed with cotton. Her vision grew more and more blurry around the edges.

"I don't...feel good."

She could just make out a grin on Brent's face—a face that had been so handsome at first. Now he looked ugly and distorted. Almost evil. Was it the booze doing this to her? Something else?

"I...I need to go...." She tried to turn and move away from the wall, but her feet were mired in something thick and sticky. She looked down, squinting at the floor as it moved in and out of focus. Lifting her head took almost more strength than she seemed to have.

"I think...I'm sick."

He laughed softly. "No babe, you're just fine. Right as rain."

Why was he smiling? Couldn't he tell something was wrong?

She needed to get home. Mama would know what to do. She'd know how to make her feel better. Ophelia closed her eyes as the memory returned.

"Mama's dead." Saying it out loud always hurt, but she could usually hide it. This time she felt the tears slide down her cheeks.

"Yes, that's right," he said as he took her arm. "Mama's dead and buried—or what was left of her."

He chuckled again and she felt herself moving as if wading in a deep stream. How could he say such a thing? Didn't he understand?

"She didn't go quietly into her good night," he continued, both hands like manacles on her shoulders as he propelled her from behind.

She tried to focus on where they were going, but the lights spun dizzily around her and his words made it hard to concentrate as she stumbled along.

"But you're a good girl, aren't you Lia? You won't fight it like she did. Not this time. This time..." His breath fanned her neck. "This time you'll help me get what I want and we'll all be much happier."

Fear slithered over her and she swallowed thickly. She was going to die.

"I want...go...home."

"Sorry, babe. That isn't an option. I need you just a little while longer. If you disappear for bit, that should send your big sister right over the edge—and I'll be waiting to catch her. I've been planning this for a very long time, but I'm a patient man. And you've been such a good girl, I hate to end our party so soon. I thank you for playing right into my hands. So predictable, really. That little fainting spell the other night was a trial run for tonight's main event—I had to make sure the drug was perfect."

Her knees buckled and she heard him curse. Then she was flying through a tunnel, only no welcoming light beckoned in the distance.

"Home."

His laughter rumbled through her like a wave scattering the sand.

"Sure, you can go home." The sensation of movement abruptly stopped as he dropped her hard on her butt. Ophelia moaned at the impact. Her head lolled back since she could no longer lift it. She couldn't see...her lids were so heavy, but she didn't dare sleep. A door closed, then footsteps and another door opened. The seat beneath her dipped as he sat at her side and leaned closer. She was in a car. She had to get away—she had to warn Camille.

"No worries, Ophelia," he crooned near her ear. "Camille will find you safe and sound at the hospital. I'll be there, of course, looking upset and distraught like any good lover would. She won't suspect a thing."

"No you can't—"

"But I can," he insisted. "I've waited ten years, I won't wait any longer." She heard the engine roar to life. "When I'm done and have bled Camille dry, you can both go home to mama, if you wish. Please do give the treacherous old bitch my love."

The words swirled about her in the darkness until she couldn't hold on for another moment...then they sucked her down...down into a fitful oblivion.

So this was what it was like to die.

§

Camille paced the worn wood floor, arms folded tightly about her middle. The muscles in her neck tensed with each step and worried thought that raced through her mind. None of them had slept but a few hours as they took turns combing the city for some sign of Ophelia. She was still missing, but the police were reluctant to do anything until more time passed.

"You're going to wear a hole in the floor."

She stopped and half-turned toward Ian. "She's in trouble this time, I just know it."

"Honey, she's a big girl and you said yourself she likes to party."

"You think I'm blowing all this out of proportion?" She watched his face for clues and noted the way his jaw tightened. "You're worried."

Ian sighed. "A little, yes, but that doesn't mean something happened to Lia. I'm not empathic. I can't tell you if she's in trouble or hurt."

"Neither am I...but I do have a really bad feeling about this whole thing." She spun around and paced to the window overlooking the courtyard. The sun shone brightly in a clear blue sky, but still that dark, nagging dread wouldn't let go of her. It had been the same way the day her mother had died.

She lifted the curtain and peered outside, her thoughts willing Ophelia to suddenly appear. Hungover and bitchy would be so much better than the alternatives her morbid thoughts kept conjuring.

"Lia...where the hell are you?"

Hands closed over her shoulders and she jumped. "God, how do you keep sneaking up on me like that?" she asked with a shaky chuckle.

"All part of the training," he said as he smiled down at her. "Come on, Cami, you've got to have faith. She's fine...probably off pouting again."

"Did you call Brent?"

He looked out the window, but not before she saw the shadow flit through his dark eyes. "He still isn't answering."

Camille followed the direction of his gaze but couldn't help but focus on the reflection of his handsome face. It hovered behind her own, casting an image like two ghosts in a loving embrace. She pushed the absurd notion aside.

"Until the other night you hadn't seen him in years...are you sure you can trust him?"

He stalked back toward the sofa. "I don't know what the hell to believe anymore. Shit. I don't even trust my own damn judgment. They should have sent someone else here, Camille. I should have told them no or—"

She rushed to him and wrapped her arms around his waist, shocking him from the self-destructive tirade. With a sigh, she rested her cheek against his back. He felt warm and firm and so very right in her arms.

"You've done everything you could to protect me—to protect us," she insisted. "Don't start questioning things now, and don't blame yourself for Lia's stupidity."

His large hands closed over hers and she felt him breathe deeply. His heart thumped erratically beneath her ear.

"It is my fault. I lost my objectivity. I lost my edge." His fingers moved over hers in gentle strokes. "How am I supposed to help you if all I can think about is getting you naked?"

Heat blossomed in her cheeks. "We both played a part in that, if you'll recall. And I'm not sorry about what happened in those dreams." She swallowed. "Are you?"

He turned in her arms, a soft smile playing at his lips. It made her stomach flutter. "No, I wouldn't give up those memories for anything, despite the way I acted. Will you forgive me for being an irrational jackass?"

Camille chuckled softly. "Of course."

Ian reached out and tucked a strand of hair behind her ear. "I wouldn't give up one moment with you."

Some of the tension eased along her shoulders and she

smiled up at him. "Neither would I."

God help her, but she wanted to repeat the experience with him in the flesh this time. She longed to take it to the next level, damn the consequences. The bed upstairs seemed to beckon. The shift in mood wrapped around them, thick and consuming. If it were true that love was blind, then lust must be deaf, dumb and thoughtless, as well.

She once thought she wanted romance with candles and wine, soft words and moonlit strolls. But at that moment, staring up into his eyes with the thick heat of desire slicking over her skin, all she wanted was hot, naked, hungry sex. *With him...only him.* And she wanted it now.

"We'd better get going," he said as he took a step back. "Sam and Davu will wonder where we've disappeared to. They've taken the hospitals and shelters so we should concentrate somewhere else."

"You're right," she replied, more than a little guilty at the thoughts running through her head when Ophelia was missing. "There are a few bars she likes. I think we should go to the Blue Moon, too. She seems to have a thing for that place. Maybe someone saw her there."

"I agree," he said with a nod. Then he took her hand in his and they set out to find Ophelia.

§

"Where's my sister?" Camille asked the bartender. He frowned at her, never missing a drop as he ran the taps.

"Who's your sister?" He flung his ponytail over one shoulder and slid a draft down the bar.

"Ophelia!" she shouted over the drone of the music and chatter. "Ophelia Bryant."

Recognition dawned on his lean face and he poured a measure of whiskey over some ice. "Oh, sure...Lia. She came in late last night and left."

"Was she alone?"

He shook his head and turned as a waitress rattled off a drink order like an auctioneer.

"Shit, slow down, Dena. I've only got two hands." He glanced back at Camille who was on the verge of screaming. "I don't know," he continued. "It's been busy as hell these last two days and we're short-handed. Doesn't give me much time to notice who's bagging who."

"Is there anyone who *might* know?"

"Yeah, I think she was sitting at Jenny-Lyn's station last night." He nodded toward a tall waitress with a bright pink bob who stood flirting with a table of male customers. "She might remember more." He turned back to the waitress and cursed. "I said slow the hell down! Do I look like an octopus to you?"

Camille turned to shove her way through the crowd. Laughter rippled around the room, grating on her nerves. She reached for the smiling waitress, grabbed her by the arm and jerked her around.

"Hey," the girl protested. "Watch it, lady."

Camille bit back her irritation and forced a smile. "Sorry, but the bartender said you waited on my sister last night."

The girl shrugged. "It's been a crazy weekend. I've waited on a lot of people."

"I realize that, but this is important. She's missing. She's about five-three, black hair down to her waist? Blue eyes?"

The girl looked at her thoughtfully. "Oh, sure, I remember her. She ordered rum and coke, drank it and almost passed out. I think she was sick."

Camille's throat tightened. "Did you see her leave?"

"No, sorry, but I'm sure her date took care of her."

"Date?"

"Yeah—tall and blond, not bad looking. Didn't catch his name, but he was a great tipper."

"Okay, thanks."

Camille glanced around the club and saw Ian talking to another waitress. His brow furrowed as he listened. Then he looked at her and his mouth turned up into lopsided smile. The gesture made her pulse spike. A moment later, he weaved his way through the room to her side.

"Any luck?" she asked.

"No, the girl vaguely remembers Lia, but doesn't have a clue when she left or if she was alone."

"The waitress with pink hair served her and a tall blond man," Camille reported. "Her description was pretty vague, but it sounds like Brent...or even Drew, for that matter. The last time she saw Lia, she was looking sick."

"Maybe she was with Brent, got feeling bad and he took her to the hospital. That makes sense." His gaze moved around the room slowly, as if he were looking for something. "We need to get back to the house in case she calls or comes home. I'll call Sam on my cell when we get to the car, I can't hear a damn thing in this place."

Ian took her by the arm and threaded their way through the crowd and out the door. It occurred to her that he seemed a lot more worried than he admitted to being. *If something has happened to Ophelia...*

They had just reached the Jag when Ian's ringtone began to play. "Yes?"

She stared at him, holding her breath as she waited.

"Okay," he said as he glanced at her. "Fine...we'll be there in fifteen minutes. Okay. Thanks."

"Lia?" She reached out to him, silently pleading for good news but unable to say anything more as her throat clogged with tears.

"Davu and Sam found her at Georgia Regional," he began. Then his hands were on her shoulders and she felt as if the ground were slipping from beneath her feet. "They were searching the local hospitals one by one, asking about any Jane Does admitted. The staff said Lia either wandered in or someone took her there, they can't be sure. An orderly found her in the emergency room late last night. She's alive, but still unconscious."

"What happened?"

"I don't know, honey. She didn't have an I.D. with her and they had no idea who to contact."

"Oh, God." Tears burned her eyes, blinding her to everything. It felt as if someone had punched her in the gut with a sledgehammer. Ian pulled her into his arms, his hands moving over her back as he gently rocked her.

"They're taking care of her, honey. We'll do everything we can, I swear it. Now come on, I'll take you over there. They're waiting on us."

Camille nodded against his chest. "Okay," she said with a sniff. Then she took a deep breath and blinked back the tears as she looked up at him. "Thank you...for everything."

Chapter Sixteen

Around nine o'clock that night, the four of them entered through the old iron gate, spirits lagging. Camille hadn't wanted to leave Ophelia at the hospital, alone, surrounded by strangers. She had looked so forlorn, so pale and ill. But everyone insisted there was nothing they could do. Until the tests came back, they weren't sure what they were fighting. It could be some kind of virus or an allergic reaction, for all they knew.

She was young and relatively healthy, they told her. She would probably be fine. Camille mustn't give up hope.

Probably. It wasn't much to cling to, but it was all Camille had.

Ian had been silent for the long drive back to the house as they followed Sam's BMW. At the hospital Samantha had tried to keep a light conversation going as they waited—speculating at how it was likely just a bug and Ophelia's bad eating habits catching up with her. She felt good about the outcome, or so she'd said. But Camille couldn't help but notice the way her friend didn't quite meet her gaze when she spoke.

Camille unlocked the door and stepped inside, staring at the empty parlor as the others filed in behind her. For a moment, she was at a complete loss as to what to do next. A large void seemed to have settled in the house. Something was missing...something that she hadn't appreciated in a long time.

"I'm sorry," she murmured. "Everyone must be hungry. I can—"

"No," Sam interjected. "Don't be silly. You go get a shower and change. I can whip up some sandwiches or omelets. What would everyone prefer?"

"Omelets sound good," Ian said.

"Anything is fine with me," Davu agreed.

"Okay, I'll get to work then."

"Nothing for me," Camille said. "I'm too tired to eat."

"Nonsense," Sam exclaimed. "You have to take care of yourself, Cami. Now go get cleaned up and I'll bring up a tray. Davu, would you mind the sofa? Otherwise there's only Ophelia's room."

The dark man raised a brow. "No, the sofa will be fine, thank you."

"All right then, Ian...you know where the linens are, I presume?" Sam asked. When he nodded obediently, she continued. "Grab a set for Davu, please. I'll bunk with Camille tonight—if you don't mind?"

She smiled at her friend and shook her head. "Not at all. It's a big bed. I think we'll both fit. But you can always take Lia's room..." Her voice trailed off as the image of her sister in the stark white hospital bed filled her mind and brought a lump to her throat.

"No, I'd rather not, if it's all the same," Sam said with a smile. "I haven't had a slumber party in years. It'll be fun." She glanced at Ian with a secretive smile. "And it'll give us a chance for some girl talk."

§

"Are you up to the Literacy Council benefit tomorrow night?" Samantha asked as they both readied for bed that night. "We can always cancel. I'm sure they'll understand with Lia being sick and all."

"No, I don't think that's a good idea," Camille said. "They've planned this for six months. I'd hate for all that work and money to be for nothing. I can go, make my acceptance speech and leave early. Besides, Lia might be feeling better by then."

Sam looked away, but not before Camille saw the doubt in her green eyes.

"Let's get these sheets changed and then I'll do your hair," Samantha said, her attempts at changing the subject less than subtle.

"Oooo...can we have makeovers next?"

Sam laughed and tossed a pillow at her. "Very funny. Come on, Cami. Play nice. I grew up with five brothers—I didn't have much girl time growing up."

Camille's smile faded. "No, I don't suppose either of us did."

They stared at each other in silence, both of them lost in their own memories.

"Hey, do you have a dress to wear tomorrow?" Samantha asked suddenly. "Something special...something sexy and sleek?"

"Uh, I don't think so." Camille felt a little swell of panic in her belly. "Oh, damn. With everything else going on, I forgot all about the dress. What am I going to do?"

Samantha just laughed. "You're going to relax and leave it up to me. I have to pick my dress up tomorrow morning, I'm sure the shop will have something suitable for you to wear." She eyed Camille up and down. "Something red, I think. Yes, that would be perfect."

"Oh, no. I cannot pull off bright colors. I'm much too pale."

Sam waved a hand at her. "Don't be silly. I think it's about time we break you out of that monotone cocoon, little butterfly. Before I'm done, you won't recognize yourself and Ian won't be able to keep his eyes...or hands...off of you."

Camille turned and yanked the covers off the bed with a quick jerk. She felt her cheeks begin to burn. How had Sam known what she was feeling? Was she that obvious? When she looked up, Samantha stared at her, a brow raised in question.

"What?" Camille asked, feigning innocence even when she knew it was a lost cause.

"Do you want to talk about it?"

"About what?"

"Ian."

Camille shrugged and avoided Sam's gaze. "There's nothing to talk about. He's macho and pushy and stubborn—"

"And sexy as hell."

Camille couldn't hold back a grin. "Yeah, that too."

"You've got it bad, don't you?"

"Don't be silly." She tossed a clean sheet over the mattress. "Yes, he's attractive and virile and can be really sweet, but...." Camille sighed. "Yeah, I've got it bad."

"If it makes you feel any better, the feelings are mutual."

"I doubt it, Sam. He's not the kind of man who falls in love let alone sticks around for the long haul. Once this mess is straightened out he'll be gone, we both know that."

"I'm not so sure." Sam tugged the corner of the sheet down. "I've known him for years, Cami, and I've never seen him look at a woman the way he looks at you. I've never seen him so protective or medieval about it. You've burrowed deep under his skin. Just please be careful. I don't want either one of you hurt."

"I'm the only one in danger of that," Camille insisted.

"I wouldn't be so sure." Samantha flung the flat sheet over the bed and they both tucked the ends under. Then came the blanket and pillows. "I think he's in deep, Cami. Just take it easy on the old man, okay? He's the best dream-walker I have at the moment, and he's already been through hell and back once this year. One of his charges wouldn't listen, wouldn't follow his advice and the young man wound up dead. Ian still blames himself for that fiasco."

"Sam, I already learned my lesson, believe me. I'd probably jump off a cliff if Ian told me to." Camille eyed Samantha thoughtfully. "Is that all you're worried about? Whether or not he can work when I'm through with him?"

"That...and other things," Sam admitted. Then she sighed and dropped down on the bed, folding her legs beneath her. "I do need to tell you something. I have gifts of my own."

Camille looked at her friend and waited, her heart picking up tempo as the silence grew between them. It wasn't as if she hadn't suspected as much, but to actually have Samantha open up made things more complicated. How could she hold anything back now? Was she ready to have a friend like this? One who shared secrets and expected the same in return?

"I have dreams, too," Sam began. "Dreams that tend to come true. I'm also empathic."

"Meaning you feel what others feel?"

"Yes, so when I tell you that Ian is falling for you, it's not just glib banter. It's the truth."

"All right, I think I understand," she answered carefully. "You're warning me not to hurt him because you feel these things in him. But Sam, if you really are empathic, shouldn't you be able to tell what I feel for him, as well?"

"I should," she admitted. "But you've always been a difficult subject to read."

Camille smiled and climbed into bed, lying back against the pillow with a long sigh. "Let's just say he can eat crackers in my bed any time...large, crumbly ones."

Sam chuckled softly as she nestled between the fresh sheets. "That's good to hear. Just for the record, I think you two will make a great couple." She yawned broadly. "I'll do your hair and makeup tomorrow for sure, okay? I want it to be a night to remember."

"Okay, it's a deal."

"Good night, Cami."

"Good night."

§

Camille walked down the stairs the next evening dressed in red silk from her shoulders to her feet. The material clung in all the right places and emphasized her hourglass figure the way nothing else could. *Except, maybe, a simple bath towel,* Ian thought.

She was a vision with her dark hair piled in an elegant twist at her crown. Samantha smiled a smug little smile at the men as they took in the lovely kitten's transformation into a tiger.

Tiger, hell, she's turned out to be a vixen in disguise, Ian mused.

She would show the world something he had figured out at their first meeting—Camille Bryant was a beautiful, vibrant woman. It would be heaven and hell to have her on his arm tonight.

The hellish part started all too soon as they arrived at the banquet hall and were met by a throng of reporters and photographers. Ian thought it must be a slow news day if the sharks had nothing better to do than circle the building, looking for fresh meat.

"Are you okay?" Camille asked quietly.

Okay? Hell no he wasn't okay!

"Why do you ask?" he snarled.

"Because you're bruising my arm."

He glanced down at his fingers and immediately loosened

his grip.

"Sorry."

"It's fine...if you kiss it and make it all better later," she whispered with a playful grin. His stomach twisted. *God, if anything happened to her...*

"I'd love to," he said, following her lead. "But the reporters will have a field day if they see a man nibbling on you in public."

She lifted her head and spoke near his ear. "Then take me somewhere private when this is over. You can nibble on me there."

Ian's cock tightened and throbbed as a very vivid picture raced through his thoughts.

"Don't do that, honey."

"Do what?" she asked, her eyes sparkling even as she tried to look innocent.

"Don't give me a hard-on in front of God, the media and everybody."

Her cheeks flamed and she glanced away. Ian grinned. She was fun—sexy, flirty and with just enough innocence about her to bring out the alpha wolf in him. Damn, he was in big trouble.

Davu moved in behind them, Samantha a regal picture in copper silk on his arm. "Sam and I will scout out the building. You get Camille seated and join me once Sam is in place."

"Fine."

He forced a smile for the cameras, his eyes burning as flash after flash all but blinded him. Hopefully, the demon would make some kind of move and soon. He hated the thought of putting Camille on display like a giant piece of cheese for the mousetrap. One wrong move...one screw up and they could lose her forever.

ς

Seafood smells circled on the fringes of the room like a scented aura. While Camille found it slightly more pleasant than the hospital aroma at Georgia Regional from the night before, she couldn't wait until the night ended. Events like this could be pure torture.

She glanced around the large room. The white tablecloths

reminded her of shrouds over morgue gurneys rather than elegant coverings. Dim lighting and the bone-chilling effect of a powerful air-conditioning system added to the feel and made her shiver. What she wouldn't give for a nice, hot beach right about now.

"You okay?"

She turned her head and smiled at Samantha sitting beside her, looking elegant and relaxed.

"Fine, it's just so damn cold," Camille replied without dwelling on the morbid images of morgue slabs carousing through her head.

"Yeah, it always is at these things," Sam said with a grimace. "I think it's to keep us from getting too comfortable. Get them in, get them out—best rule of the banquet game."

Camille smiled and twirled her water glass between her icy fingers. "Don't tell me you worked in this business, too?"

Sam nodded. "Yep, did just about anything and everything to work my way through college. If you're good I'll tell you all about the meat-packing plant someday."

Camille laughed as she held up a hand. "Uh, save it for the next time I decide to try a diet, okay?"

"Diet?" The deep voice behind her made both women turn. "Now why would either of you ladies need to diet?"

The sight of Ian standing there, dark eyes glittering, made her heart jump. God, he was beautiful all in black. The collar of his dress shirt held snug by a string tie with a polished onyx near his strong throat. The suit fit him as if it had been hand-tailored to hug every broad edge and honed muscle of his body.

"Not all of us are perfectly buff," Sam replied with a smirk as she gave Camille a knowing wink. Her attention to Ian's impressive build had been noted. Her cheeks warmed in stark contrast to the chill in the air and she reached for her water glass.

"I do believe they're about ready to start," Davu announced as he appeared from somewhere in the crowd and slid into his seat at Samantha's other side.

Cami watched him with purely female appreciation. She'd never seen a man as graceful and smooth as the ancient Sentinel. Even Ian seemed almost clumsy in comparison. Almost.

Ian slipped an arm over the back of her hard metal chair as

he sank down beside her. "Are you okay?"

She nodded slightly, not daring to look him in the eye. He would see her lie for what it was and he hadn't been too keen on letting this evening play out in the first place. But they had to go through with it. They had to figure out what disguise her demon wore before he had a chance to move on and hurt someone else. If this evening gave them that opportunity, it would be worth all the risk in the end.

Her throat tightened at the memory of Virginia's body lying in a puddle of her own blood. The image of her sister, lying lifeless and pale on cool hospital sheets followed in close succession. No one had suggested Ophelia's illness had been caused by the demon, but she couldn't help but wonder about it. She also wondered what had happened to Brent—Ian still hadn't been able to reach him by phone.

"Hey," Ian's warm breath tickled her ear. "If you want to stop this, just say the word."

She looked at him then, her heart instantly doing a somersault as she forced a lopsided smile to her lips. What she really wanted was to run off with him and find some quiet, remote spot to spend the night exploring every hard inch of him. That, however, was a fantasy for another time.

"We can't let it go on," she answered softly. "We can't let him hurt anyone else."

His dark gaze searched hers as they sat close like lovers, close enough to touch. To kiss. A spark stirred low in her belly and she glanced at his mouth, only to hear him groan softly.

"Don't get my mind wandering, honey," he whispered. "I can't afford distractions. Not now."

Camille snatched her gaze from his lips and moved away a little. Part of her felt more chilled at the loss of his warmth, the other a bit smug at what he'd admitted. He really did feel something for her, and even if that something turned out to be no more than lust, she couldn't help but be satisfied by his obvious attentions. Heaven knew every woman in the room watched him and Davu with rapt interest, many sending her envious glares in return. If only it could last.

After dinner the houselights dimmed and the wave of conversation ebbed to the quiet whoosh of the cooling system and antiquated sound system. The director of the Literacy Project, whom Camille had met several times over the course of the past months, walked onto the stage to stand in the bright white spotlight. A gentle mechanical whir brought down a large projection screen at the back of the stage as polite applause faded.

"Ladies and gentlemen, tonight we honor our Woman of the Year, Ms. Camille Bryant, for her unflagging support of the Savannah Literacy Campaign." He paused to encourage another round of applause, his wide smile lost in the bright white spot. "Not only has she donated her time and resources to our cause, but she's been a shining example to the entire state of what a hometown girl can truly accomplish if she sets her mind to it."

Another spotlight spilled over her table, sending Camille's stomach into a nosedive right to her feet. With a smile plastered to her face, she rose on shaking legs as all eyes seemed to fix upon her. Fatigue and nerves were suddenly there in crippling force and she swayed a little. Then she felt Ian's hand, firm and warm on her shoulder as he stood with her.

"Go get 'em, honey," he encouraged close to her ear. "You are beautiful."

Warmth spread through her like a dam of bursting sunshine. Buoyed by his words, she managed to make her way up the steps without tripping over the voluminous folds of her red silk dress. The master of ceremonies met her halfway and shook her hands as he led her to the podium, words of encouragement pouring from his lips. She could barely hear him, however, with the blood rushing through her veins. The spotlight combined with the stage lights made her as blind as a bat as she stared out at the gray silhouettes that filled the cavernous room.

Another beam of light snapped on and poured over the screen to her left. A slide-show presentation began, showing Camille's recent outings at local shelters, schools and hospitals where she had read to children and donated books and money to her favorite charity. She blushed under the scrutiny of Savannah's biggest movers and shakers, not to mention the press at every level. Her dedication to the literacy program had nothing to do with fame—she had initially refused the award they were giving her. But even Sam had insisted it would be a great way to get publicity for her career. She had never been the best at self-promotion. What really sold Camille, however, was the chance it would give the literacy campaign to join her in the national spotlight.

After a moment of nodding and thanking everyone, the thundering applause fueled by freely flowing liquor began to fade to a drizzle and then stopped.

Camille glanced at the large screen behind her and cringed slightly at her own smiling face surrounded by fans at a book signing. Not the best photo, but if it helped promote the campaign, then she could deal. With a deep breath, she faced her audience and smiled.

"I'm not much of a public speaker, so I'll assume everyone came for the open bar."

Laughter trickled through the audience, swelling and calming like the tide. She could see a few faces more clearly now that the stage lights had been dimmed for the slides. She caught sight of Ian's lopsided smile. Her pulse immediately spiked and settled into a more comfortable beat.

She swallowed back the nerves and bore on with her prepared remarks.

"I'm honored to have been chosen as the Literacy Campaign's Woman of the Year," she continued. Flashbulbs popped, cameras whirred and the changing lights of the slide show moved around her. "But I really don't deserve such praise. The true heroes are the men and women who spend hours a day, sometimes six days a week for weeks on end helping impart the love of reading to Savannah's men, women and children. They are the ones who should be honored this evening."

The slides continued to flicker and change, casting different hues of color across the stage and in her peripheral vision as she spoke.

"I am simply grateful that these individuals allowed me to participate in their struggle. And it is truly a struggle given the cuts in funding and..." Several gasps echoed from the audience and she stumbled to a halt, her speech briefly forgotten. She glanced around but decided to go on.

"I-I am thankful for the small way—"

Something was wrong. People stared at the screen behind her, their faces filled with a mixture of shock and embarrassment. The air at the back of her neck tingled. A tremor of unrest rumbled about her, throwing her mind off-balance.

"Leave the stage," Josiah commanded.

Her feet suddenly rooted to the spot, she watched in surreal fascination as the scene around her seemed to change in excruciating slow motion.

Men jumped to their feet. Women hid their faces or turned to whisper to companions. Still more continued to gape. The expressions melted from astonished to horrified and embarrassed. She glanced at her table where Sam, Ian and Davu had gone into instant motion, the latter racing like a running back toward the rear of the room. Sam whipped out her cell phone and Ian moved toward the stage, his face a stone cold mask even as his eyes flashed with unbridled fury.

Camille's heart seemed to stop as an idea formed in her mind. She slowly turned and looked over her shoulder. The enormous image on the movie screen made her teeter backward on her three-inch heels and into the podium. She forgot to breathe. Her lungs seized in her chest as a sharp pain in her gut almost brought her to her knees.

The photo cast larger than life showed her in all her natural glory—years younger and thinner, but the identity of the girl could not be mistaken. It looked to be a pose of haphazard seduction with her dark hair splayed across stark white sheets. Her eyes were partially opened as she gazed out at the audience with a vacant stare.

Camille finally sucked in a breath of air and her stomach tightened as if someone punched her. Then the slide clicked and changed to one even more graphic and degrading than the first. Tears blurred her vision. Bile rose up her throat. She stumbled out of the spotlight and into the dark recesses backstage. Voices roared through her head from inside and out. Everything spun dizzily as she bent and threw up prime rib and cheap Champagne all over the hard floor.

The tears burst free, burning her cold cheeks while thundering footsteps drew closer. Her throat closed up until she almost couldn't breathe with the acrid taste of vomit in her mouth.

Run. Disappear. Oh, God, she couldn't face all those people after that...after they'd seen those pictures. After they'd seen her.

She sobbed and staggered through the dark recesses of the stage away from the sounds—the voices calling her name.

Murmurs, whispers and pounding. Lights flashed like those in a carnival marquee. She had to get away. Far away from the freak show her life had just become.

Oh, God, please let me disappear, she cried silently.

Somehow, she managed to find a door that opened into a dark alley away from the hustle of the front entrance. Again the voice in her mind cried out at her, this time urging her to stop and wait, but she paid it no mind. Panic filled every cell of her being and she had to get away from the mortifying scene. She had to hide away until some part of her brain could function and she could figure out what to do next.

The pictures would be an even worse scandal than her mother's grisly murder. This time it was her fault. Her innocence and her naïve stupidity had gotten her into trouble. No one would care that she had been young, in love and drugged out of her mind. All they would talk about was the lurid details of the photographs and the tawdry presentation during what should have been a wonderful night. A glorious night—not for the fame and praise of the city, but that it might have ended in Ian's arms.

She stumbled through the dark alley and finally kicked off her heels so she could walk on the uneven pavement and gravel. The thought of him sitting there, privy to her ultimate humiliation made her want to throw up again.

Oh, God! How the hell could she ever face him after that?

In her mind, the dam was threatening to burst. Voices whispered to her through the tiny cracks and crevices of the failing barrier between the living and dead. Josiah had abandoned her along with her last shreds of self-esteem. One last warning and he had left. Just as she was sure Ian would now that he'd seen the weak-willed person she had once been. Even though she had been drugged, it didn't change what she'd done—or what she hadn't done. She should have said no the first time Drew asked her out instead of agreeing. She'd been trying to fit in at college—to become a part of the popular crowd instead of going it alone. She had ignored her gut instincts and lived to regret it over and over again.

The sound of footsteps and the creak of the stage door sent her ducking between the dumpsters in the passageway. She fell silent, holding her breath as she listened and prayed whoever had followed her would give up and leave.

Invisible. Invisible, please let me disappear, she chanted, eyes closed.

A few jogging steps, heavy breathing and a muffled curse, then the steps retreated and the door snicked shut. She waited, her lungs burning as she continued to listen for other sounds. After a moment, she realized she was alone. It was now or never. She had to escape. If running off to hide made her a coward, she didn't give a damn anymore. This wasn't something she could deal with today.

Tomorrow...well, tomorrow would have to take care of itself.

With one last glance around at the ever-darkening shadows, she crept out of the alley, retreating farther into the shaded streets of Savannah as she moved away from the main street. She would hide for a while. Just for a short time. *After that...*

But she couldn't think that far ahead.

§

The press lined the walk outside the convention center, cameras flashing, pens scribbling in frantic strokes as more and more showed up with cameras, mikes and speculations. Ian had spent almost three hours combing every inch of the center without success. Camille was gone.

Sam and Davu had finally convinced him to leave the scene with the idea that she had simply slipped out the back and gone home. He didn't know what to think except that he was extremely pissed off—and he had failed. They left the building with Samantha between him and Davu for protection. But the crowd of pariahs attacked when they recognized Samantha as being Camille's agent.

"Where did the nude pictures of Ms. Bryant come from?" The reporter shoved a microphone into Sam's face. Ian clenched his jaw.

"Was this a planned publicity stunt?" another woman asked from behind.

"Are you out of your mind?" Samantha jerked away from Davu's hold on her arm and faced the press. "Why on earth would anyone intentionally humiliate themselves in such a way? No, this was not a stunt. This was a cruel and sick vendetta being played out in a very public arena. Unfortunately, not only is Camille Bryant suffering, so is the foundation for which she's worked so tirelessly over this past year. When we find out who is responsible for this public degradation, they will pay to the highest extent of the law, I promise you that."

"Where is Ms. Bryant?" another reporter piped up from the back of the crowd.

"Yeah, why isn't she here herself?"

"That's enough questions," Davu announced, his mere presence effectively putting an end to the questioning. The reporters parted before them, somehow instantly subdued by one look from the big man's dark eyes.

Ian moved through the throng until they reached the limousine. The scene at the benefit replayed in his mind like a clip from a low-budget movie. He had been unable to move, unable to think for a long moment as those photos blazed across the screen like an ad for a porno movie.

He slid into the backseat of the limo beside the others, the door slammed shut behind him. The sound was so final that it made him want to break something in two. How could he just leave without Camille? He should keep searching... There had to be something they missed.

"God, where is she?" Samantha wondered out loud. "She must be so scared...so freaking mortified. Who the hell would do something like this?"

"An old boyfriend," Ian answered softly. "And when I find him, he'll regret the day he was born."

"We don't know that for sure," Davu intervened. "All the technician could tell us was he opened the door, someone wearing a Halloween mask hit him and he blacked out. It could have been anyone. It still could have been our demon."

Ian shook his head. "No, we didn't sense the beast or his energy. The bastard who did this to her is human."

"I think you're wrong, Spain. We need to look over every—"

"I am not wrong, *Mr.* Johnson!" he roared, patience gone with the swell of fear and anger that filled his gut. "I know a demon when I sense one and this wasn't it."

Davu's brow rose. "And you're telling me you've never made a mistake?"

A heavy beat of silence filled the limo. "Who the hell do you think you are?"

"That's enough!" Sam shouted, hands in the air. "I told you before—we don't need this macho shit right now. We need answers. Now put your egos away and let's work together here, gentleman. If anything happens to Camille..." Her voice broke and she swallowed hard before collapsing back against the seat.

The men fell silent and stared out of the tinted windows as the car rolled through traffic. Darkness had sent the sun scurrying below the horizon and the local vermin were out and about along with the party-goers and tourists. While this section of town wasn't the worst, Ian didn't even want to think about what Camille might be facing in her present state of mind.

God. Where the hell is she?

§

She ducked through the dark alley and skirted around town from block to block, jumping behind buildings and dumpsters every time she heard a siren or voices coming near. She ran until her lungs burned, her feet stung, and her side ached, and yet she couldn't seem to stop. She couldn't get far enough away from those horrible images of her naked, white flesh displayed on that screen. She couldn't get away from the humiliation and pain.

That's what happened when you let down your guard and trusted someone. Especially a man—any man. Her father hadn't been trustworthy and neither had Drew. Could Ian really be any better?

Her eyes blurred with fresh tears at the thought. He had already admitted he could never love anyone. It wasn't his thing, could never be a part of him.

Why was she always trying to make men like that care? Why couldn't she just shut off her own emotions and stay that way?

It was safer. It was so much less painful.

Camille lost track of time as she wandered the streets, her thoughts spinning. Voices shimmered near as if funneled down a long corridor, but she kept them at bay. Whether it was sheer will or something else, she couldn't be sure. But she was grateful. At some level she realized her sanity hung by the thinnest of threads. Being bombarded by the voices of the dead would push her directly into madness.

She roamed silently through the crowded streets, her skin chilled in the sultry humid air. Camille rubbed her arms with both hands, wishing fleetingly that she had worn something more substantial than the red satin confection Samantha had talked her into wearing. After a while she forgot to hide herself from view and meandered along the sidewalk feeling like Cinderella coming home from the ball. No one seemed to mind her formal attire. In fact, no one seemed to notice her at all.

She hugged herself to ward off a chilling breeze from the waterfront and slowed her pace to keep in time with the couples and groups around her. Laughter trickled through the air along with the beat of a bass from one club down the block and jazz from another. She felt like a clown in her bright red gown, the satin sliding around her body as she moved. But still no one spared even the slightest glance in her direction.

The tension along her shoulders began to soften and slowly uncoil. With peace settling into her body, her mind began to clear. The panic that had gripped her by the throat ebbed until it seemed little more than a small tremor in her memories. At last, her thoughts connected and she could actually concentrate on the world around her. It was as if her vision had cleared as well as her mind.

She sighed. Samantha must be worried sick. Ian...well, she didn't even want to think about him now though it was almost impossible not to do exactly that. He had been the only thing on her mind for the past week—the one vision in her head that didn't involve demons and dragons or ghosts from the past. He was warm and real and so sexy it made her ache just to think of those moments in his arms.

The crowd on the sidewalk thinned as she moved on and still no one paid any attention to her. At this point, she must look more like a street person than someone who had just been named "Woman of the Year".

She stopped at the plate glass window of an upscale antique shop. The reflected image was slightly distorted, but showed the street behind her and the people walking on the sidewalk. She blinked. There was something wrong, something... Why couldn't she see herself? She swallowed, her breath quickening as the panic returned. Was this insanity?

A door opened nearby, the sounds and smells from within catching her attention. She realized she stood outside the Blue Moon. She stared at the blue, crescent-shaped sign as it flashed in welcome. When she closed her eyes the glowing image of the neon light stayed with her. The beat of the sultry rock emanating from the bar called to her, pulling at something deep in her gut. It seemed to draw away the last resurgence of fear and panic. It somehow left peace in its wake.

Camille sighed and opened her eyes to look back at the window. Her image remained absent. There had to be an explanation—maybe not logical, but since when had talking with the dead been an accepted event?

She could handle this, and if it turned out she had lost touch with reality... Weren't crazy people supposed to be happier?

It had been stupid to run again. Stupid and careless and thoughtless. She cringed as she tightened her arms about her waist. Not only had she acted the coward, but she'd deserted those that could have helped—would have helped had she been strong enough to stay and face those images from the past. But she'd lost it. She had freaked out and hightailed it out of there—sneaking out into the dark by the backdoor as if she really had done something wrong.

"You are so freaking stupid," she murmured out loud.

The door burst open again as a twenty-something couple staggered out. The man bumped hard into her side and Camille yelped.

"Oh, God, I'm sorr—" The man stared right at her and blinked, then looked up and down the sidewalk. "Sheesh, I had one too many, babe," he told his companion. "We better get a cab."

The redhead on his arm frowned. "What do we do with your car?"

"I'll get it in the morning." He grinned and drew her into his arms, kissing her long and hard as if they were the only two in the world. "But not *too* early."

"Get a room," Camille muttered softly.

The girl jumped and looked right through her.

"This place is giving me the creeps, John. Let's go."

They scurried away, arms around one another as they glanced over their shoulders and ran across the street. Camille almost laughed. This might not be such a bad thing after all. Then she realized what it meant—if those two couldn't see her, then maybe she wasn't insane. Maybe she really was...invisible?

It didn't make any sense.

She continued to walk down the block, watching the tourists pass with a bit of trepidation. It might be a good time to test her newfound gift. Camille waited until an older couple came close, then she jumped in front of them and waved both arms. They kept talking and moving until she had to leap out of the way to avoid a collision.

Okay, she really was invisible or this was the world's biggest, strangest practical joke.

A young man dressed in black and sporting numerous piercings was next. She bit her lip. Was it a good idea to tempt fate? Camille shrugged. Why the hell not? If she was crazy there wasn't anything to lose.

"Hey, buddy, got any spare change?" she asked when he came near.

The boy glanced over his shoulder and frowned, then continued down the street. He should have seen her. He'd been looking directly at her. A few more trials with people of all walks of life yielded the same results. Camille shook her head and chuckled. This was real or she was dead, if not crazy.

The weight of the talisman seemed to grow warm against her skin. She had almost forgotten she still wore it, tucked beneath the low neckline of her strapless dress. The Chameleon Talisman... Could this small charm be the secret?

Is this the magic Virginia spoke of? she wondered. *Is this the promise it holds?*

"I don't believe in magic," she murmured softly. But in her heart she knew it was a lie. She not only believed in magic—she experienced some form of it every day when she spoke with the dead. Now she longed for it to be real, if only to prove she wasn't going insane.

The night wore on toward dawn but the humidity never changed. The air hung warm and damp over her shoulders as she moved through the city like a ghost. Suddenly forlorn and miserable, Camille decided it was high time she went home. A shower would be heaven—Ian's arms would be paradise.

She shook her head and turned down the block toward home, her decision made. It was time to stop running like a frightened child. It was time to face the fallout.

Chapter Seventeen

Ophelia was still unconscious in the hospital. No one saw Camille leave the banquet hall and even Davu with his superior, ancient skills couldn't find her. Ian finally gave up the search at about three-thirty in the morning after over five solid hours of patrolling oak-lined street after street, the hospitals, park benches and finally the morgue.

Camille had vanished from the face of the earth as if she'd never existed.

He didn't know where Samantha and Davu wound up for the night, and frankly he didn't give a damn. He only assumed they made it back to the small apartment Samantha kept near her office downtown since they'd been headed in that direction. She had promised to check in at the police station first thing in the morning to make sure the cops were still looking for Camille. At the moment, Ian wasn't in the mood to talk to either Sam or Davu. He knew this whole fiasco lay on his shoulders, no matter what they said. He hadn't done enough.

After scouring every inch of the house, Ian made his way back to the kitchen for a bite to eat. Although his stomach growled, he had little desire for food. But he went through the motions of making himself a plate of fried eggs and ham, knowing it wouldn't do Camille any good if he collapsed before finding her.

As he rummaged through the cupboard for a bottle of hot sauce, he stopped and stared at what seemed to be an apparition in the back of one of the cabinets—a dusty, half-empty bottle of Jack Daniel's. The label was almost completely obliterated by grime, but he knew from years of experience the exact shape of that particular brand of whiskey.

He later sat on the edge of the big bed, lights off except for the small one in the adjoining bathroom. He felt like shit and he wanted that drink so badly his mouth watered. He stared at the bottle, the back of his throat constricting. He could almost taste it, could almost feel that initial burn as it poured down his throat. A little voice in the back of his mind had protested as he lifted the whiskey from the shelf and dusted it off with his bare hand. That same voice reprimanded him as he grabbed a glass from the cupboard and carried it upstairs to the bedroom, his eggs forgotten on the kitchen table.

He gazed at the glass as if expecting some kind of sign—as if looking at it long enough would tell him where Camille had gone. But nothing seemed able to conjure her from the depths of regret that wrapped around him like a boa constrictor. She had been mortified, humiliated in such a way that she'd been pushed right over that edge he knew she'd been balancing on since the moment they met.

She put up a brave front most of the time. So brave that he'd been careless. He'd been so caught up in her success, in her excitement over the evening that he checked out every inch of the facility except the one that mattered in the end—the projection booth.

Ian reached out and poured a full glass of the dark liquid. The smell brought immediate and vivid images back to mind. They bumped and churned around in his thoughts like a reel of film clips with no particular order. The overall theme, however, did not escape Ian, despite his state of mind.

Depression. Degradation. Failure. Body after bloody body.

He clutched the glass tighter. Anger burned through him until he thought the whiskey would begin to boil. This insanity had to stop. Getting drunk wouldn't bring her back—it wouldn't bring back the kid he'd lost six months ago in Kentucky or the mother he'd lost twenty years ago. It sure as hell wouldn't do him a damn bit of good, either.

Ian lifted the glass and brought it to his lips. He closed his eyes, taking a long deep breath of the fiery brew that seemed to beckon him. Then he raised his arm and hurled the tumbler at the far wall where it smashed into a thousand pieces. Whiskey sprayed over the wall, floor and ceiling in a macabre splatter pattern any forensics expert would love to analyze.

He sank back down on the bed and sighed. Damn it, he

was weak. The only thing that kept him from taking that drink was the thought of Camille out there alone and in trouble. She needed him, and she needed him sober, not high as a kite or in a drunken stupor. Somehow, she had managed to give him the one thing he had lacked for so many lonely years—a real reason to stay clean.

"Help me find her," he whispered.

A cool rush of air coursed over him and he sat up straight, his gaze roaming over the room in quick perusal. The air conditioning was off, the windows closed. He stood and circled the room slowly, investigating every inch. Nothing unusual, but the cold feeling remained.

Could it be one of Camille's spirits trying to contact him? Looking for her? He shook his head and swiftly shed his clothes before collapsing back on the bed.

For once in his life, he wished he could actually do more than walk through dreams and battle demons. Right now he wished he could speak to the dead. Ian closed his eyes and tried to relax—tried to let his thoughts go blank. But it wasn't as easy. Too many images raced through him. Too many worries and words. Too many scenes both dreamt and real.

He finally gave up and took refuge from the cold beneath the crisp white sheet. Sheets she had placed on his bed only days ago. Sheets touched by her soft, gentle hands and which still held the subtle vanilla scent that clung to her skin.

Regret twisted in his gut like a dull blade. God, how he wished he'd been more alert, more aware of what was going on around them last night. Had he somehow missed the demon after all? He hadn't thought it possible, but he couldn't trust his instincts anymore. At least not where Camille was concerned.

He snorted. Shit, she might as well have been alone at that benefit for all the good they did her. Exhaustion pulled at him, dragging his thoughts deeper as the line between dream and reality blurred. He saw her standing there again—the lurid photo of her younger self, naked and drugged, laying across a rumpled bed that broadcast sex in less than subtle tones.

He should have killed the bastard when he'd found him earlier tonight at that hole-in-the-wall dive downtown. But at least Ian had gotten the pictures and negatives from him—they'd made a great bonfire in the trashcan outside of Drew Lee's roach hotel. Ian smirked at the memory of the other man's expression when he told him to leave Georgia and never come back. Yes, he'd meant every bit of his threat. If Drew ever got within a hundred miles of Camille again, Ian would gladly put a bullet in his brain. Sentinel rules be damned.

Exhaustion pulled at him until he had no choice but to succumb. He'd sleep for a while and then start over. There had to be something they overlooked, someplace they missed in the search of Savannah. People didn't just disappear. Not really.

§

Someone had forgotten to lock the front door. She frowned as the knob turned easily and a whisper of stale, cold air rushed out over her skin and into the night. It wasn't like Ian to be careless. Could he be gone? Hurt? Fear slithered through her and she hurried inside, closing and triple-locking the huge oak door behind her.

The house stood still and silent, even the ghosts were quiet. She wrapped her arms about her middle and moved to the stairs, listening. Hollow echoes of her footsteps seemed to rattle the walls. She tiptoed up the steps. It grew darker with each tread. Her heart beat so hard that her ears felt as if they'd burst from the pressure. God, if anything had happened to him because of her...

At the landing, she stopped again and glanced from door to door. They were all open—the rooms beyond like the black, gaping maws of uncharted caverns. She swallowed and moved toward his door. Ophelia would still be in the hospital, but Ian should be there. Asleep. Alive. She hoped to heaven he hadn't left, although she wouldn't blame him for doing just that. Why the hell stick around when she couldn't even face a little scandal?

Camille slipped into the dark room and waited for her eyes to adjust. The king-size bed took up much of the large space and seemed bigger in the darkness. It loomed solid and black like an island in a sea of shadows. The thick scatter rug muffled the sound of her footsteps as she tiptoed toward it, holding her breath in anticipation and fear.

She froze and listened. Her heart continued to thunder in her chest but then she heard another sound above that—a soft rush of breath and air, a gentle rumble of sound. He was there, sleeping in the huge brass bed. Dreaming, maybe. But of what? Had she pushed him away with this latest stunt? Would he even want to help her now that he knew what she had done?

Ian had been the only one in many years who had ever really noticed her, talked to her. He seemed to give a damn whether or not she existed, her knight in a shining black Jaguar.

She crept to his bedside, the gentle sound of slow, steady breathing assuring her that he was still asleep. Camille longed to slip into the bed beside him and cuddle up close. She felt so cold, always cold. Somehow, she knew this man could warm her despite the savage glint in his eyes and the steel edge to his soul. She knew he would be the one to calm her cold, trembling body and stroke the heat into her veins.

The bed creaked. She froze and her heart skipped a beat. His breathing settled back into the smooth, peaceful rhythm of sleep. Clouds parted and moonlight poured through the window nearby, casting a faint silver glow on everything within its reach. The mirror across the room reflected a dark silhouette of everything it faced...everything but her.

She held her hand in front of her face, carefully moving each finger. Nothing. She knew her hand was there, could feel the cool air on her skin, but couldn't see her own flesh. It was an eerie, unreal feeling like being in the middle of a bad dream, unable to wake up.

"Camille..."

She jumped, glancing toward the bed, half-expecting Ian to be sitting there, staring at her with those midnight dark eyes. Those eyes had always frightened her with their depth and intensity and yet drew her like a moth to an all-consuming flame.

But he lay flat against the mattress with his dark head nestled on a pillow. He moved, his head jerking sideways with such force that Camille cringed, wondering if he had hurt himself.

"No!"

The urgency in that one syllable struck a protective chord within her. She stepped closer. He seemed so distressed as his arms thrashed atop the covers. He groaned.

A dream. He must be dreaming, a bad one, too. Camille

wondered if this were a common thing for this powerful, frightening man. Could that be why he always seemed so tired and weary with life?

"Cami... Oh, God!"

The pain in his voice cut her to the core. He was worried about her...calling her name in a tone that denoted the deepest of a man's fears. That meant so very much, coming from a man who normally feared nothing and no one.

Without thought for the consequences, she found herself at his bedside, lowering her body to sit on the edge. His warmth reached out to her across the scant inches between their hips, then the covers slipped down to his waist. He didn't wear a shirt. Forcing her gaze upward, she could see the deep furrow between his brows. The scar on his side seemed more prominent in the silver glow permeating the room.

"Cami?"

Unable to stand his pleas any longer, Camille reached out, laying a cool hand on his cheek. He felt warm. The raspy stubble on his jaw scraped against her fingertips like sandpaper.

"Oh...oh, God... No!" He bolted upright, almost knocking her off the bed. She suppressed a scream, her fingers digging into the quilt. Ian stared into the silver gray shadows. His breath came in harsh shallow gasps.

"It's all right," she whispered near his ear, her heart loping at a frenetic pace. He stilled, his mind somewhere between the dream and reality as he blinked at the darkness. "I'm okay, Ian, it was only a dream. I'm safe, please don't worry."

He shook his head, some part of him seeming to hear and trying to function. Camille smoothed a hand over his damp forehead, brushing back a long strand from his eyes.

"Cami?"

"Yes, Ian, I'm here."

He blinked again, his dark gaze moving in her direction but seeing right through her. It was unnerving, but she held still, her hand resting on his rough cheek while she waited. What would he see?

He squeezed his eyes shut and she pulled her hand away, realizing how confusing it must be for him.

"You're really losing it this time, Spain." He scrubbed both hands over his face.

This couldn't go on. She took a deep breath. "You aren't crazy."

His head jerked up and he glanced around the room, alert and ready to pounce.

"Where are—?" He moved his legs and bumped into her. His entire body stilled, she thought he might have even stopped breathing. "Camille?"

"Yes, Ian," she said, reaching out one hand to caress his jaw. He jerked away slightly, then relaxed. "I'm here. I'm safe."

Relief and confusion followed in close succession across the rugged planes of his face. He cared. Such a joyous, peaceful feeling washed over her. Every muscle in her body relaxed with the euphoria that followed. She leaned forward, feeling his warm breath on her face. She longed to taste it mingling with her own. Camille saw the look of surprise in his midnight eyes before her lips met his.

Ian gasped beneath her mouth, then his arms were around her, his mouth moving slowly against hers, testing, probing, until some part of him accepted she was there in his arms. She was real—this was real. With his eyes closed, Ian caressed her back. His hands moved lower as his mouth trailed across her cheek and down the curve of her throat. Camille pulled herself closer, winding her arms around his strong neck.

"If this isn't real, don't tell me," he murmured against her pulse. "I don't understand...but God, I don't care...Cami...touch me honey. Touch me. I need to feel your hands on me."

She rose and leaned her weight into him, pushing him back against the mattress. His eyes started to flutter open, but she put her hand over them, gently closing the lids.

"Don't...just feel, Ian. Let me touch you." She felt his muscles still for a moment as if the decision to trust was very foreign to him. It probably was. Given his former profession, she doubted the man took anything at face value. Ever.

She knelt on the bed and stared at him. Stark white light from the adjacent bathroom mingled with the moonlight streaming in the window. Shadows outlined every curve, every sleek slope and ridge of his muscled torso. She let her gaze roam over him, committing each nuance to memory. It would sustain her during the uncertain future that lay before them.

He started to move but Camille took action and slung one leg over his waist to straddle him. She heard his swift intake of air, felt the steel of his desire against her bottom. Ian groaned her name out loud as he shifted restlessly beneath her. A rush of liquid heat pooled low within her body. Every part of her was more than ready for this man who set her blood on fire with a look.

"Don't move," she whispered.

A soft touch on his shoulder sent him into a single convulsive shudder. She smiled, his reaction giving her courage as she boldly began to stroke his smooth, dark skin.

His shoulders...biceps...forearms...and back again. Down the thick column of his neck, her thumbs skimming over his Adam's apple to feel the pulse beating like a tom-tom on either side. She continued down his broad chest, down smooth skin and over flat male nipples so similar and yet so unlike her own. She wondered if they were as sensitive, if her touch there would ignite the same erotic feel his brief caress had. On impulse, Camille leaned forward and flicked her tongue across one. His soft gasp made her smile. Perhaps they were similar after all.

The exploration continued, even more erotic and surreal as she caressed and explored with her hands. She memorized every inch of his sculpted torso from the sleek skin to the muscle beneath that contracted at her touch. Her own desire heightened at the tiny sounds of pleasure that rumbled in his throat. The spicy scent of his cologne filled her along with the musk of his arousal.

Camille bound each caress, each sight and sound to memory, for she knew this could never happen again. This might be the last moment she had with Ian. Here lay her champion, her hero, helpless and mindless with desire as her hands stroked his body.

But if he could see her, she doubted she'd have the courage to continue. Then she wouldn't be in control. That was the other gift Drew had taken from her so many years ago—not only her innocence and trust, but her ability to let a man have control of her body.

Tears burned her eyes as she leaned forward one last time to place a gentle kiss on Ian's parted lips. He jumped a little, his eyelids flew open as he stared up into the empty darkness. He was so strong...so desperately alone, just as Virginia had said. But Camille couldn't help him when she couldn't even help herself.

She didn't realize the tears had fallen until she saw one glistening on his cheek. Ian blinked up at her. "Cami?"

She shook her head and tried to smile through the pain. "Don't worry, Ian. I'm fine. I just needed to be alone for a while." She couldn't resist one more taste of him and bent to touch her lips to his. "Don't blame yourself. It's my own fault."

Camille sat back and moved to release him. When her thigh brushed against his erection, she heard him gasp. Either pain or pleasure, she didn't know, but the touch seemed to bring him fully awake again. Ian bolted upright, his hands grasping at what seemed to be thin air. One latched on to her arm; the other snagged the chain that dangled around her neck. She tried to jerk away, but the big man had strength on his side.

She saw the disbelief melt into triumph in his expression. Then he tugged at the invisible catch in his hands, pulling her taut against him. His eyes searched the empty space where his body told him she must be.

"Cami...honey...please tell me I'm not insane."

She couldn't resist touching him. She reached up to smooth the worried lines of his forehead. Ian's eyes grew wide.

"You're not insane," she reassured. Then with a sigh, she cupped the strong hand that held the talisman's chain. "Let go. I'll prove it to you."

He slowly released his hold on the chain and Camille lifted the pendant up over her head. "Hold out your hand," she instructed. He obeyed automatically. When she laid the chameleons in his large palm and let go, the air shimmered around them. Ian gasped. She looked down and saw her own, somewhat disheveled appearance for the first time in hours. Camille grimaced.

"I guess I should have changed clothes or cleaned up first," she said with a shrug. "But I've been a little preoccupied."

When she dared to look him in the eye again, he was still staring as if he'd seen a ghost. Or a woman with two heads.

"Wh-what happened to you?"

She shook her head and sighed. "I'm not really sure. After the fiasco at the benefit, I just wandered around town in a daze for a while. I remember wishing I could disappear until I could figure out what to do. Then I started to come out of the shock I...well, I wasn't *there* anymore. It worked, just like Madame Virginia said it would."

She went on to tell him the things the strange little woman had told her—things no one else could possibly know, and the special powers she claimed the talisman held. Camille talked and talked, finally trusting him as she had never trusted another human being since her nineteenth birthday and the night that had stolen both her innocence and trust.

He listened. His frown deepened. He seemed to slowly withdraw from her with each sentence of her unbelievable tale. But he had just witnessed the magic, hadn't he? How could he deny what he'd seen...not seen, with his own eyes?

The next thing she knew, he surged off the bed and paced to the other side of the room. When he turned back to stare at her, the anger in his eyes made her blanch. Had she done that?

"Damn it, Camille, you're always running. When things get messy—a little tough, you run away like a frightened child."

"That's not true."

"Like hell it isn't." He turned away and pushed a hand through his hair with a sigh. "You run from me every time we get too close. You can't stand the thought of me touching you."

"It's not that," she insisted. How could he not understand? How could he not know how much she wanted him? "I can't let myself be hurt again."

"And you think I'll hurt you."

"Yes, I know you will. You don't believe in commitment, remember? You said yourself you can't stay with one woman very long."

He shook his head. "I also said I'm willing to try even if it scares the hell out of me. But you...you can't run from life, Camille. You can't run off every time you get scared or things get hard. That isn't living, it's existing. I don't think you like that place you run off to because if you did you wouldn't keep coming back."

She stared as his words whirled through her like a dust devil. She wanted to tell him he was wrong—that she wasn't that kind of person, that kind of coward. But the words wouldn't come. She knew he saw her better than she'd ever seen herself. The knowledge stuck bitter and hard in her throat.

"God..." Tears flooded her eyes. "I really am pathetic." She swallowed and tried to turn away, but he moved like lightning and scooped her into his arms.

"Life's scary and it's messy," he murmured against her hair

as he held her. "But, honey, it is worth the risk. Believe me...it's worth it all."

"How can you be so sure?" she asked. "What if you jump in but still wind up alone? Hurting? What if nothing ever turns out right no matter how many risks you take?"

He tilted his head to look into her eyes. The emotion there took her breath away.

"Then at least you know you did all you could," he said. "At least you never regret what could have been if you'd just given yourself a chance."

"The voice of experience?" she whispered as the fight in her drained away.

His smile was slow and sweet. "Definitely."

"I can't imagine you hiding from anything or anyone."

Ian took a deep breath and tucked her close to his chest. "I wish that were true. But I did a lot of running...from physical pain, from the fear of being shot again, from the guilt."

"Guilt?"

"I was high on painkillers and a rookie took a bullet meant for me. He could have died because I had to hide from my own life. He wound up in a wheelchair for over a year before he could walk again."

"But you're clean now."

"Clean and sober for seven years, though I have to watch my step every day. I'll always be an addict, Camille. I can't let my guard down for a minute."

"But you've been clean since the dream-walker healed you."

"Yes."

She shook her head and sighed. "I know all this is true but it's still hard to believe."

"Believe, Camille," he said. "Trust your heart."

"I'm not sure I know how anymore."

"Then trust me, honey. I'd rather take another bullet than hurt you." He leaned back and gazed at her, his dark eyes soft and warm with promise. "You are so incredible...so beautiful."

She opened her mouth but the denial died on her lips. She could see her reflection in his eyes and to her utter amazement, she was beautiful. The revelation took her breath away. Could this be the man she'd been waiting for all her life? The one who could accept her? Love her, no matter what?

"I'm not running anymore," she whispered. "I don't know how you figured it out...how you saw the real me when I couldn't. But I don't want to be that scared little girl anymore. I want to feel alive, Ian. I want to wake up."

She relaxed in his arms, enjoying the way his eyes darkened with promise. Then his lips met hers and Camille sighed. She let go of the fear, let go of the past and simply let herself feel the warmth of his body, the passion of his kiss, the hard length of him pressed to her. This was living.

"I want you," he murmured as he left a trail of hot, wet kisses down her throat. "If you want to stop, you'd better say so now...I might not be listening much longer."

She smiled and slid her fingers into his long, silky hair. Ian shuddered.

"Don't listen," she whispered. "Just touch me."

His hands moved over her skin, bolder and surer with each caress. Somehow he found the zipper at the side of her dress and deftly slid it down so the gown slipped off her body and onto the floor. They fell onto the bed together, the touch of skin on skin igniting the passion that had been smoldering since that first day. Ian removed her strapless bra and she knew a moment of panic when he gazed down at her naked breasts.

"You are so beautiful," he whispered reverently.

He bent his head. She gasped when he took one nipple into his mouth, sucking gently while his fingers brushed the other in slow circles. She arched her back, seeking more of his warmth, needing him to touch her and afraid he would stop. But she shouldn't have worried. Ian was a thorough lover. His touch started gentle and slow until she sank her fingers into his silky hair. Then his hands became bolder, his mouth suckling and tasting with a hunger she'd read about, written about, but never experienced.

Her thoughts seemed to disconnect and for the first time in her life, Camille knew nothing but sensation. The world melted away and disappeared. She wondered for a brief moment if the talisman had worked its magic again, but Ian's sure exploration of her body proved he could see every inch of her. She melted under his caress and soon found he'd removed the last scant piece of clothing she'd worn. The desire to touch him pushed away everything else and she rolled over with him, straddling his waist as she had done when he couldn't see her while under the magic spell.

He stared up at her. "Oh, honey, you have me at your mercy."

"Do you want me to be gentle?" she teased.

"I want you in whatever way I can have you." He reached for her, sitting up enough to suckle her breasts again. The flame rushed right to her pelvis and she gasped.

"Tie me up, tie me down..." he whispered. "I don't care, just don't stop."

She felt a sense of power rush through her. She'd never been in control like this. Never. It made her feel sexy and wanton—so unlike her normal self that it gave her pause. But she wasn't about to stop. Not now. Not with this sexy, erotic man feasting on her as if she were ambrosia.

She pushed him back on the mattress and ran her hands over his sculpted chest and abs. "Beautiful," she murmured. "A Greek god in my bed."

"I think you're in my bed," he replied, his dark eyes alight with mischief.

Camille leaned toward him and kissed him into submission, her tongue plunging again and again inside the warmth of his mouth. Soon his hands moved over her back, down to her butt where he shaped and kneaded her as if he couldn't touch enough. That little tingle started again and she slid down his body a bit, enjoying the sensation.

Suddenly she felt his erection against her backside and rolled off to have a better look. Her eyes widened with some measure of respect. When she slid her fingers over him from tip to hilt, Ian gasped in response, closing his eyes as he went still.

"Very nice," she whispered as she continued the soft caress. "You are very nicely endowed, Mr. Spain."

He swallowed and laughed. "Thank you, Ms. Bryant." He sucked a rush of air in through his teeth as she moved her fingers again. "Now please stop before I lose control."

"I thought I already made you lose control," she said in mock surprise. She rolled on her back and sighed. "I suppose I might as well give up."

Ian rolled on top of her, silencing any protest with his mouth on hers, his hands between her thighs. With one knee, he nudged her legs apart, plying her with kisses as he slid into position at her wet heat. The tip of his erection probed her tender flesh and she moaned deep in her throat. Then she grasped his hips in her hands and showed him what she wanted. She wanted it now.

He thrust deep inside her, the sudden penetration shocking her system. Camille felt her body relax and accept his invasion. Pressure built at her core, letting her know that something else was needed...something else before this could come to a satisfying end.

She moved against him and he groaned aloud and swallowed. "I can't hold on too long..." he murmured as he kissed her cheek. "It's been so long...this is just so damn good, honey. You're tight and wet and..." He groaned again and dropped his head to her shoulder.

"Hang on... I can't...hold back." He began to move. "It'll be better next time, I swear it, honey. It'll be better."

Camille smiled at his words. He couldn't know, couldn't realize how very close she was as well. It hovered there, just out of reach. Then he moved inside her, pumping into her body with sure strokes. She met him measure for measure until they formed a seamless rhythm as if they'd done this before. Again and again they parted and collided, the force building that tension inside her until she knew, without doubt, that this was it. One last thrust and she gasped, her hands grabbing at his hips when he hesitated.

"Don't stop," she begged.

He continued the rhythm, the only sound the mingled rush of their breathing and the slight creak of the bed beneath. Camille felt the pressure break free. A jolt of power surged from where their bodies met, up her spine and down again. She cried his name out loud and held on as he increased his tempo. Then he went still for a split second, his breath caught. The tension in his face slowly melted.

Ian fell on top of her. The slick sweat on his body mixed with her own and she smiled lazily. The rush of his breath slowed after a time, along with the frantic beat of his heart. Camille kept her arms around him, stroking his back weakly until he finally stirred.

"Are you okay?" he asked softly.

She took a deep breath and smiled. "Oh, yes."

Ian chuckled and slipped away from her to lie at her side. She couldn't read the expression in his eyes, but she saw the contented smile that hung on his lips. With one finger, she traced that smile, and then raised her head to kiss him gently.

"You are incredible," he said. "I don't think I'll ever get enough of you."

"That sounds very promising."

But a shadow fell across her happiness as she remembered the benefit and those photos splashed on the screen for everyone to see. Would Drew Lee continue to lurk in the background, waiting for his chance to knock her down again? To humiliate her? How could they live like that?

"What if Drew comes back?" she asked suddenly. "What if he never leaves us alone?"

Ian gathered her to his chest with a sigh. "I couldn't find you, but I did find Drew. I destroyed the pictures and negatives. He won't be bothering you again, Cami. He's gone."

Her eyes went wide. "You...you didn't...?"

His deep chuckle rumbled against her ear. "No honey...but he knows I won't hesitate to kill him if he ever comes back to Georgia."

"You threatened him?"

"Yes, yes I did." He rolled her to her back and smiled down at her. "And I always keep my word. For instance...I vow to make love to you until neither of us can move."

It was a promise he soon fulfilled.

Chapter Eighteen

She moved her fingers over his broad chest, following the contours of his sculpted muscles with admiration. He had the physique of a god and the dark looks of an Apache warrior. Dark and dangerous, he should be dressed in metal armor or buckskin and astride a tall stallion. He was a symbol of virility and most amazingly of all, he was the kind of gentle, giving lover any woman with a pulse would dream about. If only it could last.

Camille pushed the thought away and settled more securely against his side. She felt him move a hand, sliding it down over her back and skimming her bottom before moving upward again to sift through her hair. They had just shared the most intimate of events with one another and she felt like she barely knew the man.

"Do you remember your father?" she asked, suddenly curious about his life, his heritage.

"Yes, very well, unfortunately." The edge to his tone spoke volumes, but for some reason Camille needed to know more about this man she'd come to rely on and care about in such a short time.

"Not father-of-the-year material?" She tried to keep her own voice light to dispel some of the anger she felt rolling off his skin.

"No. He wasn't." For a moment, she feared that she had pushed too hard, then he sighed. "My first memory of my father was his incredible height. He seemed like a giant to me when I was a boy. And his voice...he rumbled like a freight train. He always seemed angry. At the world, at us."

"You and your mother?"

"Yes."

"What happened to her? Is she still—?"

"She died a long time ago," he cut in. "Drank herself to death."

Instinctively, she pressed her hand to his chest, her heart aching at the pain underlying his words. She knew what it was like to lose a parent...a mother. She understood the desolation it could cause. The guilt it could leave behind. It must be even worse for someone like Ian who was a protector by nature.

"I'm sorry."

He shrugged his broad shoulders but said nothing as they lay together beneath the cool white sheets, his hand still playing through her unbound hair. He wasn't a man to share his pain easily, that she knew. But somehow she had to get him to trust her as much as she had grown to trust him.

"Were you very young when she died?"

"Fifteen going on forty."

Camille frowned, trying to picture him as a young boy on the verge of manhood, at the edge of childhood and losing the one person he loved and trusted. It was a wonder he had any tender feelings left in him. She could almost see those eyes beneath a frown, his jaw set at a stubborn angle. She lifted her head and stroked the hair back from his forehead.

"You must have missed her."

He shook his head. "Sometimes. But I was generally too busy trying to keep alive to feel much of anything." He glanced down at her, a grim, half-hearted smile twisting the corners of his mouth. "My mother died long before her liver finally gave out. Living with my father had that effect on people. He was a cruel, violent man."

"He hit her?"

"Yes, until I stepped between them. I was big for my age and once I turned eleven, I wouldn't let him lay a hand on her if I could help it. He didn't really care, except that I undermined his authority. But one punching bag was as good as another.

"So I took the beatings for her. Eventually I got strong enough to get my own licks in and he stopped. But it was too late. Mom's spirit had died already."

"What did you do? After she was gone, I mean?"

"I left and never looked back."

"At fifteen? But how did you survive? You were just a child."

"Mama C took me in once she found out I was living on the streets. Said she couldn't face her maker knowing she had let one of His children die in the gutter. She gave me a job and a place to stay so I could go to school."

"What then?"

"The police academy. Eventually I signed on with the DEA."

"And the rest is history, as they say."

He smiled. "Yeah, that it is." He glanced down at her, his expression guarded behind that infernal wall again. "Satisfied now? Do I make a good subject for one of your novels or am I completely unredeemable?"

The comment stung. After all they'd been through together—he still didn't trust her? He thought she was studying him like a bug under a microscope? She pulled away and sat up to swing her legs out from under the covers. The floor felt like ice beneath her feet and a hollow feeling chewed at her insides.

"Actually, you'd make a great hero if it weren't for one detail."

"And that would be?"

She looked at him over her shoulder, their gazes connecting with a fierce intensity she normally feared. "You haven't a clue how to let someone close to you. How can you be a hero if no woman can get past the exterior? How can you make love to me one minute and say things like that the next?"

"Maybe I don't want to be a hero," he said softly. "Maybe the stakes are too high."

"Or maybe you're scared like every other human being."

"I'm never scared."

"Bullshit."

He arched a brow.

"You're scared to death, Ian, just like me. You're scared someone will find your weakness and hurt you again like your father, or leave you alone like your mother did. You hate her for being weak, yet you have the same monkey on your back. You're afraid someone else will get hurt because you might slip up and return to old habits."

Anger darkened his features and he turned from her to climb out of the bed on the other side, his back straight as a brick wall. "You don't know what the hell you're talking about."

"Part of forgiveness means forgiving yourself," she continued, fighting to ignore the anger in his voice. "Believe me, you'll never move on with your life until you do. Your mom's death wasn't your fault. The past is written—move on and write your future."

"And you would know all this...how?" He demanded as he stood and waved a hand between them. "You hide behind an iron fence and write about fantasies you're too damned scared to try out. Don't talk to me about fear and forgiveness, honey, until you've actually learned how to live for yourself."

She ground her teeth together, fighting back the tears that burned behind her eyes. What the hell did he know about her life? Nothing. Absolutely nothing. Sadly, she thought they had actually connected on some deeper level. After what they'd just shared, she had naively thought they might have some kind of future together.

"I know a hell of a lot more than you realize," she snapped as she jerked the blanket off his bed and wrapped it around her naked body. She grabbed the talisman from the nightstand on her way to the door. "I've been there, done that and burned the freaking T-shirt. When you're ready to move on, let me know. Until then, I'll show myself out."

Head high, she walked to the bedroom door and jerked it open, slamming it shut behind her with a resounding slap. If he wanted to come after her, fine. But she didn't think he'd have the courage. No man with his magna-alpha attitude would take kindly to having a spotlight cast on his fears, his flaws.

But she wasn't sure she could deal with him after this blatant rejection. That same macho attitude made life a living hell for way too many women in the real world. She'd had too many disappointments in her own life to go begging for another, no matter how much she might care for him. Yes, she wanted him. But she needed him to trust her with his secrets and to respect her point of view.

To hell with him, she thought as she fumbled with the blanket and hurried down the hall to the safety of her own room. The door crashed shut behind her and she fell to the bed as tears poured down her face.

If he was all that stood between her and insanity, then maybe bedlam wouldn't be such a bad thing. But she wasn't about to let him see how deeply his remarks cut her. She'd been abused once by a man. *Never again.*

God help her, but she'd never give anyone that kind of power again.

At dawn she rose and dressed, then snuck out of the house before anyone could stop her. Camille couldn't stand the thought of facing Ian after their argument. Maybe she had lousy timing, but his anger still cut deep.

She slipped the talisman over her neck as she stepped into the damp morning air already tinged with unbearable warmth. It was going to be another long, hot day. But it didn't matter—Camille could always use a little extra heat.

Not sure where to go or what to do, she finally decided to check on Ophelia. She wasn't sure what the visiting hours were, but hoped the nurse on duty could at least give her an update on her sister's condition. As she wandered through the halls, the smell of antiseptic and bleach filled her nostrils. She grimaced but moved onward to a bank of elevators.

A young man in green scrubs smiled and nodded as she entered the car and pressed the button for the third floor. She'd check on her sister, then maybe grab a bite to eat in the cafeteria. The doors swished open and she stepped onto the highly polished floor. The nurse's station was deserted. She could hear the clang of metal trays and beep of monitors as she wandered down the hall toward the drink machines near a small waiting area.

Slumped in a chair nearby was a tall man who seemed a bit familiar. Then Brent Adair glanced up at her. His clothes were wrinkled and his hair stood on end in places. He offered a wan smile which didn't quite reach his red-rimmed eyes.

"Brent Adair?" she asked as she approached him. "We haven't formally met—I'm Camille, Ophelia's sister."

"Yes, I recognize you," he said. "It's nice to finally meet you."

"Are you all right?"

He rubbed the back of his neck with one hand and nodded. "Yeah, guess so. Is it morning already?"

"Yes...it's almost seven-thirty."

"Wow, I must have dozed off or something."

She glanced around before lowering herself onto a hard plastic chair beside him. "Has there been any change? We haven't been able to reach you."

"No...no change." He cleared his throat. "My cell battery died last night and I finally got his messages. Damnit! I should have stayed with her like Ian asked me to. But I swear to God, I only went to the men's room for three minutes—five, tops. I just don't know what the hell happened. I came out and she was gone. I looked everywhere."

She touched his sleeve and smiled softly. His pain was almost tangible. "We all should have paid more attention to her health. No one expected...well, it won't do any good to beat yourself up over it, Brent. I'm sure Ophelia will be fine. The doctors will take care of her."

"Yeah, got to have faith, right?" He smiled. "I probably look like a vagrant—I think I'll go home to shower and change. But I'm coming back later."

She felt bad for doubting him. "I'm glad to see she's made such a good friend."

He rose and stretched. "I don't think they'll let you visit her yet. Do you need a lift somewhere?"

"Oh, I'm fine, really..." she began, but faltered at the look of sorrow in his eyes. "Hey, you know what? I think I'd better get home, too. A ride would be great."

"Does Ian know where you are?"

She glanced down at her feet. "Um, no...and he's probably going to be worried."

Brent chuckled. "Sounds like you two have connected. That's great. He deserves a good woman at his side."

"I don't know about that, but thanks."

They rode down in the elevator without speaking, and she followed him outside to where he'd parked his sedan about a block away. Weariness tugged at her, bringing her mood to a new low. But when she climbed in the passenger seat, Camille felt a sudden urgent need to run.

"Camille...leave him!" Josiah ordered as Brent got in behind the wheel.

She hesitated for a moment, uncertainty filling her. Then Brent turned a feral smile in her direction.

"Alone at last...I've been waiting for this."

She grabbed at the door handle but he clamped down on her arm with one hand. Then a sharp jab pierced her shoulder and she gasped. The world spun suddenly out of control. Her vision wavered and dimmed.

"Now we play the game my way, child. Don't worry..." she heard the engine start, "...if you cooperate I'll make this as painless as possible."

§

Ian arose a little after eight to find Davu waiting for him downstairs.

"You are a jackass," Davu informed him as he stepped into the parlor.

"Up yours, *Mr.* Johnson." Ian turned from the other man and tried to walk away. It was none of Davu's damn business what happened between him and Camille. But try telling *that* to an ancient telepathic Sentinel with a God complex.

A hand on his shoulder spun Ian around like a top. Davu stared down at him, his dark eyes spitting daggers. He could feel the sheer power radiating off the man's skin. It stood his hair on end and sent a tingle down his spine. This was a man that could kill with a glance, or so the story went. Right now, it looked like he wanted to unleash that power on the jackass in front of him.

Shit. Go and piss off the ancient one...smooth move, Spain.

"How can you bed the girl and then treat her so?" he asked with indignation. "I know your father wasn't much of an example on gallant behavior, but surely you could have learned better somewhere along the line?"

Ian narrowed his eyes. "Don't you ever mention that son of a bitch again. I am nothing like him. Nothing. Who do you think you are? God? My conscience?"

"I thought I was your friend...once." Davu took a deep breath and stepped back. "But somehow...somewhere we wound up like this. I'm not sure I remember how."

Ian felt some of the fight drain away along with the anger. Yes, at one time they had been friends, allies. But Davu had seen things in him...things he hadn't wanted to admit were there. Weaknesses Ian hadn't wanted to own up to until it was too late. He had let that get in the way of their friendship just as he had let Camille's questions get in the way of their most intimate moment.

"Addiction to drugs is one thing," the older man told him. "Addiction to a person...to love them beyond your own life...is a far different thing. You have to take chances, Ian. Otherwise, you aren't really living."

Davu's paraphrase of his own words hit Ian straight between the eyes. He ran a hand through his hair and cursed. "I really am a jackass."

"Yes, but it's not too late," the other man said softly. "She still loves you. Go to her...crawl on your knees if you have to. Never let love get away. It might not be offered a second time."

He stared at the ancient Sentinel, his thoughts reeling. "What if I fail her?" he asked. "What if I can't make her happy?"

A small smile turned up the corners of Davu's mouth. "Then you'll be in good company along with just about every other male that has ever lived. We all fail from time to time. None of us is perfect. But I don't think the young woman wants perfection—she only wants you."

"The demon—"

Davu waved a hand between them with a grunt. "Put it out of your mind for now. The demon will wait—he's been waiting for ten years. But your woman's heart is breaking now. She can't fight him like that. He wins *only* if she's lost her will to survive."

He was right. Ian spun around to go back upstairs but stopped and turned to his former mentor, his friend. "Thank you," he said, holding out a hand. "For everything, and I'm sorry...for all the years I wasted...for being a stubborn jackass."

The man stared at him for a moment, until Ian thought his gesture might be premature or maybe too late. Then Davu smiled widely and took his hand in a bone-crunching grip.

"Forgiven," he announced. "Now go take care of her so we can get this job done. I'm in the mood for some dragon barbecue."

Ian chuckled and took the stairs two at a time. Outside her bedroom door he paused, his heart suddenly in his throat as he remembered the heartless, cruel way he had spoken after they made love. It would serve him right if she never spoke to him again. But he'd fix this somehow. He'd make it up to her if it took him the rest of his life.

He took a deep breath and knocked on her bedroom door.

Nothing. He tried again. Why did he go and screw up the best thing that had ever happened to him? Because of some asinine fear? Anger surged through him and he pounded on the door.

"Camille, please we need to talk," he shouted through the thick oak door. "I was an ass, honey. I want to apologize...I need to apologize."

He waited. Nothing. He could sense the other Sentinel downstairs, probably laughing at his sorry ass. Ian dropped to his knees on the hard wood floor.

"Honey, please...I'm on my knees here," he begged. "Let me in...let me make it up to you. I swear I'll never be so stupid again."

He heard the sound of heavy footsteps on the stairs. Davu reached the top, a frown on his dark face as he gazed at Ian. "She's gone. I don't know when...sometime while we slept. She went to see Ophelia first, then she left with him."

Ian was on his feet and running down the steps. "Who did she leave with? That bastard Drew? Where did he take her?"

"No, God help us...she's gone with the demon."

Ian almost stumbled. "How the hell do you know that?"

"Josiah...he's with me. He's come for our help."

"Shit! We have to find her. Where's Sam?"

"She went to the store for some groceries ," Davu said as they ran out the door. "We assumed everything was fine after you called this morning telling us Camille had come back." Davu pulled out his cell as they moved. "Samantha? She's gone again. The demon has her... I don't know, but I want you to call Gabriel and get him here as soon as possible. We may need him... Yes, I will."

"Who is the demon? It can't be Drew, I would have felt something when I found him last night—he would have challenged me when we were alone. But she wouldn't go anywhere with a stranger, she's smarter than..." Ian ground to a halt. Davu stared at him as a horrible feeling filled the pit of Ian's stomach. "Oh God, the waitress at the Blue Moon saw Ophelia with a tall blond man. Camille was right—it must have been Brent. The demon is someone Camille trusts or she never would have gone off with him willingly. Brent is the host. That bastard picked the one man I would never suspect and I practically invited him in for the feast."

"It's not your fault, Ian," the other man consoled. "To

disguise himself so completely, this demon must have been around for a long, long time. He has to be ancient, and you don't get that old without learning to hide your trail. But we'll find her."

Ian started the Jag's engine and they drove halfway down the street before he slammed on the brakes. "Where do we go?"

Davu could only shake his head. "I don't know. Her essence is masked from me, somehow."

"Damnit!" Ian slammed his hand on the steering wheel. "Madame Virginia gave Camille a talisman... She called it the Chameleon Talisman. Do you know anything about it?"

"Yes...yes, I have heard the legend. They say it amplifies the powers of whoever wears it. It can provide a visual or energy cloak when the owner needs one. What did Camille use it for?"

"To disappear after the benefit—literally. She didn't do it on purpose, it just happened. I couldn't see her when she sat a foot away from me."

"That must be what she wished—to become invisible. But why would she keep it on after she came home? Why would she leave..." He looked at Ian as his words faded.

They both knew why. Ian had humiliated her. His anger after they made love must have smacked of rejection in the worst way—because she trusted him so completely. She may have tried to go into hiding again.

Ian cursed. "It's my fault she left. He's going to kill her and I'm to blame for being proud and stupid." Tears burned his eyes but he blinked them away. "What the hell do we do now?"

Davu laid a hand on his arm. "Josiah can guide us. The demon is strong, but he is stronger. He's here."

Ian looked behind them but the car was empty. A car horn blared.

"How...?"

The other man simply smiled. "The demon took her somewhere quiet...somewhere they won't be interrupted until he's done with his games and siphons her powers. Josiah is the reason this demon has hunted Camille. It explains his obsession."

Now Ian understood, as well. "Because she's Josiah's daughter."

"Yes, Josiah killed this rogue Sentinel years ago when he

went against the others," Davu explained. "He chose the demon path over death and has spent centuries trying to find a way to even the score with Josiah. I'm betting he thinks he's found it now."

"Killing Josiah wasn't enough?" Ian asked. "He has to kill his heir, too."

"Yes...for that, and because she has remarkable power flowing through her veins...power that will strengthen him immeasurably." He sat silent for a moment, his eyes closed. "Yes, yes...I see." When he opened his eyes again, he looked at Ian. "Drive, I'll direct you. Josiah knows the way. He says we still have time. The talisman's magic is young compared to Josiah—it cannot hide her from him. But we must hurry."

Ian nodded. If Camille died because of him... He pushed the thought aside. She would survive. She had to, because he had a lot of repenting to do.

Chapter Nineteen

She struggled against the tide on the edge of consciousness, unwilling to take that last fleeting step over into the realm of dreams. There would be no rest there, no peace. She had to fight it—had to pull herself up from the oblivion that yawned before her.

Save me, she whispered.

Her heart slowed in her chest, her body heavy and weighted. Fear clogged her throat, filled her veins. No one could reach her here with the amulet masking her presence. A shiver slid over her skin. The dragon was near. She felt his presence. She could hear his raspy breath and feel the heat of his fire in the air surrounding her, suffocating like a heavy wool blanket.

Wake me up! Her mind screamed as she fought to swim above the murky state between one level of existence and the next.

This was why she had never agreed to take tranquilizers, despite her bouts of insomnia. With drugs in her system, she couldn't escape the dreams on her own. She couldn't leave the nightmare.

Soon the demon would take her. She would die and she could never tell Ian that she understood his reaction. That she was sorry she helped ruin the moment between them. That she loved him with every breath she took.

Ian...Ian...Ian...

She called his name, again and again in her mind, fighting to open her eyes, to move her limbs. But silence remained. Not even the whispers of the dead reached her here. The voice of her guide had been silenced. Nothing could find her but the one who wished to destroy her—as he had almost done ten years before.

The memory assailed her like a technicolor shock wave. How could she have forgotten?

She came home to find her mother bloody and lifeless. A man with an aura of pure evil and the handsome face of Brent Adair roared with anger as it tried to suck the power from the blood oozing from Marguerite's lifeless corpse. Power she had long before lost due to too many drugs and even more bad choices.

Then it turned. Blood-red eyes stared back at Camille, alight with lust and fury. She ran and ran until a man of solid build and Herculean strength grabbed her, silencing her terror with one look that had sent her into a deep, dreamless sleep. She awoke hours later. Alone. Safe in a place she had never been and with a new presence in her life named Josiah. He had rescued her from the demon and certain death, only to pay with his own life.

How long had she suspected the truth, yet denied herself the memory of it? Terror of the past mingled with the present and she felt a tremor rush through her limbs. She couldn't do this. She couldn't fight this evil alone, helpless in her nightmare.

"Ian!"

A deep chuckle filled her mind, the menace as tangible as the weight bearing down on her body and soul.

"The Sentinel cannot save you, child. He cannot find you as long as the amulet cloaks your essence. Too bad for you that its magic is so much younger than I—otherwise I wouldn't be able to find you, either. But I thank you for coming to me, Camille. You saved me a bit of time and energy. Now, you are mine at last."

"No!"

The chuckle deepened before morphing into an eerie hiss like the sizzle of grease on fire.

"I have waited an eternity for your kind of power. Your mother tried to save you, but she died in vain."

The realization of the depth of her mother's love washed over her like a balm, soothing her torment, her fear. In its place, a small voice of strength emerged. She would see this through to the end. Too many people she loved had suffered at the hands of this monster. Camille wouldn't let anyone else endure such an ordeal. She would fight him the only way she knew how and with whatever power she could muster.

"You won't win," she told him. "You may have killed my mother and my father, but you will die for what you've done. Even if I have to haunt you from my grave, you will pay until you burn in the depths of hell."

She felt a slight hesitation in the entity before he laughed again.

"Fighting words, child? Very brave...or very foolish. You have nowhere to go and you are completely alone. By the time I'm through, there will be nothing for them to bury...and no one left behind to mourn you."

"Then I'll fight you alone. You'll die with me—that's a promise."

At that thought, Camille made a decision and allowed the heaviness to pull her under, giving in to the deep sleep that beckoned relentlessly. If Ian could fight the monster in her dream, then so could she. It was her dream, after all. There must be a way to control it.

As she drifted further downward, she thought of that first encounter with the Sentinel in her nightmare. She had summoned him, somehow. He had meant to merely observe from the shadows and yet she had thrust him into a staring role. Perhaps she could do the same now, on purpose? At least she might be able to control the vision enough to defeat her adversary. All she needed was an edge.

Mists surrounded her as she felt the dream begin. Her boot-clad feet were planted firmly on hard stone...the alley again. Madame Virginia's little shop had left an indelible impression on her subconscious...or was there something more to it? Camille felt as if she were missing an important link in the equation. Why did this place keep drawing her back?

The sky hung above her like an overdone painting with an artificially bright sunset and low-hung clouds drifting over the five-story buildings that stretched down the block. A beacon of fire lit the west. She heard the sounds of a woman screaming in the distance, the rumble of thunder, the hiss of the devilish dragon that echoed off the brick walls. He was coming for her, but first he fed off her deepest fears and fantasies. She had little time to prepare.

"Weapons..." she murmured aloud. She needed something with which to fight.

Her thoughts conjured a long steel sword. Its blade shone like the moon beneath the city lights. The tip fell to the ground, wrenching her shoulder. It was too heavy. She could barely lift the blade, let alone defend herself as her dark knight had done.

It disappeared as quickly as it had come. Next, a dagger flashed into her hand, its six-inch blade of hardened steel thrust from a hand grip of brass. *Better.* In the other hand, a pair of black nunchucks dangled. These were weapons she had once mastered when her fears led her to study martial arts. These weapons felt like part of her. But would they help her vanquish a demon as old as time?

A trickle of doubt slipped down her spine. She quickly nudged the feeling aside. If she couldn't escape the dream, she would either have to fight or let him have her. Camille refused to give up, no matter the odds, no matter the consequences. She closed her eyes and whispered a silent prayer for protection. As if in answer, sturdy leather garments as black as night wrapped around her body. They were very much like those Ian had worn. They felt warm and comforting like a second skin.

"Come, demon!" she demanded, her voice steady though her insides quivered with fear. She licked her dry lips as the dank-smelling breeze whipped her long hair about her face. "Fight me. I'm tired of hiding."

The threads of sunlight had faded from the sky, replaced by a deep still blackness void of stars or the moon. The light of the streetlamps seemed muted. One of the surreal clouds grew dense and dark above her. It swirled like a tornado as bolts of yellow lightning shot from its depths. Camille swallowed back the bile that rose in her throat and took a deep steadying breath.

"As you wish," the phantom cloud hissed. Then its form shifted and undulated until the dragon, some three stories high, hung above her. She caught her breath as orange-yellow eyes opened and focused on her. The light from the street lamps showed the beast to be covered with large leathery scales. His wings fluttered about like undersized sails of a massive galleon. His teeth were two rows of razor-sharp bone that dripped with foul smelling goo. She knew that must be the odor of burning, rotten flesh.

Camille wrinkled her nose and fought the intense need to

gag. "You should really see a dentist about that."

The dragon considered her for a moment before a low, growl-like chuckle emanated from his mouth. "Jokes at a time like this? It's a pity you wouldn't join me of your own volition. I admire a woman who can laugh in the face of death."

He lifted his head and a stream of fire spewed up into the dark night sky, filling the air with the putrid smell of death. Camille held her breath, the stench almost overwhelming.

Calm...remain calm.

"Showing off again?" she queried. The demon's eyes narrowed.

"You do not fear me, child? That is your first mistake."

"I'm sure it won't be my last."

"Oh, yes. It will be."

The beast's tail swung around, knocking her off her feet as it caught her by surprise. She had expected his claws or a burst of flame first. Breath rushed from her body as she landed hard on the cold cement.

"Cheater," she muttered as she pushed herself upright, tiny bits of rock cutting into her palms.

The demon laughed. "Give up, and perhaps I'll make this as painless as possible."

"Like my mother? You didn't make her death painless, did you?"

"The bitch lied to me," he stated mildly. "She angered me."

Anger boiled in her own veins but she fought to keep it reigned in—she might need that anger later, but now she needed to think.

"And if I refuse to give in?" she demanded as she stood before him, her breathing ragged, her back and hips throbbing from the abuse.

"Then you'll be begging for death before I'm finished with you."

Camille shrugged. "You've taken everything from me already—my family, my peace of mind. Do you think I fear death? Or pain?" She took a step forward. "I know what happens beyond this life—death doesn't frighten me. I've felt more pain than you can imagine—and I know it can't last forever.

"So give it your best shot, you bastard. I will not lie down and die for you. For every drop of blood you spill, I'll take two of yours. For every bone you break, I'll rip scales from your foul hide."

"The child talks big," he snarled. "But we both know you are no match for my power."

"If that were true, you wouldn't have come back to take mine."

Again the hesitation, a slight shift of his body. Camille knew then beyond a doubt that this monster was afraid of her. Very afraid.

Before she could fathom why, the beast reared back his head and let out an unearthly roar. His tail whipped back around, but she was ready and jumped over it, rolling sideways into the gutter.

At the next lash she struck out with the dagger. The blade only nicked the heavy armored plating between the spear-like spikes.

Camille scrambled to her feet and ducked behind a parked Cadillac just as a fiery blast billowed around her. She leapt away from the auto as it burst into flame—the odor of melting metal, plastic and gasoline added to the mix of noxious fumes.

"Good thing I don't have asthma," she whispered, fighting to keep the panic from taking over as she crawled along the rough pavement.

The beast was huge and deadly, but his size and lack of agility gave her the advantage, small as it might be. Another roar of fury and the demon began to blast every car lining the street, removing any hiding spot she might have.

Camille jumped from her position near his next target—a late-model SUV—and ran to the recessed doorway of the closest shop. She knew Madame Virginia's was the next doorway down. If she could get to it and somehow make her way inside, maybe she'd have a chance. As it was, she felt like a mouse about to run out of luck against a much larger cat.

The tail swung around again, sweeping the burning piles of metal into a heap near her hiding spot.

"Come out and fight like a warrior!" the monster demanded, and then chuckled as if the very notion held infinite appeal.

Camille crouched down, said another silent prayer and sprung out from the doorway and to the right. She heard the beast's rush of breath, dropped and rolled just as a blast of fire scorched the brick building above her. Another three steps and she dove into the dark recesses of the doorway to the little occult shop. She heard a howl of frustration and felt another blast of heat. The hanging sign caught fire, creating an eerie glow like a spotlight around her.

"Come out, come out," the beast sing-songed, chuckling like a madman.

Camille tugged at the door handle, but it was locked. She took the steel nunchucks in one hand and covering her eyes with her arm, tried to smash in the glass. The loud rap ricocheted up her arm, but the window didn't break.

"Damn it!" Her eyes filled with futile tears. "This is my dream—break you stupid glass!"

Again and again she rammed the weapon into the window, but to no avail. It didn't make sense. She could speak to the dead, write stories as if the words poured from her fingertips, and yet she couldn't break a freaking window in her own dream?

"Damnit, damnit, damnit!" she cried, her shoulder growing numb from the jolts it took in her efforts.

"Now, now," a voice murmured close at hand. "Is that any way for a lady to talk?"

She froze, afraid to look, terrified of what she would see.

"I thought I taught you better than that," the voice continued. "Never give up—and cursing the darkness won't do you a lick of good."

The street beneath her feet rumbled as the beast drew near.

Camille swallowed. "Mom?"

"Yes, baby girl. Now turn around."

She pivoted slowly, her eyes burning with tears and the sulfur being spewed into the air. The ghostly image of her mother stood in the shadows of the doorway—seemingly alive, vibrant. Marguerite Bryant smiled as if she hadn't a care in the world.

"This is the end, isn't it?" Camille whispered.

Marguerite shook her head. "No, sweet child, this is only the beginning. You have the power, baby girl. You just need to use it."

Camille shook her head and tears sprung free to slide down

her face. "I don't...I have nowhere to hide and he's so much stronger."

"No, child, he's not stronger," the apparition said. "No one has ever had more strength than you, baby girl. No one. He's only...bigger."

Camille frowned as the image began to dissolve.

"Mama? Don't leave!"

"You're stronger, Camille," the sweet voice echoed as the image faded into mist. "Use what she gave you and he'll be no match for you. Just remember I love you. I always will. We'll meet again someday, don't you worry. You still have work to do."

Camille reached out a hand, but found only empty space. Had it been an illusion? A vague image conjured by some part of her frightened mind? But it had felt so real.

The building shook around her as if an earthquake rocked the city. Camille peeked around the corner of the doorframe and saw the demon hurl himself at the structure.

"Come out!" he bellowed. "I tire of our game!"

Then he saw her and grinned a terrible, evil grin. "Ah, hide and seek? You never really did grow up, did you? Still playing games with your life and your powers. Foolish girl."

Power. Her mother's specter had said to use the power "she" gave her. *What...?* The light dawned and her fingers flew to the talisman still securely hanging about her neck. Camille smiled. Yes, it was time to level the playing field.

"The demon isn't stronger—he's merely bigger."

A plan formed in her mind as the dragon paced and bellowed in front of the shop. She would need a small element of surprise on her side or he might simply vanish and leave her here. If he got away this time, she might never have another chance to defeat him.

Camille closed her eyes and thought of her surroundings, searching her memory for some place she could hide, if only for a moment. She hoped she could make it there before the beast broiled her like a steak.

When the demon paced away, his back to the doorway, Camille threw the nunchucks as hard as she could down the street. The clattering brought the beast to a standstill and she made a break for it—running to the right, heading toward the alley. Behind her, she heard a burst of flame, a bellow of anger as the demon realized he'd been tricked.

Camille rounded the corner, jumping over a broken bit of pavement as the dragon charged. Taking a deep breath, she dropped and rolled behind the large dumpster at the mouth of the alley. She leaned against its side, breathing hard as she again fingered the talisman.

"Please let this work," she murmured, eyes closed.

The ground shook beneath her. The buildings swayed and seemed to be at the verge of buckling. With her eyes closed, she thought of Madame Virginia's words, thought of what Ian had taught her of battling dragons. Then she made her wish.

"Release me from my selfish bonds," she murmured.

A tingle spread over her skin as the dumpster began to shake and the demon's deafening roar filled the little alley. Then she made another request of the talisman. Heat filled the palm of her hand until it seemed to burn her flesh and she let it go. Her body began to tingle as if an electric current filled her from head to toe. For a moment, she couldn't breathe, couldn't hear anything but a ringing in her ears.

Eyes tightly shut, she prayed that whatever happened would give her a quick and painless death. She prayed that Ian might finally know what happened to her. She couldn't stand the thought of his torment if he believed she had simply left...that he had lost another protected one. She wished she had told him how much he had helped her...how deeply she loved him.

When there was silence, Camille dared to open her eyes. She blinked, disoriented at the sudden changes around her. Then she carefully glanced down at her body, a gasp of surprise from her lips at the transformation. In place of leather and boots, her body was covered in thick, red scales. Her hands and feet were claws, a tail a block long wound around her.

"How?" The demon's voice sounded almost small, and very frightened. "How have you done this?"

Camille felt the power course through her veins and she smiled. "I used the power."

Without another word, she lunged for his throat and ripped at his neck with her razor-like claws. The demon hissed in pain as scales tore from his flesh and left him exposed. Dark blood as thick as tar oozed from the wound while the dragon's outraged howl echoed off the brick buildings.

Flames shot from his mouth, scorching her own scales as she dove around his bigger body. Camille felt her feet lift from the ground when instinct took over and her large red wings unfurled to flap against the stiff breeze billowing around them.

"You fool! You begin to think you can defeat me?" The demon's spiked tail swung about, catching her across the belly and slicing through the more tender flesh. She growled at the pain and felt the fire that erupted in her stomach rise up her throat. A burst of flame shot from her jaws. The demon spun around, grasping for her with both front claws as he tried to slice through the scales once more.

He was strong, but she was smaller, quicker. Camille writhed about in the dragon's clutches, slamming her whip-like tail straight between his back legs. The demon shrieked in pain and loosened his grip. The movement gave her enough room to lunge forward. Her talons shred more scales from the dark dragon's neck. Just what she'd been hoping for. Camille threw her dragon body at the beast, jaws open as she bent her long neck and dove for his exposed skin.

With the scent of his fury in her nostrils, she sank her fangs deep into his throat. The demon screamed—a long, howling cry of an animal caught in a trap. For a moment, Camille almost let go, but the image of her mother lying in a pool of blood flashed before her eyes, followed by that of her sister, pale and lifeless in the hospital bed.

Anger boiled in her veins, turning her vision blood-red with rage. She sank her teeth deeper into the beast's flesh, just below his jaw. A gurgling sound bubbled up from his gaping jaws as dark red blood flowed from the wounds, coating her jaws and dropping to the pavement with a sizzling sound. Camille twisted her head, severing the jugular before she ripped her head backward and released her enemy. The demon stared at her through dimly lit eyes, a large gaping hole in his throat.

"How?" he muttered in a tone of disbelief. "I am...master... I am...ancient...."

Swaying like an oak felled by an axe, the black beast teetered and plummeted backwards. The concrete shattered beneath his massive weight, sending jagged pieces of gray stone into the air like confetti. Blood poured from his mouth and throat, polluting the street with his stench, sizzling and burning all in its path.

As she stared down at the destruction, Camille felt the air around her shift and change. Her own strength seeped from her limbs as the dragon's blood continued to flow. It burned her mouth, but she barely noticed.

Had she really killed him? Was the nightmare truly over?

"Camille?"

She turned. Ian stood by the burning wreckage, clothed in black leather, sword in hand like a knight of old. His face twisted with emotion. His eyes filled with confusion and a bit of fear. He glanced from the prostrate dragon to her and back again. Only when he took a shaky step forward did she realize what she must look like and the horror of the scene at her feet.

"It's over, honey," Ian said as he stepped closer. His expression was tight with concern. "You've done it. Come back to me now...please." He stared up at her and smiled softly. "Please, honey. Let me take over now."

She stared down at him, her mind awhirl in confusion and shock. At that moment, all she wanted was to sink into his arms, close her eyes and sleep...really sleep for the first time in months. Ian would keep her safe. He should have been the one to face this final battle. But he might have died and she could never have forgiven herself if that had happened.

Camille felt a sob well up in her throat, but swallowed it back. With her eyes closed, she murmured the words to return her form to normal. The air sizzled with power. She swayed on her feet as wind rushed around and through her body. Then his hands were on her arms and she opened her eyes.

"Are you okay?" he asked, his expression concerned as he drew her closer.

The depth of feeling in those dark eyes took her breath away. She swallowed, slowly filled her lungs and feigned a smile. But the tears gave way and streamed down her cold cheeks.

"I just want to sleep," she said. "I want to sleep."

He nodded, gathered her close to his chest despite the gore dripping down her body and the tears pouring down her face.

"Take us somewhere safe, honey," he whispered. "I'll take care of everything else."

With one thought, she transported them to her house...to Ian's room.

"I can't wake up. He drugged me...a needle in my arm. I

thought he was your friend, but he's not. The talisman..." She coughed, her voice hoarse from the noxious fumes she'd been breathing. Camille tried to clear her throat and took a steadying breath. "My mother told me to use its power...that he wasn't stronger, just...bigger. I surprised him. I didn't really think I'd win. I thought...I thought this was the end. He killed my mom...and Josiah. I remember it now—all of it. Brent was the demon this whole time."

"It's all right," he assured. "I'll take care of you now. I'll never leave you again."

With that, he led her into the bathroom where he stripped the smoky, blood-soaked clothes from her body and helped her climb into the shower. While the warm spray washed the grit and grime from her, he went into the other room. Soon he came back, laid her robe on the sink as he stepped into the shower with her, his own clothes discarded. He filled his hands with shampoo that smelled of flowers and spring rain, and gently washed the grime from her hair. His hands were warm and firm on her skin, his ministrations soothing instead of erotic.

Ian comforted her with soft words as he dried her with big, fluffy towels and wrapped the robe around her shaking body. Then he led her to his bed, tucked her snugly beneath the covers and lay down beside her, spooning against her back.

"Sleep," he murmured as he stroked her damp hair. "When you wake up, you'll be home and safe in bed. The nightmare is over, Cami. You've done it. You killed the demon."

Then Camille did something she hadn't done in months...she let the darkness overtake her without reservation and she slept. It was a long, peaceful, dreamless slumber unlike any she had known. And all the while a part of her was vaguely aware of Ian's arms around her, his warm body close to hers. She snuggled into him—melding her form to his as her thoughts calmed, soothed by the gentle beat of his heart and the rhythmic rise and fall of his breath.

"*Sleep, little one,*" Josiah whispered in her thoughts. "*Now you'll have peace.*"

Epilogue

Three Days Later

Ian watched her sleep throughout the night and the next two days. Whatever kind of sedative the demon had injected, it was a powerful one. That combined with her general exhaustion had taken a toll. But she was safe now and his old friend, Gabriel, assured him she would be fine. Her body just needed time to work the drug out of its system. Her dreams would be a peaceful place with the bastard gone.

Josiah had directed them to an old estate on the very edge of town. Behind the iron fence encased in kudzu, tall oaks and maples hid the house from prying eyes. It had been easy to break down the door with their combined strength. Inside they had found Camille and Brent Adair, lying side by side on a large brass bed in a second-floor bedroom. Camille had been sleeping heavily while Brent lay dying, blood trickling from the corners of his mouth.

Clean-up had been the relatively simple task of salting and burning the demon's remains since Camille had killed the beast for them. When the demon died in her dream, the shock had been too great for the host. Brent's body died along with the evil that had possessed him. They might never know how long the demon had used the man's identity or what heinous sins he had committed. But from what Camille had told him in her dream, Ian surmised it had been for at least ten years. Anger filled him every time he thought of his old friend—or the man he had thought him to be.

Ian brushed a lock of hair from Camille's cheek and smiled. God, she had been a beautiful sight, clothed in armor and flush from battle. The image of her as a red dragon would haunt him forever. She had looked so majestic and powerful—her courage mirrored that of the ancient Celtic warriors of myth. He had thought he'd have to train her in battle, but it seemed his woman had already trained herself.

Camille's eyes fluttered open and he sat up straight, his heart suddenly in his throat. She looked around her slowly, her gaze finally coming to rest on his face. She smiled at long last and the tension coiled around him for three days drifted away like smoke in the wind.

"Hey, honey," he said as he sat on the bed at her side. "How are you feeling?"

She frowned a little. "I'm not sure. I think I feel pretty good, actually." She looked up at him then, her eyes searching. "Did it really happen? Is he dead?"

"Yes," he said with a nod. "You did it, Cami. You killed the demon."

She closed her eyes and sighed deeply. "I'm so glad. I was so damn scared." She looked at him again and smiled softly. "Not of dying, really. I was scared you'd blame yourself and that I'd never have the chance..." she swallowed, "...the chance to tell you how much I love you."

Tears sprang to his eyes, and Ian didn't try to hide them this time. He laughed as he gathered her into his arms. She felt so warm, so right there. He wanted to hold on to her forever.

"I love you, Camille," he whispered. "You are the one addiction I can gladly live with...if you'll have me, that is."

"Of course," she said. "If you think you're getting away from me, you are sadly mistaken. I have dead people on my side, Mr. Spain, and they know everything. There won't be even one place you can hide."

Their kiss was interrupted by a tapping on the door and then the sound of someone clearing their throat loudly.

"Excuse us," Davu said. "But there's someone here who would like to see Camille."

She looked to the door and gasped as Ophelia came into view—awake, alert and smiling as if she didn't have a care in the world. She rushed inside and Ian stood, allowing the sisters to reunite as he stepped out of the way. Davu laid a hand on his shoulder and smiled.

"A job well done, wouldn't you say, Ian?"

"Yes, thanks to you and Josiah," he agreed. "If it were up to me..."

"Ah, but you were the one who gave her a reason to fight. You were the one that brought her back among the living. We helped save her life, but you gave her a life worth saving."

Ian smiled. Maybe the old man had the right idea, but it would take a while before he'd forgive himself. He'd rather die before he hurt Camille again. A shadow in the hall caught his attention and he looked out the door, then smiled as he motioned the newcomer forward.

"Camille, honey," he said as he edged his friend toward the bed. "There's someone else you need to meet. He's somewhat of an old friend but... Well, he's the one that helped Ophelia."

A man took a step around Ian to stand at his side where Camille could see him. Her smile melted as a look of shock spread over her pretty face. She said nothing, but simply stared up at him.

"Hello," Gabriel said, obviously feeling a bit ill at ease. "We've never met but I believe you know me...a little too well, actually." He laughed softly before his expression turned more serious. "I wanted to meet you, Camille...to thank you for what you've done for me, for all of the Chosen. Your story gave me hope when I needed it most. Beth..." his voice faltered a bit before he continued, "...she's the best thing that has ever happened to me. If Davu hadn't told me about you, about your story..." He looked away for a moment and cleared his throat. "Let's just say, I might have missed out on someone very special. Thank you."

"Oh my God," she finally sputtered. "I-I can't believe it's you. Virginia tried to tell me the stories were true but I didn't understand. I never knew." She sat up and reached out to grasp his hands in hers. "You're a healer. You healed my sister. You're the one that saved Ian's life."

He nodded. "Yes, Samantha flew me in and I was able to help Ophelia. It was the least I could do for you. The demon gave her a virulent poison—one the hospital could not have detected in time." Gabriel kissed her hand in an old world gesture that made her smile. "Just know I am in your debt forever, Camille. I will never be able to thank you enough for what you've done for me...for Beth."

She shook her head in wonder. "You're welcome, Gabriel. Oh, is Beth with you? Can I meet her, too?"

"No, she's home, but hopefully, someday you two shall meet. I think she'd like that."

"Me, too," she replied. "Tell her she's a very lucky woman."

Ian couldn't be sure, but he thought his old friend blushed at the comment. Gabriel nodded solemnly, "Yes, I will. Thank you, again."

"All right, everyone," Samantha chimed from the doorway. "Let's leave Cami alone so she can get up and dressed. I say this occasion calls for dinner out on the town."

"Who's buying?" Ophelia asked.

"Davu," Ian suggested and winked at the older man.

"Fine, as long as I get to pick the place."

The others filed out, leaving Ian alone with Camille. As the door shut, she pulled him down on the bed and planted a long, provocative kiss on his lips. He was about to start stripping the clothes off her body when she broke free.

"Any chance we can be alone later?" she asked, her voice breathless.

"Yes, honey, I would say there's a definite possibility."

Camille smiled at him and glanced at the closed door. "I get the impression that life, as I know it, is about to change in very dramatic ways."

"I'd say your intuition is right on the money," he agreed. "I plan on making your life very interesting and dramatic from now on."

About the Author

To learn more about Meg Allison, please visit www.megallisonauthor.com, Send an email to Meg at meg_allison_author@yahoo.com or join her Yahoo! group to join in the fun with other readers as well as Meg! http://groups.yahoo.com/group/romance_ink_newsletter

Secrets and Shadows

© 2006 Meg Allison

Jason Sinclair has to keep his employer's daughter safe from evil that lurks in the shadows…but he can't forget the love she once offered.

Sabrina Layne left her wealthy father years ago, vowing to never return. But she's back for his funeral and to evade phone calls haunting her nights. Can she avoid another rejection from her first love?

Jason leads a double life working for the CIA—posing as a chauffeur while uncovering terrorist sympathizers among the elite. Murder in his home town forces him to face the friend he hurt years ago.

Together they might uncover secrets that lurk in the shadows before another life is lost. But Jason isn't sure Sabrina will forgive his lies when she learns the full truth.

Available now in ebook and print from Samhain Publishing.

GREAT
cheap
fun

Discover eBooks!

THE FASTEST WAY TO GET THE HOTTEST NAMES

Get your favorite authors on your favorite reader, long before they're
out in print! Ebooks from Samhain go wherever you go, and work with
whatever you carry—Palm, PDF, Mobi, and more.

Printed in the United States
150063LV00005B/6/P